Emerald
Alien Hunting Grounds Book 5
Kyla Breene

Foreword note from Ky

I put a part of myself into every character I write, but this one was the hardest so far. It took a long time until I could force myself to stop writing book nine (AKA avoiding) so I could finalize this one and put it out in the world. It feels like baring my soul and fears.

Olivia isn't autobiographical and is definitely her own person, but there was enough overlap that I struggled. This is for all the late-diagnosed neurodivergent people like me whose parents didn't understand. I was recently diagnosed with AuDHD and PTSD. As a child, I would sometimes hit someone if they kept touching me without permission, or have a screaming meltdown if I got overloaded. I was a force of nature. I've always been strong, and so some boys (who for some inexplicable reason think tackling a girl is how you behave with a crush???) ended up bleeding on the ground. My parents loved me, but they still brought in an exorcist. I could write pages and pages about the power of suggestion on a young mind... but suffice to say that it's the sort of experience that teaches you to mask your neurodivergence reeeeal quick. And very, very well. Now I'm a cupcake and reformed people-pleaser with an almost debilitating level of empathy and social awareness. If I didn't love the outdoors and sunshine, I would be like Kroaicho and tunnel down into a nice, quiet cave. The idea of rocks falling on top of the heads of people I don't like is pretty satisfying and I could probably live happily as a hermit (okay, that's hyperbole... sort of). Sometimes I wonder where that girl with the right hook went, but I'm slowly figuring out what person I want to be now that I'm (mostly) not fighting my brain. There was a lot of time lost trying to fit in. And yet, I was fortunate. This book is about what it might be like to have a family who doesn't love, doesn't understand, but won't let go. To feel broken and to be told you are. You aren't broken, by the way, regardless of whether your brain has the "typical" label or not. You are beautifully you. Keep being just the way you were made to be. Weird is wonderful. XO - Ky

A note on species and politics

There are a lot of alien species in this series. This will help you keep track of which ones you have come across so far.

Manticorid: once empire seeking, now mostly living peacefully. The origin of manticore mythology on Earth.

- **Abstainers**: A sub-sect of manticorids with a strong political presence in Session. They believe venom is dangerous and cut off the tip of male manticorid tails at birth.

Genali: The slimes we all love to hate. Opportunistic, with a specialty in exotic goods, including people of all species.

Braceaaer: The origin of Little Green Men mythology on Earth. Violent, small, and much stronger than they look.

Drakonid: a dragon/dinosaur-like species that was once a servitor race to the manticorid empire.

Qendi: Kuret's species. They are from a primitive desert world, with green bioluminescent marks on dark gray skin.

Zhasie: a reclusive cave dwelling species who show their emotions via bioluminescent skin. They are obsessed with treasure and many other species take advantage of this to trade worthless items for galactically sought after resources.

Wroahk's species name is unknown, and who knows when he will share it (if they have even named themselves or he bothered finding out).

1

Olivia

"She broke my daughter's nose," seethes the woman.

I'm sitting in this cold, stiff chair with my hands clenched into fists on my lap, trying to get my mind to stop punishing me. My fingers dig into my palms, and I focus on the sting to keep the tears back. I don't want anyone to see me like this. Weak. Emotional.

The fluorescent lights overhead flicker and hum, the noise bouncing around the small, bare office, making my brain burn and my skin crawl. I keep my eyes down, locked on the scuffed floor, not daring to look up. Not at the woman who's yelling, not at my boss, not at anyone.

"You need to fire her!"

I flinch at the volume of her voice, a shot of pain quickly following, wishing I could cover my ears. But that only makes me look deranged. Well... more deranged. My chest tightens, but I won't look up. I won't give her the satisfaction of seeing me upset.

"Please calm down," my boss says, his voice strained but controlled. "We're handling the situation, but shouting isn't going to help anyone."

The woman's voice gets even louder, if that's possible, and I can feel the heat of her rage like it's a physical thing in the room. "Calm down? CALM DOWN? My daughter is bleeding because of that monster. Why is she even still here? Fucking waste of space..."

I suck in a sharp breath as she continues to call me all kinds of names, trying to ignore the sting her words bring. Like mother, like daughter, it looks like. Can't keep their fucking mouths shut.

I glance over at the blonde in the chair. The blood-soaked cloth held to her face makes me want to grin, but that will only inflame things. Still. She deserved it.

I know I shouldn't have hit the bitch, but she wouldn't leave my space.

She closed the distance by fifty percent... then ninety. That was uncomfortable, but manageable. People do that all the time. Sometimes you briefly get to one hundred percent with an accidental touch, but this one was no accident, at least judging by the other data.

When I told her we didn't have her size in the back, thirty-two percent of her words became mean. Insults. Then sixty-five... but I was still holding myself back, forcing back thoughts of physical retribution, even though I knew it would feel good.

Then she snapped and wouldn't stop touching me and pushing her fingers into my chest as she screamed at me. Grabbing my arm so I couldn't escape. Still, I kept my hands fisted, but didn't use them. I reminded myself that so far I'd been kicked out of ninety-two percent of jobs and schools.

It didn't help. I lost control soon after when she called me a bastard. That word always takes me to one hundred percent rage. Nothing helped overcome the visceral way my body reacted to her touch at that point, percentages be damned.

Then there was blood. Just like always. And it felt just as good as every single time before it, and just as bad afterward.

Bastard. That word echoes in my mind, making me feel dirty, like there's something wrong with me just for existing. I didn't know what it meant when I first heard it and now people just throw it around like it's nothing. A bit of spice for their sentences.

I was seven the first time it was used as a weapon. I didn't respond well then, either.

Like usual, my stupid brain is more than willing to throw the memory back up. Just to make sure I've gotten yet another look at one of my many failings.

✳ ✳ ✳

"She's just a child, Mrs. Harper," Mr. White says in a hard voice. "Nothing was broken. Just a bit of blood. We're talking about children."

"Where is her mother?" says Mrs. Harper, her voice dripping with disdain. I feel my stomach knot up even more. "Why isn't she here, taking responsibility for this? Or her father, that hor—"

"Enough! I will not abide by racial slurs," he barks out, then takes a deep breath. There's a heavy pause, and I can almost feel him wince before he responds. "Her mother has been informed and her father is... unreachable at the moment."

Unreachable. I hate that word. It means gone. It means not ever here. I lower my head, biting my lip so hard I taste blood, my nail scraping against my inner wrist over and over.

Mrs. Harper scoffs as she paces in front of me, her heels clicking on the tile floor. "Of course she's not here," she sneers, venom dripping from her words. "Some irresponsible, rich moll who opens her legs for anyone. No wonder the kid's a violent little terror."

Though I don't understand all her words, I feel like I've been punched. Her words are sharp, jagged things that cut deep, hitting a place inside me that I try so hard to keep hidden. I squeeze my eyes shut, trying to block out her voice, trying not to let the tears spill over.

It's so hard not to break when every word feels like a weight crushing down on me. A physical pain that starts in my ears and stabs into my skull.

"Lily provoked the altercation by calling Olivia a... a deeply inappropriate name. It doesn't excuse violence, but it does explain why things escalated."

Mrs. Harper turns to me, face white, her eyes burning with some emotion I can't identify.

"People like you," she hisses, her voice low now, like she's trying to poison me with her words, "always end up just like their parents."

* * *

When I start paying attention again, the latest woman upset with me is no longer yelling and I've made a long, red line across my left wrist. I clench my hand, making myself stop before someone notices.

"You can contact the police, but her employment is my decision, not yours. If you would like to see the recording again where your daughter..."

The woman grabs her purse and storms out of the office, yanking her daughter behind her. Around the bloodied cloth, she gives me one last look before she goes, a little smirk on her face. It makes my skin crawl, and I know enough about her sort of person to know what it means. I clench my fists tighter. I wish I could wipe that look off her face all over again, but I know I can't. Not now.

When the door shuts behind them, the room feels too quiet. The tension lingers in the air like something heavy and awful. I can still hear Mrs. Harper's words echoing in my head, like a bad song that won't stop playing. On repeat for decades.

My boss lets out a long, tired sigh. "Olivia," he says softly, like he's exhausted. "Come sit over here."

I hesitate for a second, my feet feeling like they're glued to the floor. But I stand up, creeping toward the chair across from his desk. He gestures for me to sit, and I do, feeling small in the big, cushioned seat, mind distracted by the rough feel of the fabric and my attempts to get my skin away from it.

He looks at me for a moment then speaks, his voice not angry, just... tired. "You're not in trouble," he says quietly. "Well, not too much trouble, anyway."

I nod but don't say anything. My throat feels tight, like if I try to talk, I'll start crying, and I really don't want to cry. Not in front of him.

"Olivia," he says again, leaning forward with his elbows on his desk. "I'm not going to lie to you. What you did was serious. I don't tolerate violence. But..." He pauses, and for a second, he just looks at me, like he's trying to figure something out. "I understand why you did it."

That makes my head snap up. I stare at him, eyes skittering just shy of keeping eye contact, confused. "You... do?"

He nods slowly. "She shouldn't have touched you. That doesn't make it okay, but I get it."

I blink a few times, unsure of how to respond. Nobody's ever said something like that to me before. Usually, it's just "Violence is bad" or "You shouldn't have done that."

No one seems to care how many times I have communicated that I hate being touched. That it makes me feel unsafe. Overwhelmed. Out of breath. And of course angry. They seem to like to ignore that one and then complain about not having a fully functioning body afterward.

I communicate just fine before it gets to that point.

In fact, telling people seems to make it more likely they will use it as a weapon, although I have made it a habit to tell anyone who is supposed to be in charge. Like my boss, who even asked if he should make a sign and put it up so people would know. I declined, though for legal reasons I can see now that it might have been a mistake.

"I don't want to fire you," he says with a long sigh. "I mean, I think I should, but not for this. Not really. You're one of the brightest people I've ever met, and I don't know why you're wasting your time selling clothes."

I shift uncomfortably in my seat, unsure of how to react. I don't feel all that bright. Right now, I just feel like a mess. As always.

I frown at him, unsure why he's trying to make me feel better instead of yelling at me. "I'm not that smart," I mumble.

"Hitting a customer would be evidence, I guess. Please tell me that felt good, though? I've imagined hitting her a few times myself."

His blue eyes are unfocused. Is he's trying to imagine how good it felt? If he is, he's probably remembering the dozens of times she's mouthed off to him or ordered him around.

"You better come to work with a sketch of that one tomorrow. Or better yet, go back to school and just drop it off as you go out into the world to do something better than this. Oh, that reminds me..."

Before I can ask what he means, he reaches into one of the drawers of his desk and pulls out a new sketchbook. He holds it out to me, and I just stare at it, confused.

"I got this for you."

I take it from him, still not sure what to say as I run my fingers over the glossy cover.

"I'm not all that good," I blurt out, my voice small.

He chuckles. "Stop lying to yourself. You're obsessed. You're good at that. Putting your heart into things, I mean."

I stare down at the book, unsure of what to say. I don't feel like I'm good at anything right now. But the way he says it... it almost makes me believe him. Almost.

A small smile creeps onto my face, and I glance up at him through my lashes. "Thanks," I whisper, my voice barely audible.

He nods. "You're welcome, Olivia," he says in a soft voice. "You're going to be okay."

I clear my throat, confused by all of this. I thought for sure he would have tossed me out by now. "So, am I fired?"

"Will you go back to school if I fire you?"

A shudder passes over me when I remember the rigidity. The layers of social expectations that never made sense. Or how they related to grades.

"Absolutely not."

He lets out another long sigh. "Then you still have a job. Though we should keep you in the back, I think."

A snort escapes before I can stop it. "I told you that last week."

He scowls, but I'm pretty sure it's one of those ones that are fake. I think...

His tone when he speaks confirms it is and I let out a sigh of relief. "Get out of here, and when you come back, leave your cheek at home."

I stand up slowly, clutching the book to my chest, thoroughly confused. It's a feeling I've grown accustomed to. People make no sense.

I turn to leave, but he speaks up again. "I know this isn't any of my business, but do you have anyone you let touch you? Don't you get lonely?"

I flinch. Of course I get lonely, though it bothers me less than most. I clear my throat, not sure what someone is supposed to say in moments like these, so I just let words pour out. "My mum used to give me the best hugs... but that's been years now. It's just too much and I just... lose it."

"Maybe someone you trust, then? I've read a bit about..." he stops himself, and his face screws up into another expression I don't have enough context to understand.

My body is rigid, waiting for him to tell me how messed up he thinks I am, but the words don't come.

"Sorry. I'm making you uncomfortable. I just wish... It doesn't matter. I'll see you tomorrow."

As nice as he's been, my desire to be alone is at a fever pitch now, so I scramble out the door.

2

Kroaicho

On waking, the sound of my involuntary chittering resonates off the damp walls of my cave, and after a few stretches to be rid of the kinks crippling my movement, I run a claw down the side of the ancient case I've been scratching my back on lately.

To say that I am embarrassed will be underselling the sheer expanse of indignation I feel at the moment.

They have continued to taunt me.

I don't need to see my reflection to know that my pigmentation has changed. I should calm myself.

I cast a satisfied glance at the small pile of glittering, hardened, rarely found volcanic rocks to the side, and preen at the sight of them, taking pleasure in the endorphic rush that paints my skin yellow.

Braving the heights of Mount Rev'ercha to gain access to its lava pits and navigating those as well was no easy feat. Many zhasie preferred to hedge their risk by sticking to the cooled rocks that found their way to the banks of the expansive lava lake within the mountain, but a few of the more unhinged zhasie, that being myself for the most part, were more than happy to skip across the rock-littered mass of burning mountain to retrieve as much as one could carry from the more abundant rocks on the other side.

I pull out the best prize from where I tucked it before sleeping off the trials and insults of yesterday. A melted and reformed gemstone, its perfect, alluringly green, glittering depths pulling the eye in whirls of delight.

The pain in my muscles and the after effects of the red fear that pulsed through me making me feel slightly ill. I remember that final leap to get away from the whole thieving lot of them. It pushed me to my limits.

The other zhasie often weave tales, shouted from their cave entrances, that put my sanity into question. But they are the ones being odd.

Treasure is the ultimate goal. There is no risk not worth taking for this singular process, especially when there is a story to be remembered from the gathering. I certainly will never forget that leap, or the red fear and the orange triumph.

Remembering the stories behind the treasure are what give them value. It's what makes them important, which is why so many are jealous of my hoard. The risks I take and the tales they tell only increase the significance.

They call me a fool, but I know it's because they are jealous.

A gust of wind blows into the cave, quenching my mental tirade and forcing me to seek warmth behind my pile.

It also reminds me of the reason I am pouting in the first place, and almost immediately the glow of my skin turns a dark purple, taking on a more vivid than usual hue that does a proper job conveying just how annoyed I am with myself.

I look back to my most beautiful treasure, the green depths of it all but showing me the story of how I found it... but also reminding me of what I have neglected. The green mocks me in its beauty, pointing out my lack of zhannel.

Hoarding season has passed with a resounding success, but with that success came a failure I didn't even realize was a failure until I was in my cave watching the signs of the cold season trickle in.

I've entered hibernation season without securing an offspring of my own. Again.

It's not like I intended to go unmated, but my manic need to hunt for shiny things has taken precedence over something as inane as finding zhasie to collaborate with in bringing life.

This is not the first time this has happened though, nor the second, nor the third either, so even that excuse is lacking in more ways than acceptable to even my own mind.

My zhann would be berating me now if zha were here, calling me a fool for valuing the sparkle of synthetic materials over the biological imperative to reproduce. The thought of my zhann's lectures sends a red hue rippling across my skin, but I shake it off. I don't need to be dwelling on those depressing thoughts now.

A skitter of movement catches my attention. A xhenl, bright flashes of blue thrumming over its trailing tendrils as it moves farther back into the cave. My limbs twitch with the desire to capture it, but once again I hear the words of my zhann.

Never keep pets. They only distract you from your true purpose.

I let out a long sigh, returning to berating myself. This hoard is large enough to have a zhannel and yet another season passes.

Deciding to put such grim reflections aside, I settle into my hoard, a sprawling collection of shiny rocks, leaves, and synthetic materials. My skin lights up the items around me with an orange glow, signaling my joy. It's a simple pleasure, to admire the bright things I've amassed. The value doesn't matter; it's the shine that counts.

Not many zhasie would agree, but thankfully, when you're of the first brood of a Primarch zha, many would be hard-pressed to try to convince you otherwise.

Even though there was no remedy for zhasie terming you insane.

I run a claw over a particularly lustrous piece of metal, feeling its smooth surface. It glimmers beautifully under the orange light of my bioluminescence.

Then I turn back to staring in the green, whirling depths of my favorite treasure.

The urge to gather things with a zhannel in mind tugs at me. The instinct to mate is fading now, but it will surge again after the long sleep.

Once I've taken care of that, I can be back here, alone, with my treasures.

A sudden noise from the entrance of my cave jolts me from my thoughts. I turn, my bioluminescent skin shifting to a wary blue. Standing there is a genali, their heavy-duty suit a stark contrast to the natural beauty of my hoard.

I know about them; even recluse like the zhasie have heard of their bloodthirsty campaigns across the system. Ever since the manticorid empire halted their own advancement, the genali have been quick to seize the opportunity to spread their disgusting, slime-covered presence.

The genali stands at the entrance of my cave, its bulbous, wet body coiled with tension. Its skin glistens in the dim light, reflecting an array of colors that rival my own bioluminescence. It has one of my shiny objects in its grasp, turning it over as if mocking my collection.

"What are you doing here?" I demand in its deplorable language, my voice a low growl. My skin flickers with shades of violet, my anger barely contained. None of their stories are worth hearing, though the longer I look, the more are whispered to me.

No. No story associated with them is worth collecting as treasure.

The genali tilts its head, its eyes locking onto mine. "Admiring your collection," it says smoothly, the words dripping with disdain. "Such a... peculiar hobby."

"This is my home, my sanctuary," I snap, the orange glow of joy replaced entirely by the dark purple of annoyance. "You have no right to be here."

The genali's lips curl wide. "You zhasie are so territorial. I merely wanted to see what you had that was so worth protecting."

"Get out," I say, my voice trembling with barely restrained rage. My bioluminescent skin flashes a warning pulse of deep purple. "You deserve none of the stories."

The genali doesn't move. Instead, it reaches for another of my treasures, a particularly beautiful piece of synthetic material. The sight of it in the genali's grasp sends a surge of fury through me, my skin now a bright violet.

"I said, get out!" I roar, my muscles tensing as I prepare to lunge.

The genali finally drops the object, but not before giving it a disdainful toss. It clatters against the cave wall, causing me to tense. The genali steps back, still watching me with that infuriating smirk.

"No."

More genali step into my cave, their ugly eyes scanning my hoard. I hiss, my skin flashing an angry light purple. More of them swarm in, each one trampling over my precious collection. Rage bubbles up inside me as they start destroying my hoard, smashing my shiny treasures under their heavy boots.

"You filthy slimes!" I roar, my voice echoing through the cave. "Get out of here!"

But they don't listen. Instead, they continue their rampage, tearing apart the collection I've spent years building. My anger surges, and I lunge at the nearest genali, my massive arms swinging. I feel a satisfying crunch as my fist connects with its helmet, but it doesn't go down. Instead, more of them surround me, their suits glinting menacingly under the dim light.

I rear up on my back limbs, letting my front limbs dangle for a moment before launching into the fray. My hands grab, tear, and crush, but there are too many of them. Formidable as my physiology is, it's not enough against their numbers and their protective suits.

Desperation fuels me as I release a high-pressure mist from my snout, a rarely used secretion meant to make other species sleep. It's my best defense, but the genali are immune to it. Their suits shield them from my misting secretions, and instead of them falling asleep, I start feeling dizzy from the effort.

I pump more and more mist into the air, hoping to overwhelm them, but it's draining me quickly. My vision blurs, and I stumble, my body weakening. The genali close in, their hands grabbing at me, pinning me down.

I fight back with all I have, but it's not enough. They are too many. One of them strikes me hard across the head, and I feel my consciousness slipping away. The last thing I see before everything goes black is my hoard, my beautiful, shiny hoard, being trampled under their feet. The glittering green of my latest treasure fading.

3

Olivia

Along with the damn near manic reruns of *Ancients Behaving Badly*, *BoJack Horseman*, and *Rick and Morty* that had been on repeat in the background, my personal research has been the only thing keeping me sane the past few weeks as I took care of my mother. She's on one of her downward spirals.

All she let loose was that small little hint, and then left me to obsess about it. So typical.

Had I known she was going to drug herself into oblivion maybe I could have wrested more clues from her as to the second half of who I was. Not that I saw her much in between the boarding schools and all of the failed attempts to fix me.

She completely refused to explain, aside from not denying the truth of it. Now she has so many things in her system to help with her mental anguish she's rarely conscious.

It's a struggle to hold back the keening whine of frustration I want to let out.

She lies drugged in the next room, one step away from mentally checking out forever. I don't want her to leave, but that other part of me... the part that longs to be free? To explore the other half of what should have always been mine?

She's ready.

I might not be ready, but she is.

It's a thought that doesn't exactly fill me with the best of confidence. I can't seem to make myself leave this room, let alone go out into the world. Soon I probably won't even have a job anymore, so how would I support myself?

I should go, but I can't. Not until I know. I ignore that small voice saying I won't leave even if I knew. I've had enough change in my life. The thought of more makes me feel paralyzed.

But I should go. I should.

I can't help but feel a surge of guilt at my hesitation. My mother is lying there and here I am, torn between my desire to know more about my heritage and the sheer weight of the resentment I carry toward her for hiding it from me all these years. This guilt gnaws at me, twisting my insides as I force myself to shift my focus back to my research.

I turn back to my laptop, fingers hovering above the keys as I delve into the world of *tā moko*, the traditional māori tattoos. The intricate designs and their profound meanings captivate me. They're not just art; they're a declaration of identity, heritage, and belonging. The *moko kauae*, the chin tattoos of māori women, hold particular significance. Each line, each curve, tells a story, a history that stretches back generations.

I begin sketching, my fingers moving almost of their own accord. Since she hinted at my māori heritage, I've spent countless hours perfecting my drawings. It's become a way to connect with a part of myself I never knew existed. Each design is a step closer to understanding who I am.

I've memorized almost every design I've come across. The *koru*, with its spiral shape, symbolizes new life and growth. The *manaia*, a mythical creature with a bird's head, a human body, and a fish's tail, represents balance between the sky, earth, and sea. The *puhoro*, a pattern of curved lines, symbolizes speed and strength. I've learned their meanings, their origins, and the variations within each design. Yet, I know it wouldn't be respectful to create my own variants. Not until I'm accepted as māori.

I ignore the prickles of unease and the fear of not being welcomed. Drawing these designs has become second nature, a meditative process that grounds me as I wait for the inevitable end. They will kick me out soon. Once she is no longer mentally fit.

All they care about is the money. They... I stop myself before I start a mental tirade about materialism. I don't have the energy for it after all the conflict today.

I should leave.

I wonder... would a māori community accept me? After so many years lost, being outside my birthright, could I ever find a place among them?

A sharp, jarring sound breaks my concentration. The bell from my mother's room. She's summoning me again.

Reluctantly, I close my laptop and make my way to her room. The smell of alcohol is overpowering, a constant reminder of her condition. She lies on the bed, her once vibrant eyes now dull and unfocused. She mutters to herself, nonsensical gibberish that echoes around the room.

"Mum?" I say softly, stepping closer. Her eyes flicker, finally focusing on me.

"Ariki," she whispers. Her voice is a mere breath, but the name is like a lightning bolt, "His name was Ariki."

There's a moment of cluelessness as I blink stupidly before my heart begins to race.

Ariki. Is this my father's name?

"Mom, who is Ariki?" I ask, my voice trembling with excitement. "Is he my father?"

She doesn't respond. "Tell me more. Please." I draw out the last word like a petulant child, desperate to know.

But she only mutters incoherently, slipping back into her half-mad state. Frustration and desperation well up inside me. Just as I'm about to press her for more, the door bursts open, and my older siblings storm in.

"What are you doing in here?" my brother Timothy demands, grabbing my arm and pulling me away from the bed.

My brain fizzles with the contact, but I'm too distracted by what my mum just said to lash out.

"I was just—" I begin, but he cuts me off with another yank.

"She needs rest. You're upsetting her," my sister Bethany snaps. "Get out."

"But she said—" I try to explain, but they're not listening. My brother pushes me out of the room and slams the door in my face.

I stand there, heart pounding, the name Ariki echoing in my mind. It's the first real clue I've had about my father, and they've shut me out. Anger and frustration boil over, but I know there's nothing I can do. Not now, at least.

The corridor feels colder than usual, the dim light casting eerie shadows on the walls, electricity from the light buzzing even louder than usual, overloading my senses.

Shut door or not, I can still hear my mother's raspy breaths and incoherent mumbling through the shut door, each one a stark reminder that her time is running out. She's slipping away, and with her, the answers I so desperately need about my father.

I shut my eyes and lean against the door only for her frail form to flash in my eyes.

Like it or not, I am torn between a sense of familial loyalty and the bitterness that she's taking her secrets with her as she shuts us out. It'll only make it worse that she'll still be here in body for who knows how many years.

Suddenly, raised voices break the stillness. My siblings are fighting again, their voices clearly heard through the door. I begin to beat a slow-paced retreat once I realize where their conversation is going, disgust curling in my stomach as I hear them bickering over the will. Don't they realize she can still hear them?

"What about the house? It should be mine; I've done the most for her!" My brother's voice is sharp, filled with entitlement.

My sister's voice cuts through his, equally venomous. "You? Don't make me laugh. I've been the one taking care of her every day!"

She hasn't. It's been me.

I can't stand to hear anymore. Picking up the pace, I head to my room, their voices growing faint behind me. I need to distract myself, to find some sense of clarity. I lock the door before taking in the familiar, comforting sights and smells. The soft light filtering through the thin curtains, the desk with drawings scattered across it, and the distinct scent of old coffee that has long since gone cold.

Dune, a well-worn copy I fell asleep reading the night before, is on the floor. It's one of my favorites. Along with my shows, it's one of the many ways I escape while staying right here where it's safe. Although even that safety is an illusion, judging by what my siblings are yelling now.

I ignore the screeching of my siblings—vultures circling a carcass, both of them.

Sitting at my desk, I type *Ariki* into the search engine. The name my mother whispered clings to my thoughts like a lifeline.

Ariki. The results flood my screen, but they're next to useless. It's a common name, meaning "chief" or "leader" in Māori. It's impossible. Frustration gnaws at me. I was hoping for something more, some clue that would lead me to him, but it seems fate is playing a cruel joke.

I try for hours, but nothing changes. I start to calculate the percentage of success, but it is negligible. Far too many decimals. It's pointless.

I listen to make sure the vultures are done, then stop ignoring the protesting of my bladder. When was the last time I drank something? Ate? I don't remember. It doesn't matter, the best thing to do now is to go to sleep so this day can be over.

My limbs move mechanically as I shuffle toward the bathroom. I catch a glimpse of myself in the mirror, my reflection hazy. My dark hair is tousled and my skin pale.

My hand picks up the toothbrush and begins scrubbing my teeth, my movements brisk and routine. Then there's a knock. Loud, insistent, and growing more obnoxious by the second, pounding into my skull. The bathroom door rattles under the force of it.

God, I wish my brain would just let me leave. Not be warring with itself. Too anxiety ridden to leave while obsessed with the idea of being completely alone.

I feel my lips twitch, wanting to turn into a scowl, but it's not reflected in my expression.

"Come on, Olivia! Open up already!" Bethany's voice, sharp and grating, cuts through the door. My hand twists the knob, and as the door swings open, Bethany barges in, as impatient and domineering as ever. She's already in her pajamas, hair perfectly groomed, and the predatory gleam in her eyes is unmistakable.

Without waiting for me to speak, she thrusts a crumpled piece of paper into my face.

"Here," she says with that obnoxious sneer of hers. "I need this done by tomorrow before I head back."

I glance down at the paper. Research on the thermodynamic principles of non-ideal solutions. It's a chemistry assignment. Graduate-level, of course—because Bethany never asked me for anything simple. Why is she even taking this course? I thought she was going to be a barrister.

My mind races, skimming through the words, and I'm only paying twenty-three percent attention as Bethany drones on. This will take at least four hours and twenty-five minutes to complete. If I'm quick, maybe I can shave that down twelve percent.

Bethany waves her hand between me and the paper.

"What?" I hear myself ask, my tone flat, emotionless, though inside, I'm seething. I want to tell her to go to hell, to shove her assignment somewhere dark, but I know what's coming.

Bethany rolls her eyes dramatically. "Oh, come on, don't act like you've got anything better to do. I heard you hit someone again, so I figured you're free. Plus, you're good at this stuff, so it shouldn't take you long."

I feel the burn of anger rise in my chest, but I keep my face expressionless. No matter how angry I get, no matter how many mental cusses I throw her way, nothing escapes my lips.

Instead, my body moves like it's on autopilot. I take the paper from her hands without protest, scanning the assignment quickly, a routine I know all too well. This is Bethany at her worst—entitled, arrogant, and completely sure I'll do as she asks.

"What, no complaints?" she asks with a needling tone. "I don't even have to threaten to touch you?"

She's testing me, prodding for a reaction, but I don't give her one.

I open my mouth, trying to warn her about the assignment's complexity, about how she'll need to defend her work, but as soon as I begin, Bethany cuts me off, waving her hand dismissively.

"Oh, and once you're done with that," she adds, "Timothy left the invoices and receipts for you on the dining table. You'll need to sort those out and handle the tax stuff."

I don't even have the energy to respond. It's always like this with them. Bethany and Timothy, always taking, never giving. At least Tony leaves me alone. He hasn't said much of anything to me in years.

I never imagined my life would turn out like this.

I just want to be left alone to draw. The resentment in my chest grows, swelling to the point where it feels like I might burst, but my body doesn't show it. Numb and disconnected, that's the best way. My head just nods on its own accord, as if this were the most normal request in the world.

Bethany narrows her eyes at me, sensing the shift in my mood. Her lips twist into a smile. I assume a cruel one, since that's her natural state.

"Oh, and don't think you're fooling anyone," she says, her voice dripping with condescension. "We all know you're only good for this kind of thing. I mean, come on. Twenty-six and still at home. Half white, half nobody. One hundred percent crazy. You should be thankful we keep you busy."

I flinch at her use of a percentage, knowing it's meant to mock me, not just insult me. That stings. A sharp, burning pain that lances through me. I want to scream at her, to tell her how vile and wrong she is, but the words stay locked inside my head. My body just stands there, silent. Reminding me, once again, that I don't have much evidence to say otherwise.

Bethany's smile grows wider, satisfied with the impact of her words. "Anyway, get to work. I'll check in later."

She turns on her heel and leaves, slamming the door behind her. I'm left standing in the room, staring at the piece of paper in my hand. Anger bubbles inside me, hot and relentless, but there's nowhere for it to go. No one to lash out at.

I crumple the paper tighter in my hand. There is no refusing, at least not without repercussions, that much is clear, but I can make this as painful for her as possible. I'll bury her under complex theories and advanced chemistry concepts. If she's going to be lazy, I'm going to make sure she looks like a fool when asked to defend her work.

I move to the desk, pulling out my notebook and a few reference textbooks I've kept handy. My fingers fly across the page, drafting an outline for the paper. Concepts like Raoult's Law, activity coefficients, and Van't Hoff factors fill the page, with enough subtle errors in application that there will be follow-up questions.

I feel the pressure building in my chest, the anger simmering just below the surface, threatening to spill over as I work. Tears prick at my eyes, hot and angry, but I force them back. Crying won't help. It never has.

4

Olivia

I wake with a start, a jolt of panic coursing through me. I'm not in my bed. My body is bound, and I'm being carried like a sack of potatoes over someone's shoulder. A masked man. Fear grips me, then rage, and I struggle, but my movements are useless against the tight bindings.

"Let me go!" I scream, my voice muffled by the gag in my mouth. My heart pounds in my chest, a frantic rhythm of terror.

In my panicked thrashing, I catch a glimpse of Timothy. He's standing in the doorway, a smile playing on his lips. My heart sinks as I realize he's watching them take me away. My sister and other brother enter the room, see the commotion, raise their brows, but then roll their eyes and say nothing. They seem more content to converse with Timothy.

"Are you just going to let them take me? Help me!" I scream, but my voice is muffled by the gag, my words falling on deaf ears.

They ignore my pleas, their indifference cutting deeper than any blade. The front door swings open, and the cold night air hits my face. I'm dragged out, my screams swallowed by the darkness as the door slams shut behind me.

Tears blur my vision, the betrayal stinging worse than the ropes cutting into my skin. I'm thrown into a van, the door slamming shut with a finality that echoes through my soul. The engine roars to life, and the van lurches forward, carrying me away.

My mind races, trying to make sense of what's happening. Why would Timothy do this? What could he possibly gain from having me taken away? The questions whirl in my mind, but no answers come.

The van moves through the night, the vibration of the engine lulling me into a state of fearful resignation. I'm trapped, powerless to escape, and the only thing I can do is hope that somewhere, somehow, I'll find a way out of this nightmare.

I close my eyes, trying to shut out the reality of my situation, but the images of my siblings' cold indifference and Timothy's smile are burned into my mind. I've been betrayed by my own family, and the pain of that betrayal is more than I can bear.

The van comes to a stop, and the door slides open. Rough hands pull me out, and I'm dragged toward an unknown destination. The night is silent, the only sounds are my muffled cries and the footsteps of my captors.

I'm thrown into a small, dimly lit room, the door slamming shut behind me. The bindings are removed, and I collapse to the floor, my body aching from the rough treatment. The room is bare, with only a single chair and a small table. I crawl to the corner, curling into a ball as I try to make sense of what's happening.

The percentages don't align.

Hours pass, or maybe minutes—it's hard to tell. The fear and uncertainty are overwhelming, and I can feel myself slipping into despair.

***

"Aliens," I say, tasting the word. "Bugs," I add, instantly knowing that word tastes like bile.

I sniff, remembering the new scent in my cell... but, no, it isn't bile. I sniff again.

Or bug blood, either. I push down the surge of satisfaction. "Twelve bugs dead," I sing-song.

I wait for the feeling of relief that usually bubbles up after enumerating, but nothing comes. No feeling of safety. No satisfaction. Numbers aren't working on this damn ship.

One ship. Twelve dead aliens. Six by the throat. Three from pulling off enough limbs. Two from a crushed head chitin. One through the eyes.

But still... zero safety.

No satisfaction, I grumble internally.

Perhaps it is me having spent so long stuck with my own body and its variant smells and oozes in a confined space, but I am pretty sure there is something foul smelling about the cell I'm in. Something new, that is.

It's not an overpowering smell——and further, albeit demeaning, efforts to sniff myself have proven that I am not the culprit——so putting the smell out of my mind has become infinitely easier.

Well, that's an exaggeration, the smell is still offensive to my nose but only about as uncomfortable as being stuck in a room with an undetectable source of rotten egg smell that just won't go away.

Nothing too drastic, but it's the sort of scenario you could live with grudgingly.

Hmm. What could I live with un-grudgingly? Is that a word?

No.

"Doesn't matter," I chide.

Luckily I can still remember just about everything I've ever read, as much as it has served me well for the mind-wrecking periods of sound torture the bug-men have subjected me to. I can still hear the pinging echoing off the walls and my eye twitches at the memory.

Another one of my many woes since I got here.

I don't want to think about it, though. "No. No. Remember what's happening. Don't let it slip," I tell myself.

Alright. What has happened?

"Bug aliens," I remind myself.

Eerily enough, I was quick to accept the fact that I have been kidnapped by aliens because what else could they be? Giant talking bugs that seem to have a bad case of indiscriminate grabbing of parts that have no business being grabbed without permission... yes, aliens.

Traumatizing, but clear enough to comprehend, and luckily their limbs are easy to snap so there is an outlet for my rage.

The next shock point was watching in numb horror as I was partly sedated and subsequently operated on to have my body modified to be as aesthetically pleasing as an oversexualized MAPPA-drawn anime character. Drawn specifically to fit the tastes of no-life pop culture addicts who spend more time digesting *Kuroinu* than should be legal.

I grab my newly shorn dark-brown hair, yanking it to center myself.

"Not legal," I hiss out.

Again, mind rending, albeit less frightful and more existential, but still, fairly easy to comprehend and come to terms with. Even when they keep changing their minds and altering me again.

Which brings me to the recent routine I've more or less been subject to over the past couple of... days? Weeks?

I can't believe I lost count. I should have that number, but I don't. It makes me feel unmoored.

It's hard to keep track of time when all you sleep and wake up to is the sight of acerbic lights that are every bit as invasive as the short, bug-like fuckers that brought me here in the first place.

The realization that I hadn't been the only one to be taken did help dull the panic of having to process everything in the brightly lit gray central hallway they allow us to stretch our legs in every now and then. Call it what you will, but there is something about collective misery that just makes the process all the more bearable.

I'd take my own thoughts on the subject with a pinch of salt though, I am no therapist or psychologist, despite the sheer volume of amateurish self-taught information I have on the topic.

Where am I going with this?

"Abduction," I remind myself.

Right after the wholly nonconsensual body modification that we had been put through, it became apparent that not everyone's body reacted to the change positively.

By "everyone" I simply mean just me. My luck tends to be shitty that way.

Unlike the others, I had to go under the knife again and again. The first time I damn near went into anaphylactic shock barely a few hours after the sedatives wore off, and the second time I had to deal with frequent blackouts that had everything going dark when I was in the middle of something. By "something" I mean pulling books from memory or letting my imagination run freer than I would usually let it. And the next time I regained consciousness, I would be in a situation that was equal parts karmic as it was painful.

"Aliens," I say, deciding the word tastes bitter and pungent. "Blood," I mutter, deciding the word tastes sweet.

Revenge is sweet, they say.

The first time I blacked out, I woke up with a squad of the same bug-like aliens beating down on my stiff body as I throttled the last vestiges of life out of one of their own. The sod was already dead, its chitin-covered body having faded to a duller, pallid, purplish tone as its disgusting barbed tongue lolled out of the side of its stupid mouth on its stupid face.

The emotions I felt at that moment rapidly cycled from morbid curiosity, to surprise, to realization, to mild disgust from its fetid death rattle before settling on vicious glee at the realization of what I had just done.

I loved it.

I've hit plenty of people in my life, but I always held back. If I had known killing felt this good...

"Loved it. Loved it," I repeat.

I only registered the assault my body was going through shortly after that epiphany, and the few minutes I spent curled into a ball as they capitalized on my sudden porousness to pain to beat me within what I was sure was a millimeter of my life.

They didn't kill me, though, and I'm not sure why. They must not place much value on their individual lives. Maybe it's a queen and drone situation?

Ants. Bees. Alien bugs.

"Bugs. Bugs..." I trail off with a long susurration.

The punishment so far has been to limit my interaction with the others. What little time I spend with them is down to the few minutes of mute staring we get just before we are stuffed back into our cells. The rest of my time is spent in one room or the other being prodded, injected, studied, and in some truly twisted version of fate, having my fingers tightly wound around the neck of the next unfortunate piece of chitinous shit that had the fate of being stuck in the same room with me whenever I blacked out.

It feels so damn good, cathartic even to get my revenge in these small ways, not too major to warrant execution... somehow. Despite the dead bodies.

The nice little alien kill count I've wracked up since the beginning leaves me full of smiles no matter how long they spend leering at me from the observation deck with their stupid multi, concaved eyes.

I obey their instructions and allow myself to get stabbed full of vial after vial of panic-inducing substances. A good portion of that panic may or may not be due to the sheer size of the needle used to administer it.

I've learned how to placate them. Usually with crying and screaming.

So far so good, it has brought me less pain, and as any well-adjusted human in my current situation would...

How badly adjusted is not good? Thirty... ten... twenty percent.

"Five," I announce.

It's a no-brainer that less pain is better for my health than the pain that would come with stubbornly digging my heels in.

One of the other women, the one with creamy skin, and black hair, and a scowl that eerily reminded me of an unhinged animal being put in a cage, seemed to be the most stubborn of our mish-mashed bunch.

She didn't last long.

Spitfire she may have been, but between the two of us, I like to think I'm making more headway in sticking it back to these psychos by playing the role of the weak, defective human that shies away from everything and cries harder than everyone else when subjected to even the most basic of bodily violations.

Well, until I choke the life out of one of them, of course. But I don't say no.

Of course I don't say no.

"Say yes. Say yes," I nudge.

Not that bodily violations should be tolerated in any form.

"Zero percent," I hiss out, the number not helping my mind settle at all. "Can't say no."

No. It shouldn't be tolerated, but I like living. You'd think that after killing one of them that acting insane and apologizing wouldn't work, but it does.

Misdirection. Directions are missed.

"Ninety-five percent," I disagree. "Not five."

That article three years ago said that I'd struggle with making my point if I did not outgrow my timidity.

What a load of bull... bull that suddenly makes me aware that I have been silently repeating the same line in my head over and over again as my mind fills up the blanks provided by the silence with its own voiceover of memories past.

Memories... memories.

"Five percent," I mutter.

My mind is on fire.

Five fires. One fire. Ninety-five fires.

There is plenty to occupy yourself if you have a memory as vivid as mine. The fact that I seem only to have gotten better at it in captivity is just another example of how fucked up I am. Just like they always said.

All the places she sent me to get "fixed." Twenty-three places in the US. Eight in the UK. That one in Sydney. All the years living away from my only safe space. My room. It did no good.

"Cannot be reformed," I quote from the files.

Formed and reformed.

I should form something new. That would be nice.

A good thought.

"Five and ninety-five," I hiss out, then suck my teeth.

Any thought is easier to deal with compared to considering just what little remains of your sanity before it goes careening off the hills at over three hundred kilometers per hour.

"Formed and reformed," I say in my best American accent. The one I used to blend in. Then switch to British, which I was never quite as good at. "Five formed. Ninety-five reformed."

Sydney was nice.

"*Pākehā* have no right to *moko*," I recite aloud from memory, more than happy to put all rationalizations of my possible insanity behind me.

I pause, tasting the statement in my mouth to make sure I got the pronunciation right before repeating it again, this time to better grasp the concept behind the message as opposed to its linguistic structure.

The words are just as bitter as when I say "alien."

"*Pākehā* have no right to *moko*..."

It's a line I've recited multiple times, first to pass time and then to better digest its content, which I've been privy to after multiple read-throughs.

It's a dismissive statement, an absolute lodged in no doubt pre-contemporary superstition or something along those lines, and yet, I don't disagree.

Even though it always makes my heart sink.

I touch my chin, where I hoped one day to have the dark lines declaring who I am. Once I figured out what that means, of course.

It seems useless now.

It's a pipe dream—and I mean that in the literal sense that it is the sort of delusion you'd find only through repeated exposure to marijuana blowing——this obsession with solidifying identity that is.

Blame it on my existential crisis sponsored by my mind eating itself over...

What? Something. Some of a thing.

"Five of what?" I ask, jarring my memory.

Right. Whether or not I'm still the same person I was prior to the bodily modifications. That something.

"Classic ship of Theseus-type thoughts," I titter.

But with the human flesh being the object of interest this time around, I muse. *Five rounds of some.*

Like my mind wasn't a confusing hot box of identity-based issues before now.

"Cannot be formed or reformed," I remind myself, pulling myself back from my thoughts shattering.

I touch my chin again.

I don't want an empty symbol. I want a heritage, something to look back on just before I'm gone and die happy with the knowledge that it will live on long after I am gone.

"I'm already gone," I clarify.

One and gone. Just one. Thing of sums. I won't die happy.

I've read my fair share of self-help pieces advocating for individual identity or prestige amongst other flowery terms and descriptions, and while it was a good enough consolation for my teenage years, maturity did a good job disabusing me of that notion.

Humans, at our core, are more or less social creatures. The need to identify with a unique group of one's own was as much of a psychological need as it was a social one.

I cannot be reformed because I would prefer to not be part of that society.

Sum of none. One and gone.

"Alone," I mutter. "One, not five. But am I two?"

Maybe two, but one is better. Safer.

I'm having a bit of trouble finding what group exactly I am supposed to be identifying with.

I'm half white, or *pākehā*, and half māori, if her hints are true.

"Ariki, Ariki," I chant.

I know nothing of that second half of my heritage beyond what I read voraciously after she let out a hint.

Just one? One and done?

Just a small hint, but my features and all the odd looks suddenly make sense.

"Just one," I decide.

I mentally set down the article as a yawn worms its way past my lips. How long have I been here?

I stare listlessly at the single observation window a good meter taller than me and I am unsurprised at seeing nothing but the reflected light bouncing off it.

They get sick of my muttering sometimes. It's useful.

Technically speaking, the window is not the only potential exit in the room, there is a door... somewhere along the walls. It is the main entrance and has been the route through which they have brought me into the room repeatedly.

"Formed through which," I say with a snicker.

Form of sum. One and gone.

Stupid door. It has a nasty habit of fading into the monochrome singleness of the room the moment it is shut, and subsequent efforts to pry it open had me pawing at the white walls like a loon until it became clear that the door had either completely disappeared or specifically been designed to become one with the wall to deter escape attempts.

Neat. Very neat. And stupid.

Suddenly it makes sense why the psychotic bugs from the slot above me haven't bothered to bother me despite my fiddling.

"Why does it make sense?" I ask, confused.

I lay down on my back and shut my eyes as a wave of exhaustion washes over me, but not one of sleep.

It's been a while since I felt the urge to sleep without the compulsion of the containment chamber they stuff me into every... night? Is it possible to have night without a sun?

Sum of sun is none.

If nothing else, at least I'd be more alert to pay attention to what exactly my kidnap-mates spend their time doing before they go to sleep. If I could see them.

"I can't see them," I note.

Believe it or not, I haven't paid much attention to the other women prior to now, on account of my less-than-stellar mental state.

"Ninety-five reformed," I remind myself.

No. No. Five.

My brain burns, and here I am shutting down again. I resist, but then let myself slip and tumble over the abyss of unconsciousness.

***

When I wake up, I hear the chittering. They like to come in when I'm unconscious.

"Just be still," one of them says.

Say yes. Say yes, I remind myself.

But I can't. This is new. There are too many of them. Far more than ever before and I just know they plan to kill me.

The fear starts to rise. They aren't touching me yet and so there is no rage to help me. I get up from the cot shakily.

"I must not fear," I recite. "Fear is the mind-killer."

It recedes the moment the first pincher touches my naked skin, glorious rage filling the gap it left behind. I keep up the litany in between crushing whatever limbs are closest to me. The bugs pile against me, and I scream out my rage, fists and elbows flying.

"...there will be," I punctuate the last word with an elbow to a chitinous throat, "nothing."

I cry out, staggering when one lands a blow to my shoulder, then get my balance back and kick one of the fuckers right in the chest, the sound of it caving sending a fissure of ecstasy through me.

Then one of them finally manages to knock me off my feet and they rush me as I roar.

"ONLY I WILL FUCKING REMAIN," I scream out, wriggling, but not able to move the sheer weight of dozens of them on top of me.

I'm panting when a new voice speaks. "She is perfect," says someone in an oddly wet language. "I will transfer the credits now."

I try to look past the writhing bugs, but then there is a stinging pain in my neck. Another needle. My vision blurs as I curse.

One and done. One and...

***

When next I open my eyes, I am back in my sleep chamber, mouth dry, remnants of tears sliding down my cheeks, and with a copious pink slime slathered all over my body.

It takes a moment of silence for my brain to catch up with that tidy little bit of info before I squeak in horror and proceed to scrape the offensive stuff off my person with reckless abandon.

I sincerely hope this came from my mind snapping and crushing bugs, anything other than that and I am going to curl up into the fetal position and cry.

I can't get to my back because something is holding me in place.

Then I realize this is a different chamber.

There is a beep, and then I fall, my legs giving out beneath me. The ground rushes up to meet me, and I crash down hard. Pain shoots through me, but I can't focus on it. Something is in my lungs, burning and choking me. I try to cough it out, but my body is weak and unresponsive. Tears stream down my face, blurring my vision, but I can just make out someone rushing toward me.

She reaches me, her hands gentle but firm as she tries to help. Luckily I can't move my limbs or I might kill her. *Only bugs get that,* I remind myself, my lips moving but no sound emerging.

My body is heavy, my movements sluggish, but I manage to expel the gas from my lungs, each cough a battle. A vent system whirs to life, and fresh air fills the room. I can finally breathe, and my vision clears enough to see her face. She's saying something, but it's hard to focus over the pounding in my ears.

Then it clears and I wish it hadn't.

"Aren't they so delightfully powerless?" a voice says, and I flinch.

The creature I set my eyes upon looks nothing like the bugs I've been crushing over the course of the past couple of weeks... or months.

Unlike the scratchy, high chirping sounds those ones made, this one's voice is cruel and grating.

It's face and skin remind me a bit of a dolphin, albeit with the sort of consistency you'd come to expect from a slug, paired with three trunk-like legs akin to an elephant and the copious amounts of slime oozing all over. The perfect image for nightmare fuel.

I want to scream in fright, but it comes off as more of a pathetic whimper after an initial screech.

When I feel a surge of arousal, I know that I have truly lost my mind.

The woman beside me looks at me with a mix of unknown expressions. I want to scream again, to rage, but my voice is caught in my throat. The slug speaks again, and its words make my skin crawl.

"Just imagine them bent over like that for your own purposes." Suddenly, I find my voice.

"OHFUCKYOUANDYOURPURPOSE-YOUSLIMECOVEREDPIECEOFSHIT!"

The horror of it all hits me, and I can't hold back my voice from hurtling into a gibberish-filled scream. The woman grabs my shoulders and I barely restrain myself from lashing out, her voice urgent in my ear. "They won't stop pumping gas in here until you stop screaming. Just..." She doesn't get to finish before another wave of gas makes us cough.

When the air clears again, I'm making terrified moans, my throat raw. The slug keeps talking about our bodies, about how they'll be used. I can feel the woman's arms around me, her whispers trying to soothe me, her touch doing the opposite.

I had settled on the bug situation. I hate change.

Hate. Hate change.

The woman speaks again, interrupting my litany. "I have you. I know this is terrifying, but it only gets worse if you seem scared. They like it."

Tears are streaming down both of our faces now. "Wh-Where are we? What is that?" I manage to ask, my voice trembling.

"On a spaceship. Those aliens captured us," she says.

Spaceship. Another one? The words spin in my head, trying to make sense, and then I slap myself lightly to remind myself that the events of the past couple of days, weeks, or months are not a fever dream, and that I need to stop looning out before this lady figures I am a few bolts short of well-mounted engine block.

I look around, really seeing my surroundings for the first time.

Standing casket-like pods, very much similar to the pod I just fell out of, dominate the room with glass panels through which

I see other women lying still, with their features stuck in various states. I look back at the woman, and something about her eyes catches my attention.

I look to my own reflection and see I've had a similar modification. Green eyes. Green hair. That's new. A glance down at my body reveals I don't have the giant breasts and healing scars the bugs gave me anymore. I look almost... normal.

My mind stutters and I look back at the woman.

"What did they do to your eyes?" I ask, stupidly, before almost kicking myself.

They did the same thing to your eyes dipshit, I screech internally.

I feel unmoored, but then with a start I realize that my thoughts are coming sequentially. They haven't done that for a while. Not since they started drugging me.

The woman holds back a groan. Her eyes are a vivid shade of aquamarine, completely blue except for the black pupil. It's unsettling, unnatural, albeit beautiful in its own way.

She moves on to another topic before I can backtrack, and I hear the slug snigger something to his asshole colleague before an errant thought pings me at the fore of my mind.

I gesture vaguely at the slugs, careful not to make the motion too obvious. "Why can I understand it?"

Well-read I may be, but I'm pretty sure I never learned to speak snot alien. Or bug chitter, for that matter, but I was too drugged to wonder about it before.

"They put nanites in us that do lots of things, including somehow letting us understand and speak other languages," she explains.

I'd spent ages alternating between isolation and that bleak hall waiting for a crumb of info on what exactly was going on, but it's safe to say that I am not prepared for the info being piled on me.

Nanites. Languages. It's all too much.

Involuntarily, I feel myself one wrong exhale away from a shutdown and I can't. The last thing I need from her right now is sympathy, so I push the rising panic back down.

"There's a live feed running at all times, and they like it when we watch it. Don't look at it because you'll be able to read the comments," she warns me.

I stare long and hard at the nonsensical-looking strings of characters that pop up in the comments bar and sure enough, I can read the comments with all the fluency of one born into the language.

Did... that...that son of a gun just suggest I ...?

Curiosity can be a bit of a bitch sometimes. This is one of those times.

I'm shaking harder, when I turn back to her. "That's anatomically impossible."

She lets out a mirthless chuckle. "I'm a nurse, and so I was sure to point that out to them. They started showing videos of how buyers have sex. Avoid talking about it. Trust me."

At least the bugs weren't interested in that. This is a new form of hell, it seems.

I gulp, then nod. "My name's Olivia."

"I'm Ree."

The sound of the pneumatic doors hissing open is just about the only warning I get before torture gas floods my airways sending the both of us both into a hacking fit.

It's a while before I gain control of my spasming body again, and when I do, I cling on to her for dear life, my rage at the contact somehow less important than grounding my mind before it fractures for good.

Her arm is wrapped around my waist and mine around her shoulders as tears stream down our faces.

"You have no names until your buyer gives them to you," the slug says to us in a nasty tone.

He goes back to his salesperson's voice. "That concludes our special session. We will bring another of the harem out to play soon."

He turns back to us, his eyes focused on Ree. "Put the green whore back in her chamber."

Ree tries to protest. She spends a few more moments trying and failing to argue with the slime-covered fucker and only ends up choking on gas. Me right along with her.

Knowing a losing battle when I see one, I reluctantly let go of her and climb back into my pod. Tremors wrack my body, but we don't look away from each other. I really want to get another long look at the slug, but it was pretty clear already that they don't have the spindly neck of the bug men.

Doesn't matter. It'll feel just as good to kill a slug as it was the bugs. I know it.

5

Kroaicho

I awaken with a start, disoriented and alone. The walls of my prison are smooth, and cold, and seem to pulse with an eerie, otherworldly light. I shiver, feeling the chill seep into my bones. My skin begins to shimmer with an array of colors: blue, violet, and red.

Not my calmest moment.

The panic sets in regardless as I try to comprehend the situation. The air is thick with the scent of decay and something metallic, creating a nauseating cocktail that churns my stomach.

My hands instinctively reach out to touch the walls, seeking purchase, any familiar sensation. The walls are slick and unresponsive, offering no comfort. I recoil, feeling a wave of helplessness wash over me. As my senses come alive all of a sudden, I am slammed with sensory overload. The smell I perceive is acrid, bitter and I get the vague impression that were I not surrounded by walls on all sides I'd have just been witness to something truly terrifying.

It takes some time to adjust, but with that gone, my senses return to normal. With a clearer head, I pick up the sounds of distant explosions and muffled voices echoing through the walls, growing louder as I focus on them. It's a cacophony of languages I don't understand, filled with fear, anger, and desperation. I'm alarmed, that much is a given, and it takes a bit of effort to recouple my memory of all that happened to lead me to this point.

I remember that I was captured by genali. Did they sell me?

I am on my feet in an instant and with that done, I take a minute to take stock of the cave I am in.

Driven by instinct, I begin to claw at the walls, desperate to escape. My claws, durable enough for the task, dig into the material. The walls resist my efforts. Yet, with each desperate attempt, a small amount of material chips away. As the wall begins to yield, a draft of colder air rushes in, carrying with it the scent of dirt and something wild. Hope ignites within me.

The sounds of approaching footsteps echo through the prison, growing louder. Adrenaline surges through me, fueling a final, desperate push against the weakened wall. With a final heave, I break through the wall, meeting dirt, and quickly begin tunneling through at vicious speeds. The soil around me is a familiar sensation, grounding me as I dig.

I maintain the pace until I tumble into a narrow tunnel. The tunnel is pitch black, filled with the same metallic scent from before. As my eyes adjust to the darkness, I see figures moving ahead, their forms indistinct in the low light. They speak in rapid, harsh tones, their words lost in the echo of the tunnel.

My heart pounds in my chest. I am no longer alone, but the company offers little comfort. The figures ahead are a threat, their intentions unknown. I decide to remain hidden until I can determine the next best step.

Crouching low, I peer at the figures, my bioluminescent skin dimming to avoid detection. The tunnel is narrow, and their movements are slow and methodical. They carry equipment, strange metallic devices. I strain to catch any recognizable words or phrases, but their language remains foreign, alien to my ears.

It's simple though, and I know it won't take me long to figure it out.

As I watch, one of the figures stops and sniffs the air, its head turning slowly in my direction. I freeze, willing my skin to match the dark tones of the tunnel walls. The figure's eyes, glinting faintly in the darkness, scan the area where I hide. My breath catches in my throat, and I remain motionless, praying to any entity that they do not see me.

After what feels like an eternity, the figure moves on, satisfied that nothing is amiss. I let out a silent sigh of relief, my muscles relaxing slightly. But the danger is far from over. I need to find a way out of this tunnel, away from these unknown entities, and back to safety.

The distant crashes and muffled voices continue, a constant reminder of the chaos beyond these walls. I stalk forward, careful to avoid making any noise that might attract attention. The tunnel is cramped, forcing me to move slowly, and cautiously. Every step is a calculated risk.

As I near a bend in the tunnel, I pause, listening intently. The voices are louder here, more distinct. I catch snippets of their conversation, though the words are still incomprehensible. Their tone, however, is unmistakable: urgency, frustration, and fear.

I peer around the bend, my eyes adjusting to the dim light. Ahead, the tunnel opens into a larger chamber, filled with more of the figures. They are gathered around a large, cylindrical device, that dominates the center of the dug-out cavern that had been repurposed to become a room of sorts.

Now I can get a proper look at them, I feel the first vestiges of unease begin to bubble up.

Braceaaer. A whole group of the terrible bipeds.

Surely I have not displeased the demiurge so much so that zha chooses to punish me like this.

My eyes fall on the gadget in the center of the room. Its surface is covered in blinking lights and strange symbols. There are multiple metal ropes leading from it into a part of the room I can't see. The figures work quickly, their hands moving with practiced precision.

One of them, larger than the others, appears to be giving orders. Its voice is commanding and authoritative. The others respond with quick nods and movements, their focus entirely on the device. I watch, fascinated and horrified by their efficiency.

I need to find a way out of this place, but the presence of these figures complicates matters. I can't risk being seen, not until I know more about who they are and what they want.

I press myself against the cold, damp wall of the tunnel, my skin dimming to a muted blue to blend into the shadows. The figures move closer, their conversation becoming more distinct. I strain to catch their words, my mind racing to piece together their language.

One of them growls something to the other one, their tone urgent.

The other replies testily, its tone even.

A third one snaps at them and they shut up; it's obvious who is in charge of this little operation.

I take a deep breath, trying to steady my nerves. These ones are clearly afraid of something. I move closer, careful not to make a sound, my eyes fixed on the group ahead. Their faces are obscured by helmets and their bodies covered in protective gear. They carry weapons, the glint of metal visible even in the dim light.

One of them turns suddenly. I freeze, holding my breath. For a moment, I think they have seen me, but they continue moving forward, their attention focused on the path ahead.

The leader growls out something to the others, their voice steady and commanding. And with that the group disperses, their footsteps echoing through the narrow passageways. I wait until the last of them has disappeared from sight before moving. My skin shifts to a deeper blue as I creep forward, keeping to the shadows. I need to find a way out of here, but I also need to understand who these people are and what they want.

I follow the leader, keeping a safe distance. They move with purpose, their steps confident despite the darkness. I stay close to the wall, my senses alert for any sign of danger. The tunnel widens slightly, and I see the leader stop to inspect a large metal door set into the rock.

They press a series of buttons on a keypad, the door hissing open with a burst of cold air. I edge closer, peering through the gap as the leader steps inside. The room beyond is filled with strange machinery, the hum of electronic devices filling the air. I slip through the door just before it closes, hiding behind a large blinking table as the leader moves deeper into the room.

I watch as they approach a table, their fingers flying over small buttons that respond by lighting up. The machines come to life, screens flickering with data and lights flashing in sequence. I move closer, my curiosity piqued. What are they doing here?

It hunches over the console, speaking into a communicator. I can barely make sense of its growls and grunts until I heard an all-too-familiar name.

Trakeldon. My skin lights up a muted red as I suck in air sharply.

No wonder they are terrified, they are about to die... what good a supplication can I give to the demiurge to avoid the same fate?

The leader grunts out a few more sentences before a voice crackles back. I'm starting to piece together the language, upset with myself that I never tried to learn it before.

The braceaaer nods, cutting the communication and turning back to the control panel. I take a step forward, my curiosity getting the better of me. I need answers, and this might be my only chance to get them.

"Who are you?" I demand, my voice low but firm. My skin shifts to a dark-hued purple of anger as I approach him slowly.

The leader spins around, their weapon drawn in an instant.

It gives me an appraising look before it sneers, "Back off *wasur*," they counter in a perfect rendition of my zhasie tongue, their eyes narrowing behind their visor, freezing me dead in my tracks.

My skin pulses to a darker shade of purple as I stand before the braceaaer. Its weapon remains trained on me, eyes narrowing behind the visor. This alien is unlike the genali; its build is more compact but brimming with potential lethality. My knuckles twitch, the spikes ready for action.

Did this incomplete life form just call me a wasur*?*

"You intend to make me pry it from your lips? Very well then..." My words are a growling click, the irritation, and adrenaline fueling my resolve. The braceaaer responds with a swift motion, a shot firing from its weapon. I twist, my body contorting with ease, the shot grazing my side but not enough to slow me down.

The first clash is brutal. I lunge, using the full force of my muscular segments to deliver a crushing blow to its helmet. The spikes on my knuckles pierce through, drawing a spray of blood as the helmet cracks. The braceaaer staggers but doesn't fall, a testament to its resilience.

I pivot, my body coiling back like a spring before launching into another assault. My hands dart forward, seeking weak points in its armor. The braceaaer counters with a series of quick, precise strikes, aiming to disorient me. I duck and weave, my bioluminescent skin flashing lighter purple as my irritation mounts.

Its fighting style is methodical, with each movement calculated and controlled. In contrast, my approach is raw and feral, driven more by instinct and brute strength.

If there is one thing my zhann tunneled into my head from the time I was but a limbless zhannel, it was the ability to play into my own strengths with little care to flare or some misguided sense of dominance hidden under the veneer of a fair fight.

I do not need to outfight a clearly skilled fighter, I just need to surprise the fool once, and then capitalize on that to extricate its life from it in the most effective way possible.

I see an opening and release a burst of poison mist from my nose glands. The mist envelops the braceaaer, but its suit protects it, the toxin ineffective. It retaliates with a powerful kick, its deceptively spindly limbs sending me sprawling.

I roll with the impact, my back spikes digging into the ground to halt my momentum. With a snarl, I rise, my skin a deep violet as I bare my tusks at the small thing.

The braceaaer charges, and I meet it head-on, using my near-invulnerable tusks to deflect its weapon. The clash reverberates through the cavern, or maybe that's just my brain rattling in my skull from the bone-to-alloy clash.

I make a mental note never to do that again.

In a fluid motion, I grab the braceaaer's arm and twist, the spikes on my knuckles digging into its flesh. It cries out, a guttural sound of pain, but manages to break free, landing a solid punch to my middle segment. Pain flares, but I embrace it, channeling it into my next attack.

I leap, my flexible body twisting mid-air to deliver a punishing blow to its chest. The impact sends the braceaaer crashing into the console, the machinery sparking from the collision. My skin shifts to a dark purple, reflecting my determination. I cannot afford to lose.

The braceaaer rises, its movements slower now, but no less deadly. It draws a blade.

I respond by bracing myself, my back spikes flaring defensively. We circle each other, both searching for an opening.

It lunges, the blade slicing through the air. I sidestep, my hands grabbing its wrist and twisting. The blade clatters to the ground, and I follow up with a limb to its midsection. The braceaaer doubles over, gasping for breath. I don't let up, my fists raining down blows, each one more brutal than the last.

I feel the crunch of bone beneath my knuckles, the spikes tearing through flesh and armor alike. The braceaaer collapses, a lifeless heap on the floor. My chest heaves, the purple of rage slowly fading to a pale blue of confusion.

"Did I... kill it?" I mutter, my voice tinged with disbelief. I hadn't intended to go this far. I sink to my knees, staring at the broken body before me. "Fool," I berate myself, my skin shifting to a muted purple. "You should have known better. You didn't even check if it could take your hits."

I needed answers.

My self-reproach is cut short by a horrifying screech echoing down the tunnel. My skin flashes red with fear, head spikes shivering.

There is another crash, braceaaer screams, and then suddenly the lights on the control panel dim until they are all out.

Did it destroy their power supply? There is a crash behind me that interrupts that tunnel of thought.

I barely have time to react before a massive limb slams into me, sending me crashing into the wall.

Pain explodes through my body, but I don't wait to see what the limb belongs to. Instinct takes over, and I begin tunneling into the wall. My physiology, built for such tasks, allows me to burrow through the soil at high speeds.

My muscles work in perfect harmony, each segment contributing to the effort. The spikes along my back slice through the soil, creating a path for my body to follow. The dirt around me is a comforting embrace, grounding me as I flee the unknown terror behind me.

I push myself to the limit, my breath coming in ragged gasps. The tunnel I create is narrow, just wide enough for my body to squeeze through.

My skin glows a faint red, a beacon in the darkness. The scent of soil fills my senses, a stark contrast to the metallic tang of the braceaaer domain.

Minutes pass in a blur, my mind focused solely on escape. The sound of the creature's roaring grows distant, replaced by the rhythmic scrape of my tunneling. I don't stop until I'm certain the danger is far behind me.

My hands, with their four thick digits, dig into the dirt at a manic pace, pulling and pushing with relentless determination. There is none of my usual finesse in the act as I brute force my way through to get away from the murderous creature those idiots brought here, my strength and the sharp spikes running down my back were more than sufficient to carve a path. The tunnel I created is narrow but stable, the walls packed tightly by the force of my movements.

As I tunnel, the spikes on my back serve a dual purpose, cutting through the soil and providing a defensive barrier. Any debris that falls is quickly pushed aside, the rhythmic motion soothing. The walls around me are cool and dark, a soothing contrast to the chaos I left behind.

The bioluminescent glow of my skin provides just enough light to navigate, the soft blue hues casting an eerie glow in the confined space. My breath comes in steady, controlled bursts, the rhythm of my tunneling matching the cadence of my heart. The scent of dirt is a comforting companion.

Every muscle in my body aches, but I push on, driven by the instinct to survive. The terror of the unknown creature becomes a distant but all too vivid memory in the back of my mind, replaced by the focused determination to escape. My mind races, each movement calculated and precise, a knife-edge balance only those who had tempered the urge to survive and the instinct that guides it.

Finally, as the adrenaline begins to fade, I find myself in a small cavern, the walls smooth and cool to the touch. I collapse, my body trembling with exhaustion. My skin shifts to a pale orange, the relief washing over me as palpable as anything.

That was close. Too close.

Nonetheless, I'd escaped.

***

I awaken with a sharp intake of breath, pain ripping through my side as if that cursed trakeldon struck me all over again. The memory surges forward with a clarity that makes me almost keen, my bioluminescent skin pulsing violently in whirls of blue, violet, and red. The cold, damp air of the cave does nothing to soothe the agony, and for a moment, I remain sprawled against the stone floor, gasping for air, disoriented.

Where am I? My head whips around frantically, my eyes scanning the cave, but there's little comfort to be found in its jagged walls. My vision blurs slightly as my skin shifts to a soft gradient of blue that ripples across me in erratic waves before I shake my head. I need to focus. But the panic flares hotter, and I can't seem to link the story that brought me here.

The pain, the darkness, the relentless chase—I was fleeing from something, wasn't I? My thoughts are fragmented, scattered, like shards of broken glass. My body tenses, skin shifting to a deeper shade of violet as my brows knit together in a grueling effort to get a hold of my feral-fueled anger.

It's not often I lose my control like this, and the thought of allowing fear to cloud my mind, like a headless zhannel, irritates me in more ways than I'd like.

Control yourself.

I remain like this for several agonizing moments, my breath ragged as I struggle to regain some semblance of composure. Slowly, ever so slowly, I steady myself, forcing my breath to even out. The blue glow on my skin dims, replaced by the faintest hue of red as I feel a venomous steam hiss from my snout into the stale air of the cave.

The relief that washes over me is short-lived, but it's enough to bring my mind back to the present. I blink slowly, assessing the situation with more clarity now. I can't stay here. Not with the distant rumbling of the ground beneath me, growing louder and more violent with each passing second. The ground trembles as if it, too, is aware of the dangers lurking nearby. My reprieve is over.

I push myself to my limbs, wincing as the ache in my side flares up again. I ignore it. Pain is familiar, comforting, even. I can deal with pain. What I can't deal with is being caught off-guard again.

I stagger out of the small cavern, squinting as I step into the harsh light that greets me at the cave's mouth. The brightness burns my eyes, forcing me to hiss in discomfort. A thin membrane slides over my pupils, dimming the glare to a tolerable level. My vision sharpens, and I assess my surroundings with renewed focus. The terrain stretches out before me in a jagged mess of rocks and sparse vegetation. It's alien—nothing like the lush, dense forests I'm used to.

But there's no time to dwell on the unfamiliar landscape. I need to move. Fast. I drop to all six limbs, my body moving with a natural fluidity that only comes when I'm in full motion. My muscles coil and release in perfect synchronization, propelling me forward with bursts of speed that leave the cave far behind. I push through the discomfort, the lingering pain in my side no more than an afterthought now.

I'm getting a good distance away when a sound stops me in my tracks. Voices. Not far off. My first instinct is to bolt in the opposite direction, but something stops me. A scent. Sweet, enticing, cutting through the acrid taste of my fear like a blade. It wafts into my nose, and before I know it, I'm frozen in place, inhaling deeply. The smell pulls at me, urging me to find its source.

What am I doing? My brain tries to pull me back to reality, but the scent... it's overwhelming. I find myself sniffing around, eager to locate the source. I shake my head, trying to snap myself out of this strange trance. *Focus, Kroaicho.* What am I doing sniffing around like some animal? I've lost my composure. I snarl quietly, berating myself for the lapse in discipline.

But then, the smell comes again, stronger this time, making my body respond in ways I hadn't anticipated.

What in the demiurge's name?

Frustration and embarrassment flood through me, my skin shifting to a dark, virulent purple. This is unacceptable. My control is better than this. I am better than this. The fact that there exists something capable of breaking through my discipline so easily makes my skin flash purple. I clench my fists, digging my claws into the soil to ground myself, trying to regain some semblance of control over my body.

Before I can settle my thoughts, a shout erupts nearby, startling me. I freeze, instinctively ducking lower into the brush. The scent has grown stronger, almost unbearably so, and it's clear now that whoever—or whatever—is producing it is close. Very close.

My mind races as I try to focus on the more pressing matter at hand: I'm being hunted. And, judging by the increasing intensity of the scent, the braceaaer are closing in on me. *Of course,* I think bitterly.

It's not enough that my hoard was destroyed, now I have to deal with... I cut off the thought, pushing aside the rising anger. Now is not the time to mourn what I've lost.

Another shout rings out, closer this time. My body tenses, ready to move at a moment's notice. I don't like the idea of approaching the source of that scent—it's dangerous, intoxicating, and far too distracting. But at the same time, I can't ignore it. It's calling to me in a way that makes my muscles itch with the need to move toward it, no matter how much my mind protests.

I consider burrowing underground, a tactic that has saved me on countless occasions. But as much as I long for the safety of the depths, tunneling isn't always the most subtle of actions. If I want to remain unnoticed, I'll need to rely on something less... conspicuous.

I shift my weight, testing the stability of the bushes and trees around me. They'll provide decent cover, at least for now. I begin to move cautiously, creeping forward through the underbrush, my body low to the ground. The scent is stronger now, pulling me along despite my better judgment. My heart pounds in my chest, a mix of trepidation and... excitement?

I freeze again, mentally cursing myself for the traitorous surge of emotion. Excited? Now, of all times? I grit my teeth, fighting back the urge to laugh at the absurdity of it all. Here I am, on the run from demiurge-know-what, possibly being hunted, and my body has the audacity to feel... thrilled?

I push the thought aside, focusing on the task at hand. I need to find out who or what is creating that scent and why it's affecting me like this. And I need to do it without getting caught.

Creeping forward, I move as silently as possible, using the cover of the bushes and trees to hide my presence. Every step is careful and calculated. My skin shifts to a muted brown to blend in with the surrounding foliage as I move closer to the source of the commotion. The voices are louder now, more distinct, though I still can't make out what they're saying.

As I near the edge of the clearing, I peer through the thick leaves, my eyes narrowing. There, in the center of the clearing, I see them.

Genali. Again.

Of course, it had to be them. What cruel twist of fate is this?

The leader stands in the center of the group, its compact frame brimming with the same lethal energy I remember from before. My body tenses involuntarily at the sight of them, my skin flashing purple with irritation. These... incomplete life forms. I don't know what they're doing here, but if the scent is coming from one of them, that might explain why I've been so... affected.

I watch as the leader gestures to something behind them—a large, cylindrical metal-like contraption. The rest of the group moves with practiced efficiency, setting up equipment and positioning themselves around the clearing. Their movements are precise and controlled, just like before.

My eyes go back to the cylinder, eagerly taking in the details.
I must have it.

I remain hidden in the bushes, trying to make sense of the situation. My body itches to move, to strike, to *do* something. But I need to be smart about this. I can't just rush in without a plan. I need to figure out what they're doing, why they're here, and most importantly, how I can use this to my advantage.

For now, I'll wait. Watch. And when the time is right, I'll strike.

I shift from one foot to the other aggravated as the tension in my gut rises, before the familiar scent wafts into my nose again, eliciting a low hiss from the back of my throat.

The scent is not from here, but the only way to get to it is past them.

Tunneling is out of the question though, they'd be here and have a one-way path to my destination.

Perhaps now is a good time as any to plan an ambush.

6

Olivia

The cold wraps around me like a familiar blanket, numbing my thoughts as I drift in and out of consciousness. My body feels heavy, sinking into soft fabric. I blink, trying to shake off the lingering fog of sedation, but something is wrong. The cold is giving way to an uncomfortable heat that seeps into my skin. A strange mix of grogginess and confusion overtakes me as I open my eyes, expecting the sterile light of a cell to greet me.

But there's only darkness.

I blink again, trying to make sense of it. Why is everything dark? My breath catches in my throat as the realization dawns. I was in a ship. A wave of panic rises in my chest, and I struggle against the lethargy, trying to sit up. The heat is suffocating now, clinging to my skin like a thick, damp layer of fear. My pod, once a freezing prison, now feels like a furnace, the air thick and stifling.

I claw at the door, hoping to push it open, but my fingers slide uselessly over the glass. That's when I notice the glass pane is no longer smooth. It's covered in breaks and dents... and dirt?

The panic surges through me in full force. My mind races, piecing it all together, a chaotic jumble of thoughts tumbling through the haze of fear and confusion.

The ship has crashed.

A strangled gasp escapes me as I push harder against the door, my palms slamming into the glass over and over. I can feel the edges of hysteria clawing at my mind as the door refuses to budge. I cough, the acrid scent of burning electronics assaulting my senses. I can't stay in here. I need to get out. Now.

Desperation fuels me as I search for any way to escape, my hands frantically scrabbling over the smooth surfaces of the chamber. There has to be something, a lever, a button. Anything. My breaths come in short, sharp gasps, and I can feel the walls closing in on me. Trapped. I'm trapped.

A loud groaning noise reverberates through the chamber and my heart leaps into my throat. My eyes dart around wildly, trying to find the source of the sound. The chamber starts shaking, and suddenly, with a crack, something gives way beneath me and I'm falling.

I scream as my chamber jerks violently, the entire pod I'm trapped in tipping forward and plunging into a gaping darkness. My body is thrown against the glass as I fall, the impact rattling my bones and slamming me back against the back and then the glass again. The world outside my pod is a chaotic blur of debris and darkness. I'm tossed about like a ragdoll as the pod tumbles downward, and with a final, bone-jarring jolt, my chamber stops.

I hit the ground hard, and the world explodes into pain and noise. Metal screeches against rock, and I'm vaguely aware of rocks and dirt pelting the outside of my chamber as it skids and rolls to a stop a few feet away from a steep slope.

I lay there for a moment, stunned, trying to process what just happened. My whole body aches and my head is pounding from where I've been slammed against the inside of the chamber. I can feel warm blood trickling down my face, sticky and uncomfortable. I groan, closing my eyes for a moment to steady myself.

When I finally manage to gather my wits, I take stock of my injuries. My muscles scream in protest as I attempt to move, and I hiss in pain as I realize I've got more than just a few bruises. Lacerations dot my face, small cuts from where I was tossed around. My head is throbbing, the telltale sign of a concussion making everything feel far too bright and sharp. But, despite it all, I can feel something tingling within me, knitting my wounds back together at an accelerated rate. The pain dulls slightly as the healing process begins, but I know it'll be some time before I'm fully back on my feet.

With a groan of effort, I struggle to sit up, my vision swimming for a moment before it stabilizes. The inside of my pod is a mess of cracked glass and twisted metal. I reach up and try to push the door open again, but it's dented from the fall, and it refuses to give. Long locks of bright green hair are wrapped around my arms, making it harder to move, but when I yank at them there is simply an answering pain on my scalp.

It's my hair... somehow. And it's limiting my movement.

Panic starts to creep back in as I realize how truly trapped I am.

But then I noticed something else—I'm stronger. My hands, which once struggled to make even a dent in the reinforced glass, now press with a force I never had before.

What the hell? Adrenaline?

I grit my teeth and push harder, using every ounce of strength I can muster. The glass groans under the pressure, but it's slow going. The pod was designed to keep us in, and even with my sudden strength, it's not easy to break out.

Just as I feel like I'm making progress, the ground beneath me shifts again.

"No, no, no!" I shout, but it's no use.

The shale beneath the pod gives way, and with a sickening lurch, the entire chamber starts to slide down the steep slope. I scream, clinging to the sides of the pod as it hurtles downward, faster and faster. Dirt and rocks spray up around me, and the world spins wildly as the pod careens out of control.

There's nothing I can do but hold on for dear life and pray that I don't get thrown around too much inside the chamber. Every jolt sends fresh waves of pain through my body, and I can feel another bruise forming on my already tender head as it bangs against the glass.

Finally, with one last bone-shaking crash, the pod slams into something solid at the bottom of some odd tunnel. The impact is enough to knock the breath out of me, and for a moment, I just lay there, dazed and disoriented. My head throbs painfully, and I can feel the darkness creeping in at the edges of my vision.

Not again.

I try to fight it, but the exhaustion is overwhelming, and despite my best efforts, my consciousness slips away, leaving me in darkness once more.

* * *

The world around me feels like it's spinning out of control, a whirlpool of dark shadows and dim, flickering lights. I'm barely conscious, teetering on the edge of oblivion when a sudden, sharp sound slices through the haze. A distant explosion? Or was it gunfire? My groggy mind can't tell the difference. Everything feels muffled, as if I'm underwater, with a thick, syrupy fog clogging my thoughts.

It occurs to me that I can no longer hear the electricity of the chamber. I've heard it my whole life, regardless of how many people told me that's crazy, and the lack of it is unsettling. Especially if this chamber is keeping me alive in some sort of strange, alien environment.

Or am I on Earth?

I force my eyes open, but the effort is almost too much. My eyelids feel like they're made of lead, and the simple act of blinking sends the world reeling. The harsh contrast between the pitch-black surroundings and sporadic flashes of light strains my vision, making the throbbing in my head intensify. The cold metal of the cryo chamber is gone, replaced by a much more troubling sensation—a deep, stabbing pain right in the center of my skull.

Instinctively, I raise a hand to my forehead, hoping to soothe the ache. But as my fingers make contact with my skin, I feel something sharp and out of place—a small, jagged shard embedded in my flesh. A choked gasp escapes me as I realize what it is. Glass. There's a shard of glass lodged in my skull, a cruel souvenir from the chaotic fall. The skin around it is slick with blood, warm and sticky, trickling down in tiny rivulets.

I squeeze my eyes shut, trying to will the pain away. But it's no use—the stabbing sensation flares every time my heart beats, sending ripples of agony through my already foggy mind. Frustration bubbles up inside me, mixing with the pain and disorientation. I can't think clearly, can't focus on anything except the maddening throb in my head.

"Damn it," I mutter through clenched teeth, my voice barely more than a whisper. I take a deep breath, trying to steady myself. There's no room for fear or hesitation. Not now. With a sudden, rough motion, I grasp the shard of glass and yank it out.

The pain is white-hot, blinding in its intensity. For a second, the world narrows to a single point of excruciating agony, but then it starts to fade, replaced by a dull throb.

Damn. That probably wasn't smart.

My vision clears just enough for me to take in my surroundings. I'm partially out of the pod. It's cracked and twisted from the fall, the once-pristine glass shattered into dangerous shards. The air is thick with the acrid stench of smoke and burned electronics, making it hard to breathe. I need to get out of here.

I push myself up, trying to orient myself, but the world tilts dangerously. My head feels like it's full of thick syrup, every movement sluggish and delayed. I blink, trying to shake off the grogginess, but it's no use.

Just as I'm about to try and stand, a sound cuts through the haze—a strange, wet, squelching noise, growing louder by the second. My heart skips a beat, and I turn my head slowly, trying to locate the source. The movement makes me dizzy, and for a moment, I have to brace myself against the side of the pod to keep from toppling over.

When I finally manage to look up through the opening above me. My breath catches in my throat. A horde of alien creatures is rushing down the slope toward me. They're like nothing I've ever seen before, their bodies made entirely of some kind of pink, gelatinous substance. They move with a sickening fluidity, undulating and shifting as they swarm closer. Panic grips me, my muscles tensing involuntarily.

I need to get out of here—now.

With a surge of adrenaline, I push open the cracked door of the pod and stumble out. My feet hit the uneven ground, and immediately, I lose my balance. My head is still spinning, the concussion making it impossible to coordinate my movements. I try to catch myself, but my legs give out from under me, and I crash face-first into the rocks.

The impact jars my already throbbing head, sending fresh waves of pain through my skull. For a moment, I just lay there, stunned, my face pressed into the cold, damp ground. The world around me feels distant, and unreal, like I'm trapped in a nightmare that I can't wake up from.

But the sound of the approaching creatures snaps me back to reality. I push myself up onto my hands and knees, coughing as I try to get air back into my lungs. My vision swims, but I can't afford to stay down. I force myself to my feet, swaying unsteadily as I try to get my bearings.

The creatures are closer now, almost upon me. I can hear their wet, squelching movements, and can feel the ground vibrating under the force of their collective approach. My heart is pounding in my chest, a wild, erratic rhythm that drowns out everything else.

I scramble on my knees for a short while, rocks cutting into me, frantic to get away, but I'm still stunned.

Just as I'm about to start running, a sharp voice cuts through the chaos. "Get down!"

I don't have time to react before someone grabs me from behind, yanking me out of the path of the oncoming horde. I'm pulled roughly to the side, and I stumble, nearly losing my balance again. But whoever it is keeps a firm grip on my arm, dragging me away from the creatures.

I manage to get a look at my rescuer—a woman, with silver hair and black eyes that gleam with intensity. She looks familiar, though my groggy mind can't quite place her. One of the other women from the ship, I think, though her name escapes me.

She's armed, holding a blocky, unwieldy rifle that looks like it's seen better days. It's not an energy weapon—the distinctive crack of ballistic fire tells me that much.

"Stay behind me!" she orders, her voice clipped and commanding. Without waiting for a response, she takes a stance at a vantage point halfway up the slope, her rifle trained on the approaching creatures.

I'm still reeling from the fall, my brain struggling to catch up with what's happening. But her words cut through the fog, grounding me in the here and now. I nod numbly, not trusting myself to speak, and scramble to find some cover behind a large chunk of debris.

The woman opens fire, the loud crack of the rifle echoing across the desolate landscape. Each shot is precise, and measured, and nearly every time she pulls the trigger, one of the pink creatures bursts into a spray of liquid, collapsing into a puddle of goo. They make large targets, with all of that wide, jiggling mass.

But for everyone she takes down, three more seem to take their place, surging forward with relentless determination.

I watch her for a moment, awe-struck by her calm under pressure, and her efficiency in dealing with the threat. But the sheer number of creatures is overwhelming, and I can see the strain in her eyes as she struggles to keep them at bay.

I can't just sit here and do nothing. I need to help.

My eyes dart around, searching for anything I can use as a weapon. That's when I see it—a rifle, lying discarded in the dirt a few feet away. It looks like it must have fallen down the steep hill, judging my how marked up it is.

I crawl toward it, my movements awkward and slow, but I manage to reach it before the creatures close in. My fingers close around the cold metal, and I pull the weapon to me, checking it over quickly.

It's battered, clearly salvaged from one of the fallen, but it's still functional. The weight of it in my hands is reassuring. I take a deep breath, trying to steady my shaking hands, and then rise to my feet.

"Cover me!" I shout to the woman, my voice hoarse and shaky.

She glances back at me, her eyes narrowing in surprise. But she doesn't hesitate. She adjusts her position, drawing the creatures' attention away from me so I can get a clear shot.

I took aim, my heart racing. I've handled weapons before, but this is different. Clearly not made for humans hands and the stakes are higher, the danger more immediate. I can't afford to miss. My finger tightens on the trigger, and with a loud crack, the rifle kicks against my shoulder.

I missed. I try again. And again, before I figure out how to aim it.

The nearest creature bursts apart, pink goo splattering across the ground. The sight gives me a surge sense of satisfaction, a small victory in the midst of chaos. Almost sexual, I realize.

I shoot again, another kill sending a shot of ecstasy through me, the junction of my thighs becoming increasingly wet.

But there's no time to celebrate. More of the creatures are closing in, and I need to keep firing.

I grit my teeth, forcing myself to stay focused. The woman is still holding her ground, picking off the creatures with a steady rhythm, but I can see the strain in her posture. She can't keep this up forever. We need to move, to get out of here before we're overwhelmed.

"We have to go!" I shout, firing another round into the horde. The creatures are so close now that I can see their slick, gelatinous bodies rippling with each movement. The sight sends a shiver down my spine, but I force myself to keep firing, to keep fighting.

"We can't outrun them!" the woman snaps back, her voice laced with frustration. She fires another shot, and another creature collapses into a puddle of goo, but there are too many of them. We're being pushed back, millimeter by millimeter, and I can feel the desperation mounting in my chest.

"Then what do we do?" I shout, my voice rising in panic. Another shot, another creature down. But it's not enough. We're losing ground, and I can see the creatures closing in, their pink bodies undulating and shifting as they swarm toward us.

The woman doesn't answer right away, her focus on keeping the creatures at bay. But I can see the tension in her jaw, the way her eyes dart around, searching for an escape route. She knows we can't hold them off forever. We're running out of time.

"This way!" she finally shouts, her voice sharp and commanding. She fires one last shot, then turns and bolts up the slope, her movements quick and sure despite the uneven terrain.

I don't hesitate. I follow her, my heart pounding in my chest as I scramble after her. The creatures are right behind us, their wet movements growing louder and more frantic. I can feel them closing in, can hear their sickening squelches as they surge forward in a mindless frenzy.

But we don't stop. We keep moving, pushing ourselves to the limit, our breaths coming in short, ragged gasps. The woman leads the way, her black eyes focused and determined when she glances back, and I do my best to keep up, my legs burning with exertion.

We reach the top of the slope, and for a brief, blessed moment, the creatures seem to falter, their movements slowing as if they're unsure of what to do next. But it's only a momentary reprieve. They'll be on us again in seconds.

"Keep going!" the woman shouts, her voice hoarse with effort. She glances back at me, her eyes meeting mine for a brief, intense moment. There's a fire in her gaze, a fierce determination that ignites something in me.

I nod, gritting my teeth as I push myself to keep moving. The ground is uneven and treacherous, but we can't afford to slow down. The creatures are still behind us, still relentless in their pursuit.

But we're not giving up. Not yet.

The woman leads us toward a rocky outcrop in the distance, a jagged formation that juts out from the barren landscape. It's not much, but it offers some cover, and a chance to regroup and figure out our next move.

We reach the outcrop just as the creatures start to catch up again. The woman spins around, raising her rifle and firing off a few more shots to keep them at bay. I do the same, my hands trembling as I take aim and squeeze the trigger.

The creatures burst into pink puddles, one after another, but there are still too many of them. They seem to realize they've lost an advantage and back off, finding cover while we do the same.

We can't hold them off forever. We need a plan.

"What now?" I ask, my voice shaking with exhaustion and fear.

The woman doesn't answer right away, her eyes scanning the landscape, searching for something—anything—that might give us an edge. But there's nothing. Just the barren wasteland, the distant fires of the crashed ship, and the relentless horde of alien creatures.

Finally, she turns to me, her expression grim.

"It's time to run," she says, as if that isn't what we've already been doing.

I couldn't hide my snarl even if I wanted to, "Oh, you think?!"

Then we run. And somehow live.

***

The valley is eerily quiet now, the only sound is my ragged breaths and the rhythmic thud of my heartbeat pounding in my ears. We talked a bit, shared our names, which is how I know hers is Rin, then fell silent. The adrenaline is still coursing through my veins, making my limbs shake even though we've put some distance between us and the crash site. Rin and I stumble to a halt in the shadow of yet another jagged outcrop.

The creatures, thankfully, aren't visible from here.

I drop to my knees, gasping for breath, and Rin does the same, her silver hair sticking to her forehead with sweat. For a moment, neither of us says anything, just focusing on pulling air into our burning lungs. The quiet is a relief, but the silence that hangs between us is heavy with unspoken questions. The ground beneath us is rough and uneven, the dirt dry and cracked, and I can feel every sharp edge pressing into my palms as I brace myself.

We are under a bush and fighting about utter nonsense not long after, at least until I realize I can understand when she speaks a foreign language. It helps me calm down my burning brain to focus on something else besides killer aliens.

We introduce ourselves, which is how I find out her name is Rin. Then she teaches me how to clothe myself out of... nothing.

So I am now fully clothed in a spandex suit straight out of a *Catwoman* comic book. Handy.

Being naked for weeks is highly uncomfortable.

Then she's reaching her hand for me and I barely resist the temptation to shrink back. Instead, I pull from my bottomless well of useless movie facts, throw on a smile, and distract my mind from the anger.

"This makes me think of *Titanic* and how Jack could have gotten on the door with Rose," I say inanely, but then her eyebrows furrow.

I quickly sift through the possible emotions attached to that, hoping it isn't anger and just let my stupid mouth keep running on. "You haven't seen *Titanic*? Oh my God, have you been living under a rock?"

I let out a hearty laugh, one I've practiced dozens of times, playing a recording back until it was perfect and luckily it draws a chuckle from her. Good, that means she probably isn't angry.

"I have not seen it but once I can, I will," she tells me, and I nod in response.

Then I bite my tongue and pick up a rock to ground myself, sure my mask is in place with a small smile. She probably hates me.

Ninety-five percent chance, I muse.

When I look up again she's staring at me.

"Rin?" She doesn't hear me and I cringe as I place my hand on her, hoping she doesn't hit me.

"Sorry, I got lost in my thoughts," she says.

I let go of her, my smile slipping, and focus on the rock again. "I understand," I say, voice tight with my social anxiety. "I don't mean to pull you from it."

"No, don't be sorry. I finally have an actual human being to talk to and I should take advantage of that," she responds.

Did anyone else in the pods survive? Are we the only ones? "Am I the first human you've come across?" When she nods I let out an involuntary moan.

The woman with the purple hair was nice. It would be terrible if she died after trying to protect me. "So you haven't seen Ree?"

Rin gives me a sidelong glance, still frowning, but she doesn't respond. She just shakes her head, as if trying to shake off the strangeness of it all. I'm about to say something more when the ground beneath us rumbles. A deep, ominous vibration that makes my heart skip a beat.

Before I can react, the earth gives way beneath us, crumbling into a yawning sinkhole. The world lurches violently, and I let out a startled cry as the ground disappears from under my feet. Rin yells something, but the sound is swallowed by the rush of air as I fall.

I'm too scared to get angry when her hands clasp tight to mine, stopping my fall. Then her grip is slipping and I'm yelling out her name.

I can tell from her face that she won't be able to hold me for long. She looks past me, then speaks. "I can't see anything. It's all dark."

I'm about to reply when the ground shifts again and she loses her hold on me.

I scream out a yelp as I fall, then make painful contact with the ground.

The impact knocks the wind out of me. I land hard on my back, the breath forced from my lungs in a painful gasp. Dust and grit fill my mouth and nose, making me sputter and cough as I try to sit up. Everything aches. My head, my ribs—hell, even my teeth hurt from the jarring fall.

I blink through the haze, trying to get my bearings, when something massive looms over me. My heart stutters in my chest as a huge, multi-tusked creature with bioluminescent skin reaches down and grabs me. Its skin glows with an eerie, pale light, casting strange shadows on the cavern walls. I let out a panicked squeal, the sound loud enough to make the creature wince, but it doesn't let go. Instead, it pulls me closer, pressing me to its broad chest with an almost possessive grip.

"Let me go!" I gasp, anger surging, struggling against its hold, but my efforts are laughably ineffective. My fists pound against its chest, but it barely seems to notice. My face is pressed against its cold, hard skin, muffling my cries, and I can feel its deep, rumbling breaths vibrating through me.

Mixed in with my anger is arousal, which only serves to whip me up into a fury.

"Olivia!" Rin's voice cuts through the chaos, distant but frantic. I try to twist around, to call out to her, but the creature's grip is unyielding.

I'm sure she's convinced I just broke my neck, so I try to reassure her.

"I'm okay," I say back, though my voice is muffled by the creature's chest. "I'm... sort of okay," I add, struggling to breathe through the tightness of its hold.

Oddly enough, the pressure is calming me down, which is the exact opposite of what I would normally feel and at odds with how freaked out I am.

What if she jumps down if I scream for help? She'd get hurt, or worse.

I wriggle to get my face in a better position to yell. "Nasrin, I'm okay. There's... someone else here."

"Please give my friend back, please," Nasrin calls and my heart leaps.

Only a five percent chance she hates me, I correct myself, my mind whirling.

I feel my mind trying to slide into the stuttering, skipping thoughts from when the bugs held me captive, but resist.

The creature lets out a series of low hisses and chitters, its body vibrating with the sound. At first, the noise is just a meaningless jumble of high-pitched sounds, but then the patterns start to shift, and I can almost hear words forming in my mind. The translation is slower this time as if my brain is still catching up to the creature's strange language.

Or maybe I'm just slow in general.

"This one... belongs to you?" the creature hisses, its voice a strange mix of high-pitched clicks and deep, resonant growls.

"Zha is part of my hoard now," the creature announces. "Go away."

Hoard? Anger flares even higher in me at its words, and I manage to pull my face away from its chest just enough to speak. "Fuck no!" I snap, my voice shaky but defiant. "I'm no one's but my own."

The creature freezes for a moment, its grip tightening slightly. Then, it lets out a high-pitched creaking sound, almost like... surprise? The sound is so alien, so foreign, that it's hard to tell, but something in the way its body shifts makes me think it wasn't expecting me to talk back.

"If... this one talks..." the creature hisses slowly as if testing the words. "Then... zha must have it."

Before I can make sense of what it's saying, the creature tightens its hold on me and suddenly takes off, sprinting through the cavern with terrifying speed. I barely have time to let out a startled yelp before we're plunging into a freshly dug tunnel, the walls rushing past in a blur.

It's gait is odd, then I remember from the quick flash that it had three sets of limbs and shudder.

"Rin!" I shout over my shoulder, my voice barely carrying over the sound of the creature's pounding footsteps.

I almost scream out my fear, demanding help, but then I picture her bloody and broken. I would never forgive myself if she got hurt.

I pull in a deep breath, unsure how to keep her from following. "I'll be okay!" I yell out, cringing when it's just an echo of what I said before.

She's probably completely unconvinced.

Rin's voice echoes faintly behind us, growing more distant with every second. "Olivia!" she calls, desperation lacing her tone. "Olivia, where are you?!"

I yell back, desperate to make her feel better so she won't break her neck. "I'll be okay, I promise. I'll find you once I can."

"No, no, Olivia, please," she begs. "I'll dig my way down to get you out. I'll find a way. Just hold on."

"Get to safety," I yell back, suddenly realizing she must be shouting and there are enemies up there. "I'll find a way out."

"Olivia..." she says, but the sound fades as the creature races deeper into the tunnel, and soon, all I can hear is the pounding of its feet and the harsh rasp of my own breathing.

I stop trying to shout back. There's no point. The distance between us is growing too fast, and I need to focus on staying calm, on figuring out what the hell is happening. The tunnel twists and turns, the walls a blur of jagged stone and glowing lichen as the creature barrels forward with inhuman speed. My head is spinning, my mind struggling to keep up with the sheer madness of it all.

What is this thing? Where is it taking me? And what the hell did it mean by "zha must have it"?

Questions race through my mind, but there are no answers, only the hot, suffocating grip of the creature and the endless, twisting tunnels stretching out before us.
And of course my impotent, murderous rage.

7

Kroaicho

I shuffle from one foot to the one of the others, in a square pattern, my claws scraping against the rough stone, and I can't help but stare at the green-haired, green-eyed creature I impulsively brought back with me. Why did I do this? What part of my mind thought this was a good idea?

My mind supplies the answer with an image of the green lava gemstone the genali destroyed. The shifting colors of the creature's long green hair are just as mesmerizing. Zha must have a story, I know it.

But is it worth the trouble?

Zha reeks of that smell... not quite the same, but now I realize part of the same species. It was the other one's smell that drew me in, but it is this one that I chose. Zha came from the wrecked silver container I desired, which is no longer worthy of my hoard after I had to create a tunnel to divert it to me.

Instead I have this oddly signaling creature. Green? At a time like this?

The creature—zha—sits there, staring at the ground, carving strange marks into the dust with delicate fingers. Zha is small and fragile, especially in comparison to me, and yet, as I look at zha, I can't help but curse my own poor impulse control. Of all the reckless decisions I've made—topping even my foolish treasure-hunting expeditions up Mt. Rev'ercha—this one stands out.

I curse again, clicking my tongue against my tusks. What was I thinking? At the time, my only thought had been to steal the little thing away, putting distance between zha and the other one zha had been with. But now that I have zha here, alone, away from the other creature... I am faced with a glaring question.

What do I do with zha?

I consider the possibility of killing zha. It would be the simplest solution. I'd never have to worry about what to do next, about the complications zha brings. But as soon as the thought enters my mind, something ugly twists in my chest—a bitterness, a root that digs deep and snarls, making me feel sick. I discard the idea immediately. No. I won't kill zha.

Instead, I shoot a furtive glance at the diminutive creature. Zha is still busy with the dusty floor, zha's hands moving in patterns that I can't make sense of.

It is what zha started doing after zha realized trying to escape me was futile. The screaming stopped and zha froze in place for a long moment, then dropped to the ground and started... drawing.

What an odd creature.

I should be looking at what zha is drawing, trying to decipher any meaning from it, but my gaze is more intent on zha instead. There's something... compelling about zha. Something that makes me want to keep looking, to understand.

The question that lingers in my mind, though, is the one that won't leave me alone: Why is there so much green?

I tilt my head, my bone-ridged brows knitting together as I give the creature a more appraising look. Green hair, green eyes... is zha that desperate for a zhannel? It makes no sense. How does zha intend to cater to a zhannel without so much as a hoard of treasure?

It's insanity, I think. *Complete and utter insanity.*

I should stop staring. I need to act. But what should I do? Zha is here now, and I need to make a decision. I decide it would be best to put zha deep in the cave, where zha can serve as the start of a new personal hoard. After all, I must admit, zha is beautiful—easily the best of anything I've ever hoarded. The thought sends a twinge of... something through me, a warm sensation that makes me feel embarrassed, my skin lighting up in brighter shades of blue.

I take a step closer, my feet dragging across the dusty cave floor, and suddenly I'm aware of how tusk-tied I feel. Why is this so difficult? Zha is just another addition to my hoard, and yet I'm struggling to find the right words. What does one say in a situation like this?

I realize, with a growing sense of anxiety, that I have no idea how to interact with zha. My species, the zhasie, are direct, and straightforward. But this creature... At first I thought the vivid green of zha's hair must mean zha is signaling for a mate, though of course I should have known better. I have met plenty of species that do not signal like a zhasie.

What is it about this creature that has me so confounded? The sounds coming from zha's mouth don't match. They're high-pitched, like a shriek, and they sound... annoyed. Not seeking or entreating.

I don't understand. I don't understand any of this. I take another step back, feeling overwhelmed by the confusion and the conflicting signals. Should I just put zha to sleep with a quick burst of gas from my sacs? That would at least give me some time to think. But I hesitate.

No, no. That would be too easy. Too cowardly. I can't resort to that. Not yet.

Instead, I turn and retreat farther into the cave, away from memories of the creature's high-pitched tirade. I've almost heard enough of the language to make sense of it.

Zha's mumbling voice follows me, but it fades as I move deeper into the shadows. I press my back against the cool stone and take a deep breath, trying to calm myself. What am I supposed to do now? This is not how I imagined this going.

I only wanted the silver container. It would have been an excellent start. Not this.

Not this.

I peer around the edge of the rock, watching zha from a distance. Zha is still going, that strange little mouth moving and moving. The color of my skin shifts to a dark purple, a sign of my irritation. Why is zha like this? What does zha want from me? I've given zha space, I've brought zha somewhere safe—shouldn't zha be grateful?

I don't know why I expected that.

I would not be grateful.

I rattle my head, the tips of my head spikes drooping slightly. I've heard of creatures like this, ones that don't follow any logic I understand. Maybe I'm the one who's missing an important signal. Maybe there's something I'm not seeing.

I take a cautious step forward, my eyes narrowing as I try to make sense of zha's words. Zha's language is strange—there's no easy translation just yet, but I think I have enough words to be understood.

I pick up on the tone. Zha is... not pleased. I force myself to speak, even though my mouth feels dry. "You not want here?"

The creature pauses, looking up at me with those bright green eyes. There's a flicker of surprise there, I think, but then zha scowls. "Not want? What does that *even mean*? You *took* me! You *took* me *away from Rin!*"

I can't understand half of what zha is saying, but I pick up on the tone, the anger. My skin shifts to a deeper shade of purple. "Zha... bad," I say, trying to convey my meaning with a growl. How

much I don't want the green one to return to the white one. "Not...
safe."

"Not safe?" zha echoes, the words sharp. "You think *you're* safe?
You think *this* is safe?"

I feel a flash of white—an amused glimmer along my skin—but
it fades quickly. No, zha doesn't understand. I need to explain
it better. "Here," I gesture to the cave around us, "better than...
outside. Better than... zha."

Zha's eyes narrow. "So, what, you're keeping me as... what? A
pet? A *prisoner*?"

The words don't translate well, but I think I understand. I rattle
my head, frustrated. I need more of the language's words and I'm
not gaining them fast enough to be persuasive. "Not pet. You...
hoard. Mine. Keep hoard safe."

For a moment, there's silence. Then zha bursts into a sound I
quickly realize is laughter—a sound so unexpected that it sends a
shock through me. It's low, just like the rest of zha's language, but
the cadence is the same. I stiffen, my skin flashing briefly blue in
confusion.

Why is zha laughing?

"Hoard? Yours?" Zha's voice is incredulous. "You think... you
think I'm just some... some *thing* you can keep? There really is no
escaping it, is there? *Materialism exists* everywhere."

I don't know how to respond to that. My skin flickers between
purple and blue, a mix of irritation and confusion. "Yes," I say,
because it's the only thing that makes sense to me. "Mine. Now."

Zha throws zha's hands in the air in some odd gesture I assume
is defiance. "You're unbelievable," zha says loudly, then more
softly, "two is not one. Cannot be *reformed*."

Then zha goes back to drawing, dismissing me entirely, still
muttering what I'm starting to suspect wouldn't make sense to
others of zha's kind, let alone someone still figuring out zha's
language.

I feel a sting, like a slap to my pride. Purple flares briefly along
my arms. "Unbelievable... why?"

My skin shudders at the low growl that erupts from zha.

"Because you don't get it!" Zha shakes zha's head, that green
hair flashing in the dim light. "I'm not... I'm not some *object*. I'm
not something you can just... *claim*."

I narrow my eyes, trying to understand. "But... you green. You...
signal?"

"What?" Zha blinks at me. "What does that even mean?"

I hesitate, feeling awkward. "Green... for mate?"

There's a pause. Then zha's eyes widen, and zha lets out another burst of laughter. "Oh. Oh, no. You think... you think this means I want to..."

I don't understand why this is funny. I feel a flush of light blue creeping along my skin, my spikes shuddering in embarrassment. "Is not. Thought not, but ask."

Why did I ask? My skin flushes to purple as I berate myself for being stupid.

"No!" zha exclaims. "This is just... how I look. Not how I used to look, but how I do now."

I feel an odd mix of relief and irritation. So zha isn't signaling for a mate. But then... what does that mean? My mind races, trying to piece it all together. "Then... why... angry?"

"Because you took me!" Zha's voice is sharp again. "You took me from the *person* I was with you *overgrown LED bulb*!" I get the sinking sensation that if I were to come any closer then zha would do something drastic, perhaps sticking a finger into an eye, and the mental image roots me to the spot, unwilling to test the theory by coming any closer.

The creature's enchanting green eyes look positively murderous as zha finishes zha's tirade, "And now you're acting like it's not a problem. What the *fuck*?!"

I flinch at zha's tone, the sound grating against my senses. I'm overwhelmed, and I don't know how to respond. Should I try to explain again? Should I just... let zha be? I consider making zha sleep, just for a little while, just to give myself time to think. But no. Not yet.

Instead, I turn away again, retreating farther into the cave, letting the shadows swallow me up. I need a moment to think. To breathe. This is more complicated than I expected, and I'm not sure what to do next.

Behind me, zha's voice continues, echoing off the cave walls. But I don't listen. I doubt I have the fortitude. For a creature so tiny, zha's voice is raised to the point of pain in my ears when zha yells.

I need to figure this out. What do I do with zha? What do I want?

For now, all I can do is wait and see.

8

Olivia

I lose some time to my mind scattering, rage threatening to tip me into a shut down. It's the pain in my knuckles when I start beating on a cave wall that brings me out of it and I feel the exhaustion trying to take over.

"No, no, no, not now," I say as I drop back to the ground and use the dim light from the odd glowing mushrooms to find the rock I was using to draw.

Then I use every bit of what's left of my focus to draw another tattoo design. I lose myself in the swirls of the fern. The spikes rising from the central swirl an extension of my resentment, the point the whirling design ends on like the knife I want in my hand right now.

When the creature comes back, I try to use the rock as a knife, but it just bounces off the tough, glowing skin. Then I start laughing again, heart pounding as I think of how stupid it is to try to pummel something so massive. Then I try again anyway.

It chitters at me, I assume in displeasure, but simply scoops me back into its arms, rearing back its torso like some sort of giant, glowing, lizard caterpillar.

I scream out a few threats, but then suddenly feel exhausted again and I stop struggling as it runs.

The tunnel seems to go on forever, twisting and turning in a dizzying labyrinth that I can barely keep track of. I remain limp in the creature's arms, saving my strength, my breath coming in quick, shallow gasps. The walls of the cave blur past us, illuminated by the soft, bioluminescent glow radiating from the creature's skin. Every turn it takes, every sudden descent or steep climb, I try to memorize, but it's hopeless—there are too many.

I can't tell up from down anymore. I can only focus on the rhythmic pounding of its four feet against the smooth stone floor, the way its breath vibrates through my body, and the suffocating warmth of its skin pressing against mine. I should be terrified—hell, I am terrified—but there's something strangely comforting about being held like this. The creature's embrace is almost... protective.

It reminds me of how my mother used to hold me as a child. Nice and tight, just how I liked it. The only way I liked it.

But I push the thought away. Now's not the time to go soft. I need to stay sharp.

The rage rattled through me when it first grabbed me, but it was just too strong. Now, held in this tight hold, it's like something is loosening inside of me when it should be lashing out instead.

Maybe I've just finally given up.

"Five and ninety-five," I mutter, chest tight when the numbers don't help.

The walls around us are too smooth, unnaturally so. My overactive mind, still buzzing with adrenaline, starts to wander. This isn't a natural cave. The way the walls slope and curve seamlessly into one another, the almost polished quality of the stone—no, this was made. But not by any tech I know. What kind of machine could carve out a cave system like this?

My breath catches. What if it wasn't made by a machine at all? What if something living dug these tunnels? Far too large to be the one carrying me. A creature native to this planet, burrowing through the soil like an insect through fruit? The thought sends a chill down my spine, and I shiver involuntarily. The monster holding me senses it, and its grip tightens reflexively, pressing me closer against its chest.

"Ugh, not so tight!" I mutter through gritted teeth.

The contact against my skin sends shots of panic and anger through me, but I already know that hitting it does no good. I turn to numbers to help me, and this time there is a small thread of satisfaction.

"Three point one four one five nine..."

By the twentieth digit I start to feel better, the pressure of the creature's hold helping, though I still want to scream at it. Part of me also welcomes the warmth radiating from its skin. It's hot, almost uncomfortably so, but it's better than the skin-biting chill of the cave air. I feel the steady rise and fall of its breath against me, the powerful muscles moving beneath its glowing skin.

My wrists are tucked tight against me, palms curled in so I don't accidentally touch it.

I try to push away the odd sense of security creeping in, not to mention the ever-present arousal. I need to focus on the situation. What does this thing want from me?

Someone always wants something from me. Usually to take care of them and get shit on in the process. My chest tightens as I think about just how fucked I likely am at this point.

Eventually, the creature slows down, its footsteps growing softer, more cautious. We enter a spacious enclave, brightly lit by clusters of bioluminescent mushrooms clinging to the walls. They glow with a soft blue-green hue, their light casting strange shadows on the stone. It stops near the largest cluster, and I'm struck by the warmth radiating from them. It's surprising, almost like standing next to a campfire. I instinctively lean toward the warmth.

The creature slowly lowers me to the ground. My legs are shaky, barely holding me up, but I manage to stay standing. It steps back, giving me an appraising look. I feel my eyebrow twitch in irritation—its gaze is almost... evaluating. Like a merchant sizing up a new piece of rare, expensive merchandise. It shivers its large, spiked head, seemingly satisfied, and retreats to the far corner of the enclave, where it sits back on its haunches and watches me intently.

I stay where I am, too scared to move, too uncertain to run. My eyes flick to the tunnel we came through, but I can't see beyond the glow of the mushrooms. For all I know, there could be a dozen more creatures just like this one, waiting in the shadows. No, running isn't an option. I purse my lips and settle down instead, sitting cross-legged on the rough stone floor.

Instead I take a better look at the creature. It has two massive arms, each one longer than its four legs. Its body is segmented, reminding me again of a caterpillar, but only if they were incredibly muscular. I assume it must be designed for digging. A glance at the huge claws makes me question my sanity again about the whole rock attack idea.

Its feet look similar to what are on its hands and it makes my skin crawl. There are two long, thick digits directly opposite and closing in toward each other with an additional set of two fingers pointing forward. The ones on the side are oriented so they splay toward the inside and outside of its body.

It has a row of spikes starting on its head, which are oddly not spaced in the middle, but instead start on the left side of the skull, then continue in a crosswise line so they are oriented mostly to the right side by the time they disappear on its last body segment.

As I watch it, different colors light up along its skin. Glowing pink eyes stare back at me, which always remain the same color. There is a grinding sound coming from it, which it takes me a while to realize is from it rubbing together its tusks. There are multiple of them. Large ones jutting up from a massive lower lip, smaller ones inside its mouth on the top.

You'd think with all of the muttering about hoards it would look like a dragon. Or a goblin. But instead it looks like some sort of mish-mash of lizard, caterpillar, glow worm, freaking Godzilla, and bunch of other scary shit I don't have a name for.

The longer I stare, the louder the grinding becomes and the lower the sharp looking planes of its forehead descend over its eyes and its large, four holed nostrils flare.

I might be clueless when it comes to a lot of human expressions and since it's an alien, I might be completely wrong, but I'm starting to think I'm making it mad.

My lips pull wide into a feral grin. Clearly I can't kill the thing, but I'll just have to take what satisfaction I can. You can hurt people just as much without fists, though I can't say I've ever been very good at it. I've been on the receiving end enough that I should be able to come up with something, though.

For a while, we just stare at each other, but then my mind, left unstimulated, starts to wander. I think about Earth. About home. My mom. She was near the end before I got taken, her body so frail and weak from the mental illness that had been eating away at her for years.

I wonder if she grieved when I vanished—or if she was even still aware enough to grieve.

She didn't, even if she knew. I was forever a disappointment. Something to fix, which never happened, no matter how much money she threw at the latest boarding school. She wouldn't grieve.

The thought squeezes my chest, a deep, hollow ache that has nothing to do with my current predicament. She's probably mentally gone by now, I think. The reality of it settles in, a cold, heavy weight that makes my throat tighten and my eyes burn, though there are no tears to give.

Regret bubbles up, sharp and bitter. I didn't even get to say goodbye. Despite everything, the resentment I felt for her, for refusing to tell me who my father was, for keeping so many secrets, I never stopped loving her. She was a constant in my life, from birth until now, the one steady presence I could always count on, even if it was just to berate me for being weird. And now, I'll never get the chance to say goodbye. To ask her one last time who he was.

I remember being a kid, barely a preteen. My mum would let me into her locked study—no one else was allowed in, not my siblings, not even my step-dad. Just me. The room was packed with old books, their spines cracked and faded, the pages yellowed with age. I'd spend hours in there, thumbing through them, getting lost in worlds far away from our tiny apartment. It was like she wanted me to read them, to know them.

One book stands out in my memory—a well-worn sci-fi novel with a cover so faded that I could barely make out the title. It was the first one she had me read. She insisted on it. Said it was important. I can still see it clearly in my mind, the way it looked, the way it smelled like old paper and dust. Whoever owned it first had scribbled their name all over it, like they were afraid someone would steal it. Ariki.

How could I have forgotten? I'd memorized that name from seeing it so often, but it never meant anything to me. Not until now.

My mind snaps back to my mom's study, to all those books with the same name written in the corners—Ariki. And then I remember her voice, weak and delirious from the meds, calling out for an *Ariki*. It was rare, but on some nights, when she was particularly out of it, she'd whisper it like a prayer, like she was begging someone for help. I'd thought it was just nonsense, a name plucked from the fog of her deteriorating mind.

It was him. She never forgot him, but couldn't bother telling me who he was.

A mix of emotions churns in my chest—anger, confusion, a strange sort of hope. Would he have claimed me if he knew? I don't know if it's true, but it feels right. And maybe that's enough for now.

"Ninety-two percent," I whisper.

A small, almost giddy smile spreads across my face. I try the name out in my head, testing the sound of it. Olivia Ariki. It has a nice ring to it. The logical part of my brain chimes in, reminding me that now might not be the best time to be thinking about surnames, not when I'm trapped in some alien cave with a creature staring me down like I'm dinner or something worse. But I ignore it. I need this. I need something to hold onto, something to keep me from losing my mind completely.

I hum a quiet, tuneless melody to myself as I lean closer to the cluster of mushrooms, soaking in their warmth. The creature shifts slightly, its intense eyes never leaving me, but it doesn't move closer. I take that as a good sign. Maybe it's waiting for something. Or maybe it's just trying to figure me out, the same way I'm trying to figure it out.

Good luck. No one ever has.

Either way, I stay where I am, humming softly, my mind spinning with new possibilities. For the first time in what feels like forever, I feel a spark of hope. I don't know what's waiting for me in these caves or what this creature plans to do with me, but I do know one thing. I'm not done yet.

Olivia Ariki. I think I like the sound of that.

And then I see it shift, my eyes narrowing as it moves away. "Where are you going? Take me back," I say through gritted teeth.

It doesn't respond.

"Oi! Don't turn your back on me you little shit! You don't get to dump me here and walk away!"

My kidnapper alien keeps walking, and I can almost swear that it increases its pace as my voice climbs in pitch.

"Oh, fuck you, then!"

It's gone from sight by the time I get that last bit out, but even then, I can't help the surge of vicious vindication at getting the last word out.

It'd been a long time since I hurled insults at anyone besides bugs, and now that I think about it, doing this to a potentially violent extraterrestrial probably wasn't a bright idea in the first place.

But damn did that feel good. "Piss off!" I add, although I doubt it can hear me at this point.

Perhaps yelling at a six-limbed, seven-foot-tall mass of multicolored nightmare fuel wasn't the wisest of choices, but I'm frayed beyond my usual limits at the moment and the cathartic nature of my outburst did wonders for my mood.

I probably won't be doing it again anytime soon though.

I snort. "Why not? Arsehole."

A yawn escapes my lips as exhaustion crashes down on me like a tidal wave. My brain starts to fizzle. How long has it been since I slept?

9

Kroaicho

The cave is cold and quiet, save for the distant drip of water somewhere deep in its shadows. I walk aimlessly through the twisting tunnels, each step a scrape of my claws on the stone, my mind buzzing and my skin flickering with a mix of emotions that I can't quite parse. I left the little green-haired creature back in the enclave hours ago, zhas angry voice still echoing in my head. What an infuriating thing, making such loud noises and throwing zha's hands about like that. I don't know how to deal with creatures like that. And yet...

And yet, there is this strange sensation prickling beneath my skin. It twists high in my nose, surging up every time I think of those furious green eyes glaring at me. I don't understand it. This odd... heat that makes my skin flare green despite myself.

No. Not green, I will until my skin flickers Annoyance, maybe? Yes, that makes sense and my skin lights purple in agreement. I am annoyed that zha, a small, fragile creature, has made me feel... this way.

Whatever way this is.

I huff, trying to push the feeling down. I'd thought wandering the caves would help me figure something out, but it hasn't worked. I should go back. I should return to the enclave and figure out what to do with the creature. Keeping zha here has complicated things far more than I expected.

I turn, retracing my steps through the winding passages, my mind still tangled in a web of confusion and frustration. What even is zha? I've never seen anything quite like zha. The green hair, the way zha's eyes flash with such intensity—it makes no sense. And zha's words... Oh, zha's words, sharp like shards of ice thrown into my face. I shake my head, a high chitter making its way up my throat.

As I near the enclave, I slow my pace, my claws clicking softer on the stone floor. I feel silly creeping like this, but I don't want to set the creature off again. I peer around the bend in the tunnel, spotting zha in the small hollow I call my resting place. To my relief, zha seems calmer now, a bit groggy now, seemingly just rising from sleep. If nothing else that explains zha's lucid state, perhaps gas would serve as a good deterrent for when next...?

I shake off the disgusting thought, such vileness would be best reserved for enemies, and virulent temper or not, I am hard-pressed to think of zha as an enemy.

Confusing, but not an enemy. Zha still signals in green, but at least zha is no longer shouting. Good.

I stay where I am for a moment, watching zha. I don't know what to say. I don't even know how to approach zha without risking another outburst. But then zha sighs—a small, weary sound that carries over the stone walls. I feel something ease in my chest, just a bit. Maybe zha is tired. Maybe zha will not shout this time.

"Do you have nothing better to do than stare?" zha snaps suddenly, startling me. "Or is lurking in shadows your idea of a fun time?"

I bristle, the tips of my head spikes twitching in irritation. "Not... staring," I say quickly. It's a lie, and I know zha knows it. The creature rolls zha's eyes—a strange motion that makes me wince just looking at it. How can zha do that without pain?

Zha should not do that.

"Sure, you're not," zha says, as if zha agrees with me... and yet doesn't. Odd.

"So, are you going to keep acting like a multi-legged *teenage stalker*, or are you going to come over here and ask whatever it is you're dying to ask?" zha taunts.

I don't understand all of what zha just said, but I feel the sting of an insult buried somewhere in there. My skin flashes dark purple, and I let out an irritated huff. I take a few cautious steps forward, not entirely sure how close I should get. The creature's lips curl upward slightly—a strange expression I've not seen before. I keep my distance, still wary of another bout of those sharp, biting words.

Zha watches me, those green eyes narrowing slightly as if studying me. I feel a flicker of uncertainty, but before I can say anything, the creature speaks again. "I'm Olivia," zha says, "Olivia Ariki. A *human* from *Earth*. A planet, far from here." Zha gestures vaguely, and I get the sense that zha means a great distance.

I blink, taking in the information. Earth. I have never heard of such a place, nor have I ever heard of... humans? Is that what zha said? "Hyu-mans?" I echo, the unfamiliar word strange on my tongue.

"Yes," zha replies, sighing a little, "humans. That's what I am. And that's where I'm from. I was... taken from there. Kidnapped, you know?"

My skin flares blue at the word. Kidnapped. Taken. I know what those words mean. My kind, the Zhasie, knows of many worlds, many species. Some we trade with. Some we avoid. But I have never heard of these... humans. Still, I understand being taken. "Who... took you?" I ask cautiously, my eyes narrowing as I try to make sense of this.

Olivia's expression shifts, becoming darker. "Ugly things," zha says with a shudder. "Bugs and then aliens with gray skin covered in some kind of pink slime, and three legs. They must have put us on a ship. That's how I ended up here."

I hiss at the description, flashing an annoyed purple. I know the creatures zha speaks of.

"The slimes," I share.

They have raided my world before, though they have learned not to come back. Still, they take from other worlds.

"They raid and steal what they cannot make or trade for," I tell zha.

Olivia's eyes widen a bit at my hiss. "You know them?" zha asks, voice cautious.

"Genali," I say, the word heavy with disdain. "They... raid worlds. Take people."

Zha looks stunned for a moment, zha's green eyes wide. Then zha's expression softens a bit, and zha seems to study me more closely. I feel a little exposed under zha's gaze, my skin flashing briefly red before I steady myself.

"I am Kroaicho," I say, wanting to shift the conversation. "Zhasie, not human. But like you I was taken."

Olivia gives a slow up and down movement of zha's head, taking this in. "So... you were taken by them too? And ended up here?"

I mimic zha's movement, but don't explain, though there is more to the story. I do not wish to tell it now. "Yes," I say simply, then add, "You need to clean." I gesture vaguely at the grime covering zha's skin and clothing. Zha must be uncomfortable.

Olivia blinks, clearly caught off guard. "What? Clean? I mean... yes, that would be good."

I decide not to waste more words explaining. Instead, I reach out, grabbing zha's arm again. Zha lets out a yelp, but I don't give zha time to protest.

"I don't like to be—" I shudder to think what zha is going to say and instead I break into a sprint, dragging zha deeper into the tunnels. I hear zha's voice behind me, rising into that high-pitched tone that seems to be zha's way of expressing distress, but I do not slow down.

I know where I'm going. There is a small pool of water further in, one that I sometimes use to wash myself. Until I know how breakable zha is, we should avoid the flowing water. It is not far, and I can reach it quickly if I hurry. Zha stumbles behind me, trying to keep up, and I can feel the heat of zha's anger radiating off zha, sections of sentences coming out of zha's mouth as zha sputters. But I do not stop.

I can feel zha's heartbeat through zha's arm, fast and erratic. Zha is afraid, perhaps. But zha will see. I am not a danger. I just want to help. I just want to understand.

I dutifully ignore the leering voice in my head jeering that I am a liar.

***

I come to a stop at the edge of the pool, letting out a breath I hadn't realized I was holding. The cool air here is a stark contrast to the stifling heat of the cave passages behind us, carrying the scent of minerals, damp stone, and something else—something old, ancient even like the air hasn't been disturbed for centuries. I can feel Olivia's small form tugging against me, zha's grip firm yet delicate. I release zha, my clawed fingers uncurling slowly as zha steps away, and zha's face emerges from zha's hair, eyes squinting in the dim, bluish light emanating from the rocks beneath the water.

The pool stretches out in front of us, the water's surface rippling slightly with the flow of the hidden currents below. It's almost hypnotic, the way the water seems both still and alive, a mirror-like surface broken only by the soft, unseen movement beneath. Rocks at the bottom glow with a soft, cerulean light, casting shimmering patterns along the jagged walls of the cavern. It's as if the water is alive, as if it holds secrets just waiting to be uncovered. The beauty of the scene is almost otherworldly, and I find myself momentarily entranced.

Olivia's eyes go wide, and zha takes a tentative step forward, staring at the water. I watch zha closely, unable to tear my eyes away from the way the light dances in zha's eyes—those peculiar green eyes that seem to hold so much emotion at once, even though their color does not change. There's a depth to them that unsettles me, something that feels like a challenge or a mystery that I am not sure I'm prepared to face. For a moment, I feel a twist high in my nose again, but I push it back, forcing myself to focus.

"Careful," I warn, my voice echoing off the cave walls like a low growl reverberating through the space. "The water here is deep. It dips underground."

Zha pauses, turning zha's head toward me, and there's a cautious head up and down movement. I place Olivia down gently, making sure zha is steady before I let go, but I don't move far, settling close beside zha. The creature gives me a pointed look, lips pressed together in a tight line, and I can feel the tension radiating off zha. I return the look, unblinking, watching zha's eyes flicker between green and something darker, something unreadable.

A sigh escapes zha's lips, heavy and resigned. "Can you at least give me some space to clean up?" zha says, irritation evident in zha's tone.

"I am giving space," I reply, keeping my tone even but firm. "Not holding your hands, see?" I spread my clawed hands wide to show I am not restraining zha. "I assume they are capable of cleaning."

Olivia's mouth twitches, and I wonder if zha is about to argue again. There's a flicker of something in zha's eyes—defiance, maybe, or frustration. But then zha pauses, eyes narrowing slightly, considering. I watch carefully, my own breath held, waiting to see what zha will do. "Unless..." I add tentatively, letting the word hang in the air between us like a challenge, "you want me to... help clean you?"

The creature's face contorts into a strange expression I've seen before—a mix of annoyance and something I can't quite place. Is it embarrassment? Without a word, zha scoops a handful of water and splashes it right into my face. The water is colder than I expected, and I flinch back, shaking my head as droplets scatter from my skin. The shock of the cold sends a jolt through me, and I instinctively take a step back.

"Zhannel behavior," I grumble, wiping my face with a swipe of my forearm. "Immature."

Olivia's eyes flash a darker green, and for a moment, I think zha might lunge at me. Zha's small body practically vibrates with energy, a coiled spring ready to snap. It amazes me how much anger such a tiny thing can hold and how vividly zha can express it without color. My own skin flares dark purple, a warning signal I don't entirely mean to show. But I do not back away. I have a sinking suspicion that if I do, the moment I take my eyes off zha, Olivia will dart away. And I cannot allow that. Not here, not now.

"Don't touch me."

I don't, but I also don't move.

Seeing that I'm not moving, Olivia lets out a sharp sigh, a sound that seems to cut through the cool, damp air like a shard of rock. I startle and my head spikes twitch involuntarily.

After kneeling down and taking a long drink, Olivia stands again. Then I see zha's glossy black skin begin to recede, rolling down into a thin band around zha's waist. My skin flashes red without my meaning to, the sudden fear twisting through me like a knife. What is Olivia doing? Why is zha shedding zha's skin?

Olivia notices my reaction and raises one of zha's brow ridges, a strange redness coloring zha's cheeks making me realize zha is also afraid.

But zha was just angry. I don't understand this expression. I don't understand this situation. My body tenses, ready for whatever might come next. "Why are you staring at my naked form?" Olivia asks, voice tinged with something I cannot quite identify. Is it fear? Is it mockery?

I blink, my head tilting slightly as I try to process zha's words. "Naked?" I echo, not understanding. I look zha over again, trying to find what zha means, and my gaze lands on zha's chest—on two rounded protrusions, I hadn't noticed before. A peculiar, thrilling sensation runs up my spine and into my nostrils, one I've never felt before. I think to ask why zha shows fear—what is there to fear here?

But I don't get the chance.

A small rock smacks into my snout, cutting off my thoughts. I hiss in surprise, my skin flaring to an annoyed purple as I look back at Olivia. Zha's face is flushed deeper now, and zha looks absolutely livid. "Stop staring at my privates!" zha snaps, voice sharp like ice shards.

Grumbling, I shift my gaze away from zha's body, fixing my eyes instead on the cave's roof. I don't turn away completely, unwilling to let zha out of my sight, but I try to focus on the jagged stalactites hanging above. "Fine," I mutter. "I don't understand what that means, but finish so we can return."

Olivia mutters something under zha's breath as zha starts to wash zha's body with the water. I can hear the soft splashes and the muttered words that I am almost certain are more insults, though I don't understand them fully. There's a rhythm to the sound, like strange, angry music that fills the air between us. I consider responding but decide against it. There is no point in arguing more when zha is already this angry.

Instead, I keep my gaze upward, watching the shadows cast by the glowing rocks below. The shadows shift and move like creatures of their own, dancing along the walls. I focus on their movements, trying to distract myself from the awkwardness of the situation, and from the tension that still lingers in the air. The cave is quiet now, save for the occasional splash and Olivia's grumbling. I feel the tension in the air slowly ease, and I find myself relaxing a bit, though I remain alert. I cannot afford to let zha run off. Not now. Not when I am still so uncertain of zha's intentions... or of my own.

It is good that zha is cleaning off the dust and blood. Every treasure should be well cared for and clean before you can figure out its story. This feels different, though. Every treasure has come to me with a story already set, but this one feels like it is still being told. The story always ends with possession and protection, but I don't know how this one will end. It's exhilarating and unsettling, all at once.

After a few moments, I risk a glance down, careful to keep my gaze away from Olivia's body. I see zha's face, the green hair plastered to zha's skin, and zha's eyes look a little less fierce, more focused. Zha seems lost in thought, perhaps reflecting on something far away, or maybe just thinking of the next step. I think zha might be calming down, and I feel a small flicker of relief in my chest.

Perhaps this strange creature and I can find a way to understand each other. Or at least, to coexist. I can't let zha leave my hoard, so I must figure it out. There's a fragile peace here, a tentative balance that could be shattered by a single wrong move. But for now, that is enough. The cave around us seems to hold its breath as if waiting for what comes next, and I wonder if maybe, just maybe, there is a way forward from this strange place we find ourselves in.

The rippling water continues its silent dance, the glowing rocks beneath casting their soft light into the darkness. The patterns they create shift and swirl, ever-changing, like the thoughts that swirl in my mind. I watch the light move, my eyes tracing the lines and shapes, and I think about all that has led us here. How much has changed in such a short time, and how much more is yet to come.

There is a moment of stillness, a calm that settles over the cavern like a blanket. I breathe it in, feeling the cool air fill my lungs, and for the first time in a long while, I feel a strange sense of peace. It is fragile, yes, but it is there, and for now, that is enough.

10

Olivia

I keep my gaze fixed on the rippling water as I continue to wash, trying to focus on the coolness against my skin rather than the unnerving presence of Kroaicho behind me. At least my throat is no longer raw with thirst.

The dim, bluish light from the glowing rocks beneath the water casts an ethereal glow on the cave walls, creating dancing shadows that almost distract me from the weight of the creature's stare. Almost.

I need to think. There has to be a way out of this mess. Maybe, just maybe, I can convince this... creature... to let me go. I pause at that thought, scrubbing my arm absently as I mull it over. The way it moves, the way it speaks—everything about it is so... alien. It's so fucking huge and scary it just screams male, but I'm too angry with it to let it turn into a person.

My mind lands back on *it* with satisfaction and anger.

Then I feel guilty for some reason. Then angry. Frustration bubbles up, and I let out a huff, letting that line of thought die a natural death. It's a waste of time trying to pin it down with human concepts.

Instead, I go back to my original idea. Maybe I can reason with it. I've seen hints of rationality behind those unnerving eyes, those oddly hooked, slitted pupils that narrow and widen with each passing emotion. It can speak. It understands.

I still don't know what it wants, which has me on edge. Humans are confusing as hell, but one constant remains. Everyone always wants something. Homework, taxes, someone to admit they are lesser than them. Someone to torment or someone to make them feel better about themselves because they are trying to "fix" you.

I just need to figure out what it wants.

Surely that means there's some logic buried in there somewhere, right? But then I remember the way it referred to me as its property, and I grimace. I catch myself rubbing my arm a bit too hard, the skin turning red under my nails.

My gaze drifts toward Kroaicho for a moment, and I catch it watching me. Its eyes—those strange, unblinking, almost-too-large eyes—are tracing my curves. I can't help but roll my eyes. Typical. At least that much I recognize. "Enjoying getting an eyeful?" I snap, sarcasm dripping from every word.

So much for pulling out logic. I roll my eyes at myself, but I'm still too angry to push past the snark.

Kroaicho blinks slowly, its bioluminescent skin shifting to a soft shade of blue. The color pulses, faint and almost pretty in the low light—a thought I immediately stomp down with a mental boot. I don't have time to find anything about this thing "pretty." It shifts its gaze to my face, looking genuinely puzzled. "Eyeful?" it repeats, voice a low, rumbling growl that echoes slightly in the cavern. "I do not understand. How can one's eyes be full? Is that why you rotate them?"

It shudders for some unknown reason when it says it.

I feel an eyebrow twitch in frustration. So much for my attempt at teasing. "You know, for supposedly intelligent sentient life, you're pretty slow on the uptake. Ever heard of wit? The holy grail for your species, I'm sure."

I look around for a sharp rock and start hacking off the long green hair, taking out my frustration on it.

Kroaicho's blue deepens to a darker shade, and I see its brow furrow slightly. "Wit," it says slowly, testing the word like it's tasting it for the first time. "I know this. But you speak of it as if it is...somehow precious?" It tilts its head, genuinely perplexed. "What does wit have to do with treasure?"

I blink, my mouth opening and closing for a second as I process that. Holy crap, it actually knows what wit is? Then I realize it must have picked up the term from me or somewhere else, but doesn't understand the reference. It's hard to remember sometimes that I'm talking to an alien, not another human.

It's still blowing my mind that its speaking English, and getting better and better at it. It's unsettling.

I let out a breath, trying to stay patient. "It's just a saying we have back on Earth. 'Holy grail' means something treasured, something everyone wants."

Kroaicho's eyes widen slightly, and its skin glows a more vibrant blue. "Treasure..." it murmurs, the word rolling off its tongue like it's savoring it.

Then it switches to its own language. "How does one acquire this treasure of wit?"

I pause, a new thought forming in the back of my mind. This thing values treasure? That makes sense with all of the "hoard" mutterings. Maybe there's a way to exploit that. But for now, I play it off.

When I open my mouth to reply, there is a sharp pain for a moment and then I'm making the same odd chittering sound it does. "Well—"

Its skin flares a brilliant orange after the first word of its language. "You also learn languages like zhasie do?"

"Not before I was taken," I admit, mind still fucked that these clicks and chitters actually mean something.

"Anyway," I click out tersely in its odd language, "you can't just get wit. It's more like… you have it or you don't. It's about being quick on your feet. Making clever remarks. You know, saying things that make people think."

Kroaicho's brow furrows even deeper, and I can see it struggling to piece together what I'm saying. "I… see. So, wit is both a treasure and a state of being?"

I can't help but laugh, the sound echoing off the cave walls. "Sure, let's go with that. It's a treasure and a state of being. You're catching on."

It nods in a slow, deliberate motion. "And how does one know if they possess wit?"

This is ridiculous. I shake my head, feeling a smile tug at the corners of my lips despite myself. "Usually, people with wit don't have to ask if they have it. It's pretty self-evident."

The creature's face twists slightly, its bioluminescent skin flashing a brief purple before settling back to blue. "Self-evident." It nods again, as if deep in thought. "This seems… inefficient. There would be guessing and some of those would be wrong. So how could it be self-evident?"

I bark out another laugh. "Inefficient? Seriously? You have a lot to learn about humans. I go through all of my life guessing."

It tilts its head again, eyes narrowing slightly. "Indeed. Your kind seems very perplexing. You use many words to convey simple ideas. Some of them contradictory."

I smirk. "Being steady and clear would be boring. Life's too short to be boring."

Kroaicho's eyes narrow further, and I can see the confusion etched into every line of its alien features. "Your lifespan is short, yet you choose to complicate it further? This does not seem wise."

I roll my eyes again. "Yeah, well, wisdom's overrated. And besides, some of us prefer to enjoy life, not just survive it."

I cringe, hoping it doesn't recognize my bravado. As if I would leave my room if I could get away with completely shutting myself away forever.

The creature falls silent for a moment, its eyes fixed on me in that unnerving, unblinking way. I can't tell if it's pondering my words or just trying to figure out if I've gone mad. The truth is, it's probably a bit of both.

We lapse into a tense silence, and I go back to washing myself, hoping the cool water will help clear my head. I'm not sure what's worse—the conversation or the fact that I'm actually starting to feel like I'm getting through to it, even if just a little.

"You speak of enjoyment," Kroaicho says suddenly, breaking the silence. "Is this a human form of treasure? For us, the treasure is what brings the enjoyment."

I sigh, deciding to play along. "Sure, why not? Enjoyment is a kind of treasure too. Different from wit, but valuable in its own way."

Its eyes flicker with a hint of understanding. "Many treasures exist among your kind."

"Yep. Wit, enjoyment, freedom... the list goes on." I feel a pang of something sharp in my chest as I say that last word, my mind drifting back to my initial thoughts. Freedom. Now there's a treasure I'd give anything for right now.

Kroaicho's head tilts again, more sharply this time, like a bird of prey zeroing in on its target. "Freedom," it echoes, voice softer, almost contemplative. "Another treasure. But this one you do not possess."

I stiffen, feeling the hairs on the back of my neck rise. "Not yet," I say, trying to keep my voice steady. "But I will."

It stares at me for a long moment, and I can see a strange flicker in its eyes—curiosity, maybe, or something else I can't quite place. Then it shakes its head, almost like it's shaking off a thought. "This is... confusing," it mutters, more to itself than to me. "Where is the story in that?"

"Well, welcome to my world," I say dryly as I try to figure out what it means about a story. "You think you're the only one confused here?"

It gives me that same odd look, and I see the color on its skin start to shift again, a gradient of blue swirling over its skin and between the spikes jutting from its shoulders.

"You are confused also," it chitters slowly.

"I don't know what you want from me," I retort.

I'm feeling more and more desperate to know with each passing moment.

"Nothing," it chitters back, limbs twitching, lighting up blue. "You are here to shine."

"What the fuck does that even mean? Don't lie to me. Just say it," I chitter back, unsure of how I know that the clicks I'm adding mean I'm angry.

Swirls of red join the blue and it gets even twitchier. "Perhaps it is better to be... elsewhere."

I get a sinking feeling in my stomach. I've seen that look before, the way its eyes dart around, the way its skin flares slightly. I have a hunch about what it means, and I can't let this conversation end like this. Not when I'm starting to get somewhere.

"Hey, hey!" I blurt out, trying to keep its attention. "You're not leaving already, are you? What's wrong? Too much wit for one day?"

It glances back at me, and I swear I see a flicker of something like annoyance in its eyes. "It is not wit that confounds me," it says slowly. "It is... you."

I narrow my eyes at that, feeling my cheeks heat up slightly. "What's that supposed to mean?"

I've heard a version of it my whole life, but for some reason it feels like even more of an insult from such a lumbering alien oaf.

Kroaicho looks me over once more, but this time its gaze is different—more hesitant, more guarded. "You are... unpredictable," it says finally. "This is unsettling."

I feel a smirk tug at my lips. "Well, get used to it. That's just how I roll."

"Is that a method of conveyance?" it asks.

"No. I mean that is how I operate. My main state of being," I tell it.

"Unpredictable?"

"Yes," I say, my chittering firm, though I'm lying.

I'm pretty simple, actually. I like peace and long stretches of quiet. Not a whole lot matters more than that. But I can be unpredictable if that's what gets under its stupid light-up skin.

It watches me for another long moment, its skin flashing with an almost imperceptible glow. Then it turns away, its muscles tensing as if preparing to leave. "I will be... elsewhere," it says, sounding flustered.

And just like that, it starts to move away, the tension in its posture clear as day. I get the feeling it's more confused than ever—by me, by this whole situation. Maybe that's a good thing. Maybe.

It's a crack in the armor I can use.

I watch it leave, a thousand new thoughts swirling in my mind. The water ripples around me as I stand there, my body still half-submerged, but my brain already working on a new plan. If I'm going to get out of here, I'll need every bit of wit and every ounce of treasure I can muster.

Freedom. Yeah, I'm coming for you. Just wait and see.

***

The water is cold against my skin, a numbing chill that keeps me alert even as I scrub the last of the grime from my arms. My bath is done, and I've stretched my time as long as I can without drawing suspicion. The glowing rocks beneath the surface flicker softly, like underwater stars, casting shifting patterns on the cave walls. I can feel Kroaicho's presence behind me before I see it. There's a slight tremor in the water, a shift in the air that prickles the back of my neck. I turn, squinting against the darkness, and there it is—its towering, shadowy form looming over the dimly lit cave.

"Finished?" its voice rumbles out, echoing in the space. I give a curt nod, biting back a retort. No point in pushing it any further right now. It steps forward, its bioluminescent skin pulsing a dull, steady blue—a sign of calmness, or at least neutrality, if I've interpreted its moods right.

Without another word, it grabs me by the arm—not harshly, but firm enough that I know better than to resist. We make our way back to the enclave, the cave twisting and turning like a stone labyrinth. My feet, still slick with water, slip a little on the wet stone, but I manage to keep pace. Kroaicho is quiet, its focus seemingly elsewhere, muttering under its breath in that guttural language of its kind. I only catch fragments, words like "treasure", "centerpiece", and "hoard", but I don't bother deciphering its gibberish. I'm more concerned with my current state—trapped, cold, and plotting a way out.

When we reach the cave from before, Kroaicho releases my arm and, without a backward glance, turns to leave. "I will return," it growls, as it often does, as if I have any choice in the matter. Then it's gone, its heavy footsteps fading into the winding passages beyond.

I exhale, letting out a breath I hadn't realized I was holding. This bigger cave isn't much better than the bath cave—dark, and damp, with only the soft glow of bioluminescent mushrooms scattered around the walls to provide light. There's a larger cluster near where I'm sitting, their soft blue hues casting strange shadows across the ground and thankfully also the same heat as before. I find a patch of softer soil nearby and settle down, reaching for a sharp-edged rock.

I feel the numbers and the mind stutters wanting to push back up into my mind from where I shut them away. I need to keep my mind busy, so I resume drawing.

* * *

For hours, I've been etching out designs—small, intricate patterns reminiscent of the māori tattoos I memorized on Earth. I draw them small, not only to conserve space but also to test my ability to maintain detail. My fingers trace the lines, carefully carving them into the soil. Each drawing feels like a lifeline, a tether to a past life that seems so far away now.

One is a *koru*, a spiral that symbolizes new life and growth. Another is a *hei matau*, a fishhook pattern representing strength and good fortune. I work on a third, a *manaia*, the guardian symbol, with its beak-like curves and intricate inner swirls. The ground around me is slowly filling up with these tiny pieces of art, and as I finish the last one, I find myself staring at it for a long moment. The realization hits me like a punch to the gut—I've just been sitting here on my behind like an idiot, completely unsupervised.

I freeze, a wave of embarrassment washing over me.

Stupid, Olivia. Really stupid.

Who knows how long Kroaicho will be gone? I could've used this time to plan, to escape. I glance around the darkened cave, my heart starting to pound. Now's as good a time as any.

I move quickly, scooping up several of the larger bioluminescent mushrooms. Their soft glow barely lights the way, but it's better than nothing. Holding them like a makeshift lantern, I pick a direction—any direction that isn't the one Kroaicho took—and start moving.

The cave air is cold and damp, the walls slick with moisture. Each step echoes in the emptiness, and I find myself straining to hear anything beyond my own breathing. The cave splits off into countless paths, some leading into narrow crevices, others opening into larger chambers filled with strange rock formations and more clusters of those glowing fungi. I keep moving, keeping my eyes peeled for anything that looks like an exit.

After what feels like an eternity of winding through the dark, I come across a part of the cave where the overhead stalactites drip consistently. The water trickles down, pooling onto sheets of rock that look almost like glass. I step carefully onto the slippery surface, testing my footing. The rock is smooth, wet, and incredibly treacherous. I take it slow, moving one foot after the other, keeping my balance steady.

Then I hear it—a faint skittering sound coming from somewhere to my left. My head whips in that direction, muscles tensing. Big mistake. My foot slips out from under me, and I'm sent sprawling onto the slick rock. Pain flares up as I roll across the jagged sheets, a dozen sharp edges cutting into my skin. I let out a yelp, instinctively reaching for something—anything—to stop my fall. My fingers catch on a crevice in the rock, and I cling to it desperately, hanging over what looks like a dark, bottomless chasm.

My breath comes in ragged gasps, and my fingers burn where they grip the rock. I look down, and a sick feeling twists in my stomach as I see one of the mushrooms I'd been holding slip from my grasp. It tumbles over the edge and falls, its bioluminescent light slowly swallowed by the blackness below. I swallow hard. I don't hear it hit bottom.

Okay. Deep breath. Focus.

I force myself to calm down, my heart hammering in my chest. I can't afford to freak out now. I painstakingly pull myself up, inch by inch, feeling my way along the rough surface. The rock cuts into my palms, blood trickling down my arms, but I grit my teeth and keep moving.

I finally manage to haul myself onto a smoother patch of rock, and I collapse against it, breathing heavily. My whole body is shaking, adrenaline coursing through my veins. But then I realize—there's no light. I've lost my last mushroom. I'm in total darkness.

Fear grips me, cold and sharp. I've always hated the dark—too many childhood nightmares, too many memories of being in new places.

The sound of skittering comes again, closer this time, echoing off the cave walls. My breath catches in my throat, and my mind races. I can't see it, but I can hear it—something moving, crawling, getting closer.

Panic sets in, my thoughts scattering like leaves in a storm. I have to move, have to get away, but where? Which direction? My hands shake as I press them against the cold rock, trying to steady myself. The skittering is almost right on top of me now, a rapid clicking that sends a shiver down my spine. My breath comes out in short, shallow bursts, and I feel the walls closing in, the exhaustion threatening to overwhelm me. Shut me down.

No. I can't lose it now. I bite down hard on my lip, forcing myself to think, to focus. I push the fear down, locking it away, and breathe deeply. The skittering noise grows louder, more insistent. My heart pounds in my ears. Then, just as suddenly as it started, the noise stops.

Silence. I stay still, barely daring to breathe, waiting for the next sound. When none comes, a shaky sigh escapes me. Relief floods in, and I feel a half-crazed giggle bubble up from my chest. I can't help it—after everything, after nearly dying, I'm here, alive. Somehow, that seems almost funny. My laughter echoes off the cave walls, a little wild, a little broken.

The adrenaline starts to drain away, leaving me feeling hollow and exhausted. I lean back against the rock, the darkness pressing in on all sides. My eyes are useless here, but my ears are still ringing from the tension, an ache that won't quite go away.

I don't know how long I spend laying there but it's long enough to cycle between pretty much all the emotions I've got on my emotional spectrum and once that's done, all that's left is extreme apathy.

As I lay there, a persistent, throbbing ache in my ears keeps me from fully relaxing. I shake my head slightly, trying to ignore it, but it only grows worse, like a pressure building inside my skull. I force my eyes shut tighter, praying for sleep to come, to escape this nightmare for just a little while. Eventually, mercifully, I feel myself slipping away, the darkness pulling me under.

Fuck it, if I'm dying here, I'm dying in my sleep.

There's no ceremony to the thought, just stony acceptance, and with that concluded, I close my eyes and let myself shut down. Maybe things will be clearer when I wake up—if I wake up.

11

Kroaicho

I return to the enclave with my arms full—an array of gleaming rocks, stalactites, and other shiny treasures gathered meticulously from the deeper cave systems. Each piece is carefully chosen; each represents a piece of a hoard I am building back after losing so much in this foreign place.

One stalactite among them is particularly desirable. It glows in the most lovely striations of green among the brown. The story of each drip of mineral building it layer by layer stretching back long before I was alive. Each streak a moment in time as creatures passed by it, fought under it, nestled against it, while it changed slowly, almost imperceptibly.

It will provide such a long, rich history. A steady presence among the rocks made of incredible forces; much stronger, but less steady. A product of violence rather than a slow expansion.

Each perfect in their own way.

I cradle them close to my chest, feeling their solid weight, and imagine how they will gleam under the pale glow of the bioluminescent mushrooms scattered throughout the enclave. They are humble beginnings, yes, but even a small hoard can eventually grow into something vast and worthy.

But as I near the enclave, a sudden absence registers—a cold, creeping emptiness that sends a jolt through my core. The human. I sense it immediately. I lower the rocks gently, body twitching to full alert. The atmosphere is wrong and unbalanced.

I scan the darkened cave, my eyes narrowing into slits as I process the space. No Olivia. No muttered insults or sarcastic quips echoing in the damp air.

Just silence.

My nostrils flare, drawing in the cool, musty cave air, searching for zha's scent. Thankfully, it hasn't faded yet. Zha is nearby, but moving away—fast. I grind my teeth and clack together my tusks, my jaw tightening with irritation.

Zha is always trying to escape. Always complicating things. Why does zha make everything so difficult?

I drop to all six limbs and break into a dead sprint, my claws clicking against the damp stone as I dart through the narrow passages. The echo of my own breath reverberates against the walls, but I ignore it, focusing on the scent trail winding its way through the cave network. Zha is heading deeper into the caverns, toward more treacherous terrain. I push myself harder, muscles burning as I weave through the maze-like tunnels.

Stupid, impulsive human.

The scent grows stronger, and soon, I reach a familiar section of the cave. My momentum slows as I near a portion with a glassy, slippery rock floor, a naturally dangerous area even for creatures as agile as myself. I approach cautiously, claws gripping the wet stone.

The dim light from the bioluminescent fungi reveals zha's prone form a few feet away from a massive chasm, zha's body is limp and dangerously close to the edge. My irritation spikes, followed by a tight, uncomfortable feeling I can't quite identify.

"Foolish, foolish human..." I mutter under my breath as I approach zha's still form.

Zha's eyes are closed, breathing steady—zha is asleep. I stand over zha, my shadows stretching across the glossy rock. I should leave zha here, and let zha learn the consequences of zha's reckless actions. But my body moves before my thoughts can catch up. I reach down and scoop zha up, tucking zha against my chest.

Zha is so light, fragile even.

Almost immediately, zha unconsciously shifts closer, seeking warmth. Zha's small body presses against mine, head nestling against my skin. My bioluminescence flickers, shifting into a deep orange, a reaction I quickly tamp down by thinking of my irritation until the purple glow returns.

I glance down at zha, feeling my lips pushing against my tusks to reflect my annoyance.

"This is why a hoard never includes pets," I grumble, my voice a low rumble in the silence. "Never."

Zha does not respond, zha's body is limp and zha's face is relaxed in sleep. I sigh and begin the long trek back to the enclave, navigating the slick, uneven terrain with more care this time. The human is warm against me, zha's soft breath tickling my chest with each exhale. I try not to think about it, about how natural it feels, carrying zha like this.

The journey back feels long, and my mind starts to wander despite myself. Why can't I just leave her? Zha is troublesome, always asking questions, challenging me, and running off when Zha knows nothing of the dangers of this place. Zha complicates my life in a hundred small, frustrating ways. And yet...

I glance down at zha, watching the way zha's face twitches slightly as if zha is dreaming. Zha's small body is so easily broken, so vulnerable. I could end zha's life right now if I chose to. The thought passes through my mind like a shadow, unbidden but not entirely unwelcome. But I don't. I can't.

Why am I so fascinated by Olivia? Zha is unlike anything I have ever encountered—bold, reckless, unpredictable. Somehow completely uninterested in treasure.

It makes no sense, and yet part of my mind wonders what it would be like if there wasn't that competition between two zhasie. Or, well, a zhasie and a human.

Everything about zha defies logic, and yet there is something about zha that keeps pulling me back, making me want to understand zha. To understand this...human.

I shake my head, trying to dismiss the thought. Zha is nothing but a distraction, a complication I never asked for. And yet... I can't help but feel a small flicker of something—curiosity, perhaps? Or is it something more insidious, something I dare not name?

Before I can delve deeper into this uncomfortable line of thought, I feel a stir against my chest. I look down to see Olivia's eyes fluttering open, zha's body tensing as zha wakes. Zha's eyes go wide, and zha jerks upright, looking around wildly.

"What—" zha starts, zha's voice groggy and confused. Then, realization sets in, and zha scowls up at me. "What the *hell*, Kroaicho?"

I set zha down on zha's feet with a huff, my irritation flaring back to the surface. "What exactly did you intend to achieve by falling asleep a few feet from of certain death?" I snap, each chitter strident, my voice echoing through the enclave.

Olivia lets out a growl, rubbing zha's eyes. "I don't know, maybe I was tired?" Zha wiggles out of my grip, zha's feet unsteady on the uneven ground. "Ever think of that? Why must you always be *schlepping* me around?"

I narrow my eyes, my patience wearing thin. "You were tired, so you decided to risk your life on a ledge?" I click, my voice rising with each word. "That makes no sense, even by your baffling standards. I keep my treasures safe, but you have purposefully put yourself at risk."

Had I only realized it would be this difficult to keep a treasure safe... from itself. It's baffling to suddenly have a greater concern than theft. My skin lights up purple as I remember just how close zha was to ending zha's story.

Zha moves zha's shoulders, not the least bit bothered by my anger. "I was *bored*, okay? So I went exploring. Big deal."

I freeze, the word catching in my mind. "*Bored*?" I echo, tasting the unfamiliar term. "What is this... *bored*? Does it mean seeking death?"

Zha looks at me, exasperated. "You know, *bored*. When you've got nothing to do, and your brain starts turning to mush?"

I tilt my head, trying to parse zha's meaning. "You... turn to mush? This is not possible. You are solid."

Olivia stares at me for a moment, then bursts into laughter. "No, not literally. It's a feeling. Like when you're restless and need something to do."

I blink, still not quite understanding. "So, *boredom* is... a disease of inactivity?"

Olivia laughs harder, doubling over. "No, no, it's not a disease. It's just... ugh, it's hard to explain."

I tap my arms against each other, feeling my annoyance flare again. "Your human concepts are needlessly complex."

Zha straightens, wiping liquid from zha's eyes. "You know what? You're right. Let's just say it's a thing we humans experience and leave it at that."

I huff, but the heat of my anger dissipates slightly. "Alright. If this *boredom* is such a problem, what do you do to cure it?"

Olivia's eyes brighten at that, and zha gestures toward the small pile of shiny rocks I had gathered. "Well, what do you do for fun?"

I straighten up, pride swelling in my chest. "I go treasure hunting." I gesture grandly to my modest collection. "I have gathered these today. They are quite remarkable, are they not?"

Zha gives the pile a skeptical look, raising an eyebrow. "These? These are what you call treasure?"

I feel a twinge of self-consciousness, my skin flickering to a faint blue. "Yes, they are treasures," I insist, perhaps a bit too loudly.

"All I see are dull, dusty rocks," zha chitters back and I look over to the gleaming, multi-colored pile in confusion.

"There is nothing dull about them. They each have a rich story," I argue. "Back on my home planet, we gathered these to add to our hoard. It is a practice of great importance."

Zha snorts. "Fair enough. On Earth, for fun, we have things like *television shows*."

I grind my tusks, the word unfamiliar, and I assume meaning nothing of true value. "What is this?"

"It's a kind of entertainment," zha explains, "where you watch stories on a screen that lights up. Like tiny, moving pictures."

"Stories?" I chitter back, surprised.

"Yes, of course," zha says in a dismissive tone.

I tilt my head, trying to visualize what zha is describing. "I have seen screens, but only used by visiting aliens. And not... moving stories?"

"Yes," zha says with the up and down head movement, "some of them are really good. You get to see different worlds, different lives, all from the comfort of your home."

"That sounds intriguing," I admit. "But nothing you can hold or organize?"

"A long time ago, maybe," zha says with an odd twitch of shoulders. "The story is in your mind, not in your hands."

I let out a snort. "Your species truly is strange. So, you watch these moving pictures instead of actually gathering things for your hoard. The screens are your treasure?"

Zha shakes zha's head back and forth. "No, the stories are what make the screens fun. The screens aren't important. It's what is on them. For example, my favorite show, *Rick and Morty*."

The name sounds odd to me, but I prompt zha to continue. "Explain this... *Rick and Morty*."

Zha's eyes widen, and zha launches into an enthusiastic explanation. "So, it's about this mad *scientist*, Rick, and his *grandson*, Morty, going on crazy adventures across different *dimensions* and universes. Rick's kind of an *alcoholic*, super genius, and Morty's this awkward, *naïve teenager* who gets dragged along."

My skin lights up to show my bemusement. Most of the words didn't translate, but I don't want zha to explain it again. "This sounds chaotic."

Zha moves zha's shoulders. "Yes, that's the point! It's wild, unpredictable. Like... uh... me. What about you?"

"I am neither mad nor chaotic," I tell zha.

Zha gives me a long look. "Oh, you definitely have the mad part down. And the chaos? I think that's a given."

For a moment, my skin lights up orange for some inexplicable reason. That should be an insult, why would it make me happy to hear it?

"Perhaps," I tell zha. "But I still do not understand how such a thing could relieve this *boredom* you speak of."

Olivia snorts. "Maybe one day I'll show you."

The thought of seeing these moving pictures with zha is strange, but I nod. "Perhaps. But until then, you are not to leave the enclave again without my express permission."

Zha opens zha mouth to protest, but I cut zha off with a glare and a flash of purple. "I will not always be there to drag you back from the brink of death. Understood?"

Zha mutters something under zha's breath but nods. "Fine. But if you expect me to sit here and twiddle my thumbs, you've got another thing coming."

For some reason, I don't like zha's anger. I want to see wide eyes and hear excited chitters again. They make me want to glow orange, even though what zha says is strange.

"Tell me more about these *television shows*, Olivia," I urge, suddenly excited about how many layers to zha there are.

Zha is too mercurial to be like the slow build of a stalactite, too layered to be like a rock made of earth forces. Something in between.

Zha blinks at me, brow lowering. Then, as if on cue, zha's eyes brighten, and zha seems to shake off zha's earlier annoyance. "You want to hear about more shows? That's what you want from me?"

Zha's tone is confused, though zha's green eyes are still bright.

"Yes," I respond, more firmly than I intended. "If these *shows* cure this... 'boredom,' then it's in both our interests for me to know more about them. You will tell me now."

Olivia smirks and rolls zha's eyes, making my skin shudder. "All right, all right. Let's see..." Zha pauses, tapping zha's chin thoughtfully. "Oh! Have you ever heard of *Red versus Blue*?"

I tilt my head, the words strange and nonsensical. "Red versus blue? Are those two... adversaries? Why would fear and confusion battle one another?"

Zha laughs and shakes zha's head. "Oh, thank you for letting me know what those colors mean. Not exactly. It's more of a comedy than a serious fight. It's about two teams of *soldiers*, one red, and one blue, who are supposed to be fighting in this huge war. Except, the war doesn't really matter because they're all stuck in this canyon with nothing to do. So, instead of fighting, they just spend most of their time arguing and getting into ridiculous situations."

I blink slowly, absorbing this. "So two emotions do not fight? They just argue? How is that entertaining?"

Olivia's mouth widens, which I'm starting to realize is zha's equivalent to orange, clearly enjoying zha's chance to explain. "Well, they do fight sometimes, but it's mostly about the banter. The red team is always scheming and trying to one-up the blue team, but they're all kind of idiots. And then there's the blue team, who are just as bad but in different ways. It's all about the characters and the stupid things they get into."

I can't help but snort, my skin flickering white with amusement despite myself. "So, you watch a group of incompetent emotion soldiers argue with each other instead of engaging in actual combat? This sounds absurd."

Zha crosses zha's arms and narrows zha's eyes at me. "It's funny because it's absurd. It's not supposed to be serious. It's all about the humor in the situation. You'd probably find it funny if you gave it a chance."

I challenge zha with a skeptical look and deep click. "I highly doubt it. My species values precision and efficiency. Wasting time with incompetence is not something we find humorous."

"Not everything has to be about efficiency, though I do enjoy it myself," Olivia says, clearly enjoying zha's chance to challenge me. "Sometimes, it's just about enjoying the chaos. You could use a little of that, you know. Loosen up a bit."

"Loosen up?" I echo, feeling a flicker of dark purple irritation flash across my skin. "I am perfectly loose."

I wriggle my arms to demonstrate.

Olivia bursts into laughter again and this time I notice that it sounds different. Less harsh.

What is the difference? For once I realize the disadvantage to emotions not being clearly on display. Can I trust this laugh or the other one?

I don't know.

"Kroaicho," zha continues, clicks still sounding different. Less strained, maybe? "I like order just as much as anyone else, but chaos is fun. Of all the creatures to end up with on this planet... how is it that you seem to understand even less than I do?"

I narrow my eyes, though the irritation is already dissipating. Zha has a point, even if zha doesn't understand my circumstances. "My life has always been about survival," I say, a bit more quietly. "Gathering treasures, protecting what's mine. That is how I have lived. There is little room for... the opposite of *boredom*."

Olivia's expression softens a bit, and zha tilts zha's head to the side. "I get that. But maybe that's why you should try something different? Like, what do you do for fun? Besides gathering shiny rocks?"

I bristle slightly at zha's dismissive tone, but I don't let it show. "Treasure hunting is not simply gathering rocks," I say, my voice firm. "It is an ancient tradition of the zhasie. From back before the Sundering."

"Sundering?" zha asks, brows lowered again.

"Yes. When our world burned and the zhasie shifted our lives to the safety of the caves," I explain. "There was little left afterward and each item had a history that would have easily been forgotten if not gathered, protected, and passed from zhann to zhannel."

"Burned? And I thought we had it bad. But I don't see what that has to do with gathering rocks," zha clicks back.

"We seek out the rarest, most valuable items to build our hoards. Pull out their stories. It is a matter of pride and status," I explain, wondering how that isn't known.

Even the alien travelers seemed to have understood and agreed with that.

Zha raises one brow, giving my collection of shiny rocks a skeptical look. "Right... and you're sure those rocks are the rarest and most valuable?"

I flicker briefly to a faint shade of purple before I catch myself. "They are the beginnings of my new hoard," I say defensively. "It will grow in time. Soon there will be many stories here. The best so far is that stalactite," I tell zha, pointing with a claw.

Zha looks over, brows low, then one flicks up higher. "How?"

"The layers, Olivia," I prompt, my skin lighting up blue in my consternation about how little zha seems to notice. "The passing of time as creatures such as us shift around it. Living, dying, breathing, fighting. Each drip another striation of glow and variation."

Olivia clicks, clearly unimpressed. "Well, if that's what you enjoy, more power to you, I guess. I don't see the appeal or the entertainment value. On *Earth*, we have different ways of having fun. Like, we have food. Really good food. Something that is one hundred percent missing right now, I might add."

After a quick glance at all of the layers of food surrounding us, I decide this must be another example of zha being odd.

I flash white when I think of there being other options, curiosity piqued. "Food? What kind of food?"

Zha uses zha's orange-like widened mouth, clearly pleased to have my attention. "Lots of things. We've got *burgers, pizza, sushi...* you name it. My favorite? *Pizza*, hands down. You have no idea what you're missing out on. What about you? What kind of food do you eat?"

I pause, considering how to explain my species' dietary habits. "We zhasie primarily consume a variety of bioluminescent fungi and small cave creatures. The fungi provide necessary nutrients and help maintain our bioluminescence, while the creatures offer protein."

Olivia wrinkles zha's nose. "Fungi and... small creatures? Like bugs?"

I move my head up and down in zha's human movement, not entirely understanding zha's reaction. "Yes. They are a vital part of our ecosystem. We also have large fungi that grow deep in the caves. They are rare, but when found, they can sustain us for weeks."

Zha makes an odd face. "I don't think I could survive on a diet of mushrooms and bugs. No offense, but that sounds gross, which is saying a lot because I'm starving right now."

The blue of my confusion gains flickers of dark purple irritation. "Gross? You call our sacred fungi gross? They have sustained my species for millennia."

Zha raises zha hands in a placating gesture. "No offense meant. I'm just saying, it's not exactly my idea of a good meal."

I huff, my skin flickering from dark purple to blue again as I begrudgingly accept zha's apology. "Humans have strange tastes."

Olivia's orange signal lips widen. "You're not wrong there. But if you ever get a chance to try *pizza*, I bet you'd like it."

I snort, dismissing the idea. "I highly doubt that. But perhaps one day, you will have the chance to prove me wrong. In the meantime, you are surrounded by food."

Olivia doesn't respond, just wrinkles zha's nose again.

We lapse into silence for a few moments, the sound of dripping water from the cave walls and the flow of the stream the only noise. I find myself glancing at zha, studying the way zha moves, and the subtle expressions on zha's face. Zha is so different from anything I've ever encountered, yet... there's something oddly compelling about zha's presence. Something that draws me in, despite my better judgment.

Eventually, Olivia breaks the silence. "So... what other customs do you zhasie have? Besides treasure hunting and eating mushrooms?"

I pause, considering how to explain my culture to zha. "We have many traditions. The hoarding of treasures is one of the most important, but we also place great value on our connection to the caves. We believe that the caves are alive, that they protect us and guide us. We honor the caves by caring for them, ensuring that they remain strong and unyielding."

Olivia nods, listening intently. "That's... actually kind of cool. So, you guys are like, cave guardians?"

I blink, the term unfamiliar. "Guardians? Perhaps. We see ourselves as caretakers, ensuring that the balance of the caves is maintained. If the caves thrive, so do we."

Zha seems to consider this, and then zha smiles. "You know, humans have some traditions like that too. Like, we have Earth Day, where we focus on taking care of our planet. It's not quite the same, but it's similar, I guess."

I tilt my head, intrigued. "Earth Day? What is this day?"

Zha shrugs. "It's a day where people try to be more environmentally conscious—*recycling*, planting trees, stuff like that. Not everyone takes it seriously, but it's supposed to be a day to remind us that we need to take care of the planet."

I nod slowly, seeing the parallels. "Perhaps your species is not so different after all. Though I imagine your Earth Day is far less significant than our cave rituals."

Zha laughs. "Probably. We humans aren't always the best at sticking to our traditions. But we try."

I flicker briefly to orange. "I doubt anything with such a weak constitution as yours could do more than that."

Zha lets out a long breath and zha's features suddenly become different. Far more.. neutral.

"We have plenty of traditions," zha grumbles, "I'll explain... I guess we'll start with school."

I lean in, curious despite myself. "That word does not translate."

"It's where humans learn things, Kroaicho," Olivia says, then presses zha's lips together for a long moment. It's clear zha is having a hard time figuring out how to explain it in a way that will make sense to me. "I imagine a place where *children*... young humans, I mean, gather together to be taught."

I frown. The concept of zhannel is not foreign to me, but gathering them all in one place to teach them simultaneously seems... inefficient. It is a rising theme among humans. "Why not just teach them individually?" I ask.

Olivia sighs. "It's not that simple. There are too many of us. Schools let lots of *children* learn together at the same time."

I tilt my head, my spikes twitching with confusion. "That sounds chaotic."

Olivia laughs again, though it's a softer sound this time. "It is. Sometimes. To be honest, I hated it, but don't let that color how you think of it. It's the best way we've figured out how to teach large groups."

I'm still not convinced. "But why would you want so many humans in one place? Wouldn't that cause problems?"

"Well, yeah, sometimes it does," Olivia admits with a shrug. "But it's also how we socialize. We form connections with others, make friends, and learn how to be human."

I frown deeper. "You have to learn how to be your species? Why would you want to be around so many other humans? You've spent most of your time with me. Alone. Is that not preferable?"

Olivia gives me an odd look. "Kroaicho, just because I'm stuck here with you doesn't mean I don't miss other people. Humans are… social creatures. We need each other. I didn't really realize until now just how much."

I don't fully understand. The idea of needing anyone beyond myself after growing up is foreign to me. I shift uncomfortably, my glow flickering between blue and purple as I process what Olivia's saying. Zha's need for companionship, for these… connections with other humans—it baffles me.

But before I can voice my confusion, Olivia breaks the silence with a new topic.

"What about the others?" zha asks softly, zha's voice heavy with something that sounds like hope. "The other humans that crash-landed here. Have you looked for them?"

I fight the urge to chitter aloud. I know zha wants to find them, to connect with them the way zha insists humans do, but… I'm not eager to go looking. It's not my responsibility. My focus has always been on my hoard, on exploration—not looking for humans.

Olivia doesn't let up, though. Zha presses on. "Please, Kroaicho. There were other pods. They're out there somewhere. You could help me find them."

I stare at Olivia, my glow darkening to a deeper purple as irritation floods through me. I don't want to upset zha, not when we've managed to avoid an argument again, but… I don't see the point.

With a frustrated sigh, I concede—partially. "I will… look," I say, though I don't fully commit. "But you will stay here. Do not wander. This cave is safe."

Predictably, Olivia doesn't agree. "I'm not staying behind while you search for my people. I'm coming with you."

I blink. I'm trying to protect zha. This planet is dangerous—far more dangerous than zha understands. "No," I say firmly. "You will stay. It is safer."

Olivia's face hardens. "I can handle myself, Kroaicho. I'm not some helpless *kid* you need to keep hidden away."

We lock eyes, the tension between us thickening. I feel my spikes twitch in irritation, my glow deepening as I struggle to keep my temper in check. Why is zha so insistent on defying me? Does zha not understand the risks?

"No," I say again, more forcefully this time. "You will stay."

Olivia stands up straighter, zha's fists clenched at zha's sides. "I'm coming with you. I won't let you go out there alone. Not when my people could be in danger."

I feel my irritation flare, my glow turning a deep, pulsing purple. But I know this argument is going nowhere. Olivia won't back down, and I... I don't want to lose zha's trust. Not completely.

But still...

"The only reason I am agreeing to this is on the condition that you stay here." I fold my limbs to signal my urging. "The most beautiful, complex part of the hoard should remain the safest."

Olivia raises an eyebrow. "You are so officially weird. Stay here? Seriously?"

"Yes," I click back. "Stay. Here."

"No way," zha shoots back, zha's voice rising with defiance. "I'm not just going to sit here while you—"

I cut zha off, my spikes flaring slightly. "It's dangerous out there."

"I can handle myself," zha argues, stepping closer to me, zha's glow brightening with stubbornness.

"You'll slow me down," I snap, my irritation flaring again. "Stay here."

We stand there, locked in a silent standoff for what feels like an eternity. I can see the determination in zha's eyes, the way zha jaw is set, and the pink flush of zha glow as zha refuses to back down.

Olivia lets out that odd growl, then speaks again. "You make it really hard to *pretend* to be cheerful, you know that? I'm going back to sleep."

I let out a breath, relieved to have won this small battle, though the dark-purple glow still lingers around me as I turn to leave.

My irritation simmers just below the surface, but beneath that... there's something else. A strange tug, a pull, as if something is shifting between us. I try to ignore it, focusing instead on the task at hand, but it's there, lingering in the back of my mind.

I don't understand this human. I don't understand zha's stubbornness, zha's persistence. But for some reason, I find myself doing things for zha that I wouldn't do for anyone else.

And that... that's confusing.

12

Olivia

I seethe as Kroaicho stalks out of the cave without another word, its tall, spiked form silhouetted against the cave walls, flickering purple. My fists clench at my sides, knuckles turning white, the sharp prickle of frustration clawing at my insides. At the same time, hunger surges. Great.

I ignore it. I'm not some fragile thing that needs protecting, and yet, here I am, being treated like exactly that. Again.

Part of the hoard, my ass. A prized possession that needs to be hoarded alongside a precious collection of treasures. I hate it. I hate it.

The thing is, it's not just Kroaicho. It's always been like this. My entire life on Earth, I was caged in by the people who possessed more than I did. It started with my family, always making decisions for me, and always keeping me on the sidelines. They said it was for my own good. Bullshit.

I pace the cave, the odd soles of the black suit crunching against the rocky floor. Kroaicho doesn't understand. It can't. Not when it's a towering mass of alien strength, built to survive in the harshest conditions. It thinks it's doing me a favor by "protecting" me, but it's the same thing I've been dealing with my whole life—being treated as less.

A bubbling rage rises in my chest, hot and consuming. I've reached my limit. My hands are trembling now, and I feel my breath coming in short, ragged bursts. It's like the walls of the cave are closing in on me, suffocating me, trapping me in this endless cycle of being kept safe—but never free. Never my own person.

My emotions are all over the place like I'm teetering on the edge of something dangerous, something I can't quite control.

I take one step, and my vision swims. Everything feels hot, too hot like I'm going to explode. The rage is boiling, and blistering, and I'm not sure if I'm about to scream or break something. The thought of tearing this entire cave apart crosses my mind, a wild, irrational impulse that makes my skin crawl with anticipation. I clench my teeth, trying to hold it all together, but it's like trying to hold back a tsunami with a paper cup.

But then, something snaps.

I let out a guttural scream, not caring if Kroaicho hears it. My fists slam into the wall of the cave, sending a small spray of dust and pebbles cascading down around me. The pain of impact briefly clears my head, grounding me for just a second. My vision narrows, and I feel the burn in my throat from the scream. I've crossed a line.

I gasp for air, trying to calm myself down, but my thoughts keep spiraling.

Done and undone, my mind chants.

I feel like I'm drowning, even though I'm still very much standing. Tears threaten to spill, but I choke them back. I will not cry. Not again. I've cried enough in my life, and it's never changed a damn thing.

I squeeze my eyes shut, forcing myself to take deep breaths. But I can't let myself fall apart.

No.

Not here. Not now. I have to be stronger than this.

With a loud, furious exhale, I mutter under my breath, "Fuck it." I don't care what Kroaicho says. I don't care about the dangers. I'm done being locked away. If this planet is dangerous, so be it. I'll face it head-on.

I grab a random piece of metal from the stupid, fucking hoard and grip it like a knife. A terrible, dull knife.

And then I'm off.

The cave's tunnels stretch on into the darkness, winding and twisting in ways that are still a mystery to me.

Time to explore.

And possibly die. One and done, I think, inanely.

The tunnel ahead is dark, but the mushrooms provide a soft, warm glow, enough to see by. Kroaicho probably thinks I'm sitting quietly in the cave, sulking or something. He has no idea I'm about to defy its orders entirely. Good. I need this. I need to prove I'm capable, even if it's just to myself.

As I descend deeper into the cave system, I notice the strange, otherworldly beauty all around me. The walls are coated in a thin layer of glowing moss, its bioluminescence casting eerie patterns of light across the stone. Overhead, small, worm-like creatures cling to the ceiling, their soft blue glow reminiscent of stars in a night sky. I stop for a moment, mesmerized by the sight. It's beautiful—almost serene, like the universe has folded itself into this tiny space.

Further in, the tunnel opens up into a wide cavern with a shallow pool of water at its center. I kneel at the edge of the pool and dip my fingers into the water, watching as eyeless, pale aquatic creatures swim just beneath the surface. Their ghostly forms glide through the water, and for a moment, I forget the chaos in my mind. It's peaceful down here.

My thoughts begin to slow, my breathing evens out, and I feel a strange sense of calm wash over me. Maybe Kroaicho was right about this cave not being safe, but it's beautiful in its own way nonetheless. I take in the beauty around me—the glowing mushrooms sprouting from the walls, the soft hum of the cave's natural rhythm. Everything here feels alive, pulsing with a quiet, ancient energy.

There is a warm feeling inside me. Happiness? When was the last time I felt that? After almost losing my head just now? Typical.

I let out a small, disbelieving laugh. It's been so long since I felt anything resembling joy, but down here, in this alien world, surrounded by these strange and wondrous things... I guess I do feel a little bit of happiness. It's like a tiny ember that's been hiding beneath all the anger and frustration.

I let my mind wander, leaning back against the cool stone wall. I close my eyes, letting the memories flood in.

The crash. The genali attack. Rin.

My siblings. God, they were cruel sometimes. Always treating me like I didn't belong, like I wasn't good enough. Anger bubbles up again. They never understood me. They never tried to. Everything I did was wrong in their eyes, and I was always the odd one out. Even now, trapped on an alien planet, I'm still fighting that same feeling.

Then, my thoughts drift to my mother. I wonder what she'd think of all this—of me being stranded on an alien planet, of Kroaicho and its constant attempts to keep me contained. Would she be proud? Or would she be scared for me?

She's probably glad to be rid of me.

I sigh and open my eyes, staring up at the cave ceiling again. The glowworms above seem to pulse in time with my thoughts. And as I sit here, surrounded by the quiet beauty of this place, I realize something important.

For the first time in a long while, I feel... lighter.

But I can't stay here forever. Eventually, I'll have to face Kroaicho again, and when I do, I'll be ready. Maybe I'll even try to explain things from my perspective, in a way it can understand. Because as much as I hate being confined, I can't deny that its intentions aren't... all bad. It's just... different. Alien.

I mean, completely fucked up, but I get the impression that it doesn't know what to do with me.

Everyone always wants something, I remind myself.

Then I let out a long sigh. I might need to let that go. Or at least the version I had of it before.

I've railed against materialism from the first time someone explained the concept and it was obvious how much it has affected my life. Just how much it was the reason for so much of the pain and anger of being shifted from one place to the next as my mum talked about me like I was some broken vase that just needed money thrown at it.

All my siblings seem to talk about is money and when they'll get what they are owed. If I never see another tax document it will be too soon.

But the whole concept doesn't seem to apply to how Kroaicho thinks. Nothing about what it has said suggests there is a system of exchange. What does it keep saying?

Treasure, stories, gathering, and protecting. Shockingly simple and I keep waiting to catch it out on the lie... but it remains consistent. Like there is a beauty there that I can't see and a story I don't know.

Its motivation still doesn't make sense, but I have to admit that whatever it is, exactly, isn't my world enemy materialism.

That doesn't excuse the fact that it still sees me as an object.

I stand up, stretch my legs, and start making my way back toward the main cave. For once, I'm calm. Ready. Whatever comes next, I'll face it head-on. I'm done hiding. Done being locked away.

Done being treated like less.

And if Kroaicho thinks it can stop me from taking control of my own life, the overgrown flesh flare is in for a surprise.

13

Olivia

My eyes flutter open, and I let out a deep yawn, stretching against the cold rock floor, trying to work out the knots. My muscles ache in that way they do after sleeping in a cramped position, and I shift to try and loosen the tightness. It takes me a second to remember where I am, but once the memories come flooding back, the familiar chill of the cave air nips at my skin.

I scowl, shaking my head as I recall the strange dream I'd just had. Why now? Of all the things my brain could dredge up, it picks a nightmare about Bethany, of all people, from years ago. I can't help but wonder if it's because of how trapped I feel here. The similarities are eerie, and that thought alone sends a wave of discomfort crawling down my spine.

Is this karma for all of the times I wished to never have to see people again?

"Ugh," I groan, sitting up slowly, fully waking up to my present reality.

Kroaicho. And the hoard. All still here, me along with them.

That peace I somehow found before I slept last night seems completely inaccessible and instead I do what I do best... cringe about how I interacted with someone.

My inane chattering about shows, chaos, and food did nothing, except for make me hungrier. I mean, it never worked for me on humans, so why did I think that schtick would work on a LED alien? I'm weird no matter where I go, no matter which ways I pretend to be chirpy and fun.

I doubt anything I said or my stupid, pretend laugh made it... him... something... more inclined to let me leave.

I reach up to rub at my eyes, still groggy, and try to stifle a cough—but it doesn't come out right. The rough, raw sensation in my throat catches me off guard. It's like I'm trying to swallow broken glass. Panic flares as the cough turns into a series of violent hacks, each one ripping through my chest and throat like barbed wire. I double over, clutching my stomach as my body convulses, forcing something up from deep inside me.

With a sickening lurch, I spit out a wad of something thick and wet. It splatters on the cave floor, and for a split second, all I can do is stare at it, wide-eyed. Blood. A lot of it. And it's... glowing. Faintly, but unmistakably. A dull bioluminescence seeps from the thick mixture of blood and spit, casting a faint shimmer on the stone.

"What... the hell?" I whisper, my voice raspy and weak.

The sight of so much blood sends my mind spiraling. I feel the telltale signs of panic swelling in my chest, threatening to overwhelm me. My heart races and my breaths come out shallow and quick. I'm bleeding. From the inside. There's something wrong with me. The air feels too thick to breathe, and for a second, I think I'm going to pass out.

"Calm down. Calm down, Olivia," I mutter to myself, squeezing my eyes shut and taking slow, deliberate breaths. Just breathe. It takes a minute, maybe more, but slowly, the panic subsides enough for me to think clearly again.

When I finally open my eyes, I expect pain. If I've hacked up this much blood, there has to be something seriously wrong. A throat injury? Internal bleeding? My hand trembles as I touch my neck, but there's nothing—no sharp, searing pain. Just a dull ache, fading now as if it never really happened. My chest feels fine too. I roll my shoulders experimentally, but apart from the stiffness from sleeping on cold stone, I feel... okay.

"That's not normal," I whisper to myself, swallowing carefully to check for any lingering pain. Nothing. The blood on the ground remains, an unnerving reminder of what just happened, but my body seems fine.

With a start, I realize the stupid green hair is just as long as it was before I slept and let out a groan before taking the time to braid it, muttering curses about change the whole time.

I push myself to my feet, though my legs are shaky beneath me. A full-body stretch sends a few satisfying pops through my joints, but something feels off. I feel... loose, and more flexible than usual. My muscles seem to move with an ease I haven't felt in years as if I've shed years of tension.

I'm always wound tight, anxiety pumping through me. I can still feel it rattling around in my mind, but for some reason, it isn't making its way into my body.

Just as I'm starting to appreciate the feeling, my arms brush against something rough near my ears. The sensation is jarring, and I freeze mid-stretch. What the hell was that?

My hands instinctively fly to my ears, fingers probing cautiously. I nearly jump out of my skin when I feel it—three hard spikes on each ear. They're not large, just small enough to blend into the curves of my ear, but the sharpness is unmistakable.

I panic. What the hell are these? My fingers tremble as they trace over the spines, confirming their existence. I rush to find a reflective surface, frantically searching the dimly lit cave. Of course, there's nothing. No mirrors. Nothing but stone and bioluminescent fungi casting their eerie glow.

In the absence of a mirror, I keep feeling the growths, trying to make sense of them. They're not tender or sore, and they don't hurt, which should be comforting but only makes it worse. Are these tumors? Am I growing spines? Is this some kind of mutation?

Then I remember the sound of water, and follow it. There's some sort of glowing stream at the far end of the cave. I remember what Kroaicho said about water disappearing underground and carefully move to the edge, hoping to see my reflection, but there isn't enough light to see any details.

I have three pointed... elf ears? No. The shape isn't right. Or the texture.

My mind jumps to the worst possible conclusions. Cancer. Radiation. God knows what kind of substances are in the air down here. I'm on an alien planet, for crying out loud. Who knows if this place is even remotely safe for humans? Radioactive caves, toxic gases, unknown pathogens—it could be anything.

I try to steady my breathing, but my mind keeps racing. Every part of me feels more sensitive and more aware of my surroundings. I can feel every little draft, every tiny change in the air around me. It's unnerving.

A sudden shift in the air signals Kroaicho's presence before I even hear it. It stirs from its resting place with a low grunt, and I don't even have time to collect my thoughts before I snap.

"Get me out of here!" I shout, my voice hoarse from the earlier coughing fit. I whirl around to face the towering form of the alien. Its bioluminescent skin pulses with a deep, muted blue as it watches me with what I can only assume is confusion. It glows that color a lot.

Kroaicho doesn't respond immediately, which only fuels my frustration. I stomp toward it, jabbing a finger in its direction. "I said get me out of here! I don't know what's in this cave, but my body is reacting to something in the air. I'm coughing up blood, I have weird... growths on my ears, and I feel like I'm turning into something else," I hiss out.

Kroaicho tilts its head, its glowing eyes narrowing slightly. "There are no poisonous compounds in the air," it says in its deep, rumbling voice, calm and measured as if I hadn't just screamed in its face. "If there were, I would have sensed them long ago."

Its indifference only fuels my anger. "Yeah, well, maybe it's not poisonous to you," I snap, crossing my arms. "But I'm not exactly built like you, am I?"

Kroaicho's skin flashes a dark shade of purple, a sign of... frustration, I think? It's that color a lot too.

It towers over me, eyes glowing slightly brighter. "You shine like a treasure just the same as always and there is no danger here. Your body may be adjusting, but it is not under threat."

I grit my teeth, fighting the urge to scream at its calm, detached tone. "Oh, so my body just coughing up blood is normal? Right. That makes perfect sense. And what about these?" I gesture wildly to my ears. "Are these supposed to be normal, too? Am I going to wake up tomorrow with spikes all over me?"

The alien huffs, its glowing skin flaring. "Your demands are redundant. Your biology is..."

"Your stupid face is redundant!" I snap back, not even thinking before the words leave my mouth.

Kroaicho stops mid-sentence, its glowing eyes widening in what I can only describe as shock. For a moment, the cave is silent as it processes what I just said.

"My... face?" Kroaicho repeats slowly as if trying to understand the insult. It draws itself up to its full height, skin flickering with a sharper light now. "My face," it continues, with rising indignation, "is a product of millions of years of zhasie evolution, perfectly suited to the environment of our home planet. Every feature, from the contours of my jaw to the ridges on my brow, is an adaptation for survival. To call it redundant is scientifically inaccurate!"

I stare at it, dumbfounded. The sheer passion with which it defends its face—its evolutionary masterpiece—is almost comical. I can't help it. The corners of my mouth twitch, and before I know it, I'm snorting. The sound echoes off the cave walls, loud and absurd in the silence.

The swings in my emotion in this place are even worse than when I was a kid. I thought I had outgrown that. I pinch my nose, then think of the indignation and snort out a laugh.

Kroaicho watches me, eyes narrowed and skin dimming to a confused, muted shade of blue. "You find this amusing?" it asks, its voice tinged with wariness.

"All of this is either the worst thing that ever happened to me and I am going to fall apart, or it's comical. Only one of those seems wise right now," I tell it.

Kroaicho remains silent for a moment, its head tilted as it observes me. I can tell it's trying to make sense of my reaction, but its alien mind clearly isn't equipped to understand why I'm laughing.

Eventually, I manage to calm down, wiping tears from my eyes as I straighten up. "Sorry," I say, still smiling. "You're just... you're the strangest alien I've ever met." I pause, then add, "Not that I've met a lot of aliens, to be fair. And the rest of them I killed before we got to know each other."

I moan when I remember the elation that caused and Kroaicho's skin lights up again with confusion.

"Killed which aliens?" it asks, clicks betraying deep interest.

"Well, the bugs, of course. They died with the most lovely cracking sound." I mimic it as I chop the air with one hand. "And the genali explode in a rain of goo when you shoot them."

I close my eyes for a moment to savor the memory, then open them. "And then there's you. Stabbing didn't work, and so now I'm stuck with the conversation trap."

Kroaicho's eyes narrow further, and it huffs again, its skin flashing with faint amusement, though I doubt it fully understands the joke.

But as the last echoes of laughter die down, I realize something else—something that hits me like a punch to the gut. I feel... strange. My body, already more sensitive than usual, now feels like it's buzzing with something else. Something... more.

Damn. I shouldn't have thought about killing. It makes the stupid arousal worse.

I swallow hard, forcing myself to ignore the warmth spreading through me and fight down the blush creeping up my cheeks.

I turn away from Kroaicho quickly, trying to regain control. Great. Just great. As if everything else wasn't bad enough, now I'm full-on horny? Fantastic.

Kroaicho flicks a funny look my way, its bioluminescent skin flashing between a light blue to orange, to white as if it can't decide which color to settle on. Finally, with a huff, it sticks to its normal shade, the steady blue glow fading into the cave's dim light.

"You're strange," it mutters, still watching me like it can't quite figure out what to make of me.

I let out a sigh. I've heard that before, but for some reason it hurts even more coming from someone as odd as Kroaicho. "That's nothing new," I tell it.

Kroaicho disagrees vehemently, leaning in slightly as it chitters, "No. You are particularly strange. One moment you seem angry, the next you are calm, then playful. I cannot predict what you will do." It tilts its head, genuinely perplexed. "Are all humans like this?"

I chuckle, feeling a mix of amusement and exasperation at its confusion. "You don't even know the half of it."

At this, Kroaicho's skin flares dark purple, the rapid change of color disorienting me for a bit before it grumbles deep in its chest. "That sounds like a wholly inefficient way to live."

I can't help but snort at the bluntness of its remark. "Yeah, well, humans are amazing like that and I am a master of chaos."

Kroaicho snaps back immediately, its voice sharper, more clipped. "There is nothing amazing about a species that has the emotional control of newly lifed zhannel."

The alien word pulls me up short, and I raise a brow in curiosity. "Zhannel?" I ask, glancing up at Kroaicho. "What does that mean?"

It tilts its head, a look of mild confusion crossing its features. "Do humans not have offspring?"

I blink, surprised, then quickly realize what it's referring to. "Oh, yes. Of course, we have babies. How else would the species keep going?"

Kroaicho blinks at my choice of words, then lets out a low huff. "Babies? Zhannel. It would not be surprising if your kind fumbled something as simple as reproduction." It shakes its head, skin flashing faint purple as if to underscore its disdain.

Before I can stop myself, I grab a small rock from the ground and chuck it at its chest. The stone makes a satisfying thud as it bounces off its broad, muscled torso, eliciting a low hiss of pain from the alien. Its skin flickers between a light violet and dark purple, a swirl of discomfort and annoyance dancing on its surprisingly expressive face in a manner that makes me snicker.

"Thanks for the light show," I say dryly, folding my arms.

Kroaicho's skin shifts to a frustrated blue as it grumbles under its breath. "You are the most infuriating creature I have ever encountered."

I flash it my sweetest, most sarcastic smile. "If I'm such a pain, why not just let me go then? I'll be out of your... uh, tusks in no time."

Its eyes narrow sharply, the bioluminescence along its jaw dimming to an almost threatening shade of purple as it hisses, "No."

I roll my eyes, more out of habit than anything, and instantly see its reaction. Kroaicho stiffens, its posture going rigid. It takes a step back, eyes wide, skin flaring a distressed mix of colors.

"Stop doing that," it snaps, its voice edged with genuine alarm. "The thing with your eyes. It is unsettling."

My smile turns vicious. "This?" I roll my eyes again, slow and exaggerated, just to see its reaction.

Kroaicho lets out a distressed hissing sound, its skin flashing a panicked purple. "Yes! That! It is... unnatural."

I let out a short, sharp laugh, then do it again. "Well, I'll stop if you let me go."

Kroaicho huffs, visibly agitated, its skin flickering rapidly between different shades of purple, red, and blue. "I will not be coerced by your strange eye movements."

"Fine," I sigh dramatically, tossing my hands in the air. "But just know, I can do this all day." I roll my eyes again, a slow, exaggerated motion that draws another hiss from the alien.

I hope it doesn't call my bluff because it's starting to get uncomfortable. But still worth it.

Its frustration is almost palpable as it growls, "If you continue, I will have no choice but to cake your face in mud. You will learn what it means to be difficult."

I give it a flat look, then, without hesitation, flip it the middle finger. Kroaicho's eyes flick toward my hand, confusion flickering across its features as if trying to understand the gesture. I keep rolling my eyes as I retreat to my little corner of the cave, somehow managing to not fall and break my neck before settling myself down by the bioluminescent mushrooms.

The soft, glowing light from the fungi casts eerie shadows on the ground, and I lean back against the cold stone, letting the tension in my muscles ease. My body still feels strange—like there's something bubbling just beneath the surface—but I force myself to ignore it. Whatever's happening to me, there's nothing I can do about it right now. Not without help, anyway. And considering Kroaicho's attitude, I'm on my own.

Kroaicho watches me for a moment longer, probably trying to decide if it should continue the argument or just leave me be. Finally, it lets out a low clicking, a sound somewhere between resignation and annoyance, before turning away and settling back into its spot in the cave.

I sigh softly, staring at the strange glowing mushrooms around me, their soft blue light pulsing faintly like tiny stars scattered across the cave walls. It's almost peaceful, in a weird, alien way. But my mind is far from calm. The strange sensations in my body, the spiky growths on my ears, and the weird, almost giddy rush of adrenaline coursing through me—it's all too much. I need answers, but right now, I'm stuck.

I shoot a glance toward Kroaicho, who seems content to sit in brooding silence across the cave, slowly and carefully sorting through the rocks and bits it calls treasure. Does it ever stop obsessing with things?

And I'm apparently part of that hoard. How would it organize me if I let it? It's disgusting.

Its skin has settled into a steady, muted hue, a sure sign that it's calming down, or at least no longer on edge. I wonder, not for the first time, what its deal is. Why keep me here? What does it want?

What does it gain by keeping me here? It's made sure I had a bath, gave me space, hasn't tried anything hinky or sexual, talked with me when I said I was bored. All it has asked is that I stay where it is safe.

I mean, that's basically keeping me captive, but for what purpose? Why can't it just let me go? I'm clearly more trouble than I'm worth.

I've tried being cheerful, angry, annoying as fuck... nothing is working.

Despite the ridiculousness of our exchange, I know it's not going to let me go anytime soon. And even if it did, where would I go? The thought makes my stomach clench. I have no idea what's out there in this alien world. The caves seem endless, and who knows what kind of creatures or dangers lurk in the darkness.

Still, a part of me—maybe the stubborn, rebellious part—wants to try. I want to escape, to get out of here and find a way back home, even if the odds are stacked against me. But right now, I'm stuck, with only this strange alien as my captor and the constant, unsettling feeling that my body is changing in ways I don't understand.

I lean my head back against the cave wall and close my eyes, taking a deep breath.

One step at a time, Olivia. One step at a time. One, two, five—

I stop myself with a vigorous shake of my head. I'm not going back to that mental spiral.

After a few moments, the cave falls into a tense silence, broken only by the occasional drip of water from the stalactites above. Kroaicho shifts slightly, its bioluminescent skin flickering faintly as it settles into a more comfortable position. For all its bluster and stubbornness, it almost seems... relaxed.

The calm doesn't last long. My mind keeps wandering back to the unsettling sensation running through my body, the odd warmth pooling deep in my gut that I can't quite place. It's distracting, and no matter how hard I try, I can't shake the feeling. Worse, every time I glance at Kroaicho, the sensation only intensifies.

I force my gaze away from the alien, staring hard at the glowing mushrooms on the cave floor.

Focus, Olivia. Focus.

But it's no use. The strange warmth in my body is impossible to ignore, and I can feel my skin heating up, my breath coming in shallow, uneven bursts.

It's not someone... something that can help me with this. Clearly those fucking slimy aliens did something to me.

And even if they hadn't, and Kroaicho was perfectly normal, it's not as if the couple times I let a guy stick it in was pleasant.

They just called me stiff and a bad fuck.

I squeeze my eyes shut, trying to will the sensation away, but it lingers, buzzing just beneath the surface, relentless.

This is so unfair, I moan internally.

Kroaicho, oblivious to my struggle, remains across the cave, its attention elsewhere. It hums softly to itself, a low, rhythmic sound that echoes faintly through the cavern. The noise should be soothing, but right now, it's only making things worse.

I bury my face in my hands, willing the heat in my cheeks to fade. I've been through hell for weeks, fought for my life, and faced unimaginable dangers, and this—this ridiculous, embarrassing problem—is what's throwing me off balance.

I let out a shaky breath, trying to calm the rush of adrenaline coursing through me. "I can't deal with this right now."

Kroaicho glances in my direction, its glowing eyes narrowing slightly, but it doesn't say anything. Good. The last thing I need is another awkward conversation with the alien.

I shift in my spot, pulling my knees up to my chest and wrapping my arms around them, trying to focus on anything other than the strange, unwelcome heat in my body. The cave remains silent, and for now, that's enough.

***

I glance over at Kroaicho, who is now silent in its corner of the cave, its skin dimming to a soft blue-gray. For now, it seems content to ignore me, and that's just fine... except I'm starting to feel lonely and desperate to talk.

I didn't think I would ever feel like that and it's setting my teeth on edge. I've never been particularly successful at getting along with people, but ever since Kroaicho trapped me here I keep thinking about people. I need someone to connect with who understands.

Someone to talk to about how I think I'm losing my mind. That I'm aroused by... that multi-color oaf. About how messed up my head is with the fact that it doesn't seem to be having the same issue or even be the slightest bit interested, which is not what I would expect from a kidnapper.

This arousal is infuriating. The strange warmth pooling in my gut refuses to subside, and I need something—anything—to distract myself.

My eyes land on a thin rock near the edge of the cave floor, half-buried in the dirt. I lean forward and pick it up, the rough texture familiar under my fingers, and before I know it, I'm dragging the tip across the cave floor, sketching lines into the dust.

At first, it's just random squiggles, but soon, I find myself drawing something more intentional. A pattern I remember from my childhood, a tattoo my cousin had shown me once when I was younger. It was a traditional māori design, an intricate mix of spirals and curves representing fertility.

I wish I knew then just how important it would be to me... when it was already too late.

I pause for a second, staring at the lines I've etched into the dirt, my brow furrowing. Fertility. The irony isn't lost on me, given my current situation. A reproduction tattoo seems painfully relevant right now, considering the strange sensations roiling inside me.

Of all the things to come to mind, Olivia. Seriously?

I shake my head and continue the drawing, forcing myself to focus. The pattern is complex, a blend of *koru* shapes representing new life, and thick bold lines that twist and intertwine like vines. As I work, the irritation bubbling inside me, both from being stuck here and from the damned physical reaction I can't seem to shake, begins to dull.

I've never felt this before. I've lived my entire life thinking I was aromantic, never once feeling the pull of attraction or desire that everyone around me seemed to experience so easily. After my mother got sick just after my high school homecoming, I didn't even have time to think about it. Taking care of her became my world, and I had no interest in anyone else. I just assumed that was my life.

But now, on this alien planet, with Kroaicho hovering around me, I'm suddenly dealing with feelings I don't fully understand. Arousal. Curiosity about my kidnapper. Stockholm syndrome in space up next?

Great.

A part of me feels... intrigued, even thrilled by the sudden awakening, but most of me is just frustrated. I only really tried sex before because I was curious and it was the "normal" thing to want.

Of course, this would happen now, when I'm stuck in a cave with an alien captor. My life couldn't get more fucked up if it tried.

I let out a huff, dragging the stick harder against the cave floor, and mutter under my breath, "This is just bloody brilliant, isn't it? Trapped on an alien planet, my body doing god-knows-what, and the only other sentient being I have to talk to is a glow-in-the-dark creep. Fantastic."

The scratching of the stick against the dirt is soothing, though. The more I focus, the more the world around me fades away. It's like the drawings pull me into a trance, blocking out everything—Kroaicho, the cave, the weird sensations creeping through my body. I can forget for a moment that I'm trapped here, that my life has taken a sharp left turn into insanity.

I'm so deep in concentration that I don't notice Kroaicho moving until it's right beside me.

"Fuck!" I jolt, dropping the stick as I whip my head toward it. The alien has crept up on all six limbs, now crouching just a few feet away. It halts in place, its eyes wide, skin flickering between red and dark purple. The startled look on its face would almost be funny if my heart wasn't hammering in my chest.

"What the hell, Kroaicho?" I snap, giving it a scorching look.

Its skin pulses again, this time a deeper shade of purple, clearly picking up on my irritation. With a soft huff, it drops down into a sitting position a few feet away, its limbs folding neatly under its body.

"Apologies," it mutters, its voice unusually low. "I did not mean to startle you."

I let out a slow breath, trying to calm the rush of adrenaline. "Yeah, well, maybe don't sneak up on people like that."

Kroaicho remains silent for a moment, its glowing eyes fixed on me before they flick downward to the floor where my drawing lies half-finished. "What... is that?" it asks after a long pause, its tone laced with curiosity.

I blink at the question, thrown off by the sudden shift in topic. For a second, I consider snapping back, but something about the genuine confusion in its voice makes me hold my tongue. Instead, I follow its gaze to the drawing, realizing I've run out of inspiration to keep going. Once I lose focus, getting back into that mental space is nearly impossible.

I sigh and lean back on my hands. "It's... a drawing," I say simply, figuring there's no harm in explaining.

"A drawing?" Kroaicho repeats, sounding even more confused. "Why?"

I frown at the question, unsure how to explain something that feels so fundamental to me. "I don't know... because it's what I'm good at. I wanted to be an artist before all this." I wave vaguely around me, gesturing to the cave and the general mess that is my life right now.

Kroaicho tilts its head, the purple hue fading slightly from its skin. "An artist. What is that?"

Of course, the alien wouldn't understand. I purse my lips, thinking for a moment before rephrasing. "It's someone who makes... treasures." That seems like a simpler way to explain it.

Kroaicho's eyes narrow, as if it's trying to puzzle out the meaning of my words. "Why not just find them?" it asks, the concept of creating something seemingly foreign to it.

I let out a soft laugh, despite myself. "Because it's more fun to create than to find."

It shakes its head, clearly not convinced. "There is no greater joy than discovery. To find something long lost, something rare and precious. That is true fulfillment."

I raise an eyebrow, unable to argue too much. "I guess you're not wrong. But why make that your only purpose?"

"Because of the Sundering," it chitters back. "We moved to caves to survive, but we still needed to salvage the remaining treasures of our civilization. I only know of that because of the treasure story passed on to me by my zhann. Treasure is a means of reclaiming something that might be otherwise unappreciated and respecting the value of that story."

"Huh," I say, caught off guard by how... interesting that sounds. It challenges everything I've thought of about possessions. "But what does that have to do with me? With me as part of your hoard?"

"You are the most beautiful of it and your story is unique," it responds. "Your story is still being told, not like the rest of my hoard."

I blink, then blink again, absorbing what it is communicating, trying to bridge the gap between what I thought it has been saying and this new explanation. I look at the rocks surrounding us, but I can't imagine much of a story for them besides them sitting around.

Instead, I try to think of an item attached to my own memories, and it doesn't take long. "I always liked looking for these swirling purple shells on the black beaches near my childhood home." The memory slips out before I can stop it, a bittersweet pang following close behind.

Kroaicho's head snaps up, its skin flickering to a curious blue. "Purple shells? Where did you find these?"

I snort, surprised by its sudden, very intense interest. "I don't really remember. It was a long time ago," I admit, shrugging.

The alien's bioluminescence brightens, a light teal spreading across its skin. "You do not remember where you placed something so precious?"

I stare at it, half amused by the intensity of the question. "I was a kid, Kroaicho. It's not like I cataloged every shell I picked up."

It huffs, a sound that almost resembles a scoff. "Humans," it mutters, shaking its head. "Such a disorganized species."

I snort, giving it a sidelong glance. "And what about you, then?"

"Highly organized," it says as it grinds its tusks. "You at least remember the story?"

"Oh, yes," I say, closing my eyes. "It was a perfect day. The wind was crisp and smelled like salt and was just hard enough to help keep the sand flies from biting. I had built a sand castle, which was glittering in the sun as the tide came in to obliterate it. My mum was mostly ignoring me, talking on the phone to her financial advisor."

I stop the story there, my stomach suddenly dropping. I hastily try to move the conversation back to more neutral ground. "I bet you've got every shiny rock and shell you've ever found tucked away somewhere, right?"

Kroaicho's eyes narrow, the color of its skin flickering between orange and purple. "Yes, every treasure has a story," it says, every chitter showing its longing for wherever it stashed those items.

I laugh, the tension between us easing for a brief moment. It's a strange feeling, this odd camaraderie forming between us, even if it's laced with snark and frustration.

It still has that longing, dopey look on its face. I think back to what it said about stories and their lost civilization. Nothing about being greedy about purple shells and wanting to know the stories associated with them fits in with what I think about materialism.

Does that mean it keeps me around because it wants to know my... story? My stomach drops again, but this time not from grief, but from a sudden shifting of my world. It wants to know about me? No one asks my story. They just assume.

That I'm weird. Violent. Broken.

There's a lump in my throat and I try to clear it. Do I get the chance to tell my story? Will it listen?

The warmth bubbling in my gut resurfaces, and I shift uncomfortably, my skin prickling with heat.

Not now. Not again.

I steal a glance at Kroaicho, who's now sitting quietly across from me, its skin dimmed to a soft white-blue mix, a sign of amusement and confusion. The alien hums softly to itself, seemingly content for the moment. But as I watch it, the strange sensation inside me only intensifies. My arms itch, my skin feels too tight, and the warmth pooling low in my stomach refuses to go away.

I bite my lip, trying to ignore the rising heat in my body, the way my breath is coming in shallow bursts. Why is this happening? I've never felt this way before. Nothing to this depth—certainly not around anyone, let alone an alien—and it's starting to mess with my head.

I squeeze my eyes shut, willing the sensation to disappear. I need to get a grip. Whatever this is, it's just some weird biological reaction. It has to be. It doesn't mean anything.

It might listen to your story, the most critical part of my mind warns me, *but ninety-nine percent chance it will judge you.*

That number hurts my stomach, but it doesn't help dispel the arousal. No matter how hard I try, the heat lingers, buzzing beneath the surface like a constant hum, growing more persistent the longer I sit here.

Finally, after what feels like an eternity, Kroaicho stirs, its attention drifting away from me as it rises to its feet. Its skin flashes white with a hint of blue, a combination I haven't seen before, and I'm not entirely sure what it means.

Without a word, it moves toward the entrance of the cave, its long limbs carrying it out into the open air. I watch as it pauses by its pile of knick-knacks, leaving me alone with my thoughts, my racing heart, and the strange, unwelcome warmth spreading through my body.

I let out a shaky breath, dropping my head into my hands. I think I'd rather be throttling the life out of bugs right now. I let out a bark of a laugh.

"Of course I would," I mutter.

My eyes return just in time to watch Kroaicho slink out of the cave, its long limbs moving with an eerie grace. Even with its size, it's nearly silent, the soft scrape of claws against stone the only sound marking its departure. As soon as it's gone, the cave seems to grow colder, and more oppressive. I wrap my arms tighter around my knees, willing myself to ignore the uncomfortable heat still buzzing beneath my skin.

What the hell is wrong with me? The question loops through my mind, but no answer comes.

I've asked that question every day of my life.

But there's nothing natural about this. I'm human, for crying out loud. This isn't supposed to happen. Certainly not with an alien like Kroaicho. The thought sends a fresh wave of frustration through me, and I push myself up, pacing in tight circles around the cave.

I glance at the half-finished drawing on the floor, the swirling māori design glaring up at me. Fertility. I almost laugh at the absurdity. But the laugh dies in my throat. The truth is, my body is reacting in ways I don't understand, and the more I try to ignore it, the worse it gets.

Kroaicho has been... nice enough. Well, as nice as a massive kidnapping alien can be, I suppose. But it's still keeping me here, watching me like a hawk, and I can't help but wonder what it wants. The thought leaves a bad taste in my mouth.

14

Kroaicho

I needed to gain space again, my mind still whirling with all of the new concepts and strange ideas that have entered my life along with the best——and absolute worst——addition to my hoard I have ever made. The only reliable cure for anything is finding a new item to add to the stash, and so I tunneled into new territory.

It took a while to get through the final layer of rocks and I'm concerned I made too much noise for too long in my haste to replace this... odd feeling I have.

I listen carefully before slowly moving my head out of the tunnel I have dug so I can scan the surrounding forest. Hearing nothing, I move higher, becoming more confident until I realize that it's far too quiet for the upper world.

My skin swirls purple and blue as I try to decide what to do. After the time spent with Olivia, I have nothing to show for my efforts today. Nothing amazing to add to my pitiful hoard. The need to expand it keeps me in place, undecided.

A crack of foliage behind me makes me whip around. There is a flash of blue. Some giant beast, I realize. Far too large to fit in my tunnel and so I don't retreat right away. Then I notice the black figure on top of it as it runs toward me.

A human, I realize, though with pink hair instead of green like Olivia's. From the look on the human's face, the coloring doesn't match zha's mood any more than Olivia's.

Then I see the weapon in zha's hand, quickly being raised and hastily shift back into the hole I just dug.

"Wait!" the human yells out in the same language as Olivia. "Just give *her* up, you *bastard*."

I pause for a moment, and then decide to keep moving. Soon after, there is a explosion of rock right where my head was and I start moving faster.

"You *fucker*. I am going to *fucking* kill—"

I don't know what other threats the human makes. Zha's voice is drowned out by the sound of rocks falling as I collapse the tunnel behind me. I cave in two more sections before I feel safe again.

They can't get to my hoard.

I press my palms to the rough, damp stone beneath me, feeling the jagged edges scrape lightly against the softer undersides of my fingers. The cave yawns ahead, darker now, the further I push into it. The air is thick with an acrid tang, and it sticks to my skin, my nostrils flaring as I take another cautious breath.

I shift my weight to all six limbs, keeping my longer arms poised, fingers flexing unconsciously. My senses sharpen, catching the scent again—something unsettling, primal, buried beneath the mineral staleness of the cave. It's been following me for a while now, this creeping dread.

Yet, despite it, I find my thoughts drifting elsewhere.
Olivia.

The thought of zha comes unbidden, and with it, the familiar irritation blooms within me. My skin flares a deep shade of purple, a brief flicker of color that I quickly smother. I should not be thinking of zha. My focus should be on the cave, on potential treasures, not on the strange human who seems to have lodged in my life with reckless abandon.

But even as I try to force my attention back to the task at hand, Olivia's image lingers, zha's sudden mood swings flashing in my memory. One moment compliant, the next, yelling. A zhasie is not meant to endure such volatility. We evolved to thrive on efficiency, unburdened by complex emotions or illogical attachments. One zhann and one zhannel, not whatever it is that has become of my hoard. Self-sufficiency is our legacy, honed through countless cycles of evolution.

So why do I feel this? Why does the very thought of leaving zha alone in the cave claw at my mind, digging deeper into my consciousness as if it were some vital, primal urge? I have never feared losing any one item of my hoard as much as this moment.

It isn't right.

I let out a low, frustrated click, my tusks pressing against the inside of my lips. This... nonsense... is starting to terrify me. There's no reason—none at all—for me to be concerned about Olivia. It's illogical. Ridiculous.

I pause for a moment, settling back on my hind limbs, using one of my upper arms to rub the back of my neck, easing the tension. I can't afford to lose focus, not now. The further I stray from the area of the cave that I've claimed, the more dangerous it becomes. I should be worrying about myself, not the human. Yet, despite myself, I can't help but acknowledge the truth gnawing at me: Olivia's survival instincts leave much to be desired.

My skin shifts, this time tinged faintly red with the memory of zha's last attempted escape—if one could even call it that. The silly thing had barely made it anywhere, collapsing in exhaustion mere moments from a treacherous pitfall. The image of zha sprawled on the cave floor, oblivious to the danger around zha, flares in my mind, and I suppress a shudder.

I force myself to move again, walking deeper into the cave system, using the rhythmic thud of my limbs against the stone to drown out the persistent thoughts of Olivia. My focus sharpens as I move further into unfamiliar territory, and soon, the walls around me shift, revealing a new portion of the cave.

The crystals catch my attention immediately.

I halt, momentarily taken aback by their gleaming surface, their fractal patterns capturing what little light seeps into this part of the cave. They're made from a dense, crystalline rock, something I haven't encountered in this system before. I reach out with one of my larger hands, my fingers grazing the cool surface. It's beautiful. Rare. Worthy of my hoard.

They must have been here for... eons. To capture the time represented by their growth fills me with a thrill.

For a moment, I allow myself the distraction. I crouch lower, examining the intricate structure of the crystal, and the way it refracts light into subtle colors. I decided I must have it. With renewed determination, I press all four of my forelimbs against the stone and attempt to pry the crystals free. The rock resists, solid and unmoving beneath my strength.

They are difficult to break and it impresses me. Makes me even more determined to have something so unique for my hoard.

I chitter in frustration, but then, a thought crosses my mind. I glance around, and a few paces away, a loose stone catches my eye. I pick it up, testing its weight in my hand before swinging it down with force against the crystal. The impact sends vibrations through my limbs, but the crystal chips away, just as I hoped.

Pleased, I settle into a rhythm. The steady sound of stone striking stone echoes in the chamber, and over time, my pile grows. I gather each chunk of crystal carefully, arranging them in a neat pile by my side. My thoughts, thankfully, remain focused on the task for once, the satisfaction of adding to my collection outweighing any lingering concerns.

The story of how hard I had to work is adding such a pleasing layer to the crystals. They will be a perfect addition to my collection of treasures.

I don't notice the shift in the air at first. It's subtle, just a tingling at the base of my neck, a sense of something... off. My skin shifts uneasily, flashing pale blue. I pause, my body instinctively tensing, my ears straining for any unfamiliar sound.

Then I hear it.

The low, almost inaudible growl—followed by the sharp clack of something moving swiftly behind me.

Instinct takes over.

I throw myself to the side, my muscles coiling as I leap just in time to avoid the snapping jaws that close on the air where my neck had been moments before.

I twist in midair, landing on all six limbs, and skitter backward, my heart pounding in my chest. My skin flashes violently purple, tusks bared in an instinctive display of threat.

The creatures step into the dim light.

There are a dozen of them, sleek and muscular, their dark fur blending seamlessly into the shadows of the cave. Their eyes glow a harsh amber, devoid of pupils or whites, their narrow, slitted gazes fixed on me with predatory intent. Their claws scrape against the stone as they prowl forward, the slime that drips from their jagged teeth casting an eerie glow across their maw.

They don't look like cave creatures, which means we must be close to the surface.

My first thought is how unsettling they look. Not quite recognizable, but close enough to remind me of the predators of my home world—only more vicious, more... wrong.

I count them quickly, assessing the threat. There are too many of them to face head-on, but they seem uninterested in the crystals strewn across the floor. Their attention is solely on me.

Good.

I lower myself closer to the ground, my limbs bending as I prepare for the next strike. The room narrows here, giving me little room to maneuver, but it also limits their ability to flank me. I bare my tusks again, hoping to intimidate them, though I doubt they'll be so easily cowed.

The air hums with tension.

One of the creatures, larger than the rest, lets out a growl that reverberates through the cave, the others following suit as if responding to an unspoken command. I watch their muscles coil, readying for the attack.

My heart races, blood pounding in my ears as I tense for the inevitable.

I can't afford to lose here. I need to get back to Olivia. The thought of her, alone and defenseless, spurs me into action.

The tension in the air is unbearable. I can feel the sharp prickling at the base of my neck as the creatures circle me, eyes locked, muscles coiling, ready to strike. The acrid stench of the cave mingles with the smell of their bioluminescent slime, and I hiss lowly, positioning myself to minimize any chance of being flanked. My fingers flex against the stone floor as I crouch, keeping my body low, and prepared.

With a final snarl, I brace myself on all six limbs, ready for whatever comes next.

And then, they lunge.

It happens in a blur. The largest one lunges, its body cutting through the air with frightening speed, maw snapping with a wet, sickening sound. I barely twist out of the way, but not before it grazes one of my rear limbs. I chitter in response, my skin flaring violet with anger as pain shoots through me. No time to dwell on it. Another one is upon me, slashing with jagged claws that glisten with the same eerie glow. I manage to catch its limb with two of my upper arms, but the strength behind its strike surprises me, nearly knocking me off balance.

My tusks press hard against the insides of my lips as I snarl, thrusting the creature away with a violent push. It skids across the stone, but more are already closing in. There's no stopping them now. The fight has erupted in full force, and I am at the center of it.

I swing with one of my arms, catching one of the smaller beasts mid-leap, sending it crashing into the cave wall with a satisfying crunch. The others pause for a fraction of a second, assessing my strength, but they don't relent. They come at me from all sides now, claws flashing, fangs bared, moving in a coordinated attack. I twist and spin, lashing out with all of my limbs, trying to keep them at bay, but there are too many of them. Each time I fend one off, another sinks its claws into my flesh, leaving burning gashes along my limbs and torso.

My body surges with pain, but I push through it. *Zhasie are resilient*, I remind myself, and I've faced worse than this. I slam my forelimbs down onto one of the creatures that gets too close, crushing it beneath my weight with a sickening crack. I hiss in satisfaction, but there's no time to celebrate. Another creature leaps at my back, and I barely manage to throw it off before it can sink its fangs into my neck. My skin shifts to a dark, seething purple. Irritation and frustration course through me as I struggle to keep my focus.

One of them is particularly fast. It darts between my limbs, slicing at my underbelly with razor-sharp claws. I howl, the sound more of a high-pitched hiss than a growl, and twist my body, trying to catch it, but it's already gone, vanishing into the shadows before I can retaliate. My middle section flares with a dull, throbbing pain where the claws left their mark, and I know I've taken damage that won't easily heal.

I rear up on my hind limbs, towering above the pack, and let out a screeching hiss, hoping to intimidate them, but they are unrelenting. Their growls echo in the cave, low and guttural, as they prepare for another coordinated strike.

The leader—larger, more menacing than the others—steps forward again, its amber eyes locked onto mine. It lunges, faster than I expect, and its claws rake across my chest. I roar, swinging one of my massive arms in retaliation, catching it across the face and sending it sprawling. But the effort costs me. Another beast leaps onto my back, claws digging deep into my flesh.

I screech and thrash, managing to throw it off, but not before it tears a chunk of my skin away. My whole body burns with pain, but there's no time to stop. I can feel my strength waning, my movements slowing, and the creatures know it. They're circling tighter now, sensing victory.

I slam my forelimbs down again, sending a shockwave through the ground that makes the creatures pause for a moment, but it's only temporary. They're back at me in an instant, their claws and fangs a blur of motion as they tear into my flesh. I manage to crush two more, my powerful limbs splintering bone and flesh beneath my weight, but it's not enough. There are too many.

My vision blurs as another swipe catches me across the side of my head, sending me reeling. I stumble, my limbs buckling beneath me, and for a moment, I think I'm going to fall. But I can't. I won't. I have to get back to Olivia. The thought drives me forward, even as my body screams in protest.

With a final, desperate surge of strength, I throw myself into the thick of them, my arms flailing, lower limbs kicking, tusks bared in a primal display of fury, my skin casting a bright purple glow on the cave walls around us. I manage to knock several of them away, but not without taking more hits. My skin flashes red now, fear and desperation mixing with the burning pain that courses through me.

Then, in the midst of the chaos, something shifts. The creatures pause, their heads turning as one, ears pricked. I don't know what they sense, but they suddenly retreat, disappearing into the shadows as quickly as they came. I'm left alone, panting, blood dripping from a dozen wounds, my body trembling from the exertion.

I drop to all six limbs, the adrenaline fading and the full weight of my injuries hitting me at once. I'm not dead, but I'm close. My skin flickers a dull, exhausted orange for a moment before settling into a deeper purple. I glance around the cave, my vision still hazy. The crystals... my hoard... they're scattered across the floor, a glittering reminder of why I came here in the first place. But I can't take them with me now. Not like this.

I know I can't make the journey back to Olivia in this state. Even if I could, there's no guarantee those creatures won't come back. I need to heal, and quickly. I scan the cave, looking for a solution, and my gaze settles on a loose patch of ground near the far wall. It's soft enough.

Without hesitation, I begin to dig, using my powerful limbs to tear into the ground, creating a large enough hole to accommodate both myself and my treasures. My movements are sluggish, each stroke of my arms sending sharp jolts of pain through my body, but I don't stop. I can't.

Eventually, the hole is deep enough. I gather the crystals—what little I managed to collect—and place them inside, careful not to damage them further. Then, with a groan of pain, I crawl into the hole beside them. My body protests every movement, but I force myself to curl up tightly, pulling some of the loose soil over myself and the crystals.

The darkness closes in around me, and for a moment, I wonder if I'll wake up again. My wounds are severe, and though my body will heal, it will take time. Time that I might not have if those creatures return.

But there's nothing more I can do now. I close my eyes, my body sinking deeper into the ground, and allow myself to drift into a deep, healing sleep. My skin flickers one last time, a faint pulse of red fading into black as I let the darkness take me.

15

Olivia

It's been hours since Kroaicho left, and the silence in the cave is deafening. I sit in my little corner, arms wrapped around my knees, trying to suppress the growing unease gnawing at the edges of my mind. I took another long drink, but it didn't do much for my hunger. The mushrooms pulse faintly beside me, their soft glow casting ghostly shadows against the walls, but even their calming presence is starting to lose its charm.

I doubt they are edible, dammit, no matter what Kroaicho says.

At first, I tried sleeping. That lasted all of ten minutes. My mind wouldn't shut up, images of home, of my mom, and, disturbingly, of Kroaicho flickering behind my eyelids. Then I tried talking to myself. That went even worse. Something about hearing my own voice echoing in this creepy cave made me feel like I was one step away from losing my grip on reality altogether.

I shake my head.

This is ridiculous. I am not going to go insane here. I refuse to. The bugs couldn't break me and neither will this damn cave, I chide myself.

I've been stuck in here for days now, kidnapped by a weird, glow-in-the-dark handsy alien, and, on top of that, my body is changing in ways I can't even begin to comprehend. First the spiky growths on my ears, and now... what?

I glance down at my arms, holding them closer to the mushroom light. At first glance, everything seems normal. I mean, as normal as it can be when you're stranded on an alien planet with a giant glowing captor. But then I notice it—a shimmer. A faint, silvery glint across my skin, like someone dusted me with microscopic glitter. I hold my breath and bring my arms even closer to the glow of the mushrooms, twisting them back and forth in the eerie blue light.

"Great," I mutter, biting back the rising frustration. "Just great. First the ears, and now this. What's next, wings?"

I resist the urge to scratch at the strange sensation prickling beneath the surface of my skin. It's like the texture has changed—softer, but not in a good way. More... alien. A shiver runs down my spine as I stare at the silvery glimmer on my arms.

Either I'm turning into some freak of nature, or I've contracted alien cancer. Probably both, I decide.

I huff, tossing the thought aside. I'll wait for Kroaicho to come back, whenever that may be, and I'll demand—no, beg—it to take me somewhere else. I can't stay in this cave much longer. I refuse to sit here and let my body morph into something unrecognizable.

But as more time passes, and the familiar rhythm of the cave's dripping water returns, my patience wears thin. Every moment that Kroaicho stays away, I grow more restless, more convinced that sitting here is a waste of time. I glance toward the cave entrance, my mind buzzing.

Screw this. I need to get out of here. If Kroaicho won't help, I'll figure it out myself.

I push myself up onto my feet, swaying slightly from sitting too long. The cave stretches ahead, dark and oppressive, but now's as good a time as any to make my escape. I let out a quiet groan, massaging my temples.

Last time didn't go very well, but...

Before I leave, I consider grabbing some of the bioluminescent mushrooms to light my way, but the memory of the last time I tried to handle them comes flooding back—more specifically how quickly I lost them the last time things went to shit. Yeah, not going through that again.

Instead, I glance over to Kroaicho's pile of "treasures". He once called freedom a type of treasure, but clearly doesn't value it for me. Not enough to let me go.

I'm just another addition to the pile.

"Treasures," I scoff. "More like a hoarder's nest of random shiny junk."

There has to be something useful in there, right?

I rifle through the pile, tossing aside strange objects—polished stones, oddly shaped bones, bits of metal that look like they might have once been part of some ancient machinery. Then, my hand closes around something smooth and cold—a roll of rough twine. I hold it up to the faint light, my brow furrowing. Where the hell did Kroaicho find twine? On an alien planet?

Shaking off the question, I tie a bundle of mushrooms together using the twine, making sure the stems are tightly secured. The soft glow from the mushrooms gives me just enough light to navigate without attracting too much attention. Satisfied with my makeshift lantern, I sling the bundle over my shoulder and make for the cave's exit.

This time, I take a different route, one Kroaicho hasn't shown me. If I can avoid running into the big beast, all the better. The path ahead is narrow, the air thick with the scent of damp soil and moss. My footsteps echo as I venture deeper into the labyrinth of caves, each turn feeling like a step further away from my already fragile sanity.

Time stretches on, the silence punctuated only by the sound of my own breathing and the faint, otherworldly hum of the glowing fungi scattered across the walls. I walk for what feels like hours, every twist and turn looking more unfamiliar than the last.

That's when I hear it—a soft rustling sound, like something scraping against the stone. My heart skips a beat, and I freeze, holding my breath. The sound grows louder, and more distinct. It's coming from behind me.

I whip around, the glow from the mushrooms casting long shadows across the cave floor. For a moment, there's nothing. Then, from the darkness, a shape emerges—a creature, hunched and grotesque, skittering toward me on spindly legs. Its body is a sickly blend of insect and reptile, its carapace glistening with an oily sheen in the dim light. Multi-jointed limbs click against the stone as it moves, mandibles snapping in rhythmic intervals, while beady black eyes focus intently on me.

"Shit."

The creature lets out a high-pitched chitter, its segmented body undulating as it moves closer. Panic surges through me, but I force myself to stay calm. I've faced worse things in these caves. I can handle this.

Without thinking, I grab a nearby rock and hurl it at the creature. It clatters off its hard shell harmlessly, but the creature pauses, hissing in frustration. I take the opportunity to dash past it, skirting around its side as it lunges in my direction.

My heart races as I dart down another tunnel, the creature hot on my heels. I glance over my shoulder, my pulse hammering in my ears. *Think, Olivia, think.*

Ahead, I spot a narrow crevice in the cave wall—just wide enough for me to squeeze through but too tight for the creature. Without hesitation, I dive toward it, scraping my arms and legs against the rough stone as I force my way through.

The creature slams into the crevice behind me, its mandibles clacking furiously as it tries to reach me. I wince as I feel its sharp claws swipe at my back, narrowly missing. With one final heave, I pull myself through the other side, tumbling onto the cave floor in a heap.

But before I can even catch my breath, I feel a sharp, searing pain shoot up my leg. I cry out, twisting around just in time to see one of the creature's barbed stingers embedded in my calf.

"Fuck!" I scream, yanking the stinger out, but it's too late. A burning sensation spreads from the wound, and I feel my muscles start to stiffen.

I scramble to my feet, adrenaline surging through my veins as I stumble away from the crevice. Behind me, the creature lets out another chittering screech, but it can't follow. At least I've managed to trap it. But the sting... my leg throbs with a fiery intensity, and I can feel the venom working its way through my system, making me lightheaded.

No, no, no, not now.

I force myself to keep moving, limping through the tunnel as fast as I can. The cave seems to spin around me, my vision blurring at the edges. I clutch the wall for support, my breath coming in shallow gasps.

After a few more agonizing steps, I collapse against the stone, my head swimming. I try to steady my breathing, but the venom makes it hard to focus. My limbs feel heavy, and sluggish, like I'm sinking into quicksand.

I can't stay here. I push myself up, my legs trembling beneath me. I've come too far to give up now. But as I take another step forward, the realization hits me like a punch to the gut.

I'm lost. Again.

Panic rises in my chest, but I bite it back, refusing to let it take hold. I look around frantically, trying to get my bearings, but everything looks the same—dark, damp, and endless. The tunnels stretch on in every direction, twisting and turning with no rhyme or reason.

Which way did I come from?

I can't remember. My mind is a fog of pain and confusion, and I don't know which way is up anymore.

Then I hear it—a soft, distant chittering sound. My blood runs cold.

It's not the same as before. This sound is fainter, more distant, but unmistakable. There are more of them.

"Fuck," I whisper, my voice trembling.

I stagger forward, my heart pounding in my chest as the chittering grows louder and closer. The creatures are coming, and I don't have the strength to run.

I don't see the dark figure on the floor of the cave before I trip over it. After a painful crash to the ground, I have to swallow down the screech of terror that wants to rise when I see the gaping, green glowing maw.

Then I realize it's dead, large scores across its black hide. There's something even worse in this cave than the stinging bugs that are after me.

This is bad. This is really bad.

With my last bit of strength, I clutch the bundle of glowing mushrooms tighter, their soft light flickering as if mocking my futile attempt at escape.

Just as my legs give out beneath me, and I collapse against the wall, I hear something else—a different sound, deeper, more familiar.

Footsteps. Hurried, familiar.

That god awful chittering again.

I grab a nearby rock and lash out blindly, making contact with something solid.

Warm fluid splashes across my face and a vindictive scream bubbles past my lips as I repeat the motion again and again, screaming myself hoarse.

The feeling of life fluid splashing over my face is more cathartic than I care to admit. Too bad it doesn't stop me from keeling over after what feels like the thirtieth strike.

I can't feel my limbs.

Fuck...

16

Kroaicho

I wake slowly, the tightness in my limbs easing as I become aware of my body, no longer wracked with pain but sluggish with exhaustion. The familiar cold dampness of the soil surrounds me, cradling me like the deep cave system has done many times before. I flex each of my limbs, one by one, testing my strength. To my relief, my wounds have closed up. The ache is still there, a lingering reminder of the battle, but my body has done what it does best. Heal.

Faster than normal, judging by my lack of hunger, which is odd, but I don't linger on the thought.

I push myself up, the soil sliding from my back and limbs as I rise out of the small pit I had dug. The crystals, my treasure, remain beside me, gleaming faintly in the dim light. I gather them, all four of my arms working methodically, gently brushing dirt from their surfaces before clutching them close. My hoard is safe, and I'm alive. A small, fleeting satisfaction flickers through me, but it's dulled by the nagging awareness gnawing at the edges of my thoughts.

Olivia.

The name surfaces in my mind unbidden, and immediately my skin flushes a deep, irritated violet. I know I've overslept. I know. I should have returned earlier. But my injuries... I needed time. Still, I can't shake the feeling that something is wrong. It crawls up my spine as I shove the last crystal into my arms and begin the journey back, my pace quickening with every thudding step against the stone.

The cave is familiar, but I choose the shortcuts this time, the narrow tunnels that twist and turn but cut the distance down. My claws scrape against the jagged walls as I maneuver through the tight spaces, cursing under my breath. How long has it been? Did zha stay put? Probably not. Foolish, reckless human.

I push myself harder, my heart thudding in my chest. The air in these tunnels is damp, thick with the mineral staleness that clings to the back of my throat. But even that doesn't calm the irritation bubbling up within me. Why do I care? She's not my responsibility. The thought is ridiculous, and yet it's there, pulsing, undeniable.

When I finally emerge from the tunnels into the main cave, my arms full of treasure, my breathing ragged from the hurried pace, the first thing I notice is the emptiness. The silence. My eyes scan the cavern floor, the dim light making it hard to see at first. But then it hits me.

She's gone.

I feel a surge of frustration, so powerful it nearly makes my tusks ache. I toss the crystals to the ground in a fit of rage, the clattering noise echoing off the cave walls as they scatter wildly across the floor. I've never done that before. Not once have I treated my hoard with such carelessness, but right now I can hardly bring myself to care. I stalk across the cave, muttering curses in my native tongue, the sound low and sharp, but they do nothing to ease the storm inside me.

"How—how did I ever let zha into my life?" I snarl, the words hissing through my clenched teeth. My skin flares purple, then deepens into a dark, bruised shade as the frustration coils tighter in my chest.

This is why I shouldn't care. This is why. I lean against the stone wall, taking deep breaths to steady myself. After a long moment, I force myself to calm down, force my limbs to be still and push the rage back. It doesn't do me any good, not now.

With a resigned sigh, I move to gather the crystals again, handling them with more care this time. Piece by piece, I place them in my corner, where they belong. Normally, this would fill me with pride—admiring the shiny rocks, adding to my collection. But now, all I can think about is the human. The irritating, illogical human. Olivia.

My attention drifts to the empty space again. I know I won't be able to sit here for long. How can I enjoy my collection when the centerpiece is missing?

With a frustrated huff, I rise to my feet. Fine. If zha won't stay put, then I'll find zha. Again. My tusks press against my lips as I let out a sharp breath, focusing on the task at hand. I trace the ground carefully, searching for any sign of zha's passage. The soft dirt and stone floor show little, but I find the faintest of footprints after a few agonizing minutes. They're fresh, leading deeper into the tunnels.

I follow them, my pace quicker than before, irritation spurring me on. My heart pounds as the trail grows faint in places, almost disappearing entirely, and for a moment I feel panic rising. What if I can't find her? What if something's already happened? My skin flickers violently purple at the thought, but I push it down. I won't lose zha. Not yet. No... never.

After what feels like an eternity of tracking zha by scent, I spot something—signs of a struggle. The ground is disturbed and scuffed in a way that sends a chill down my spine. My muscles tense as I hurry forward, my senses straining. And then I see it. The faint blue glow of bioluminescent mushrooms ahead, casting their eerie light on the tunnel walls.

There, in the faint glow, sits Olivia. She's resting against the tunnel wall, zha's head tilted upward, eyes closed. Relief floods through me, but it's quickly followed by annoyance. Zha doesn't look hurt, not even slightly. If anything, zha looks irritated.

I approach cautiously, but before I can say anything, Olivia's eyes flick open, and Zha gives me a flat, unimpressed look that freezes me in my tracks. Zha's voice cuts through the air, dry and sharp.

"You took your sweet time getting back, didn't you?"

The accusation hits me square in the chest. I snap back, unable to hold back the frustration any longer. "I had to fight off aggressors! Do you think I was just lounging around?"

She doesn't flinch, doesn't even blink at my words. Instead, Zha sucks zha's teeth, an imperious look crossing zha's features as zha rolls zha's eyes making me flinch.

"You should know better than to leave me alone in this cave, unsupervised, Kroaicho. What did you think would happen?"

My skin flashes deep purple with anger, tusks pressing hard against the inside of my lips. "You shouldn't be wandering around like a fool, human. You know how dangerous it is."

Her response is immediate, dripping with sarcasm. "Oh, I'm sorry. I didn't realize I was supposed to be remain still while you ran off to do whatever it is you do. Next time, try not to leave a *lady* by *her* lonesome, hm?" Zha stands, brushing off the dirt from zha's clothes as though it's the least of zha's concerns. "And for the record, I wouldn't be so annoyed if I wasn't so hungry."

I stare at Zha incredulously, the cave lighting blue broadcasting my emotions. I'm still processing zha's words when zha gestures lazily toward a dark shape lying not too far away. My eyes focus on it, and I realize it's the carcass of one of the creatures I fought earlier, its body limp, fur slick with its own blood.

"Carry that, will you?" zha says, zha's voice casual as if zha is giving a mundane request. "We're heading back to the cave. I plan to make a meal out of it."

Without waiting for a response, zha picks up a makeshift torch made from one of the glowing mushrooms and starts walking back toward the cave. I stand there, momentarily dumbfounded, the audacity of this human leaving me at a loss for words.

"Unbelievable," I mutter under my breath, a string of unflattering complaints slipping out. But despite my irritation, I move toward the carcass and lift it with one of my larger arms.

Of course. Of course, she's the one giving orders now.

I follow after her, the weight of the creature barely registering compared to the weight of my growing annoyance. As we walk back toward the cave, zha's form illuminated by the faint glow of the mushrooms, I can't help but think that this human is more trouble than zha's worth.

And yet, I can't seem to leave zha alone. Instead, I follow, skin flashing my jumble of thoughts. Blue, purple, orange... when will I return to a steady white?

***

As I follow Olivia back through the winding tunnels, the creature's carcass slung over one of my larger arms, I can't help but glance at zha. Zha's steps are light, though zha is clearly tired, the glowing mushroom zha uses as a torch casting a pale blue light across zha's features. I clench my jaw and grind my tusks, irritation still simmering beneath the surface.

I have so many questions, so much I want to say, but I hold back for now. The silence stretches between us, punctuated only by the rhythmic clack of my claws on stone.

Finally, after a few minutes, I can't help myself.

"How did you kill this thing?" I ask, my voice a low rumble. "With your—" I hesitate, searching for the right word, "—constitution?"

The question is genuine, but the moment it leaves my mouth, I see Olivia's shoulders stiffen, and I know I've struck a nerve. Zha whips around, glaring at me over zha's shoulder, eyes narrowing.

"What the *hell* is that supposed to mean?" zha snaps, voice sharp and cutting. "You think just because I'm human, I'm weak?"

I hold zha's gaze, trying to suppress the flare of white amusement that wants to light up my skin. "Well, you *are* human, and you haven't demonstrated any noticeable strength or endurance."

I gesture toward the creature's body hanging over my arm. "This creature is twice your size. So yes, I'm curious. How did you manage it?"

Olivia's face flushes with the red that is not fear, zha's lips pulling down at the edges. Zha turns fully to face me now, planting zha's hands on zha's hips. "I'm sorry, do you think I need brute strength to handle myself out here? Is that it? Maybe you're forgetting I've survived just fine on my own before you showed up."

I snort, tilting my head. "Survived, yes. Thrived? That's another matter."

Zha's eyes flare with annoyance, and I can see zha clenching zha's teeth. "You know, you have a lot of nerve. I may not have your giant *monkey caterpillar* arms, but I've gotten pretty good at using what I've got." Zha's voice is steady but heated, and there's a flash of pride there that surprises me.

I expect zha to be glowing yellow at this point and it's ridiculous. False yellow is the worst.

But what do I know?

"And what exactly did you use?" I ask, more curious than condescending this time. "Your wit? Charm? I'm sure that's what really won the beast over."

Zha scoffs, rolling zha's eyes dramatically, and the way zha's lips purse makes my tusks clack in amusement. "Very funny, Kroaicho. But no, it wasn't my 'charm,' as you call it. I used a trap. Dug a pit, lured it in, and let gravity do the work. Not everything has to be solved with brute force."

I pause at that, genuinely impressed despite myself. Zha's voice is still biting, but there's a fierce intelligence behind it. I hadn't considered that zha would use strategy over direct confrontation. "Interesting," I mutter, the sound grudging. "That's... not bad. Resourceful."

Olivia raises an eye fur at me, zha's lips twitching. "What's this? A compliment? From you? Should I be honored?"

I huff, attempting to imitate zha's eye-rolling and cringing as a result. "Don't get used to it. Just because you managed one clever trick doesn't make you invincible."

Zha laughs, but it's a dry, humorless sound. "Yeah, no joke. Look, I don't need your approval, okay? I'm not out here trying to impress you." Zha turns back around and starts walking again, the mushroom light bobbing ahead of zha. "I'm just trying to survive. Same as you."

I take a step, then a thought occurs to me. "How did you get it out of the trap? Where is the trap?"

Zha doesn't answer, just keeps stomping off ahead of me. The cave walls light up purple again, but it quickly dies back.

I take another long look at the creature and recognize the wounds as coming from my own claws.

My mouth opens to confront zha about the lie, but then I clack it closed. Suddenly, I find it amusing again.

I watch zha for a moment, my annoyance fading slightly into something more complicated. The back and forth with Olivia... it's always like this. A constant push and pull, each of us batting at the other. And yet, there's something almost enjoyable about it, as much as I hate to admit it.

Zha doesn't back down and doesn't turn away from a challenge. In some strange way, it's... refreshing.

But still, I can't let go of the irritation entirely. The fact that zha wandered off alone grates on me. I shake my head, clicking low under my breath as I trudge after zha, the weight of the carcass shifting slightly in my grip.

We continue in silence for a while longer, the winding tunnels becoming more familiar as we near the main cave. My mind drifts to my crystals, my hoard. The thought of returning to them, admiring the new additions, brings a flicker of orange contentment. But it's fleeting. I can't enjoy my treasure properly while Olivia's reckless actions still linger in the back of my mind like a thorn.

By the time we reach the cave, the air has cooled significantly, and the dim light from the bioluminescent mushrooms fades as we enter the open space. I toss the carcass onto the ground with a dull thud, not caring where it lands. Olivia, clearly exhausted, barely spares it a glance before slumping down onto a nearby rock, zha's head resting in zha's hands.

My eyes flick to zha for a moment, but then I turn my attention to my hoard. The crystals I gathered earlier are still scattered across the ground where I'd tossed them in my earlier fit of rage. I kneel down, carefully gathering them one by one, dusting off the dirt, and arranging them with the precision and care they deserve.

"These," I say, holding up one particularly beautiful shard, its surface glimmering faintly in the low light, "are the finest I've found in weeks."

I glance over at Olivia, expecting some kind of response, maybe a snide comment, or at least a flicker of interest. But zha is just staring at the ground, eyes half-lidded, looking utterly uninterested. A wave of irritation pulses through me.

"You could at least *pretend* to care," I mutter, holding the crystal up a little higher. "This is rare material, even by my standards."

Olivia doesn't even look up. Zha just waves a hand dismissively, still slouched on the rock. "Yeah, that's nice, Kroaicho. Really. I'm sure your shiny rocks are very impressive."

My skin flashes dark purple in annoyance. "They're not just 'shiny rocks', human. They're—"

"I've been pretending my whole life, Kroaicho," Olivia interrupts, cutting me off mid-sentence, zha's voice edged with exhaustion. "Surely here in this stupid cave I can let all of that go? I'm hungry. And tired. I don't really care about *materialism*, alright?"

I open my mouth to snap back at zha, to ask what that word means, but then I catch myself. Zha sounds genuinely worn out. The sharpness in zha's tone is more from fatigue than actual malice, and I suddenly feel a pang of guilt. I sigh, turning back to my crystals and setting the last one down with more care than I did earlier.

"Well, if you're so hungry," I grumble, "you could've just said so."

Olivia shoots me a flat look, but doesn't respond. Zha just slumps further, looking more miserable by the second. I glance over at the carcass, knowing it will take a while to prepare. Too long, especially with Olivia in this state.

With a resigned sigh, I rummage through one of the small alcoves in the cave, pulling out a handful of dried lichen. It's not the best of meals, all things considered, but it'll have to do for now.

"Here," I say, tossing the bundle of lichen toward Olivia. "Eat this. It will satisfy you until you can eat the creature."

Olivia catches the lichen, staring at it like I've just handed zha something rancid. "You can't be serious."

"Do I look like I'm joking?" I snap, crossing my arms over my chest. "It's edible. Stop complaining."

Zha eyes me skeptically before taking a tentative bite. The moment zha starts chewing, zha's face contorts in disgust, and zha begins to cough and gag, struggling to swallow. I can't help but signal my amusement.

"Tastes as bad as it looks," I supply with no small amount of vindication.

Olivia glares at me, still coughing. "What... the *hell*... is this?" zha wheezes between gasps.

"Lichen," I reply matter-of-factly, my skin lighting a brighter white. "Good for you. Plenty of nutrients."

Zha groans, forcing down another bite, and I can see the revulsion in zha's eyes. But zha keeps eating it, desperate enough to endure the taste. I lean back against the cave wall, watching zha with a mixture of amusement and sympathy. I didn't expect zha to actually eat it.

"Keep in mind," I say after a moment, "if you'd waited a bit longer, I could've made something a little more... palatable."

Olivia shoots me another death glare but says nothing, too busy trying to choke down the lichen. I let out a quiet chitter, my skin briefly flashing a brighter white. Zha's stubbornness is almost admirable. Almost.

When zha finally finishes the bundle, zha sits back with a groan, rubbing zha's stomach as if zha just endured some great trial. "That... was awful."

"Was it really, now?" I quip. "You ate the whole thing."

"Because I was starving," zha mutters, shooting me one last withering look before leaning back against the rock, zha's eyes fluttering closed.

I watch zha for a moment, the cave falling into an uneasy silence once again. Olivia's breathing steadies and I can see the exhaustion weighing heavily on zha. Zha is not as indestructible as zha pretends to be, not even close. I know that, but I also know that I can't help but be... concerned. As much as I hate to admit it.

I push the thought aside, returning my attention to my hoard, but the satisfaction I usually feel when admiring my collection is muted. My mind keeps drifting back to the human, to zha's fragile, infuriating form slumped against the rock.

Annoying little thing.

17

Olivia

I'm staring at the dead creature, wondering where to even start. My leg still throbs from where the stupid bug thing stung me, and every step sends a sharp reminder of just how close that thing came to finishing me off. I'm still a bit dizzy from the venom, but it's steadily getting better.

I can't believe the sting didn't kill me. What else knocks you out that fast and you just wake up dizzy and with a headache? Scratch that... I don't want to know.

But there's no time to dwell on it—I need to keep moving, keep my hands busy. Especially with Kroaicho watching me like that, arms crossed over its chest, radiating impatience.

Then I look back and Kroaicho and realize I can't keep thinking *it*. I've been stubborn about it, just like I usually am, but it isn't right.

"Alright, big guy," I mutter, stretching my sore limbs, "we need to prep this thing, and I'm gonna need your help."

Kroaicho's deep-violet skin shimmers in the low light, his tusks twitching in annoyance. "My help?" His voice rumbles, incredulous. "You expect me to help you eat another creature?"

"Yes," I deadpan. "Lower yourself to the horrors of basic survival."

He narrows his eyes but doesn't argue. Good. That's a win.

I hobble over to the dead creature, studying its oily hide. My makeshift glowing mushroom light casts weird, shifting shadows over it, making it look even more grotesque than it already is. "First thing's first," I say, glancing over at Kroaicho, who hasn't moved an inch. "I need something sharp. A knife."

"I have no such crude tools," he replies, his voice thick with disdain.

"Well, that's a problem." Great. I glare at my empty hands, then my eyes land on the pile of random trinkets Kroaicho calls a treasure hoard. "What about that?" I point to a jagged piece of metal sticking out from the pile.

Kroaicho follows my gaze, frowning. "That is not for cutting."

"It is now."

With a groan of protest, Kroaicho strides over and plucks the object from his pile, holding it pinched between two long claws and handing it to me with exaggerated reluctance, like I'm asking him to part with his firstborn. "This is a piece of ancient machinery," he grumbles. "Far too valuable for... whatever it is you are about to do."

I take it from him, turning it over in my hands. "Valuable? It's a rusty scrap."

"Very valuable," he snaps, his skin deepening to a purple hue. "You know nothing of its history. This was a tool held in the limb of someone ancient. Made for a specific task we have yet to figure out, but I assure you it was not made for this."

"History, huh? Maybe it should be in a fucking museum, but that's not helping right now, if it ever did. Well, lucky for it..." I grin, testing the edge of the metal on the creature's hide. "...it's about to make history as the first-ever tool to slice open alien cat thingy guts."

Kroaicho lets out a long-suffering clicking sigh, and I get to work, slicing the creature open as best I can with my makeshift knife. The stench hits me immediately, and I fight back the urge to gag. Ugh. I turn toward Kroaicho, who's watching me with thinly veiled disgust.

"I'm gonna need some other things too," I say, continuing my messy work. "Like sticks. Dry ones."

Kroaicho's heavy brows knit together. "Sticks?"

"Yeah, you know—wood, branches, twigs." I can already see this is going to be a hard sell.

"Ugly things," he mutters, shaking his head. "They don't belong in my cave."

"Ugly?" I pause, incredulous. "They're sticks, not fashion accessories. What's your problem with them?"

Kroaicho straightens, his voice heavy with indignation. "They clutter. They add nothing of value to my hoard. I won't allow them."

I give him a long, flat look. "Clutter? You're telling me that," I gesture wildly at the haphazard pile of rocks, crystals, and random metal bits in the corner, "isn't clutter?"

"That," Kroaicho huffs, "is an organized collection of treasures."

"You're impossible," I mutter, shaking my head. "Look, I need the sticks to make a fire, alright? Otherwise, we can't cook this thing."

He scoffs, clearly unimpressed. "Fire out of sticks? There are better methods."

"Not for humans!" I snap. "This is how we do things, Kroaicho. I'm not one of your fancy multi-limbed not-quite-a-dragon-but-not-a-bug species. I need fire."

He looks unconvinced, but at least he's thinking it over. I'm about to keep pushing when a thought hits me—what if I can just show him why we need fire?

I pick up a couple of rocks from the ground, clunking them together experimentally. Sparks. Just a little, but enough to catch my interest. If I can get him to understand the need for flame, maybe the stick argument will get easier.

Kroaicho's brow furrows as he watches me. "What are you doing?"

"Just trying to start a fire," I mutter, knocking the rocks together again. Sparks fly, and I can't help but grin. "Look, sparks! We're getting somewhere."

He squints, watching me with clear confusion. "This is yet another form of human entertainment?"

"Uh... sure," I say, trying not to laugh. "Let's go with that."

I strike the rocks together again, sending a shower of sparks into the air. "See? I can't do much with just sparks, though. I need dry sticks and leaves to get it going."

Kroaicho tilts his head, clearly still not understanding the necessity. "These sticks are crucial to your plan?"

"Very crucial," I nod, feeling like I'm trying to explain advanced calculus to a toddler. "Without them, no fire. No fire means no cooked food. And no cooked food means I'll starve. You don't want that, do you? A dead human stinking up your hoard?"

He hesitates, clearly torn between his disdain for sticks and his grudging concern for my well-being.

"Ugly," he mutters again, but I can see him wavering.

"Look," I say, lowering my voice to something more conspiratorial. "I get it. Sticks aren't as shiny or cool as your crystals, but think about it this way—if I have to keep eating raw monster, I'm going to get really cranky. You don't want cranky Olivia on your hands, trust me."

"How would this be different?"

I let out an exaggerated, frustrated groan, slumping down on the cold stone floor of the cave. Kroaicho is still standing there, all four legs rooted in place, his arms crossed tightly against his chest. That perpetual look of mild disgust hasn't left his face since I mentioned sticks, and honestly, it's starting to grate on me.

"Come on, Kroaicho," I say, rubbing my temples. "Why are you being so stubborn about this? I just need a bundle of dry sticks. You act like I'm asking you to fetch molten lava."

He remains silent, eyes narrowing slightly. I notice the faint hue of dark purple beginning to ripple through his violet skin—annoyance, no doubt. This entire conversation has been like pulling teeth, and I don't have the patience for it right now.

I stop talking, biting back the next sarcastic remark that's bubbling up my throat. Instead, an idea flickers in my mind. Slowly, I stand, brushing the dust from my backside. A glint catches in my eyes as I turn to face Kroaicho, and I watch as he shifts uneasily, clearly picking up on the sudden shift in my mood.

"You don't get it, do you?" I say, voice lowering. I begin to pace in front of the dead creature, gesturing with my hands like a storyteller about to weave an epic. "Fire, Kroaicho. Fire is more than just warmth or a way to cook. It's beauty. It's life. Do you know what it feels like to watch a flame dance? To hear the crackle as it devours wood, the glow it casts, the power it holds?"

Kroaicho stares at me, visibly perplexed. The blue of confusion flashes across his skin, but I don't let up. I'm gaining momentum now, and my words flowing faster.

"I know of fire and it is not special," he says, but I ignore him.

"Fire," I continue, "is the heartbeat of survival. It's primal, yet it holds the essence of everything. Do you know what it feels like to sit beside a fire, the warmth seeping into your bones, to watch the flames flicker and twist, casting shadows that seem to breathe?"

I can feel the passion in my voice building, and I know I've got his attention now.

"It's not just about cooking, Kroaicho," I add, moving closer to him, my tone conspiratorial. "It's about control. About turning chaos into something beautiful, something... necessary. Fire is freedom. It's everything."

Kroaicho's expression has shifted, and I don't miss the way he leans slightly forward, curious despite his earlier reluctance. I press on, hoping to seal the deal.

"Imagine," I whisper, "how valuable fire could be. How much it could add to your collection? A living, breathing thing of beauty you can command. That's what sticks bring. That's what I need."

For a long moment, Kroaicho doesn't move. His massive arms remain crossed, but there's a flicker of light beneath his skin, the faintest glow of orange beginning to spread from his chest outward. Without a word, he lowers onto all six limbs and, with a sudden burst of energy, sprints out of the cave, his six limbs moving in unison like a machine.

I blink, stunned by the suddenness of his exit. It's so quiet now, the only sound is the gentle hum of the glowing mushrooms on the cave walls. I exhale slowly, a grin pulling at my lips. That worked a little too well.

Kroaicho's gone for only a surprisingly short amount of time before I hear the familiar sound of his claws clacking against the stone floor. I turn to see him re-entering the cave, a huge armload of sticks piled high in his arms. His skin is glowing brightly now, a mixture of white and orange, as he strides toward me with an excitement that I haven't seen before.

"These?" Kroaicho asks, dropping the sticks with a dramatic flair that sends a few tumbling and clattering across the cave floor, puffs of leaves falling more slowly.

I stare at the pile, momentarily speechless. "Uh, yeah. That... that's perfect, actually."

Kroaicho's face is lit up a bright yellow glow. I almost ask about the color, but decide I'm more hungry than curious.

"Good," he says, almost puffing out his chest. "Now... what's next?"

I suppress a laugh, nodding appreciatively at him. "Now," I say, reaching down to gather a few of the sticks, "we build the fire."

As I set to work arranging the sticks, Kroaicho settles beside me, clearly fascinated by the process. His tusks twitch with excitement, and I can't help but smile at how completely different he is compared to just a few minutes ago. I've never seen him this animated before.

"You seem awfully interested in this fire now," I tease, glancing up at him.

Kroaicho looks down at me, his orange glow intensifying. "You made it sound... significant. Like a treasure of sorts."

"Fire's more important than most treasures," I reply, flicking the stones together to create sparks. "Speaking of treasures, though..." I pause, looking at him as I keep striking the stones. "Tell me about your home. You know, before you ended up here."

Kroaicho's expression shifts slightly, his orange glow dimming just a bit. He seems to consider my question for a moment before answering, voice low and heavy.

"My hoard," he begins, his eyes distant, "was vast. It filled an entire cavern—a cavern much larger than this." He gestures around the cave as if comparing the meager space to its former glory. "There were piles of gemstones, metals from worlds you can't even imagine. Each item carefully selected, and meticulously placed. I had ancient relics, machines that hummed with power, weapons forged by civilizations long dead."

I strike the rocks again, sparks flying, but my mind is captured by Kroaicho's words. His voice takes on a reverent tone as he continues, the details pouring out like a dam breaking.

"The walls of my hoard glittered with crystals that caught the carefully reflected light of our planet's twin suns. It was not just a collection—it was a legacy. The heart of my people, the zhasie. Each treasure had a story, a history. And I was its keeper."

I listen, mesmerized by the richness of his memories, but I notice a subtle shift in his tone—a dark undercurrent of anger. His skin darkens to a shade of violet, and he grits his tusks.

"What was your favorite?" I ask.

Suddenly, his skin lights blue and light purple, signaling... embarrassment? He wiggles, then sighs. "It was my most recent addition. Snatched in a dangerous trip to the lava fields. Such a rich, whirling, complex glow of green..."

He trails off, skin still lighting up in that odd combination. My brows furrow, then I glance down at the long green hair draped against my chest. "Green, huh?" I ask him. "Like me?"

He grinds his tusks. "Almost exactly like you, but far less interesting."

I blink. Am I his favorite? No way. I've been as difficult as possible.

"But it was destroyed," he growls, distracting me, voice deep and vibrating with fury. "The genali came. They took everything. Burned my cavern to ash before they captured me. How could scavengers like them not see the value of it? My treasures, my home—gone."

I freeze for a moment, caught in the weight of his words.

I mean, I can empathize, but I don't know how I feel about being the favorite of a collection.

A huff of breath escapes as I circle back around to how terrible it must have felt to lose everything. He was kidnapped too, and his life's work destroyed. Even more than that, I realize, since he has mentioned that it was passed down. Is he trying to make up the loss?

The fire I've been trying to start suddenly feels insignificant in the face of Kroaicho's loss, but I don't have time to dwell on it, not right now.

"I'm sorry," I say quietly, unsure of what else to offer.

Kroaicho doesn't respond, his eyes now focused on the growing flame as it finally catches, spreading through the dry sticks with a soft crackle. He watches, entranced by the fire I've built, the orange light dancing across his skin.

For a few moments, we sit in silence, the only sound the crackling fire and the occasional shifting of Kroaicho's limbs as he watches.

"You like it?" I ask after a while, unable to resist a smile.

He nods, a rare look on his face, which I realize with a start has somehow stopped looking odd to me. "It is remarkable," he says softly. "I never thought of it this way. A living thing, as you said."

His skin glows an even brighter shade of orange than the fire.

I chuckle and my mood shifts lighter. "So," I say, leaning back and stretching my sore leg. "Tell me more about your people. What were they like? What did you all do, you know, besides hoarding treasures?"

Kroaicho's gaze snaps to me, and I can already see where this conversation is headed. His skin glows white again, a sure sign that he's about to launch into another long-winded speech about his precious hoard.

"The treasures," he begins, "were everything. Every zhasie had a collection. Some were small, but mine... mine was the greatest. We competed, of course. Who could gather the most, and who had the rarest items. Our way of life keeps the treasure's stories intact."

He's stuck on a treasure loop and I'm beginning to think their culture doesn't extend much past it. That fact grates against my long-held distaste for materialism, but I push the thought away. I don't have the energy for it right now.

I shake my head. "You don't say."

"And the hoards," he continues, undeterred by my sarcasm, "were our history. Each piece was a chapter in our story. A reminder of what we had conquered, what we had survived. The oldest zhasie had the grandest hoards—thousands of years old, passed down from zhann to zhannel."

I sigh, half-amused, half-exasperated. "Right, but... what about, you know, culture? Art? Music? Anything other than treasures?"

Kroaicho looks at me, blue lighting his skin, genuinely confused. "Why would we need anything else?"

"Figures," I mutter under my breath, shaking my head.

Despite the circular nature of our conversation, there's a strange charm to it. I continue cleaning the creature in front of me, my knife making slow but steady progress through the thick hide. Every now and then, I have to stop to retch—the smell is unbearable—but I keep going, determined to make the whole process worth it.

Finally, after what feels like an eternity, I manage to get the creature onto a makeshift spit, propping it up over the fire. I sit back, wiping sweat from my brow, and glance over at Kroaicho, who's still staring at the fire with wide eyes.

"Stay with me, Kroaicho," I say, giving him a nudge. "Don't stalk off to treasure hunt. I'm going to go wash my hands."

I make my way to the underground stream that runs along the far side of the cave, plunging my hands into the cold water and scrubbing furiously. When I return, the fire is still burning strong, and Kroaicho hasn't moved a millimeter.

I sit back down beside him, the warmth from the fire already making me feel better. The creature begins to cook, the smell of roasting meat filling the air.

"So," I say, trying to find another way into the conversation. "Where did you get that rusty piece of metal, anyway? You said it was valuable."

Kroaicho's eyes snap to mine, and he brightens again, eager to tell the story. "Ah, that. It was part of an ancient machine, left behind by a species long gone. I found it in an abandoned room, on an odd little shelf. It reminded me of an item I traded some useless, ugly rocks to get. They said it was from a long-extinct culture. I couldn't figure out the writing, but it was still crisp and new, a testament to how advanced they must have been.

I raise an eyebrow. Crisp... but ancient? I have my doubts, but I don't share them. As excited as he sounds it would be like kicking a puppy. More and more I'm having to throw out my assumptions about what things mean to him. He sounds more like a nerdy museum curator than a pirate. Or day trader.

"That sounds... interesting," I say instead of crushing his dreams. "What were the rarest items from your previous hoard?"

And just like that, the floodgates open. Kroaicho begins to tell me story after story, each item in his old hoard connected to some far-flung world, picked up by this trader or that. Some forgotten piece of history. Slowly, I start to piece together bits of information about Kroaicho's home world, the zhasie culture, such that it is. Everything, of course, seems to revolve around treasure.

As the creature cooks, I lean back, absorbing everything Kroaicho says, my mind whirling with the new information.

After a while, Kroaicho stands, his six limbs stretching. "I should go," he says, glancing toward the cave entrance. "There may be more treasures to find tonight."

I hesitate for a moment, then speak up. "Kroaicho, if you're going out again... could you keep an eye out for the others? The other women who were with me when we crash-landed here, I mean?"

He tilts his head, considering my request. "Humans," he murmurs. "Like you, but with different... colors?"

I nod, wondering how he knows about the variation in human coloring. "Yes, exactly. It would mean a lot to me if you could find them."

The alien looks doubtful, and my brain does what it does best. Clutch for straws.

"Humans... yes, they would make excellent additions to your collection."

Kroaicho gives me what I can only rationalize to be a flat look before it mutters something under its breath and summarily turns around its six limbs stretched out as it prepares to leave, my mind whirling. This is my chance, I think. I need to convince it to help me find the others, but there's that nagging thought—what I just said about humans being "additions" to his collection. I should feel ashamed, right? After all, I've basically just offered up my fellow humans like objects to a creature whose only passion is hoarding. But I can't summon up guilt right now.

Clearing my throat, I approach it from a different angle. "Look," I say, adopting my most persuasive tone, "I know humans might not sound like much, but think about the variety. You like unique treasures, don't you? Humans are incredibly diverse. Each one is like a completely different piece in a collection."

Kroaicho pauses, turning his violet face toward me, the orange glow from the fire still reflecting off his skin, but no longer lit up orange from within. I can see him considering, so I push harder.

"Imagine," I continue, stepping closer, my voice dropping low like I'm sharing some grand secret. "A hoard with not just one, but multiple humans. It would be unlike anything you've ever collected. Rare. Unpredictable. You'd be the only one with a collection like that."

Kroaicho's expression shifts, and for a moment, I think I've struck gold. The glow beneath his skin brightens, flashing orange as it thinks over my words.

But then, his response cuts through the air like a slap. "No!" Kroaicho snaps, its voice suddenly sharp. "You... are... are the worst addition to a hoard possible! I will not seek out more of your kind."

I blink, stunned by the vehemence in its voice. What?

Kroaicho shivers, his glowing skin now turning a deep violet, the tell-tale sign of growing irritation. "Your kind are pests," he says, his voice dripping with horror. "Annoying. Loud. I will not collect more of you."

I narrow my eyes, crossing my arms in return. "Oh, I'm sorry. Did my human-ness offend your delicate treasure-collecting sensibilities?" My words are practically dripping with sarcasm, but I can't help it. I've already lost the argument. Now I'm just pissed.

Kroaicho huffs, the noise something like a growl mixed with a snort. "You are more trouble than you are worth. You and the others are no treasure. You're—" He gestures wildly with one of his clawed limbs, "—broken things. Not worthy of hoards."

His words cut deep, bringing up memories of the similar words uttered by family, teachers, employers... but I slip on my mask, refusing to let him see.

I laugh, the sound harsh and humorless. "Broken things? Is that your expert treasure-collector opinion?" I take a step forward, not backing down, despite the fact that Kroaicho could probably squash me like a bug if he wanted to.

"Listen, if I'm so worthless, then why are you still hanging around me? You know what I think?" I lean in, lowering my voice. "I think you like having someone to talk to."

Kroaicho recoils, his glowing violet dimming into a sullen blue. "I do not," he says, but I can tell by the way his skin flickers that I've hit a nerve.

I press on, refusing to let up. "Oh, really? Because for someone who's so determined to call me a pest, you sure spend a lot of time with me."

"You are part of my hoard," he grumbles, tusks grinding in annoyance.

"Right. Just a shiny human rock, right? That's why you helped me gather sticks and started getting all philosophical about fire?"

The creature's skin shifts, the colors swirling in frustration. "I will leave now," he says, and there's a finality in his tone that lets me know I've pushed too far.

I watch as Kroaicho turns toward the mouth of the cave, all six limbs moving in that smooth, predatory motion he has. Part of me wants to yell for him to stay, but I'm too tired to keep arguing.

"Fine, go then!" I shout, the words bouncing off the cave walls. "See if I care!"

Kroaicho doesn't respond. His form fades into the shadows, leaving me alone in the cave with nothing but the crackling fire and the faint hum of glowing mushrooms. Well, that went well.

I exhale sharply, rubbing a hand across my face. My breath comes out ragged, and I realize I'm shaking.

That's what I get for being vicious. My eyes sting, a dull ache starting at the back of my skull. I try to blink the feeling away, but it lingers, an ever-present weight pressing down on me. Fear and pain, I think, though it feels strange to put a name to it. I've been holding so much in. For a moment, I feel it welling up, like a dam ready to burst.

Five and ninety-five, that shattered part of my brain starts to chant. *Cannot be reformed.*

I lose myself for long moments, before I smell the smoke, the coughing bringing me out of my daze of repeated sayings. A quick glance up confirms that I forgot about a very important part of building a fire. A chimney.

My hunger takes precedence though, and I snatch the meat off of the fire. Hissing as it burns my mouth, then groaning when the flavor is terrible.

I choke as much down as I can, determined to not let this place starve me to death.

Then I gather myself to figure out the smoke issue, but before I can get up the ground beneath my feet shudders.

The fire flickers as the stone floor trembles, a low rumble echoing through the cavern walls. I freeze, my heart pounding as the tremor grows stronger, and then—CRACK.

The ground splits open with a jagged, thunderous tear, and something bursts through the surface, sending chunks of rock flying in all directions. I scramble backward, my hands clawing at the ground as I stare at the thing that's emerged.

It's massive. Easily twice my height, and covered in thick, slimy scales that glisten in the low light. Its body is long and serpentine, with dozens of legs—more like claws—that dig into the stone beneath it. Its head is elongated, with a wide, tooth-filled maw that stretches unnervingly far when it opens its mouth. Two eyes, a sickly green, lock onto me, studying me with an eerie, calculating stare.

My heart races in my chest as I freeze, barely daring to breathe. The creature doesn't move at first, just hovers there, its eyes narrowing as it watches me. I can hear the low hiss it emits, like steam escaping from a pressure valve, and the scent of sulfur fills the air.

This is bad. But I don't move. Maybe if I stay perfectly still, it won't see me as a threat. Maybe it'll just go back to wherever the hell it came from.

The creature tilts its head, then moves closer, its claws scraping the stone with each step. The tension builds in my chest, my lungs screaming for air, but I still don't move. I don't even blink.

And then, without warning, the creature lunges.

I dive to the side, just barely avoiding the snapping jaws as they slam shut where I'd been standing moments before. My heart is hammering now, the adrenaline surging through my veins as I scramble to my feet. I can feel the heat from the creature's breath, rancid and hot, as it rears back for another strike.

I'm not going to outrun this thing. It's too fast, too strong. My eyes dart around the cave, searching for something—anything—that can help me. My gaze lands on Kroaicho's pile of treasures, glittering in the low firelight. The hoard!

Without thinking, I sprint toward the pile, throwing myself into the chaotic mess of rocks and trinkets. My body crashes into the mound, sending pieces clattering everywhere as I burrow deep into the treasure, pulling as much of it over me as I can for cover.

I hear the creature's growl behind me, followed by the sound of claws scraping over the stone. It's searching for me, sniffing at the air, but I keep my breathing shallow, curling up as tightly as possible beneath the treasures.

It's no good, though. It wasn't fooled

"Kroaicho!" I scream, my voice hoarse. "KROAICHO!"

There's no response. Of course, there isn't. The stupid alien left, and now I'm stuck here with this... thing, buried in a pile of useless trinkets.

I push up slightly and start throwing anything I can grab in as many directions as possible. It seems to work, the creature whips around to each new sound, looking more and more confused.

Then I carefully lay back down.

The creature's claws scrape closer, and I bite my lip, willing myself not to scream again. I can hear it sniffing, growling, its hot breath so close I can almost feel it. It's circling the hoard, searching for a weak spot. For me.

I press deeper into the treasures, my hands brushing against something sharp—one of Kroaicho's supposedly valuable pieces of scrap, I'm sure. I grab it instinctively, clutching it to my chest like some kind of talisman.

The creature lets out another growl, and then—silence.

For a moment, I think maybe it's gone, that I've somehow managed to hide well enough. But then I hear the faintest sound—like a crackle. Like the fire...

The fire.

It must have wandered too close to the flames, distracted by the thing I had started. My pulse quickens as I realize this might be my only chance. Slowly, painfully, I shift beneath the hoard, trying to reach the edge where I can see the flickering light. If I can just get the creature to move closer to the fire, maybe...

But my movements make noise, multiple clinks of metal against metal. I freeze, my heart slamming in my chest as the creature whips around, its green eyes narrowing in on my hiding spot.

"Dammit," I whisper, gripping the sharp object tighter in my hand.

The creature lets out a deep, menacing hiss, and then lunges straight toward me.

18

Kroaicho

I pull in a deep breath of above-ground air as I berate myself for the things I said. Why did I say zha was broken? Zha's body and face instantly changed to that odd way zha could be. It made me realize that what zha was showing before——in zha's exhaustion——was the truth.

Why did I say something so terrible? Why did I bring back the lie? The way zha looked changed so quickly. Emotion colors would make this so much easier.

How do I even know it's the lie, though? My skin is a swirl of purple self-hatred and blue. My zhann did not prepare me for this. Well... aside from being very firm that a hoard did not include pets.

I let out a series of clicks. Olivia isn't a pet. There was no wisdom passed down that could ever help me right now. My mistakes are my own.

A snap of a branch brings me out of castigating myself. Then I hear a language I hoped I never would hear again. Manticorid.

My skin instantly lights up red, but I try to mute it. I would be a beacon in the darkness, but it is hard. I have never been so terrified.

"I know I smelled a human, my Ree," comes the harsh voice, and I swallow thickly when I recognize a native speaker. "And I just heard clicks and smell a new type of prey."

If I don't run, I'm going to die, but then something else catches my attention and a different emotion rises up amid the fear. A human...

They want to take Olivia. Just like the pink human wanted.

Anger starts to displace the fear, but it doesn't make me reckless. I creep slowly back to the cave entrance.

"There..." a roar comes next, then the sound of breaking branches, rapidly coming toward me. I can't help the flare of red and I abandon stealth, instead dropping to all six limbs, running as fast as I can deep into the cave. It's cavernous here. Far too open to block off, not to mention dangerously stupid to try.

I increase my pace, heart pounding, making my way toward the smaller tunnel I just dug.

Another voice calls out, this one with an accent that suggest they aren't manticorid. "We just want to talk," zha cries out.

No manticorid just wants to talk. My zhann passed on the stories. I run faster, recklessly crashing through pillars of minerals, relieved to finally see the fresh dirt of my tunnel.

The next frantic movements I barely remember, except that I spend far more time collapsing the tunnel in my panic than needed. I'm still panting, the cave section I'm in lights up brightly with my red fear when I get back control of myself.

Something catches my eye, my mind more than willing to focus on something else besides terror. I'm piling rocks into my arms frantically a moment later.

Then I crouch down, gazing at a delicate tangle of glowing vines nestled in the crook of the stone wall, their light casting a soft glow across the cave. The way the light plays off the jagged rocks reminds me of a childhood memory, a distant echo from when my zhann would lead me through the caves of my home world, teaching me how to spot treasure.

The vines seem like a perfect find—almost too perfect. They thrum faintly, in sync with my heartbeat, drawing me in like an insect to a pulsing trap. The tendrils reach into the rock, as if they are embracing it, bolstering it, as if the story of its existence is to integrate itself with what is around it. Fascinating.

A part of me longs to pluck them from the rock and add them to my growing hoard so I can study how they integrate, but I'm already carrying too much. The pile of gleaming rocks balanced precariously in my arms shudders with every slight movement, and one more item might topple the whole lot.

I chitter in frustration, my skin flashing light purple as the irritation mounts. The soft flicker of color reflecting off the cave walls only amplifies my annoyance. I shouldn't be this bothered, but the thought of leaving these glowing vines behind gnaws at me. They could make a beautiful addition to the growing pile—a glowing centerpiece that would outshine everything else. I shift the pile of treasures I'm holding, trying again to wedge the vines in between two of the larger rocks. For a moment, I think I've managed it, balancing them just so. But as I take a step, everything teeters dangerously. A stone clatters to the ground, and I hiss under my breath.

"Demiurge curse it," I mutter, the sound low and bitter, echoing off the cave walls. The sound feels strange in this stillness, the silence of the cave swallowing up my voice almost instantly. I'll just have to come back for the vines later. For now, I need to secure these treasures back in my hoard. With a few more muttered curses about the inconvenience, I make a mental note of the vines' location. My memory is flawless when it comes to treasure. I'll be able to trace my way back easily, and when I return, they'll be waiting for me. I hope.

With the vines abandoned for the time being, I begin the trek back to the main cave, my six limbs working in unison as I move through the narrow tunnels. The rocks underfoot feel more jagged than usual, each step pressing the uneven surface into the soft pads of my feet. It's not painful, but it's enough to distract me. I adjust my hold on the treasures again, feeling the weight of the stones pressing into my chest.

As I walk, my mind drifts to the earlier conversation with Olivia. I still don't understand why zha's words sting the way they do. I've dealt with biting remarks from others before—zhannel who thought they were superior to me, mockers who ridiculed me after my zhann passed on—but Olivia? Zha lights my skin purple in a way I can't explain. It's as if each sarcastic comment zha throws at me sticks somewhere deep, making my skin flash with irritation that I have to fight down.

"Stupid human," I grumble, adjusting my grip on the stones as I navigate a tight turn in the tunnel. The walls close in here, a narrow passage I've walked countless times before, yet today it feels suffocating. Zha is probably still sitting by the fire, glaring into the flames with that angry look on zha's face.

The image is oddly amusing, and I feel my skin glow briefly with white before it returns to a more neutral hue. I should have left long ago—treasures wait for no one, after all—but something about the way Olivia clacks, the way zha refuses to back down, keeps me circling back to zha.

Why do I even care? Zha is the most chaotic, difficult to keep, disruptive treasure imaginable. Zha has zha's own ideas about treasure and I should simply let zha go to gather zha's own hoard of "wit" and "freedom". Zha's own sense of value does not match my own.

I pause in my stride, shaking my head at the ridiculous thought. Zha is not a treasure. Not even close. I've spent enough energy on zha for one day.

As I continue through the tunnel, something catches my eye—small, freshly drilled holes dotting the cave wall. I stop, my limbs going still as I lean in to examine them. The light from the vines, still visible from the distance, flickers faintly against the dark stone, casting an eerie glow on the strange markings. The holes are uniform, lined in neat rows, and I can smell something acrid lingering in the air, like the faint scent of burned meat.

My skin flashes dark purple, and I pull back, uneasy. These tunnels weren't here before. I know this part of the cave system very well, and there's something wrong about these holes. Something... too new. Too fresh. And that smell. It's biological. Unnatural.

A shiver runs down my spine, my skin flickering between colors as I take in the sight. I've never encountered anything like this in my years of exploring the caves. The thought crosses my mind that something new has entered this space—something dangerous, perhaps. My breath catches for a moment, and I find myself considering what sort of creature could have made these. Something new to the cave? Something that could pose a threat to my hoard? My skin darkens further as I contemplate the possibilities.

I should check it out, but—

"KROAICHO!"

The scream hits me like a physical blow, echoing through the tunnels. My head snaps up, my heart pounding as Olivia's voice slices through the cave. The panic in zha's tone makes something tighten in my chest, an uncomfortable, foreign sensation. I freeze, torn between continuing my exploration of the tunnels and rushing back to the human.

It's just a human. The trouble is likely one zha found. Zha is not part of my hoard. Zha is not valuable.

I shift on my limbs, the pile of treasures still balanced awkwardly in my arms. I could drop them. I could run faster without them. But I just collected these... I need these.

Another scream tears through the air, and my decision is made before I can even think it through. With a growl of frustration, I let the stones clatter to the ground, some of them shattering on impact. My skin flashes a deep violet as I hiss, angry at myself for abandoning the new treasures so easily. I'll have to come back for them later. But Olivia's screams echo again, louder this time, and I push aside my irritation, spinning on my many limbs and racing toward the main cave.

The tunnels blur as I move, each step sending a jolt through my body as my limbs carry me at full speed. The acrid smell from earlier clings to the air, but I shove it out of my mind, focusing instead on the path ahead. I don't know what's happening, but

Olivia sounded terrified, and that tight feeling in my chest refuses to go away. It's a strange sensation, a gnawing discomfort that I can't quite name, but it drives me forward nonetheless.

As I near the cave, I hear more sounds—growling, the scraping of claws against stone, the unmistakable hiss of something large. My skin flickers between purple and red, fear creeping in as I slide to a stop at the cave entrance. I peer inside, my heart hammering.

The scene before me is chaos. Olivia is backed into a corner, zha's eyes wide with terror as a massive creature looms over zha, its scales glinting in the firelight. The thing is larger than anything I've ever seen in the caves, its body coiled and ready to strike. Its eyes, glowing faintly in the darkness, lock onto Olivia, and a low growl rumbles from its throat.

My chest tightens again, and without thinking, I rush forward, the glow of my skin flaring bright red as I charge at the creature. I have no plan, no strategy, just an overwhelming urge to protect zha.

It's not about value anymore. It's about something else.

I burst into the cave, my six limbs moving in rapid unison as I skid to a stop, nearly slipping on the slick stone beneath me. The dim light of the cave flickers against the creature's scales, its long body slithering menacingly across the ground. Olivia is huddled at the far edge of my hoard, barely visible beneath the piles of shiny trinkets I've so carefully amassed.

Zha is frozen, wide eyes locked on the creature as its massive, elongated head turns in zha's direction, its maw stretching open far too wide, revealing rows of sharp, needle-like teeth. The acrid stench of burned flesh clings to the air, and my skin flashes an intense violet in response—fear and anger mingling, coursing through me.

This thing. It's too big. Too strong.

I hiss loudly, the sound echoing off the cave walls, and the creature swivels its head toward me, its two glowing eyes narrowing as if sizing me up. Its body is long, insectoid, with far more clawed legs than should be natural that scrape against the stone as it moves. It's nothing like anything I've ever seen in these caves—more dangerous, more... unnatural.

But Olivia—zha is valuable in a new, mysterious way. One I need to figure out. That thought is enough to push me forward, despite the chill of fear tightening my chest.

I lunge, my bottom four limbs propelling me as my two upper limbs stretch out to grab hold of the creature. My claws rake across its scaly hide, but it's shockingly durable—my hands barely leave a scratch on its dark, iridescent body. With a furious hiss, I throw myself against it, using my weight to drive it back. But the thing is fast. Faster than I expected.

With a snarl, the creature twists its body, whipping its tail at me. I duck just in time, feeling the wind rush past as it smashes into the cave wall. Stone cracks under the force of the blow, sending shards flying in every direction. My skin flashes red—fear pulses through me, but I push it down. I can't afford to falter now.

I swipe at the creature again, aiming for its legs, but it's already moving, darting to the side with an unsettling speed that belies its size. I'm forced to rear back, my two larger arms raised defensively as it snaps its massive jaws at me, missing my head by mere inches.

"Stay back!" I roar, hoping Olivia understands as my skin flickers between violet and red. Zha shouldn't be here. Zha is too close.

I can feel the pressure mounting in my chest as the creature coils and uncoils, its glowing eyes fixed on me now. It's testing me, watching for an opening. Every instinct screams at me to run, but Olivia's still cowering behind the pile of treasure—zha is frozen in place, terrified.

I can't let zha die.

With a frustrated growl, I lunge again, this time trying to drive the creature back toward the tunnel. If I can just get it away from Olivia... if I can just...

The creature moves faster than I anticipate, its many legs scrambling across the stone with an almost eerie fluidity. It darts around me, its tail whipping out to strike. I manage to block it with one of my massive arms, but the impact sends a jolt of pain through my body. My skin flares violet as I stumble, my feet scrambling for purchase on the uneven ground.

I let out a low growl, my teeth bared as I rush the creature, slamming into its side with as much force as I can muster. It screeches, an awful, high-pitched sound that makes my ears ring, but I manage to drive it back toward the tunnel.

"Out!" I hiss at Olivia, jerking my head toward the deeper recesses of the cave. Zha is frozen, eyes wide with panic, but I can't focus on zha right now. I just need zha to move.

The creature's claws scrape across the ground as it regains its balance, its glowing eyes narrowing in anger. Before I can react, it rears up, its massive jaws snapping toward my face. I manage to dodge, but not fast enough. Pain explodes in my arm as its teeth graze me, tearing into the flesh. My skin flashes an intense red as I pull back, hissing in pain.

It's stronger than me.

Fear tightens in my chest, but I refuse to let it show. I can't let it see my fear. I can't let Olivia see.

With a guttural snarl, I release a burst of color—a bright, flashing violet—as I rush forward again. This time, I aim lower, sweeping my claws at its legs in an attempt to unbalance it. The creature screeches again, its body twisting unnaturally as it dodges, but I manage to catch one of its legs, yanking it hard. It stumbles, all of its claws scrambling for purchase, and I seize the opportunity to drive it further back toward the tunnel.

"Go!" I bark at Olivia, my voice harsher than I intend. "Get out of here!"

Zha finally moves, scrambling out of the cave and into the safety of the tunnels. Relief washes over me, but it's short-lived. The creature recovers quickly, its tail whipping out again. This time, it strikes me square in the chest, sending me flying back into the cave wall. The impact knocks the breath out of me, and for a moment, my vision wavers. My skin flashes a deep violet as I struggle to stand, the pain radiating through my body.

It's too strong.

I push myself to my feet, panting heavily as I face the creature once more. It's watching me, its glowing eyes gleaming with something that almost looks like amusement. I grit my teeth, my skin flickering between violet and red. I can't win this fight. Not like this.

But I have no choice.

With a frustrated growl, I lunge again, this time feinting left before darting right. The creature falls for the bait, its massive head swinging toward my fake attack, and I seize the opportunity to slam into its side, driving it deeper into the tunnel.

The narrow passage works to my advantage—its large body can't maneuver as easily in the confined space. I dart around it, slashing at its legs and sides, trying to drive it back further. It screeches in frustration, its glowing eyes flashing as it swipes at me with its tail, but I manage to dodge, my smaller, nimble form giving me the edge in the tight tunnel.

I know I can't keep this up for long. My body is already aching, the pain in my arm throbbing with every movement, but I can't stop. I won't stop.

The tunnel narrows even further, and I finally see my chance. With a final burst of speed, I dart around the creature, positioning myself behind it. My skin flickers between violet and red as I release the knockout gas from my nose, the thick, sweet-smelling vapor filling the air around us.

The creature hesitates, its movements slowing as the gas begins to take effect. I can see it shaking its head, trying to clear the fog, but it's too late.

With a snarl, I lunge forward, wrapping my arms around its thick neck and yanking it toward the glowing blue stream that runs through the deeper part of the cave system. The creature thrashes, but its strength is fading fast.

With a final, desperate heave, I toss it into farther down the cave, carefully away from where Olivia fled.

It staggers, moving away erratically, but quickly, crashing into the sides of the tunnel in its haste to get away.

Panting heavily, I collapse against the cave wall, my skin flickering between violet and red. I'm exhausted, my body aching from the fight, but it's over.

For now.

I take a deep breath, forcing my skin to return to a more neutral hue as I push myself to my feet. Olivia is safe. That's all that matters.

But as I turn to make my way back to the cave, I can't shake the tight feeling in my chest. That creature—it wasn't natural. It wasn't like anything I've ever encountered before.

And I have a feeling this isn't the last time I'll see one of these.

The exhaustion hits me all at once. I can barely feel the jagged stone digging into my palms or the sharp bite of the cool cave air against my skin. I steady my breathing, trying to calm the wild flickering of color that I know is betraying every emotion I've been trying to suppress. My skin flashes between violet and red, anger mixing with fear. But I'm alive. That's something.

I try to focus on the tunnel where the creature left, but my eyes keep roaming back to where Olivia ran. The stillness of the cave, after the chaos of the battle, feels almost too quiet. My head spins, and the tightness in my chest remains, pulsing faintly.

Then, a sound behind me—a familiar sound—small footsteps, uneven, moving toward me. My limbs tense as I spin to face the sound, my body already primed to fight again.

19

Olivia

I don't know how I avoid breaking my neck as I careen around corners, but I run until my breath comes in gasps and my mind finally stops screaming at me to flee.

Then I put one hand on the glowing moss on the wall and suck in long, greedy breaths. I can still make out the sound of fighting, which means I haven't run nearly far enough to be safe. My muscles bunch to run, but then I stop myself.

That sound of pain was Kroaicho. I wince, then shake my head.

What am I doing? This is my chance to actually escape the kidnapping non-dragon thing.

"He thinks you're a possession, you idiot," I chide myself. "Just run."

But I don't. I can't.

"Fuck," I say in an explosion of breath, then turn back around and start running back around the same corners.

We are both probably going to die, but I won't die a coward. Besides, he shouldn't get all of the satisfaction of killing that thing.

I've worked myself up into a completely delusional lather by the time I get back to the cave with Kroaicho's scattered hoard in it, utterly relieved when there is no giant snake-bug thing in there anymore.

I exhale sharply, trying to calm myself. Kroaicho looks equally rattled, pink eyes wide, skin a thrumming, vibrant red.

"Where is it?" I ask, voice shaky.

He raises a wavering arm and points down a dark tunnel.

"Are you sure it's gone?" I press. "What if it—"

"Feel free to go down it and check if you're dying to be sure."

My jaw clenches, but I can't muster the energy for a full argument. I sigh and lower my gaze to the ground.

"It's gone," he says in a lighter tone. "For now."

Then he gets himself up with a groaning heave, all of his limbs shaking. I rush over, not sure how to help, but he motions me back.

"I need to collapse the tunnel," he explains in a pained voice.

With a gulp, I back up. Then back up some more when he drags himself down the tunnel. A few moments later there's a crash and a cloud of dust plumes out from the tunnel, making me cough.

When I clear my lungs and my vision, I remember the fire and smoke, but a frantic glance reveals that it was scattered, only a few pieces still burning. Once I see that Kroaicho is slowly moving back toward me, I jog to the nearest item that will hold water and make a few quick trips to douse any remaining smoldering sticks.

The meat is still gurgling in my stomach, a heavy weight, especially now that I consider that cooking is likely what drew the creature to us in the first place.

So many layers of dumb. I was so busy arguing...

I stop myself there. I was also shaky and starving. No one thinks well at moments like those.

One last toss of water and my job is done, just in time for Kroaicho to make his way back to his precious hoard. He reaches down to grab a crystal, but loses his balance, tipping sideways with a crash.

"Kroaicho!"

I rush toward him, hands reaching out, but completely clueless about how to help. He's massive.

"I'm alright," he says in a weak chitter. His skin flickers a pale violet. "I think... I've overextended myself."

I grit my teeth, hating the vulnerability I hear in his tone. But I pretend not to notice it, and definitely don't comment. Instead, I loop my arm under one of his massive forelimbs and try to help him up. I'm too exhausted to feel embarrassed by how ridiculous I must look or how absurd this scene must look with me trying to support his weight.

Except, it does feel like I help because we get him standing and we slowly make our way over to his usual sleeping spot.

Each step feels like a battle in itself. My limbs ache and the world tilts slightly with every movement. But I'm determined, working to steady him as best I can. I focus on the rhythmic sound of our footsteps, on the feel of the cave floor beneath me. It's all I can do to keep moving forward.

When we finally reach his spot, it feels like a victory. I slump down, grateful for the support of the cold stone beneath me. Kroaicho releases a small sigh of relief as I help him settle into a comfortable position, propping him up against one of the larger stones.

"Stay here," I murmur, then race off again.

20

Kroaicho

My body protests the moment zha's warmth is gone.

When zha returns, I expect zha to sit across from me or maybe start fussing over the fire. But instead, Olivia does something I never would have predicted. Zha carefully lays down on my chest, zha's small body curling up against mine.

I stiffen in surprise, my skin flickering between blue and orange in confusion and something else. My many limbs freeze in place, unsure of what to do or how to react. I glance down at zha, baffled, but zha only murmurs softly, "I need you near me right now. I don't really like being touched. Not softly, at least. But if you squeeze me hard... well, not too hard. I don't want to die."

The fragility in zha's voice catches me off guard. I don't understand it. Zha doesn't make sense. But for some reason, I don't push zha away. The feeling of zha's tiny body pressed against mine is strange. Unfamiliar. But not unpleasant.

My arms hover awkwardly, unsure of what to do with themselves. I'm not used to this kind of... closeness. Zhasie don't touch like this. We're solitary, always keeping our distance. My zhann taught me that. But Olivia—zha is different. Zha doesn't seem to follow those rules. And for once, I don't mind.

Zha said to squeeze, and so I make my limbs stop hovering and do as zha asked. Zha lets out a high-pitched sound and I stop, skin lighting up red when I think I have harmed zha.

"I'm alright. Just not quite so tight," zha says.

With a delicacy I reserve for my most prized treasures, I move my limbs back around zha's small body, slowly increasing pressure until zha speaks again.

"Yes," zha tells me. "Just like that."

I can feel zha's trembling start to ease as zha settles against me, zha's breath becoming more even.

"Two and not one," zha mutters.

I open my mouth to ask what zha means, but zha speaks again. "I'm shutting down," zha whispers to me. "Sorry."

I don't understand what that means, but don't ask zha to explain. I realize I've had enough explanations and arguments for the day. There's no energy left for anything at all.

Zha's heartbeat, which had been rapid with fear, gradually slows, matching the rhythm of mine.

It takes me a moment to realize that zha is getting covered with my blood—my wounds are still seeping, and the dark, sticky liquid is smeared across zha's skin and clothing. But Olivia doesn't seem to care. Zha is too focused on finding warmth and comfort.

Zha's head rests against the larger section of my chest, right near the bioluminescent patches that faintly glow with each breath I take. Zha's eyes flutter shut as zha finally starts to drift off, zha's body limp with exhaustion.

I watch zha sleep, feeling my skin shift between colors again, a confused mix of blue and orange that I can't quite control. It's unsettling, this whole experience. I've never let someone be this close to me before. Not since my zhann. I've never wanted someone to be close to me. Not like this.

And yet, here zha is, this fragile human, curled up on my chest as if it's the most natural thing in the world.

I think of my zhann—of the way zha used to protect me when I was a zhannel, how zha would teach me about treasure and the importance of building my own hoard. I lost zha before I ever got the chance to learn everything zha had to teach. With Olivia, it feels like I'm learning something I never knew I needed.

It feels... strange. But not bad.

I let out a slow breath, the tightness in my chest loosening a little as I relax into the moment. My limbs, awkward at first, find a more natural position, curling slightly around Olivia without fully enclosing zha. I want zha to feel safe, even if I don't quite understand why it matters so much.

The warmth of the fire mixes with the warmth of Olivia's body, and despite my confusion, I feel a strange kind of peace settle over me. My skin glows a soft orange, brighter than it's been in a long time.

It's not just the relief of surviving the fight. It's something more. A quiet contentment that I've never experienced before.

I can feel Olivia's steady breathing, the way zha's small body rises and falls with each inhale and exhale. The warmth of it seeps into me, and I find myself watching zha's peaceful face as zha sleeps. Zha looks so fragile, so vulnerable, and yet there's something about zha that feels... strong. Resilient.

The thought is odd, but I can't deny it. I've seen the way zha faces the world—fearlessly, even when everything seems against zha. Zha's like a tiny flame that refuses to go out, no matter how hard the wind blows. A living thing, zha's fire, just like zha said about the sticks.

I would have never known about the sticks if I hadn't listened. Hadn't had zha to teach me.

And here zha is, resting on me as if zha trusts me completely.

My skin glows a little brighter, the colors shifting gently between blue and orange. I don't fully understand what I'm feeling, but for the first time in a long while, I don't feel the need to hoard. I don't feel the pull to go out searching for treasures. Not right now. Right now, this moment feels like enough.

Eventually, my own exhaustion catches up to me. The aches and pains from the battle still throb in the background, but they feel distant now, muted by the warmth and comfort of Olivia's presence.

I let my eyes close, my limbs settling more comfortably around zha. I'm not used to this. I don't know if I'll ever get used to it. But as I feel myself drifting off, I can't help but think that maybe, just maybe, I don't hate it.

Sleep pulls me at me slowly, and the last thing I see before I slip into unconsciousness is the tiny human still resting against me, zha's breath soft and even, zha's body warm against mine. My skin flickers one last time, a soft, contented glow of orange before everything fades to black.

For the first time in a long while, I sleep without dreaming.

21

Olivia

I wake up to the most glorious pressure and then I come to myself enough to realize it's because I'm lying on top of Kroaicho. I brace for a reaction, but there is no answering anger.

Oddly enough, the pressure loosens something within my chest, and although he's restricting my movement, I feel like I can breathe better.

It takes me back to the hugs my mum once gave me and that feeling of safety. I don't understand what the difference is between this, and being touched in other ways, but I don't pull away from it. There's not that visceral reaction that has hounded me from my first memories.

It's... nice.

The arousal surges again, of course, but I ignore it. That's not what this is about. Instead, I focus on the pressure of his arms on my back. The steady rise and fall of his chest as he sleeps under me. The oddly slow pace of his beating heart.

It's easily a third of the speed of my own and at first that worries me, but then I start counting it, the sound lulling me into peaceful drifting.

I'm not sure how much time passes before he starts shifting under me. I shift my head so I can look up at his oddly curved neck. He stiffens and straightens his head, bright pink eyes popping open in alarm, limbs squeezing me just a little too tight.

He blinks once, twice, then relaxes again.

"How are you feeling?" I ask him.

"Mostly healed," he replies, and my eyebrows shoot up.

"Truly? Those wounds were deep last night. I really should have figured out a way to dress them, but it was just too much and I—"

"No need," he says, interrupting me. "All they needed was for me to sleep."

I snort. "You are so strange."

His skin lights up in his outraged purple, but it's muted so I know he isn't particularly offended. "You are the strangest creature here, Olivia. Probably on the whole planet."

I clack my teeth together, mimicking what he does with his tusks when I am being particularly vexing and his skin lights up to his amused white.

"I didn't expect you to return," he tells me, skin shifting to blue.

I take a moment to appreciate just how obvious emotions are with him, then respond. "I didn't either," I admit.

I pull in a deep breath, then speak again. "Are you really going to keep me here?

For the first time, I see something other than irritation or frustration flare on his skin. Some odd mix of pink and purple I've never seen before.

"No," he breathes out, closing his glowing eyes.

I feel a pang of something in my chest—something unfamiliar. It's not anger, not irritation. It's softer and gentler, and I don't know what to do with it.

"Why do you want to find other humans so badly?" he asks, voice quiet and lacking his usual irritation.

"I just... I don't want to be alone," I say in a whisper, surprising myself. " I never thought I would, but I miss being part of something."

His skin lights up blue again. "But you're not alone. I'm here."

"I know, Kroaicho," I tell him. "But it's not the same. You don't understand."

"I don't," he admits. "I don't understand why you can't just be content with the hoard.

Then he looks at me with intensity. "I am starting to understand the... value of connection. I feel that value with you, and it helps me imagine how it might mean you need more than just the embrace of treasure and the whisperings of their stories. But... would you just stay?"

I look over at the scattered pile, once again annoyed that it always comes back to a pile of junk with him. "I just... can't," I reply, my voice rough. "I need more."

It's always things that are more important and I'm so sick of it.

"A human?" he asks, breaking me out of my thoughts.

"Yes, I—"

I break off with a yelp as he shifts from under me, mind reeling at the odd movements of a multi-segmented body with six limbs.

Next thing I know, he's placing me on my feet and stalking out of the cave. It seems like the end of almost every conversation we have and this time I don't have it in me to yell after him.

Instead, I huff out a breath and look around for the source of the terrible stench. It's the damn carcass, I realize and steel myself to haul it to the stream and toss it in.

"Fuck," I say, summing up the whole situation, pressing my fingers into my aching eyes.

* * *

I've finally cleared out all of the blood and gore and I'm trying not to gag as I toss the long green shorn hair into the water that I used as a mop when I hear screeching.

I freeze.

Human screeching… Farsi human screeching. It's Rin. I recognize her powerful voice, as if she's practiced yelling at people for years or something.

I groan, thinking back to the conversation with Kroaicho and how I didn't pay attention when he didn't say "humans," but instead said "a human."

She is going to kill me and I completely deserve it. Dammit. She'll turn that practiced yell on me and I'll fucking wilt.

I swallow hard, mind flitting over all of the failed social interactions I've had in my life. Then to the small bit of elation I felt when she called me her friend.

Ninety-five percent hates you, I think, with a grimace on my face.

By the time the yelling is close enough to let me know they are almost in this part of the cave, I have my mask firmly in place. Hopefully she won't notice that my smile is wobbly.

I turn, body stiff, as Kroaicho walks in. His skin is the darkest purple I have ever seen on him, his pink eyes partially closed, the spikes on his head flinching to the side each time Rin's voice reaches a particularly loud peak.

"He is going to cut you into so many tiny little—" Rin suddenly breaks off when she catches sight of me, mouth opening in shock.

"Olivia!" she cries out, voice completely different now. I flinch again when I hear the happiness there. It won't last long.

It truly doesn't, but it's not on my account, but instead because Kroaicho takes a few more quick strides and then dumps her unceremoniously on top of a pile of trinkets.

She growls out her rage, then switches to a barking language I've never heard before. "I am going to enjoy it when he finds you."

Kroaicho doesn't respond, but simply whirls around, two of his limbs stumbling over the others in his haste, and heads back the way he came.

"Zhann knew best," he mutters. "No pets. Terrible, terrible pets."

Rin scrambles up, running toward me. "Olivia! I thought we'd never find you, thank *Allah*. Are you hurt? Did he hurt you? That... that—"

I cut her off before she can get rolling again. "I'm not hurt."

"Good," she says briskly, her new green, glowing markings thrumming under her skin. The braids are new, too. "Let's go."

She marches over and grabs on to my arm and I hold myself rigid so I don't lash out.

"What's wrong?"

"N-nothing. It's just... just that there's no use. I've tried and all I ever did was almost die trying to escape," I say.

It's a deflection, but it's also the truth.

Her shoulders slump. "Are you sure?"

"Yes. There are so many deadly things in these caves. Venom bugs, things that look like cats with dripping green slime, and this really big..." I shudder. "...something that almost killed Kroaicho it was so strong."

"Kroaicho. Right. So the terrible kidnapper has a name," she says, her lip lifted in... disgust?

It's so much harder to tell with humans.

I shake my head at the thought. This is exactly what I wanted. Humans to be with. And here I am being incredibly ungrateful.

I let out a long breath and let my mask drop. It's no use. "I'm the reason you're here, Rin."

"Of course you are," she replies. "We've been looking for you."

I blink. "You have?"

"Yes! Why do you sound surprised?" she shoots back.

I shrug. "I just... I don't know."

"Kira and Ree came really close to grabbing Kroaicho and beating the information out of him, but he kept getting away."

My jaw drops. He didn't tell me something that important? "He saw them?"

"I assume so, since he ran off like a coward and caved in the tunnels behind him," she replies.

She's cursing in Farsi about his ancestry as my mind whirls.

I shouldn't have expected anything else. I close my eyes and push it out of my mind, heart aching.

"Tell me what's been happening," I grit out.

***

It's been at least a day. Rin ran out of stories to tell and aside from periodically trying to leave the way Kroaicho brought her in and being blocked by him, she hasn't done much beyond pace and mutter in Farsi.

It's making me want to shut down, but I keep pushing it off, especially since she won't seem to listen to my attempts to implicate myself in her kidnapping. My guilt is like a steady wound and as long as she denies it, the wound remains.

Finally, she plops down beside me and pulls a braid over one ear. My eyes widen when I recognize the shape.

I pull my hair back and turn so she can see. "Do my ears look like yours?"

She snorts out a breath. "Well, at least you haven't had sex with him."

"What?" I say a little too loudly. How could she know about these strange urges? And what does that have to do with anything?

"You're going to change until you have sex. Ree explained it to me. It looks like you got some of Kuret's traits by coming in contact with me. Those are Qendi ears. Any other changes?"

I will my sleeves to pull back and she grimaces. "Those are from some sort of elf-like alien. They are not friendly."

She shows me similar silver glittering on her skin, which is really pretty mixed in with the green branching marks. I point at one. "What about those?"

"Also from Kuret. I uh, slept with him." She looks down at her hands.

Is she feeling shy about it? Or ashamed? Ugh... I can't tell and my heart starts beating faster as I think of what to say that won't give it away or make her angry.

Luckily, she starts talking again.

"I'm not making rational decisions anymore, Olivia. I used to be so careful and thoughtful... My parents would be so disappointed in me and how I've thrown away all the things they ever taught me."

Oh no, I think, panicking. She needs comfort and I'm pretty sure even Kroaicho would be a better choice for this moment.

I try for a neutral topic instead. "Is your family still..."

I trail off, realizing I don't know how to end that sentence.

"Alive? Not my parents. And the rest of them clearly aren't family. They sold me. They're why I'm here."

I might not understand what I see on her face, but her raw voice tells me how upset she is about that. Of course she's upset about it. I scramble to think of a response, annoyed with my useless brain.

"We are walking statistics," I blurt out, then cringe.

"Come again?" she says, voice confused now instead of gutted, at least.

It wasn't what I was aiming for, but I lean more into it. "It was my family, too. Statistically speaking, they are the ones most likely to sell people into trafficking."

She grunts. "Right." She shakes her head, white braids clinking. "It doesn't matter. What I'm trying to say is... I'm going crazy here."

"Well, I think that is pretty normal when—"

She cuts me off. "No. You don't understand. I can't make up my mind about anything. I'm going in circles. I followed the first alien that seemed like they were protecting me around like a puppy and they ended up being a terrible, terrible person. Then Kuret, the person who saved me from them treats me really well and is pretty much the most understanding person I have ever met... I really mean that, too. I never thought a man would actually listen, but he does. Without judgement and with this incredibly flexible personality that just... sticks with me, no matter how much I vacillate. You know?"

I nod. I don't know, but I also would rather she keep talking while I try to figure out how to respond.

"I went from being a virgin, to deciding to jump him in all of about two seconds, Liv. As in hating his guts to giving away something that should have been precious."

She pauses, but luckily I've thought of a response by now. "Do you regret it?"

"What? The sex?" she asks.

I nod and she purses her lips and thinks for a moment.

"No. No I don't. He's patient, and kind, and he takes all of this crazy that is going on in my head right now in stride. He's steady. All the time... and it's exactly what I need right now. What I need for the rest of my life. But... I just don't feel like myself anymore."

"In what way?" I ask her, stalling.

"I can't make up my mind, Olivia. I hate violence, but next thing I know I'm killing a bunch of aliens. Then I give the person who saved me from a... terrible person a hard time about violence. Next thing I know I'm giving him my virginity. And then still giving him a hard time about the same things, over and over. I'm losing my mind."

I finally stop panicking when I realize that this is just simple psychology. Maybe I can help her after all."Are you expecting to be rational after waking up in another part of the galaxy?" I ask."More rational than I have been," she mutters.I snort. "If life has taught me anything, it's that people don't make sense. Why expect your actions to make sense after your world literally disappears when we, humans I mean, didn't make sense before we came here?"She turns fully to me, and I struggle to maintain eye contact, wanting to let her know that I care.

"What?" she asks, brows low.I look away, no longer able to handle my brain screaming at me. "You made choices," I clarify. "Some of them bad. Some of them good. Some didn't align with what you usually would do. Or the beliefs you thought you had. Right?""Right," she says, voice more sure now.

It gives me confidence to keep pushing my point. "Stop trying to explain the why and instead ask if it led you where you wanted.""I'm a prisoner in a cave, Liv," she says, her voice dry.

It draws a laugh from me. "I can't help you there. I mean with this alien you jumped. Do you regret it? You said you didn't, but then you circled back to guilt. You need to decide about the regret so you can let go of the guilt... or drown in it. Your choice, but do you regret it?"

"No. I don't," she reiterates.

"Then stop thinking about what was rational for you on Earth and start thinking about what is rational for you right now," I conclude.

She clucks her tongue, then sucks her teeth as I wonder if she's going to finally get mad at me now. I talked for a really long time. Surely I said something wrong in all of that. I just know it...

It's so much easier with Kroaicho. I just say whatever I want, since everything is going to sound strange to him anyway. And he lights up with clear emotional responses. Mostly purple or blue... but, still.

I'm terrible with humans.

Stupid, stupid, stupid, I chant to myself.

"How did you get so smart, Liv?" she says and my chanting stops instantly.

Wait. I said something right?

She huffs out a breath. "I see your point, but... well, that elf-like alien... he tried to um, well you know."

I blink, then catch up to what she means and anger surges. "Did Kuret kill him?"

"Yes," she says, voice firm. "It was the most violent thing I have ever seen in my life. It was like he... enjoyed it."

I gulp, then decide to admit to some of my own guilt. "I killed when they held me in the cells. I... I really liked the way it felt too."

My eyes are locked to my hands, afraid of what she will say, shoulders tense.

She puts a hand on mine and luckily I see her movement in time to keep myself from flinching.

"It's okay, Liv," she tells me in a gentle voice. "I didn't understand it then, but I do now. I mean, I don't think I feel quite the same thing Kuret does, but I can't deny that there is satisfaction when I see one of the hunters die."

My anger surges even higher, and not just because she's touching me. What she's told me about this being a hunting ground makes my blood boil.

"Anyway," she says with a huff. "Sorry to lay all of this on you, but you are so easy to talk to."

I am? Usually people just tell me how stiff I am and I avoid them. I'm not sure that she's being objective about me...

"I can let go of that guilt. What still bothers me," she continues, "is that it was no time at all between someone trying to force me that I slept with Kuret. It doesn't feel right."

"Come on, Rin," I challenge. "You're acting like there is only one way someone can respond to trauma. That's just what society says, not what actually happens."

"But jumping straight into bed with someone right after..." She shudders, seeming lost for words for a moment before continuing without naming it. "...that?"

"Why not?" I ask. "Are you supposed to be afraid of it your whole life? Is that the 'proper' response?"

"Some people are! You shouldn't mock them," she chides.

"I'm not, Rin. I would never mock someone's fear. All I'm saying is you're going to process it the way you need. Again... we are circling. Do you regret sleeping with Kuret? Choosing him?"

"No. But..."

"Alright, then let's stop the nonsense, Rin! Maybe you wouldn't have done it so hastily outside of a crash landing on a fucking alien planet and someone almost taking it from you forcefully. But... can't you see how those very things might make it seem even more important for you to get to choose?"

She blinks slowly, absorbing my words, but her body is still tight. A frisson of anxiety goes through me as I wonder if I've gone too far, not sure what her face is trying to tell me, but I ignore my fear.

I take a deep breath and double down. "It's like with grief. Society says you're supposed to show up for the funeral, act in certain ways, speak certain ways. But the person is dead. They don't care; it's just all the other people there expecting something from someone. Except, what about the people who know, deep down, that the funeral will make their grief process worse? What about the people whose grief shows up as being reckless?"

Her face twitches. "I did that," she whispers, "after my *bābā* died."

"Sure," I tell her, on a roll now, "and it was what you needed at the time. Or what about people seeking relationships as quickly as possible to fill the void their partner left behind? Be too quick and people judge, wait too long and they nag. We're talking about people's judgement, not about what someone needs or what is 'normal,' because there is no one certain way to process trauma, Rin. It's messy and terrible and we just get through it."

She lets out a long breath. "I see what you mean, Liv. I was reckless when I came here, too. It was a form of grieving, except not just my parents, but... my whole life. But that doesn't mean I need to punish myself for it, does it?"

"Exactly," I respond, glad she can see my point.

"You really are the most—"

She doesn't finish her sentence because there is a splash from the nearby stream and we both freeze.

22

Olivia

When a yellow tentacle smacks onto the bank, we both yelp and Rin clutches me close to her. There's too much fear pumping through me to be angry, and, just like with Ree, I clutch her back, squeezing tight just like I prefer.

This place is the scariest fucking planet…

I'm pulling in a breath to scream for Kroaicho when a head pops above the stream, the flow of water splashing up and over on one side.

It's a human head, though the eyes are just as black as Rin's but somehow… far creepier. More predatory.

"The fuck…" I whisper.

The head keeps rising and we both breath out a relieved breath when we see a mouth rise out of the water. With the widest grin I've ever seen on anyone.

"Yes!" the figure says in a voice as sunny as her hair. "I knew it!"

Rin's still shaking beside me and she starts talking in a wavering voice. "Will the tentacle monster… hurt us?"

The woman looks down. "Oh, no! Those are mine."

She rises out of the water more and I realize that the tentacles are coming from her head. My stomach lurches at the sight of them wriggling from somewhere that shouldn't ever…

I stop the thoughts there, chiding myself for suddenly being judgmental. Not being that way is something I've prided myself on and doing that to someone as sweet… and alright, also fucking scary… looking just isn't right.

"My name is Eli, by the way," she chirps.

"Nice to meet you, Eli," I say automatically.

"Oh! Are you Australian? That is so cool!" she gushes, and my eye twitches.

I should be used to it by now, but Americans are the worst at telling the difference.

"No, I'm from New Zealand," I correct her, "but I did spend a lot of time in other countries when I was young, including Australia, so my accent is mixed."

"Oh, sorry." Her tentacles droop for a moment, but then perk right back up. "That is even cooler! I knew I would find you! Wroahk was all grumpy and 'you can't go' about it, but we tasted your blood in the water and I knew this was the way to find you. Oh, hi, you must be Rin. Kira came to get me after you were snatched and after she saw the water coming up out of the ground and just let me tell you that Wroahk is going to be so pissed," she draws out the last word and adds a flair of drama to it.

"But I knew that I was—"

I feel bad about it, but I cut her off. I don't know how she managed to say all of that without taking a breath, but I think if I let her keep going she won't stop. "Who is Wroahk?"

"Oh. Well, he's sorta my shark-octopus uh, boyfriend. He's really sweet, and also the biggest possible jerk ever. He has some anger issues that we are working on right now. So I really, really think you shouldn't mention that I almost died. I—"

This time it's Rin who cuts her off. "You almost died?"

"Oh... right," Eli says, two tentacles coming up out of the water and wrapping around her shoulders like she's comforting herself. "I got caught against some rocks and the water was going through my gills so fast it hurt... But I got free! Totally safe and sound and I am so happy that I found you. I am going to taunt Wroahk about how much bigger he is and how he couldn't fit and how I was able to trick him to... oh, you shouldn't probably bring that up either. He might kill something if you do. I mean, not you. Well, not you as long as you make sure I say you're community. You'll be—"

"Can you take us back that way?" I interrupt.

"Oh, no, no," Eli says, more tentacles wrapping around her. "You would definitely die. And I don't really think... Don't tell Wroahk I said this, but I don't think I should get back in there either. It was really scary."

She stops talking suddenly, shivering and my brain is finally able to catch up with all of the chatter to realize that she risked her life for me. I feel doubly guilty for thinking about how odd she looks, and I don't know how to ever repay her for what she did.

For now, I just offer what I can. My name. "Please call me Liv," I say in a quiet voice. "And thank you so much for searching for me. You didn't have to and I appreciate it."

She makes a *pshhh* sound, which oddly sounds more like a whale than a human. "Of course I had to! I just—"

It's Kroaicho who interrupts her this time. "No, no, no. No more humans."

"Oh!" Eli says, raising her small fists in the air. "It's you! You are a terrible person keeping Liv here without—"

"It's alright, Eli," I say to stop her breathless tirade. She has gills, it seems, which means she can speak forever without taking a pause.

"Just let us go," Rin hisses at Kroaicho.

I open my mouth to tell her it's no use, but Kroaicho responds before I can. "Alright."

What? I whip my head over to him, mouth dropping open.

"I will find one of your others. I will need their help carrying," he says.

"We can walk... Hey, wait!" Eli says, but Kroaicho isn't listening.

He's doing his six-limb gallop, the passage lit up pink from the glow of his skin as he runs away from us.

My chest hurts and I don't know why. This is what I've wanted the whole time, but I somehow thought he would keep resisting.

And what does the pink color mean?

23

Olivia

I kept expecting him to want something from me. Kept waiting for that shoe to drop and for him to reveal his angle. Instead, he's giving me what I want. It's almost like... he sees me as valuable without considering what I can give or what he can take?

The thought stabs through me, a thrill rising, then quickly transitioning to pain.

Why do I feel like I'm going to cry? I rub at my aching eyes, but instead of making them feel better, it just gets worse. And worse. Soon after I'm hissing, then moaning out in pain.

Someone grabs on to my hands. "Stop, Olivia. They are changing. You're just going to hurt yourself."

My heart starts pounding. "I hate change," I mutter.

"I don't blame you," Eli says in a soothing voice. "Just breathe through it, though."

When I feel a wet pressure, then an odd suction and realize it's probably a tentacle, the anger starts to build higher, but the pain overtakes it instead.

Long minutes later and multiple sharp intakes of breath and it's over. I blink once—then twice—and then not at all, as my brain expects the usual bleariness to set in, the normal sensation of sluggish eyes adjusting to a dim cave. Except... I can see everything. Clear as day.

What the hell?

It's disorienting, like waking up and realizing you've grown an extra limb overnight. I blink again, hard this time, but nothing changes. I can see the shapes of stalagmites, the blue glow of mushrooms faintly pulsing in the shadows, and even the tiny glimmer of water droplets hanging from the ceiling. All of it is sharp and vibrant.

Eli's muted coloring is suddenly a canary yellow and the green of Rin's markings are beautifully vibrant. So vibrant it's on the edge of pain.

What... is going on?

My heartbeat picks up, and I start to push myself up, but there's something warm and firm holding me down. I look down, realizing there is a tentacle wrapped around me. Supporting me.

The anger is mixed in with fear and panic.

"Okay, Olivia," I mutter under my breath. "No need to panic. You've survived worse."

Gingerly, I try to wiggle out of Eli's grip and look around the cave, which is lit mostly by those damn, bright bioluminescent mushrooms. They glow a deep, serene blue, but as I move toward them, I wince, eyes stinging from the glare.

What the...? I raise a hand to shield my face, surprised by how harsh the light feels now. It's like I'm staring into the sun, except I know these mushrooms weren't this bright before.

Squinting, I turn away, navigating toward a small pool of condensation that's gathered on one side of the cave. The water is still and clear, just enough to catch a glimpse of the light reflection.

And that's when I see it. The pink glow.

The reflection staring back at me isn't entirely mine anymore. My eyes are glowing. Not just reflecting light, no. They are glowing. Bright pink, like two neon signs in a sea of darkness.

I frantically turn back to Eli and Rin. Eli is bouncing up and down in the water. "Oh, they are so pretty! And I can tell you are seeing better, aren't you? Mine are really useful too, but they are scary, which I guess has other uses... but yours!"

My stomach does a flip. "What the hell is going on?"

A few strides and I am over at the stream to get a better look. The face is still me—still Olivia, same freckles, same slightly crooked nose—but my eyes...

I lean closer, my reflection rippling in the water. I wave my hand in front of my face, but the glowing pink stays, vibrant and unnerving. It's not... bad, exactly. Just unexpected. Kind of like a really creepy party trick I didn't ask for. Just like the weird fully green ones, though I suppose Eli is right. These are far more useful.

Okay, breathe. This is weird. But it's not the weirdest thing that's happened.

The moment of panic flares then dims as I see Eli's one simple, undeniable truth: at least I can see. And, apparently, I can see in the dark.

"That's... something, I guess?" I mutter, staring at my reflection a little longer. "Glowing eyes and night vision. Yeah, okay. Not the worst thing."

Rin *tsks*. "Are things overly bright? I got braceaaer eyes and they hurt in bright light sometimes."

"Yes," I say distractedly.

Useful, yes. Still, it's unnerving. I splash a little water on my face, half-hoping the pink glow will fade. It doesn't. But at least the cold water feels good, grounding me. I can handle this. I can figure out what's happening. After all, surviving this planet has pretty much been one long string of weird stuff.

Why stop now?

I turn my back on the puddle, deciding not to dwell too much on my new ocular upgrades. There's something else catching my attention now, and it's hard to explain exactly why, but...

Kroaicho's hoard.

I greedily look over at the pile of glowing rocks, twisted vines, and scrap metal that Kroaicho has obsessively collected. Up until now, I've always thought it looked like a bunch of junk—a magpie's dream gone horribly wrong. But now? Now it's like I'm seeing it for the first time.

The rocks are glowing more vibrantly than I remember, hues of orange, green, and violet blending together in intricate patterns that shimmer with life. The vines, too, have taken on a strange beauty, their twisted shapes creating delicate, interwoven designs that seem almost artistic.

And the scrap metal, the random bits and pieces I once thought were useless, now catch the light in a way that makes them sparkle, revealing layers of detail I never noticed before.

"Pretty..." I breathe out as I take a step closer, my eyes wide. "How did I not see this before?"

It's like someone turned up the saturation on the entire world. Colors I didn't even know existed seem to dance across the surfaces, every object in the hoard radiating with a sort of... well, magic. I crouch down next to it, reaching out hesitantly to touch one of the glowing rocks. It's warm to the touch, pulsing slightly beneath my fingers.

It's almost like they are whispering to me. Trying to tell me something. Their story? Is this what Kroaicho means? Can he perceive even more than this? Is this how he learned my language so freakishly fast?

Even with these new eyes, I still don't understand how that could work...

But I can't deny the evidence before me. Everything has changed. Nothing in this pile is ugly anymore and each one teases me with the suggestion that there is... more.

What does he see when he looks at me?

There is this sudden, overwhelming desire to know what Kroaicho knows. For him to share what I can't sense.

"Okay, this is seriously weird," I mutter, but there's a smile tugging at the corners of my mouth. Despite the strangeness of it all, there's something oddly satisfying about the way the light plays across the objects.

As if Kroaicho's random collection is more than just a hoard. It's a masterpiece.

I run my hand over the surface of a twisted vine, feeling its rough texture beneath my fingertips. "I'm starting to get why you're obsessed with this stuff," I say softly, glancing over my shoulder to where Kroaicho disappeared.

There's no logic to the assortment of rocks, vines, and random scrap metal, but there's something thrilling about it. Each piece feels alive under my fingers, glowing faintly with hues I didn't even know existed.

"Liv?" Rin asks hesitantly, but I ignore her.

Suddenly, the urge to rearrange things hits me, like a burst of inspiration I can't explain. Before I know it, I'm sifting through the pile, carefully stacking rocks and vines in new patterns, arranging them just so... everything should feel balanced. There's a rhythm to it, a flow, and I find myself humming softly as I work, completely absorbed in the task.

"Olivia the decorator," I murmur under my breath, amused at myself. "If only people could see me now."

"Liv?" Eli calls out, but I'm too busy to pay her any mind.

I pause for a moment, taking a step back to admire my handiwork. It isn't quite right. Too much green on that side, I decide. Then I'm shifting it all over again.

The hoard looks different now, more purposeful. Like I've helped it become what it was always meant to be. There's a strange satisfaction in it, a sense of completion.

But then, reality catches up to me, and I realize I've just spent the last several minutes fawning over Kroaicho's hoard like it's a piece of fine art. I blink, pulling my hands away from the glowing rocks, a sudden flush of embarrassment creeping up my neck.

"What the hell am I doing?" I mutter, shaking my head as if I can snap myself out of whatever spell I've fallen under.

Eli and Rin are laughing and I feel my face flushing with my embarrassment. "Are you with us, Liv?" Eli says with her cheerful voice.

It helps soothe my self-consciousness. I gulp, and then try to explain. "Well, I'm guessing all of this looks like a pile of trash, right?"

They look around. "Well," Eli drawls, tentacles waving.

"Yes," Rin says, voice as decisive as always.

I smile. "I thought so too. But now I... quite literally have different eyes. And I think I understand Kroaicho a bit more..."

I trail off, not sure what else to say. It's super weird and not something that can be explained.

I can't deny the weird pull I feel toward the hoard now. It's like something in me has shifted, like I'm starting to see the world the way Kroaicho sees it. I glance over to the same passage, my thoughts drifting to the alien's earlier words about hoarding and treasure. Maybe there's more to it than I thought.

With a sigh, I stand up, brushing the dust from my hands. The hoard gleams in the dim light, and I can't help but feel a small sense of pride at how neatly it's arranged now. Maybe Kroaicho won't even notice.

Or maybe he will, and I'll have some serious explaining to do.

"Great," I mutter. "Just what I need."

Still, there's a part of me that can't quite shake the fascination. I take one last look at the hoard, then turn away, the strange warmth of the cave settling over me like a blanket.

As I walk back toward where the women are. I can't help but feel like something fundamental has changed. Not just in me, with my new freaky glowing eyes, but in the way I see the world—and Kroaicho. There's something more here, something deeper than just survival. Something I'm only just beginning to understand.

And as unsettling as that realization is, there's a small part of me that's excited by it. Curious, even.

"One step at a time," I tell myself, glancing back at the pile of glowing treasures with a hungry look in my eye.

There's a prickle of desire, then I berate myself that I'm being the same sort of materialist I've always hated. Then desire surges again.

"Okay, fuck it," I grit out and head back to it, the sound of laughter starting up again.

As I sink my hands into Kroaicho's treasure pile, I can't help but giggle like an idiot. It's ridiculous, but it feels like I'm swimming through someone's junkyard in zero gravity.

There's more laughter in the cave and I feel like it should matter, but it doesn't

I pick up a twisted piece of metal that looks like it came off an ancient spacecraft and wave it around like a sword. "Captain Olivia, intergalactic pirate," I declare, grinning to myself. "Fear my junk saber!"

Another laugh bubbles out of me, uncontrollable. My brain knows this is absurd, but it's like something inside me just snapped—maybe the glowing eyes are making me giddy? Who knows. Either way, it's nice to let loose for a moment, to forget about the constant life-and-death stakes of surviving on this planet.

I dig deeper into the pile, uncovering a rock that pulses between shades of violet and green. "Oooh, pretty," I coo, holding it up to the dim light of the cave. My glowing pink eyes reflect back at me on the rock's smooth surface. For a second, I think about taking it as a souvenir, but then I remember it's Kroaicho's hoard. Even though I'm having a blast playing around, I'm not ready to start swiping things. Yet.

"Liv?" calls out another annoying voice.

A few more minutes pass in a blur of giddy giggles, rearranging rocks into little towers and vines into spirals. It's oddly satisfying, like organizing the world's strangest puzzle. Eventually, the high wears off, and I realize I'm sitting in the middle of a glowing mess, giggling to myself like a lunatic.

I stop and glance around. "Oh, God," I mutter, feeling heat rush to my cheeks again. "What am I doing?"

Then I hear the laughter again and look over to Eli and Rin clutching their stomachs and wiping tears from their eyes.

I scramble out of the pile, trying to regain some shred of dignity. "What the fuck, you two? Couldn't you have stopped me?"

As I stand up, I catch myself almost drooling over the now perfectly arranged pile of glowing treasures. There's this nagging part of me that wants to dive back in, to lose myself in it all again. But no. I resist. I'm not a magpie—or, at least, I wasn't before today.

"Okay, Olivia, focus," I mutter, forcefully turning my attention away from the hoard and back to the two women still laughing at me.

"You think we didn't try?" Rin gasps out. "Oh, I needed that laugh, though. Thank you, Liv."

"Yes," Eli says, still chuckling. "That was incredibly entertaining."

"Dammit," I mutter. "Did you pick up some seriously weird urges when your eyes changed?"

The two of them look at each other, then back to me while shaking their heads.

Of course not.

24

Kroaicho

The wind blows against my skin as I step out of the cave, my arms close against my torso to shield myself from the onslaught of dust and grit whipping through the air. My glow is still a deep pink, and I am steadily ignoring it and what it means. The sharp rocks and twisted trees of the landscape loom in the distance, barely visible through the haze. I squint, my spikes twitching with frustration as I begin the search for more of Olivia's people—humans, fragile creatures who seem to always be in danger.

How will they be of help carrying? I realize my error now, but it was really just an excuse to get away. To try to get my pink glow under control.

I don't understand why zha can't be content with just us. We've been here, in this cave, for days. The hoard is safe, our surroundings are stable, and I've seen no sign of threat... for at least a partial day.

Yet every time I suggest zha stay put, zha refuses, always insisting on finding the others, always pushing to go beyond what is safe. Zha doesn't understand this planet the way I do. It's not just the land or the storms. There are predators, ones that hunt by nightfall—vicious creatures that even I know to avoid, I'm as much a stranger here as zha is, and despite my superior physiology, you'd think zha would be more open to taking advice.

But zha doesn't listen. Zha never does. I am better off without zha.

I know it's a lie before my skin flares a brighter pink.

I trudge through the rough terrain, each step a reminder of how much I'd rather be back at the cave, sorting through my treasures. Instead, I'm out here, looking for other humans—people who may not even be alive anymore. I grumble under my breath, pushing through the storm, feeling the weight of the situation pressing down on me.

Time passes. I search, moving farther and farther from the cave, but I find nothing. No signs of life. No humans...

I feel the hackles on my neck rise at the realization that the gouged soil below that I am certain was once occupied by something huge.

The scattered pieces of debris down the gouged pit tell me that true enough something large once dominated the landscape, but whatever it is has long since left...

I feel my stomach drop and I don't need to look to see that my skin has begun to signal red.

Only one creature, to the best of my knowledge at least, in this world had the capacity to do something like this.

How could you forget that there's a trakeldon loose?

I frantically survey the area, and sure enough, there are a few tracks indicating the beasts presence. Thankfully none of them are recent, but I am not willing to test the demiurge any further than I already have and figure now's a good time as any to make myself scarce.

Once I've put enough distance between myself and impending death, it's only a matter of time before I feel myself calming down enough to allow my thoughts to wander to other things.

Naturally, the first thing they wind up on is Olivia.

The glow of my body dims to a soft, dull blue as confusion overrides my barely restrained fear and settles in. I don't understand why zha insists on this search. I don't understand why it matters to zha so much. If zha can't be content with just the two of us... what else is there?

The other humans can just walk away. Why won't they?

Pointless questions with no answers, utterly impractical, yet for some inane reason my mind chooses to agonize over them.

... was it possible that the human must have infected me with something?

The anger I feel at myself for the perfectly rational suspicion is aggravating.

None of this is the way of the zhasie. The hoard must always be my priority, just like it has always been. Zha will have to decide.

My middle segment aches. Zha will not choose the hoard. Zha will choose freedom, zha's own most desired treasure.

I realize my error in letting the thoughts whirl when I hear the battle cry. I whip around, certain I'm about to meet my end, but instead of striking me, the large black and green figure deflects its sharp blade to the side at the last moment.

Zha yells out again, a harsh coughing sound of a language and attacks before I have a chance to start making sense of it.

Except when I try to swipe back, I can't make contact and zha's knife misses again. Long braids of thick black hair whirl as the figure tries to strike again, once again changing the angle of the blow at the last moment.

I take an experimental swipe and find myself doing the same. We can't hit each other for some inexplicable reason. Now that I'm not facing imminent death, I take a closer look at the figure. Zha is tall, and vaguely human shaped, but the similarities end there. Zha's glowing green eyes are narrowed at me, hatred clear in them.

This time I don't make the mistake of assuming the green means signaling to mate. If it was, zha would be from a very violent culture indeed. The marks are familiar...

They were on the white-haired human, I realize. I was uncomfortable with zha's green signaling as I took zha to Olivia, but I need to keep reminding myself that other species don't signal this way.

I rarely dealt with traders on my home planet, but now I am wondering how anyone was able to trade with outsiders without knowing their emotions. It's incredibly annoying.

When this one flings zha's arms to the side and yells out its rage, though, I have to concede that there are other ways to figure out emotions.

I grind my tusks together, then hold out my arms in a placating gesture, then wave zha toward me, take a few steps back the way I came, then wave again. I don't know the words yet, but I don't need to, to know zha is cursing me, but zha follows.

My skin has time to transition back from purple and red to pink by the time we wind our way back to my hoard. My zhann would be horrified to know just how many are there right now... and me bringing another.

Lunacy.

But I keep trudging along, my chest tighter and tighter with each step, the pink all but blinding at this point.

When I enter my hoard, I take dull note that it has been rearranged. I seek out Olivia, but then take my eyes back away before I look closely.

The dark one lets out a shout, then the white-haired one shouts back and they are running to each other and embracing in the most odd manner, both speaking that low, harsh language in a torrent.

I turn to my hoard, but my vision blurs and it brings me no comfort.

I hear Olivia padding up to me, the pattern of zha's footfalls seared in my mind.

"Will you come, Kroaicho?" zha asks, voice hesitant.

My skin flares orange for a long moment, then reality reasserts itself. "A zhasie does not leave the hoard," I grit out, tusks grinding.

"Right. I can see now that it is beautiful, and I get the desire to have more... but it is still just things. They are replaceable. People aren't, Kroaicho," zha tells me.

Zha's words strike deep and my skin lights up red. Zha is right and it scares me. Nothing should be as terrifying as this. No one part of your hoard should cause so much fear and anxiety.

I don't respond and instead sink into the mound, hoping it will help center my confused, racing thoughts.

"Alright," zha says, with an odd click to zha's voice.

Those familiar footfalls walk away, there's a moment of splashing and grunting and then all of them move down the passage. I open my mouth to say something, but don't know what to say, then close it again, tusks snapping together.

I hear zha's footsteps behind me again and a long intake of breath, then exhale. My middle segment aches as the footsteps recede. I know my zhann would be proud of my choice, but I feel miserable.

Soon, it's as quiet as a hoard should be, but everything is lit up pink. The worst color imaginable.

25

Olivia

Will my last memory of Kroaicho be of a big, hulking pink glow amid a pile of glittering junk? I've been asking myself that question over and over, but there is no answer. I want to turn back, but each time I think of it my mind pulls up every page I've ever read about Stockholm syndrome.

To think I scoffed at it, never understanding how anyone could grow that attached to anyone, let alone their kidnapper. Life has a way of humbling us. I shift through all of the pop psychology I've read, then the research articles, and even pull up the few lectures I listened to at college before I was kicked out.

None of it helps. All it does is make me far more prone to trip over things as I shuffle in the middle of the group of humans I've spent days longing to for, headed for the freedom I thought was the most important treasure possible.

Is this what that saying means? The one about things tasting of ash?

My mum told me I was never satisfied and I always hated it because it felt like they were the ones who were that way, always wanting more money. More things. But maybe she was right, because right now I have exactly what I thought I wanted and it feels… terrible.

I barely pay attention during the walk out of the caves, or the short trek through the thick forest. At first, Rin and Eli try to engage me in conversation, but I just can't get my mind to stop swirling long enough to understand their words.

Even the fake cheerfulness in their voice, which would normally put me on edge, doesn't make an impression. My mind just keeps spinning on how easily he turned his back. How easily he sunk into that pile of crap like it was the only thing that mattered. Just like everyone else in my life.

I thought he cared? He risked his life for me… and then rocks are what matter the most in the end? I try and I try, but I can't make sense of it. None of the patterns I have memorized to help me deal with humans help in this situation.

I'm finally jarred out of my mental looping when we stop and I realize it's so Kuret can gently place Eli down. She is frantically scratching at her skin as he moves a few giant logs so we can pass through a cave.

My heart constricts as we go through the familiar cool depths, once again looping back to Kroaicho, but it doesn't take long until we are in an odd valley that is ringed in by cliffs.

It should be impressive, but I just can't muster any awe.

As soon as we get on the other side, Rin breaks the odd silence we've been under the whole time. "I forgot I was strong, Kuret. So stupid. I should have fought..."

"Hush, not now," Eli whispers, still digging at her skin.

I find myself digging at my own arms, most of my body itching as well, likely in some sort of odd solidarity. Eli's skin is visibly dry and cracked in a few areas. It looks painful.

"Oh, right," Rin says, voice clipped.

Then it's pandemonium, with so much going on that my brain can hardly keep up. There's a blue dinosaur bounding up and complaining about how long Kuret took and that they could have done it faster. A woman with a shock of pink hair cursing and telling him to shut up.

A very angry sounding whale call from down the valley and the crashing of... trees? Then Eli giving her regrets and telling Kuret he better get her to water really fast or there wouldn't be anything left to give them shade.

Soon after, giant blue... spider things come bounding up, bellowing and Rin is telling them how they are the best ever. They weave in and out of the group, the smallest of them bumping me, and I feel terrible, but I shudder and it scampers away.

I want to call it back, to treat it like I should and apologize somehow, but I don't have the words.

Then a giant cat arrives and I... sort of recognize the woman riding on its back, but by then my brain is an inferno. There are five people all talking at once in a new, gravely language and I can't take it anymore.

My hands are over my ears before I can stop myself, but it doesn't help much.

"Enough!" someone calls out and there is blessed silence right after, but I'm still reeling.

Right before she embraces me, I realize it's Ree and stop myself from striking out, but I can't stop my body stiffening.

She pulls back quickly, looking me up and down, trying to make eye contact, but I keep mine just to the side of her face, already too overwhelmed to care if I'm being rude.

"Hello, Olivia. It is so good to see you safe," she says, voice breaking. "You don't like to be touched, do you?"

I shake my head, then lower it, feeling ashamed and awkward.

"Oh, Liv," Rin whispers. "I keep doing that. I'm sorry."

I clear my throat, finding my voice. "It's alright. I didn't tell you and I know that sometimes people need to be touched. You were scared and I wanted to help."

"Well, I appreciate that, but I'll stop," she replies, her voice heavy with regret.

My stomach clenches. I knew I'd mess up and ruin my chances of fitting in. I just didn't think it would be the moment I met the whole group.

Stupid, stupid. One hundred percent...

Ree's voice breaks me out of another thought spiral. "Drasuk," she says, dropping her gentle tone, "go tell Eli to tell Wroahk that if he keeps breaking trees Kira won't hunt with him for the foreseeable future."

"Yes, Commander," the dinosaur says in a distinctive, rock-grinding voice, then the ground trembles as he turns and bounds away.

"Rin, I think you should go check on Eli. She's losing her cool," Ree says.

I listen closely, but I can't hear Eli at all and I can hear electricity... Strange.

"Olivia should use our cave," Rin says. "I'll keep the argila occupied."

Rin gives a little wave and then strides off through the purple grass, the giant blue spiders cavorting around her, still braying as she laughs.

"My name is Thivoll, little green human," the orange cat rumbles. "We will talk more later, but know you are welcome."

I nod, not sure how you respond to alien cats and not up to trying to figure out how right now.

"Kira," Ree says and I wait for her to issue another order, but instead she just gestures. She puts a hand to her lips, points off down the valley and then makes some more mysterious gestures that probably only make sense to the two of them.

If I had to guess, I would say these two are really close.

"Got it," Kira says tersely.

"I'll visit with you sometime tomorrow, Olivia. Kira is going to show you to a place you can rest. She'll be on guard, just in case, but no one will bother you. Does that sound good?"

I clear my throat again. "Yes. Thank you."

Kira stalks off without a word and after a moment of panic, I jog to catch up. I look behind me to see Ree leaning against Thivoll's shoulder, some mysterious look on her face. His tail is wrapped around her legs and she is stroking his fur.

I look away quickly, afraid I am staring when they are trying to have a moment alone, then stumble to keep up with Kira's purposeful strides.

Her hair is a wild halo of blazing pink, bone spikes catching the last rays of the sun. I glance up, my mind still not settled on the new color of the sky, then quickly look back down.

So much purple... it makes me think of how often I irritate Kroaicho and my stomach twists again.

Luckily Kira is moving so fast it takes most of my focus to move through the long, thick blades of grass without tripping. It doesn't take long for us to reach a shallow cave, which is piled high with the same purple stalks in a makeshift bed.

I move inside, noting the tufts of blue and brown fur that suggest the... what was it? Argila? Yes, that's right... they must sleep here.

I feel bad again, the guilt trying to overtake my thinking, but I push it back down. I don't have the energy for it and if I entertain it I'm just going to spiral until I shut down. I've already embarrassed myself enough as it is.

Kira moves a respectful distance from the cave, turns her back to me and sits down, moving a rifle from her back to across her knees and scanning the valley.

I can't take my eyes off her pink hair. I get momentarily distracted by the row of bone looking spikes coming from her forehead like some sort of crown, and I can't believe I somehow missed that she has a blue tail... but then I'm right back to staring at the pink.

Why was Kroaicho pink? What emotion does it mean?

I can't figure it out, but when I come back to myself, I realize I've been scratching my wrist raw. My shoulders slump. Not that again...

Then I realize it isn't just my usual nerves. My skin feels terrible. I ask the black suit to recede and I see why. Interspersed in with my natural olive tone and the silvery skin I picked up second-hand from Rin are patches of bioluminescence.

Just like Kroaicho's and also shining out in the same mysterious pink.

I let out an inarticulate cry and a short moment later Kira is rushing over to me.

She pulls in a sharp breath. "Alright, I wasn't supposed to fucking talk, but that's some shit right there, Olivia."

"Liv," I mumble, distracted. "Everyone can call me Liv."

"Okay. Right. Serious shit, Liv. Was it blood or did you do the nasty with the burly glow bug?" She lets out a bark of a laugh. "You don't need to answer that, I'm just fucking with you. Damn. I'm not supposed to fuck with you. Fuck."

My skin shifts to a white glow to signal my amusement, but then to blue when I think over what she just said. "What do you mean about the blood?"

"Have you noticed that you start changing when you come in contact with aliens?" she asks.

"Yes, I've picked up things from Kroaicho," I explain. "And from Rin."

She nods. "It's from DNA contact, as far as we can tell. No one knows for sure."

My brow furrows. "But I cut up some cat creature thingy and a bug stung me and I didn't..."

"No," she says, shaking her head. "We aren't sure why, but animals haven't made us change. Otherwise Rin would be covered in blue fur and we'd all probably be trying to suck each other's fucking blood after getting bit by all of the damn bugs on this planet."

"Gross," I respond.

"Really fucking gross, Livie. Not gonna lie though, I kinda like it here. Bugs and all. It's simple and the enemies are clear," she says, tone wistful.

My skin lights up white again. "I like you, Kira," I blurt out.

"Is that what pink to white voodoo glow shit means?" she quips.

I grunt. "I guess so. I can't say for sure and while I agree that it's simple here, I'm getting sick of all the changes."

"I fucking feel that, Livie girl. But look at this shit, you'll be fine," she says, voice light.

I look up and she's naked. I quickly divert my eyes, but then they go right back to her, my eyes wide as I take in all of the alien traits on her body. Along with small patches of her natural cinnamon skin tone, she's got rough blue and red skin, black scales, spikes...

"Alright, I see your point," I concede.

"See? I always was good at cheering people up by pointing out how completely fucked things can get," she says with a laugh.

"Is it that bad for you?" I ask, wincing.

"Oh, no, no," she says with a decisive wave of her rifle. "Not at all. I fucking love it. I've never been deadlier. It's fucking great."

"You like killing?" I ask, and then cringe again.

Her eyes narrow. "That's a surprisingly specific question I've been asked a million times, but never in that tone of voice. Spill, Greenie."

I let out a mirthless chuckle. "When you were held by the bugs—"

"I wasn't, Liv. None of us were." She crouches down, suddenly so incredibly intense even I can pick it up. "What did they fucking do?"

"Nothing I want to talk about. But I killed them. And I..." I trail off.

"It felt good, didn't it?" she says, voice softer now.

I moan. "So, so good. It's wrong, I know it's wrong."

She barks out a laugh. "No it isn't. It's just another fucking emotion. Have you gone around killing everyone who pisses you off?"

"No," I say, elongating the vowel.

"Do you have empathy?" she asks.

"Yes," I reply, though I leave out my struggles with facial expressions.

"Great. You aren't a psychopath. You'll be fine," she says in the same brisk tone as when she stripped naked.

As if it is a completely settled topic.

"I'll teach you how to hunt," she adds. "It'll be a fucking riot. Now get some rest. You need it. I won't let any of the fucking idiots in."

With that, she strides out of the cave, and I realize that somehow she made me feel... better. Like I'm not a complete, colossal freak. Maybe just a partial, normal-size freak.

"Wait!" I call out, and she turns around. "How is all of... that," I say, gesturing to let her know I'm talking about all of the changes to her body, "helpful?"

Her lips stretch in a grin. "Well, the bone crown is pretty clutch if I need to headbutt something like a fucking dinosaur, I guess, but it's mainly the blue and red hide that's awesome. I'm mostly bullet proof. Then there's the extra strength."

I blink, letting my world shift again as I think through just how deadly it is here.

"Great for crushing necks?" I ask, voice hushed and sounding like a horny teenager.

"The best," she says with a laugh in her voice.

It pulls an answering laugh from me. "Blood, you said?"

26

Kroaicho

When I finally tunnel my way through into the valley I hope they took her to, I draw in a relieved breath when I smell overlapping alien scents and hear the odd sounds.

My skin——which has been lit red ever since I realized that not a single thing in that hoard was as precious as the one that walked away——transitions back to pink. I follow zha's scent, which smells strangely like... zhasie now.

And a lot of other scents. And... blood? My skin lights up red again and I increase my pace.

I don't bother to hide my presence. I can't live with this constant pinkness and from the smell, Olivia might be in danger. The risk is worth taking. Then I consider how stupid that is and start moving toward the nearest cliff side as I try to gauge how to tunnel close to the scent.

A metallic clicking sound stops me. I turn to see the pink-haired human. All the human colors lie and I know this one is one moment away from doing something painful.

Zha lowers the weapon, surprising a blue flash across my skin.

"Are you here to talk with Olivia?" the human says in my language.

"Yes," I chitter back.

Zha points in the direction of Olivia's scent. "Fix what damage you caused or next time I won't miss, *fucker*."

My skin pulses to purple, but the anger is only directed at myself. Hopefully zha realizes that or zha might shoot me in my upper segment as I walk away.

Yes. Zha might take that shot, but I don't turn around once I walk past zha or look back. My eyes are trained on the shallow cave I can see now.

When I get close, I see that Olivia is laying prone, with zha's small arms raised, poking zha's fingers at the patches of...

I stop in my tracks, my back limbs tripping over my middle limbs.

Beautiful.

Zha is glowing and a thrill passes through me. But then I take note of the color. Pink.

Just like me. It gives me hope and gets my limbs moving again. Zha lifts zha's head as I get close and there is a bright flash of orange on zha's new patches and an answering flash on my own when I see it.

Joy. Zha feels joy when zha sees me.

"You left the hoard?" zha asks in the human language, tone incredulous.

"I... well... yes. I did," I admit, though my skin is twitching to get back to it and make sure it's still intact.

Add to it. Fluff it. The desire ripples along my segments, but I don't give in.

I resist, eyes roving over zha's skin as the orange glows even brighter, then I suddenly realize there is something else new about zha.

"Your eyes..." I trail off, somehow more stunned to see zhasie eyes than the patches of orange.

"Right," zha says briskly. "Well, thanks to them I have a newfound appreciation for what you see in the hoard, but I still want to leave it."

I grind my tusks. "Why, again? I am not saying no... but why? We have a hoard. It could just be two of us. I was taught that one is better than two, and you are no zhannel to make up the exception to that... but we could be two, regardless. You could help add to the hoard, even."

Zha's skin flashes pink again. "It's funny, actually. Not that long ago I would have agreed with you. I would have reveled in the idea of hiding myself away, though not to gather treasures, that still makes no sense... but to just... it doesn't matter, actually. You taught me that I couldn't hide away anymore. That I do, in fact, need people. Even if they are confusing and I don't think I'll ever fit in. I need more than just one. More than two, even, Kroaicho."

I'm not sure how to respond and the silence stretches on.

The tension between us is thick, but I have grown accustomed to it, grown accustomed to zha. For a species so small and fragile, zha is resilient, determined even, despite my constant objections. But what I feel now... this new emotion stirring within me is not something I'm familiar with.

A glance down and I see the orange and pink mixing with green and I know how to identify it.

When I look back to zha, Olivia is signaling again... but not with just the green hair or eyes. Zha's skin is glowing that unmistakable green. And I feel my own spikes twitch, a response to something deep within me, something primal.

I narrow my eyes, studying the soft green flicker playing along zha's skin. It's more vibrant now, almost as though zha's emotions—whatever they are—are strengthening with each passing second.

"I thought it was just another way we miscommunicate," I say, my voice lower than I intend, deep in thought. "But you are signaling again."

Olivia startles, blinking up at me. A soft blue now mingles with zha's green, a blend of curiosity and bewilderment. "Signaling what?"

My spikes stiffen as I search for the correct way to explain it, but the direct path seems the most honest. "You want to mate."

Zha's face flushes a bright red—an odd contrast to the green that still glows faintly. I tilt my head slightly, noticing how zha breathing picks up, zha's heart rate quickening. Zhasie species have many ways of expressing emotions, but red mixed with green? Fascinating.

My spikes twitch, and I blink at Olivia. "You are red," I observe, feeling the shift of blue creeping into my own glow. "Have I frightened you?"

"No, no." Zha rubs the back of zha's neck. "I'm just... human skin turns red when we're embarrassed. Anger, too, but I'm not angry. Just..." zha trails off with cheeks darkening even more.

I narrow my eyes. "That is inconveniently contradictory."

A soft laugh escapes zha, the tension breaking slightly. "Yes. Tell me about it."

Yet, despite zha's oddly red embarrassment, the green glow remains, pulsing softly in rhythm with zha's emotions. There's a deep hum resonating through me now, and my own body reacts instinctively. The soft, internal heat I've been ignoring flares, and I notice a strange sensation creeping across my own skin—something unexpected, something familiar.

I blink and glance down at my arms. Definitely green. The same green that pulses from zha's skin still blooms across mine, steadily becoming stronger.

"You want a mate too?" Olivia asks with a quiet voice, almost teasing, but I hear the undercurrent of genuine curiosity.

I stiffen, unsure how to respond. This... this was not something I had anticipated. Zha's tone, the way zha is laying there, staring up at me with that strange color mixture of confusion and interest—it stirs something in me that feels entirely unfamiliar, yet undeniable.

"It is not something I am opposed to," I murmur, feeling the weight of my own words, surprised I utter them.

I do not understand how this has escalated so quickly, how zha's presence has stirred a reaction in me that I've never experienced before. Zha is fascinating in ways I hadn't fully acknowledged until now.

Zha's lips quirk and the green on zha's skin seems to brighten as zha gets up and steps closer. "You don't seem too shocked by it, though."

"No," I admit it without hesitation, though I am unsure of what to do with this new information. My glow deepens, and I catch a flicker of something else across zha's face—something playful. The interaction is strange, the energy between us shifting into something almost... charged.

We remain in silence for a few more moments, but there's an odd tension now. Zha keeps glancing at me, zha's expression curious, as though she's trying to read something off my skin, but my glow remains a steady green. It's distracting. I don't fully understand what's happening, but I cannot deny the pull I feel toward zha.

"Are you... well?" I ask, feeling unsure of how to approach this. "Is that blood I smell?"

Zha looks down. "Yes, but not mine. It's for... I don't know how to explain it, but apparently you'll see tomorrow."

I blink a few times, thoroughly confused, then shake off those thoughts and narrow back to what's important right now. "What are we going to do?"

Olivia doesn't answer immediately. Instead, zha gets up and takes a step toward me, zha's expression unreadable. I watch zha closely, my body tensing as zha gets closer and closer. Something in zha's eyes has changed—a new intensity that sends a strange jolt through me.

I don't fully understand what's happening, but I know one thing for certain: I do not want it to stop.

By the demiurge, I do not want it to stop.

27

Olivia

I don't know how this is going to work. I don't want to be touched and haven't ever found pleasure in it and he seems to lack any of the parts too...

Wait a minute... whoever said Kroaicho was a he? "You know, now that I think about it, I never asked if you were a male or a female."

Kroaicho gives me a funny look, "I am me. Stop asking such redundant questions, Olivia"

I blink. "I meant to ask if you were masculine or feminine."

The insipid stare remains.

"He or she? I mean, I hate to break things into a binary that doesn't really exist, but at least it's a place to start, maybe?"

"Olivia ..."

"What? You zhasie have no gender identities?" I ask, feeling out of my depth again.

"All zhasie are born equal, Olivia; your funny language makes no sense."

My funny language makes no...? Oh, you little...

I close my eyes and pinch my nose. "I thought you had met more sapient species than I have. Surely you have noticed there is variety?"

After a slow grind of tusks, Kroaicho responds. "I have noticed, but it does not apply to the zhasie."

"You don't have gender," I state.

"No, and that word does not translate," he... she... they... respond.

"What's the pronoun, then?"

"That also does not translate. Should we speak in my language instead?"

"No," I respond, then try again. "When you are angry with me because I just ran off down a tunnel, how would you finish this sentence? 'I can't believe—word missing here—ran off again. I am going to kill—word missing.'"

"Zha," Kroaicho answers instantly and I smack my forehead when I remember him—zha—saying that before. It was lost in the craziness of everything being new.

"Alright. Zha. So how do zhasie actually mate, then? What parts touch... you know... what parts?"

"My species does not touch to mate and we only do it twice," comes the chittering reply.

I blink, unsure how that even works. "Twice? Not just for pleasure?" I blurt out before I can think better of it.

It's not like I found much of that the few times I tried. It's hard to feel good when you just want to hit someone.

From the colors lighting up on zha's skin, the confusion is shared. "It feels good, I am told. But for just that? It would be insanity. You would lose your whole hoard!"

"You would? But... it isn't worth the risk?" I hold up a hand. "Nevermind, we are getting off track."

I push aside the comment about treasure. And I thought I had a one-track number-reciting mind...

That gives me pause. I haven't been using numbers all that much lately, have I? Huh. I wonder what...

I shake my head, not letting myself side-tracked.

"What risk?" I ask. "A zhannel?"

"No, that is why you take the risk," zha explains. "A mating leaves you prone to being tricked and losing part of your hoard."

"I don't want your hoard, Kroaicho," I groan. "How many different ways do I have to say it?"

"I believe you," zha responds. "It is strange, of course, but also very... appealing somehow."

"It's simple psychology," I explain. "Nothing mysterious."

"How so?" zha asks.

I snort. "You have discovered what it feels like to not be on guard and you like it. It's what I feel with you, too, actually. I have a hard time recognizing emotion when I look at people. I can hear it in voices and it's not like I completely lack emotion or anything..." I stop myself there, realizing I'm getting defensive and zha wouldn't even know why. "What I'm trying to say is you light up with your emotions and I can tell the difference. It's... soothing."

"I am glad our communication can be clear," zha replies, orange lighting up with the green and blue. "It is odd that it would be any other way. But many things are odd. Are you saying that humans mate just for pleasure?"

"Yes, for pleasure and with no hoard lost. Well... I guess for people paying... never mind." I shake my head, recentering my thoughts and resisting my usual urge to over-explain how things work. It would take us years to get past the misunderstanding about paying for sex. "I don't see how it can possibly work without touching. Do you just toss something at the other? Is your uh, thing, detachable?"

"Detachable thing? Is what detachable?" zha asks, blue taking over the green now.

I huff out a breath and fall back on anatomy. "A penis."

My eyebrows shoot up when I realize there isn't a translation, so I try some synonyms. And more. Every millimeter of zha is lit up in blue and I know I'm adding confusion when my face starts burning.

Nothing translated.

I try again. "Well it is an appendage that the male person pushes inside of inside the female person."

"What's a male?" Kroaicho asks, voice exasperated. "Put what in where? No, do not tell me. That is too terrible to contemplate and I do not want to know. What a violent species you come from..."

I clear my throat. "I can't argue with that, I guess. But how are we going to...you know? Deal with all the green we are signaling?"

Zha takes a deep breath and grinds zha's tusks together. "The way of my species. The only correct way."

I let out a snort. "You are gonna have to be a lot more specific than that or no way."

"All you have to do is breathe it in."

"Breath what in?" I say, voice rising in exasperation.

"We should not do this," zha says, skin lighting pink. "It is only for a zhannel."

"There is no way we are going to have a zhannel," I say, grinding my teeth now like zha grinds tusks.

"Of course we are not. They are only for ourselves."

My brow furrows, trying to make sense of that, repeating it back and then realizing the emphasis was put on *we*.

I don't even want to try to unpack what that means. It doesn't matter. "My mother... my zhann paid someone to make sure I never got pregnant," I explain, throat tight. "Ever."

"How is that possible?" I say, shocked.

I shrug. "A lot of money and a surgeon willing to do something illegal and immoral. It's more common than people think."

"You agreed to that?" zha asks, confused.

"No. I was a child, a zhannel, still."

"That is terrible," zha says, skin lit up pink.

After a hard swallow, I respond. "It was, but I don't want to talk about it.

"I will not speak of it... except to say that while you may not be able to have yours, I still want to have mine."

"Yours? Are you telling me that you have the zhannel? I thought you were male," I hiss, annoyed with myself. "Arg, sorry. You just said you weren't, but you are enormous and look so... nevermind. I still don't get the reproduction differences, clearly. Not a male, right."

"I said I do not know this word. Or the other. There are none of either. There are not two types of zhasie. Just one."

I remember the singular pronoun, feeling stupid and judgmental somehow. "Right. Zha."

"Yes. Zha."

"Still. How would I get you pregnant? I can't."

"True. You don't have the expellant."

I pinch my nose, my head suddenly feeling too full. Nothing is stable here. Not even biology.

"This conversation is not only completely the opposite of sexy, it's also giving me a headache. Just forget I brought it up."

"No, I want to try," zha says, skin flushing with a green glow again.

"But try what?"

"Will you not just trust me? Like I did with the treasure sticks?"

I cringe, thinking of how much excitement came from me lying about sticks to get a fire. "Well... That might not be the best example."

"What do you mean?"

"Forget I said anything." I say hastily. "Yes, I trust you. Let's try the... Breathing thing? Whatever they did to me, if I don't have sex I feel like I might die."

"I do not know what sex is, but I will use my expellant and see if that helps."

Zha raises a clawed hand toward me then sweeps it to the side, and I see myself flash red in fear, then green, then purple when I think of others who have touched me.

"I do not understand your signals."

I gulp. "I am still learning. I don't react well to being touched, but I liked it when you squeezed me. I know you said that you don't touch to mate, but will you hold me?

My heart pounds, more afraid that I won't like it than afraid I will, but I ask anyway. "Real tight. Like I showed you before?"

"It is strange, but I will."

Then zha is stepping forward and I'm shaking. I'm a kaleidoscope of colors as thick arms wrap around me.

When the rage starts to build up, I remind myself that I gave permission. Then zha is squeezing me and I'm no longer angry.

Then a panicked thought occurs to me. "Wait. You can only use your expellant twice?"

"No. Many times. It is a defense at other moments. But only for a zhannel twice."

"So are you putting this in the defense category?" I ask, intrigued despite myself.

"You are thinking too much," zha chides as zha takes a long breath.

My eyes dart to zha's four nostrils, from where a mist is now wafting.

I try to wriggle away, alarmed. "Of course I am, I—"

No more words come out because suddenly my mouth is filled with a cloying scent. Slightly caustic, but also sweet. Like persimmon, with cinnamon, and some sort of alien musk.

I haven't decided if I like it before it hits my lungs and instead of the cough I expect, I'm taking a deeper and deeper breath. Like I can't stop myself.

My exhale is a moan as my entire body convulses, stomach muscles rippling and my thighs clenching as the place between my legs throbs. One more deep breath in and my back is arching, an explosion of pleasure racing up my spine.

Kroaicho makes a startled sound and releases zha's grip and I feel the wrong sort of nerves firing up at the lighter touch.

"No," I gasp out, anger tinging my tone. "Harder."

My ribs creak in protest when zha complies and the pleasure rushes back in. Every breath of the mist sends pleasure racing along all of my neurons, but not in the unpleasant way I associate with things that stress me. There is no answering risk of a shut down.

For once, it's my body on fire and not my mind.

I understand now. This is what other people have experienced, but something touch could never bring me before.

"Again," I slur out, mind spinning in the best way possible.

My whole body is glowing green and throbbing soon after. A bright pink eye is watching me intently when I come back to myself. Ripples of pleasure loosening my muscles in all the right ways.

I hadn't realized just how wound up I was. Now I feel wonderfully loose, which is further helped by just how tight of a hold I'm in.

My mind drifts for a moment, but then I call my attention back sharply. Kroaicho seems just as calm and unaffected as usual and it makes me feel self-conscious.

My skin shifts to pink, with a little bit of purple mixed in, fully directed at myself. "I can't give you that? No place I could touch?"

"No. Well, there is... No."

"There is, isn't there? Where?" I push.

"It matters not."

"It does," I hiss out, suddenly realizing that I was so desperate to end the nonstop arousal that I agreed to something one-sided. Zha said it would be and I should have listened. I hate feeling like I owe something I don't know how to repay.

It's like almost every social interaction where I know they're disappointed that I don't know what they want. Except way, way worse.

At least the couple times I let a guy stick it in they got off on it. I mean, they made me feel like shite about being stiff, but it didn't stop them from cumming. Better than the girl who said I couldn't find a clit if it bit me.

I push the memories aside before I get lost in castigating myself.

"I want to reciprocate."

"That word has no meaning."

Dumb alien non-dragon things. Everything is to be taken, I guess. And hoarded. Though I have to admit that hugging me doesn't fit that stereotype.

I let out a huff. "I want to give you treasure. Uh... expellant treasure. In return"

I cringe at the thought of mist coming out of my nose while a rumble of laughter vibrates against me.

"You are the treasure," zha says with skin lighting green and orange. "Annoying, but very shiny."

My own skin lights up orange. It's the oddest compliment I've ever received, but I can tell by zha's tone that zha means it.

"Wait," I say, something suddenly occurring to me. "How is it that you know about a bunch of different aliens, that you had items in your hoard from galaxies away... and you don't know that there are multiple genders in other species?"

"I wasn't interested in them beyond the stories that came with the item or if they were the kind to steal," Kroaicho responds.

"So you have no actual way to know if any of those stories are true or if they were just lying to you to get a sale?" I ask, dumbfounded.

Zha clicks dismissively. "They took items of no value in exchange. Ugly things. Why would they lie?"

I pinch my nose again, imagining all kinds of precious resources being handed over for plastic beads. I'm positive it's happened and I think back to the stories zha told me before and throw all the information I thought I gleaned from them out of my mind. Useless.

I open my mouth to share that, but I just can't get the words out. Kroaicho is annoyingly sure about all zhasie beliefs, and a large part of me wants to poke holes in them until logic prevails... but I don't. Would I want my whole world upturned and every beautiful thing I thought I could rely on tossed out?

No way.

If zha truly does go with me—and I can't let myself think of any other option now—zha will slowly realize. As many times as I wanted to poke those smug eyes out since Kroaicho snatched me, I just can't bring myself to be the agent of that change. I'd rather be the support zha needs to weather it.

That feels right. Good, even. I've never served in that role for anyone, I realize. I've just been shuffled from one place to another once my "behavioral issues" became too much. It's always felt like, no matter how much I observed, no matter how much I read, everyone always knew more about how to be human than I did.

Who would have thought it would take meeting an alien—someone even more socially clueless than I am—to finally feel comfortable in my own... suddenly glowing... skin.

The good feelings flee and my usual anxiety surges. What if zha just can't handle being around all of us? What if zha ultimately chooses a cave. Alone. With a hoard. I'd probably never find another being as easy to read... or so completely oblivious to how fucking weird I am.

Well, I suppose everyone but a zhasie is weird to Kroaicho, but it ends up being the same.

The good feeling is back and I grab hold of it tight, the glow of my skin shifting back to orange.

"Is this uncomfortable for you, Kroaicho? Keeping up that pressure?"

"No."

"Can we sleep like this again?" I ask. "That was nice."

"I would enjoy that," zha says and I settle in with a long sigh.

28

Kroaicho

My mind is too full of what just happened to sleep, but my skin is still lit up bright orange, despite the odd tangles of my thoughts.

At first I thought I was hurting zha somehow, but the bright flaring of green and orange zha showed where the black clothing didn't cover helped settle my red fear. Now zha is sleeping... all of the confusing words and explosive energy settled and contained.

Zha is beautiful. The greatest treasure I've ever found. So I just keep staring, losing myself in the swirling shifts and odd, twitching human expressions.

But then the twitching becomes more violent and not long after zha is moaning out zha's pain sound, skin lighting in reds and blues.

Wait... is that a steady purple on zha's neck underneath the shifting colors? I look closer, my segments trembling as I watch zha's usually perpetually amused white-brown skin transition to a rougher, purple... hide?

When zha starts moaning loader and thrashing, I fully panic, lighting the cave red as I shift my segments so I can lay zha on the purple grasses. Then I shoot up to my four back limbs, unsure what to do for a long moment before dashing out of the cave, looking for the nearest human to explain what is happening to Olivia.

Surely they will know?

Luckily the pink one is crouched not far from the cave, back turned, and then zha scrambles around, raising the metal weapon as I run toward zha.

"Come quickly," I urge. "Something is wrong with Olivia."

I turn, limbs tripping over each other in my haste, and run back to the cave, the pink human coming up beside me at an impressive speed.

Zha skids to a stop beside me as I chitter inanely, arms reaching out to Olivia, but unsure of what to do. Zha would not want me to touch zha, I know it.

"*Fuck,*" the pink one mutters, then clears zha's throat. "It's alright, big *guy. She* is just changing. You two must have had a fun time, right?"

Zha punches one of my limbs with zha's small arm and it hurts more than I expect.

"This is... normal? For humans?"

"Not really, but on this *fucking* planet it is. Although..." the pink one bites zha's lips, the pause making the red on my skin flare even brighter.

"What?" I chitter harshly.

"My changes happened while I slept and weren't all that bad," the pink one says. "Drasuk would have told me if I was thrashing around... trust me. *She* is taking on changes from you and me. *Fuck.* I should have told *her* no about the blood."

I blink. What does that mean? I grind my tusks, then startle when zha starts yelling.

"Thivoll!" the pink one yells out. "Get Ree here now!"

Then the pink one moves over to Olivia and holds zha down, containing zha's thrashing. I want to protest, to tell the pink one that Olivia wouldn't like that, but I don't know what humans need.

I hear a thundering sound, like something heavy running before the pink one's blue beast appears. Right after comes the purple human with the manticorid. None of the pink on my skin is from the sight of it, though my mind is telling me to flee.

The purple human slides off the manticorid's back, stumbling over to Olivia, then also starts touching zha. I'm shuffling from two limbs to another two, unsure what to say, or how to help.

I think over everything I've seen while I was here, scouring my mind for anything that might help, then remembering where I woke up.

"There was a place," I chitter, voice high. "With screens and technology, and braceaaer. It might have something that would help."

"What is *he* saying?" the manticorid rumbles in zha's native tongue.

I switch to zha's language and repeat myself.

The manticorid and the blue beast both turn to me, eyes intense. "Come," says the manticorid. "My name is Thivoll. This is Drasuk. Ree and Kira will help Olivia. *She* will be well, but you are correct that something in the facility might help. Tell us everything you know."

I resist for a moment, but then the manticorid wraps a black scaled hand around one of my upper limbs and gently pulls me away.

"Humans are hard to kill," the blue one... Drasuk, says. "They just keep coming back so they can confuse and annoy you. Olivia will come through this even stronger... what is your name?"

"Kroaicho," I chitter.

Drasuk repeats it back, mangling the pronunciation, but I don't protest, letting them lead me out of the cave.

"Tell us," the manticorid rumbles, and so I do.

29

Olivia

My mind is a raw nerve of pain, the sensations overloading me, but not letting me shut down either. I know there are people around me. Hands on me, holding me down. I start screaming out my rage, mind going back to that terrible cell. To pinchers and needles.

"Only I will fucking remain," I choke out, wriggling, trying to gain the upper hand.

Suddenly, I do, but the sounds of bugs that I expect are instead a very human cry of pain and suddenly my mind is clear.

I shoot upright, shaking off the anger and pain, frantically looking around, panicked that I did something terrible.

Kira is groaning and rubbing at the back of her head at the far side of the cave. Ree is hovered over me, eyes wide.

"What did I do?" I wail.

"Fuck," Kira grits out. "That was fucking awesome, Livie. You picked the perfect angle to find my soft spot with a fucking cave wall. Ouch."

"I'm so sorry. I..." my voice trails off as I look at the hands I'm holding up. The ones with some sort of thick, purple hide, and long, curving claws coming out of the wrists. They look like Kroaicho's claws, except his... zha's... come from the tips of zha's fingers.

My hands...

I'm shaken out of my horror by the feel of something fluttering along my sides, right under my armpits. I look down, and there is something moving there and I shriek out in fear, purple hide lighting up red.

Kira gets painfully to her feet. "Take a deep breath and just go ahead and pull the suit back. Do you want us to go outside?"

I shake my head, not wanting to be alone, then will the suit to recede. My mind stutters when I see what it was... a small, stunted, second set of limbs. I gag.

"What the fuck," I hiss out. "How is that useful, Kira?"

"Just calm your fucking tits," she replies. "When Ree and I grew tails, it took time. I bet those will be long and strong and kicking ass in no time."

Ree clears her throat. "Speaking of tails..."

It takes me a moment to catch on and I scramble up, then crash back down to the ground when something heavy attached to my butt swings around and pulls me off balance. I lay there panting for three long breaths as both women stand there with arms outstretched, clearly wanting to touch me, but being respectful.

It helps put things into perspective, somehow, and I close my eyes and calm myself down. If I keep this up, my brain will start burning.

When I open my eyes, I calmly and slowly sit up, then reach behind me and pull my... tail around.

It looks odd, but the bright yellow color gives away where it came from. "Is that a tentacle... or?"

"If I had to guess," Ree responds, "I would say that's a mix of Eli's tentacle, Drasuk's hide, and Kroaicho's shoulder spikes on the bottom of it instead of suckers."

"It's too bad there isn't a manticorid tip," Kira says.

"Give it time," Ree responds. "Yours took a bit, remember?"

I'm staring at my... first... set of arms, not really understanding what they are talking about because I've just now noticed that they are longer than they should be and not just because there is a second smaller set under them. They grew... not just in length, but also in thickness. Purple hide stretches down the top and outside side of each one, with black scales on the inner. Then of course there are the thick, sharp claws that extend out of my wrists.

I experimentally pull my fist back and down and swipe out with them, instantly seeing the appeal.

"Purple hide?" Kira murmurs. "A combo of my red and blue? That seems a bit... kindergarten paint time, doesn't it?"

"It's anger," I murmur. "The color is perfect."

Kira clears her throat. "Well, can't argue with that."

I look down my front, noting that the hide extends all the way down my body, even my breasts. I look like some sort of purple Mystique. The hide transitions to black scales at my ankles, and when I think about it, black claws extend from where my toes... used to be.

"Damn," Kira mutters. "None of us have changed this much, this fast."

"I agree," Ree whispers back. "We should figure out why."

I push the observation and the apparent need to figure out why I'm a freak aside, still needing to know what I look like. "What can't I see?"

"You have bone spikes," Ree shares. "Sort of like Kira's, but in Drasuk's shape and Kroaicho's pattern."

"On the left part of my skull down to the right part of my spine?" I ask.

"Yes, exactly," Ree responds. "There is purple hide covering everything except where the spikes extend and your uh... tail comes out."

I take a deep breath, absorbing my new changes, trying to adjust as fast as possible with my head screaming out in protest. "Could I have a moment alone, please?"

"Of course," Ree says softly, then pads out.

Kira stays a moment longer. "You look fucking amazing, Livie," she growls out, voice raw. "There aren't many people who would take on something like this on purpose. We are a special breed," she finishes, voice rough with pride and affection.

I smile, her acceptance helping me make the disorienting transition to new changes. "Thanks, Kira. That means a lot," I tell her, feeling every word.

She pads out, leaving me to my rumination. It takes me a while to finish working through my mental process. There is a soft murmur of multiple voices outside, but I know they won't rush me, so I just take my time.

This would have been some seriously scary shit to wake up to alone and even Kroaicho's presence wouldn't have been enough to help calm me down. Zha wouldn't know what was or wasn't natural for a human.

It is nice having them here.

It makes me think about how things were before being snatched. I've gone my whole life with people around me, most of them people I didn't want surrounding me. I never understood how much it could mean to not be alone or to be around people who aren't looking to use me for their personal gain. Or fix me so I will stop making them look bad.

I'm used to spending time with ridiculously wealthy people. The sort that never seem to have enough, even though they have everything. They were always out to get more things... More notoriety. More fame.

But here? These people only have each other. I can already tell that they place their value in each other and it seems so... right.

The realization makes me want to go out to them, which is the opposite of my usual impulse: to be alone. To retreat. I'm ready to face the world and it feels good. I get up, tell the suit to cover me again, and make my way out of the cave.

It's quite a process. I stumble around, new extra small limbs flailing along with my suddenly longer arms, trying to figure out my balance and overcorrecting where I'm holding the new... tentacle? Tail?

Then I extend my toe claws and it helps. I find my balance in time to get out of the cave without face planting and to start paying attention to what everyone is talking about.

"We've left Rannek alone long enough and we should check on Silver and see if Szhe'ka has returned, but we need to check out this facility. I mean, it shouldn't even be here, should it?" Ree asks.

"Maybe Kroaicho was confused," Kira responds.

"I was not. I never mistell a story," Kroaicho says decisively, then makes an excited chitter. "Olivia! You look... well."

"Uh, thanks? What are we planning?" I ask.

Ree gives me a wave and a smile. "Kroaicho woke up in a facility, which is odd, because technology isn't supposed to work on this planet."

"It was working," Kroaicho grinds out between zha's tusks. "There were braceaaer and screens. I regrettably... broke the braceaaer I planned to get information from and was not with zha long enough to find a story in the blood."

Kira lets out a bray of laughter. "Not sure I understood all of that, but I can certainly approve of broken braceaaer and blood. Let's just go take a look. We have plenty of muscle and weapons."

"I want to fight," I hiss out, claws twitching on my wrists.

"That is no way to protect a hoard, Olivia," Kroaicho starts to protest.

"I'm going, and so are you it sounds like," I retort.

Zha's skin lights up purple and the tusk grinding starts up again, but zha offers no further argument.

＊＊＊

While everyone else prepared, my body decided to make more painful changes as Kroaicho held me tight in zha's arms to help calm me as I screamed... not that I'm complaining now. The useless arms grew longer and while I'm still trying to figure out how the fuck my mind even knows how to send signals to four different arms, I now have an identical, although somewhat smaller lower pair. Complete with wrist claws, purple hide, and black scales.

Kira was disappointed when my tail developed another hooked claw instead of a manticorid tip, which apparently has the deadliest venom in the known universe. That sounds nice and all, but as we walk through the dark tunnel toward the facility and my tentacle tail dances along behind me, it's hard to feel like I've been ripped off. I practiced using it on some of the long purple grass and left behind a carnage of innocent blades.

I'm more than ready to see if there are any genali to cut with it.

"It is close," Kroaicho chitters quietly from up ahead.

Zha is in front, Kira and Drasuk right behind, then Kuret in the middle to provide light with his green markings, then Ree and Thivoll, then me.

Rin was content to stay behind with the argila and Eli was still fussing at Wroahk. Kira whispered to me before we left that Wroahk loved it when she did that, so apparently everyone back in the valley is content.

"I smell braceaaer," Drasuk rumbles.

"It's on, motherfuckers," Kira responds with glee.

There is an answering grin on my face and my tail dances more wildly behind me, pulling me off balance for a moment before I get my excitement under control.

"Get behind me, Kroaicho," Drasuk orders and then there is a long moment of shifting as they squeeze by each other in the tunnel.

"Go already, Lizard Brain," Kira hisses out... and then it is pandemonium.

30

Olivia

Drasuk lets out a roar and barrels out of the end of the tunnel. There is a crash of glass and screech of metal, then pops of gun fire and Kira's cackling laughter. I'm bouncing on my heels in my impatience, claws digging into the soil, as everyone boils out into the facility.

Thivoll lets out a roar that makes me shiver and soon after I stumble out into the room, taking a quick look around at a carnage of broken screens and some sort of interfaces, then Kroaicho is beside me, shielding me with zha's body as we run into a hallway to catch up.

There are multiple dead bodies in the hall, none of them genali, just what look like the little green men Kira said braceaaer look like. Some have been shot, some completely crushed, others slashed with the knife I can see Kuret holding as he dashes down the hall in front of us, yelling his own war cry.

It seems insane to run in like this, but I can't deny it feels pretty amazing. Or it will be if there is anything left to fight. I increase my pace, Kroaicho grinding zha's tusks together loud enough beside me to be heard over all of the sounds of battle.

A moment later we burst through into a large room. There are multiple fights happening. Kira has abandoned her rifle and is holding on to Drasuk's spines as he rears up and crushes a pair of aliens. Kuret is slicing another. Thivoll and Ree's tails are whipping around them, eliciting keening screams from the few braceaaer they have engaged.

"Dammit," I mutter once it's clear that nothing will be alive long enough for me to get over to it.

Then Kroaicho chitters, pushing me to the side right before a chunk of the display next to me shatters. I fall, my extra limbs hard to balance, but then scramble back up. Kroaicho's large limbs are swinging, the braceaaer dumb enough to take a shot at me screaming as it flies through the air before crunching against the wall on the other side of the hallway we just left.

I dig my claws in, running into the hall to help zha. Kroaicho is lit up bright purple, anger clear in every swing into the group of braceaaer that flanked us. But from where?

I stop thinking about it and hurl myself into the fray, screaming out my rage as my own limbs start swinging.

As my claws rake through the alien closest to me and the blood starts flowing, I feel just as amazing as I remember with the bugs. Not as good as it was to be with Kroaicho... but close.

Then I hear a sound of pain from Kroaicho and my skin lights up with such a bright purple every one of the braceaaer's wide, overly large black eyes reflect my whirling outline. I whip my tail around and slice through the alien about to stab Kroaicho's back segment. They are still screaming as I use the momentum of my tail to swing my body, holding all four arms out, fists tucked back and wrist claws positioned to gut the one to Kroaicho's right.

Another crash lets me know that Kroaicho has launched another one into a wall and I have a vicarious shot of pleasure.

It's over far too fast for my liking. The hall falls silent for a long moment before Kira skids back into the hall.

"The fuck? Where did they come from?" she calls out harshly.

I shake my head, trying to slough off the pleasure and move over to check Kroaicho's wound. "Are you alright?"

"I am. It will heal," zha responds

Thivoll slides past us, pulling in a long breath before pacing up and down the corridor. "There's too much blood."

"From there," Kroaicho says, a claw pointing at a section of the wall.

"Are you sure?" Kira says skeptically. "It just looks like stone."

I take a closer look, then see where the striations of the cave move from the subtle blue glow that seems to be common in the rock here to a dull, obviously fake section.

"It's not real," I tell her.

"Oh. Nice eye, glow bug," she says before whacking Kroaicho's middle right limb.

Kroaicho's skin moves from purple to bright blue and zha looks down at zha's arm, then to Kira, then back. I have a feeling zha will mostly be that color when Kira is around and it makes me smile, the glee of the fight rising again now that Kroaicho is no longer under attack.

"We'll get this opened up," Kira says with a dismissive wave. "You all should check out the main room. Maybe there is something you can salvage in there."

Ree comes up behind us. "It would have been nice to see what it was like before it was crushed, I agree."

"You're a fucking wrecking ball, Drasuk," Kira mutters. "We've talked about this over and over again."

"You are quite welcome," Drasuk replies in his usual rumbling voice.

"Idiot," Kira mutters, then turns to the wall, poking at it in random spots.

We leave Kira and Drasuk behind to work on getting access to the hidden room, moving back into the much larger one. I take a closer look around, noting the broken panels with large metal wires running into an even larger area. Bodies litter the area and it's hard to believe there is nothing but scrapes and the odd stab wound on everyone.

One of those scrapes is on Ree and Thivoll is inspecting it, growling.

"So there really is tech. Is this from the failed colony?" Ree asks.

"No," Thivoll answers. "It's too recent."

Ree hums. "Why have all of these displays without power?"

I close my eyes and concentrate, but, no, I can't hear the hum. "There's no power," I share.

"Oh, there wouldn't be," Ree says distractedly. "Technology doesn't work here."

"What? At all? Then why the machines?"

"I don't know," she says, biting her lip. "I thought you said the atmosphere destroyed tech, Thiv."

He stops growling and turns to look at the displays. "No, it's just power sources that don't work. They degrade or explode."

"Fuck, fluff brain. You're just saying that now?" Ree gripes.

Thivoll lets out a series of chuffs and his tail dances over to Ree to tap her shoulder from behind. She jumps, yelping, and Thivoll's chuffing gets even louder.

She lets out a growl, claws extending and swiping at his tail but he's already dodging.

"We don't have time for playing, Commander," Drasuk says in a needling tone from behind us as he enters the room.

Ree lets out a huff. "Later, superkitty. Alright, so why aren't we running?"

"Because there is no power source," Drasuk answers with his usual superior tone.

I'm still trying to catch up. "But why do power sources explode, Thivoll?" I ask.

The big cat stops chuffing and settles down on his haunches, tail still twitching like it wants to get up to no good.

"I have no idea. I never looked into it," he admits.

"Useless felines," Ree grumbles, but there is a laugh in her tone and my lips quirk.

I turn a more critical eye on the structure. Panels, screens, long wires, chains...

"Was something really big held here?" I mutter out loud.

"I think so, yes," Ree says.

Kira stalks in, foot falls light and with a giant smile on her face. She glances around. "Something big? Holy fuck it must be enormous."

"Hmm..." She draws out the sound, then glances around. "It's a battery."

Thivoll and Drasuk both hiss, then Thivoll groans.

"Yes, I see it now," Thivoll grates out. "The leads are like a cryogenic chamber pumping nanites through a large body and then through a generator. How did you know, Kira?"

She shrugs. "Seems obvious."

Drasuk breaks in. "A large body wouldn't be enough to be a power source. Whatever it was will be highly intelligent and I assume also very angry."

"A trakeldon," Kroaicho adds suddenly, skin lit up red.

"Really?" Thivoll asks, all trace of amusement gone. "How do you know?"

"I recognized the tracks," zha replies.

"You got out of your hoarding cave long enough to learn some tracking, glow pop?" Kira teases.

"So far Kroaicho seems like a walking encyclopedia, Kira," Ree breaks in. "He's essentially a treasure trove inside that mind."

"Zha, not he," I interject.

"Sorry," Ree says with a grimace. "Zha knows a lot and I respect that. It will prove very useful."

I glance over to Kroaicho and notice that most of the red on zha's skin has been replaced with thrumming orange. Zha's eyes are big and zha is blinking slowly, like some realization is coming.

"Stories are important," is all zha says in response.

"Not right now they aren't. We should leave," Drasuk says forcefully. "Regroup."

"I agree," Kira says, grin dropping. "But there's what looks like a lab behind that fake cave wall you two meat heads should look at first."

"Which two what?" Drasuk grumbles. "Speak plainly for once."

"Oh, I only meant the wisest and strongest among us. Obviously you and Thivoll," Kira drawls.

"Well, why did you not just say?" Drasuk replies, puffing up his spines and stalking out of the room as Kira turns and rolls her eyes at us.

I blink, suddenly feeling far more at ease in the group. Just like Kroaicho, Drasuk is even more socially oblivious than I am and everyone still somehow likes him. Even though he's also a giant ass.

I mean, I mostly just struggle with facial expressions and it's starting to feel like not that big of a deal now that there are so many different types of faces with a whole range of different meanings.

It feels... good and I give Kira a grin.

"Lead the way, small human," Drasuk calls back imperiously.

Ree holds her arm out to Kira, mouthing something, raising her eyebrows and wiggling her head and even I can get that she's making fun of Drasuk and I burst out laughing along with them. Thivoll is still chuffing as we move out of the room.

We make our way down a long hall, the dead bodies of aliens making me smile, then move into a smaller room. Thivoll rushes over to a storage shelf, big scaled hands grabbing at silver canisters, turning them like he's reading something.

"Nanites. Translation and healing," he says, voice betraying his excitement.

"Wouldn't they be destroyed, though?" Kira asks.

"No, they just need a host body," Drasuk replies.

"But you said to never disconnect from the black suit, Thivoll," Ree adds.

"The suit is different," Thivoll says. "Manticorids didn't design it. It has to be calibrated and manually connected when it's attached to a spine. These will have base, inert coding that simply needs a living battery."

"But why?" I ask, not fully understanding, but knowing enough about systems to know that doesn't make sense. "Wouldn't the process be the same?"

"No," Thivoll rumbles out, distracted by piling canisters into Ree's pack. "Manticorid design is superior."

I blink, not quite sure how that explains it.

Kira chuckles. "No need for clothes when you have fur and scales, right? You let the 'inferior' species design those?"

"Exactly," Thivoll says, purring as he starts filling another pack. "Now let's get out of here."

***

"He won't do it," Eli explains, her tentacles drooping.

She doesn't need to translate for the group, but I can tell she's stuck in the habit. Everyone in the clearing, with the exception of Wroahk, agreed to use the translation nanites if they didn't already have them.

We can all understand his whale calls as he slaps the water in the stream. "Don't want to hear. Don't want to know all of the endless, endless words. This water is terrible. Even worse than the lake. Terrible."

"We get it, big guy," Kira sings out to him in whale voice. "You'll be back in your favorite muddy-ass water as soon as possible."

He lets out a series of clicks and hits the water even harder, but at least he stops complaining.

"What kind of water does he want?" I ask, suddenly putting it together that Kira is goading him.

Judging by how deadly he seems and pissed off he is, it seems crazy.

"Salt water," Eli says. "Fresh water just feels... wrong, somehow."

Rin stirs, flipping long white braids over her shoulder and stepping away from the argila, all three of them staring at Wroahk like they don't know what to make of him. "There's a dock," Rin exclaims, voice excited. "I forgot all about it in all of the commotion of finding Olivia. It's up north and, from what I gathered, I think that's where the hunters come from."

Drasuk nods, the motion oddly stilted. "That would make sense, yes. There is usually an island in between two large continents on a hunting ground, though it was impossible to tell if we were on the northern or the southern one. We must be southern."

Ree lets out a long breath. "That sounds like an important objective, then, but first we need to get back to the island. There are more women to gather before we take that sort of risk. For now, let's gather up anything of use here."

Ree looks up at the purple sky. "We'll head out at dark. Tell Wroahk, Eli. Hopefully he'll be in a better mood before we need to truss him up again or Drasuk might bite one of his tentacles off for real this time."

Kira snorts. "He should. It'll just grow back and even I'm getting fed up with the tantrums."

"He's working on it," Eli says in a cheerful tone. "It's getting better every day."

I look over at her huge smile, then at the murderous bared teeth behind her, tentacles wrapped around her like he can't let her take one step away from him. Even I can see the mismatch between them… but it must work for them.

Somehow.

Everyone starts to move away and I crane my neck, looking for Kroaicho. Once we got back and zha allowed Thivoll to use the nanites, zha hustled off, likely to check zha's hoard although zha wouldn't admit it. My shoulders slump as I slowly make my way back to the little cave, then make a detour, wanting to take advantage of the peace and open air while I can.

31

Kroaicho

By the time I make it back to Olivia, exhaustion is pulling at my limbs. I step inside, shaking off the dust and dirt that's clung to my skin, but the moment I enter, I notice something off.

I glance around, my eyes scanning the dark corners, but there's no sign of Olivia.

Zha is gone.

I feel my body tense, a wave of irritation crashing over me as my glow darkens to purple. Of course, zha didn't stay somewhere I expect.

For a moment, I stand still, letting the dark purple glow pulse from my body in time with my rising frustration. I will always be dark purple as long as I'm with zha. As long as zha is part of my hoard...

No other creature has ever stirred such an endless stream of irritation in me. Zha is like a constant storm, always shifting, always pushing against me.

Red fear thrums again and I take a deep breath, forcing myself to calm down. To realize that this isn't really about zha, but far more to do with how few items I was able to carry here. I place the precious treasures gently on the ground, then turn back around.

I let out a long breath, but then think back to what Ree said at the facility. My stories, my knowledge, has value to them. Zha called me treasure... does that make me part of Ree's hoard? Can that happen simultaneously?

For a moment my skin whirls in shades of blue, but then orange replaces it. That feels... very satisfying. I have value to others and they have value to me. I will have to think on this more as I shift what a hoard means or how I could be part of one that is bigger than I am, while also claiming it as my own.

I look down at the items.

The impulse to find more is still there and I still embrace it, but I can feel it shifting back in priority. I can do more than gather items.

There is a more important goal, with far richer, if sometimes very confusing, stories.

It makes my middle segment feel warm.

This shift of thinking is new, but there is one thing I know for sure. Olivia has the most value. Zha will always be the most important part of my hoard. I will always follow, or how will I know zha is safe?

My red glow dims slightly as I step back outside, scanning the area for any sign of zha's tracks. It doesn't take long to spot them—depressions in the grass, leading away from the cave and toward the cliffs beyond. Zha's confusing, multi-species scent wafting toward me from the same direction.

With a sigh, I follow the tracks, moving faster now, my spikes twitching with each step. Why does zha always do this? Why can't zha just stay where it's safe?

The terrain is rougher as I approach the portion of the valley that tapers off into cliffs, the wind biting at my skin. I push forward, determined to find zha and bring zha back. As I round a corner, I see zha in the distance, staring up at the sharply rising cliff face.

For a moment, I just watch. Zha's colors are different now, shimmering in the light. Zha glows brighter, not the dull, pale pink of before as I walked away, finally giving in to the need to check the hoard, but something more vibrant. Something beautiful.

I blink, momentarily caught off guard. I've never seen zha like this before. There's a lightness to zha, a glow that's mesmerizing. My own body reacts without thinking, the usual confusion returning as my skin flickers to blue.

The purple hide underlying it all fits zha. Simmering anger, regardless of what other colors zha might show, it's right there, waiting to jump out.

I move closer, my eyes locked on zha. Zha is beautiful. More than I've ever noticed. The way zha's light flickers across zha's skin, the way the colors of purple hide, yellow tail, green hair blend together... It's captivating.

I catch myself staring, and I quickly look away, my spikes twitching with discomfort. No. I can't let myself be distracted. I need to get zha back to the cave. That's all that matters.

But when I look again, I can't help but think that no other treasure I've ever found—no gem, no piece of rare metal, no artifact—could ever compare to the sight before me. Even all of my treasures together would not match the way zha shines.

Why do I have to keep reminding myself of this?

As I draw closer, zha turns, noticing me. A soft, high-pitched sound escapes zha's mouth, and I feel a strange sensation rise up from deep within me—a rumble, a vibration that echoes through my chest.

I blink in surprise, watching as zha lets out another sound, this time louder, and my body reacts again, the blue light shifting, flashing orange as joy sparks in my chest.

Zha looks over at me, and the moment our eyes meet, I see it—a flash of orange on zha's skin, matching my own. It's brief, barely there, but I see it. And for some reason, it makes my middle segment tingle with a sensation I've never felt before.

I move closer, standing beside zha now, but I don't speak.

Zha doesn't say anything either, but I can feel zha's presence next to me, warm and glowing. For a long time, we just stand there, side by side, watching the valley.

The thought lingers in the back of my mind as we stand there in silence again.

"We should return. Predators will soon be up and about. We should rest before it is night."

Zha hums lowly in the back of zha's throat and I resist the urge to shiver.

"I doubt they would live long, but alright," zha concedes.

We don't talk after that, both lost in thoughts, both exhausted by the day's events, but the orange glow as we settle into the cave communicates everything that needs to be said.

* * *

"No one is carrying rocks for you, Kroaicho," Ree tells me again. "And we don't have time to go into your cave even if we had space for your... treasure."

The way zha says the last word sounds like just what I have come to expect from humans. No respect for history and an obsession with ugly things. I grind my tusks, opening my mouth to argue again, then shut it.

I keep trying to think of different ways to explain to them, frantic to convince them, my middle segment twisting in pain at the idea of losing another hoard. I can't do it again. I can't...

"I need your help, Kroaicho," Olivia grits out.

Zha is trying to keep a bundle of weapons from shifting off zha's back, but even with zha's newly enhance strength, zha is too small to effectively carry it. I look down at my collection of beautiful items clutched against me, then back to the ugly mass of metal and hand-woven grasses keeping it all bundled together and my middle segment hurts even more.

My upper limbs tremble as I slowly, painfully, place my treasures on the grass, chittering out my pain as I do it. Then I exhale a long breath and move over to help.

It's no trouble to carry the weapons, but I can't move my eyes away from the pile I'm leaving behind, careful to not think of the mounds of similar items deep in the caves beneath us.

"I can carry one of them," Olivia says in a soft voice. "Which one?"

How will I decide?

I choose hastily, knowing that if I linger, I may not make myself move. Instead, I use one of my middle limbs to touch one of the crystals and then start following the rest of the group out of the valley, my skin lit fully pink as I trudge along.

The journey is long. Long enough that I have time to think, especially since everyone is being carefully quiet. Even the argila somehow know to not let out their usual braying, though Rin's constant fussing is likely the cause.

Olivia seems worried about me, skin lighting up with blues and reds when zha looks over. Zha asks me to tell zha stories of my lost treasures back in the cave behind us and I comply in a low voice. Each one I tell makes it feel like the treasure is not lost; the story remains.

After the fourth story, I realize zha knew that all along. Zha's skin is lit up white with amusement and that inner whisper lets me know this shift in zha's story.

At first, my skin thrums purple at being led in such a way, but then I decide that I have been ignoring too many of the signals and whispers.

It's always been a bad habit that my zhann liked to point out. Whatever doesn't fit how I want to think about the world, such as gender in other species, I ignore.

Life is far less confusing that way... but it isn't going to help me right now. I already left my hoard—which is the source of the tight feeling in my middle segment—I should try to shift my thinking so the decision is worth it.

I start looking around at the group, paying far closer attention than I ever have to other beings.

I remember how differently I saw Olivia earlier and try to apply the same new vision to the rest. To the way the dappled moonlight moves along Drasuk's blue hide, signaling just how confusing zha always finds Kira. Then to the shifting orange and green fur that wafts from Thivoll's long mane, also fitting for how playful and completely absorbed zha is with Ree, zha's purple, orange, and black treasure that rides on zha's back, issuing silent commands to the group.

Then to the black and green of Kuret, a fitting combination to how focused zha is on Rin. The lightness of green, mixed with the pure black a zhann would signal for a zhannel... except in a new orientation. One I'm still beginning to appreciate as I think of how to become two with Olivia.

Except... we aren't just two, are we? I look around at the dizzying array of colors moving around me, opening my vision up to catch more details in the dark... and I finally see it. What Olivia has been trying to communicate. A glittering, living hoard.

My middle segment leaps as orange lights up my skin, but then red quickly takes over. A living hoard means a mobile hoard, I realize in horror. A hoard that is easily lost. That won't stay in one place, just like Olivia won't. That can be... killed.

How could I ever, possibly protect a hoard such as this?

How?

My skin pulses red and blue as I think of all the ways each of the bright treasure beings around me could die. No, no, no. This is far worse.

"What's wrong, Kroaicho?" Olivia whispers to me, skin lighting with concern.

After a deep breath, I settle my middle segment, reminding myself that the greatest treasures are the hardest to keep from being stolen. That a zhasie just has to fight all the harder, be all the more vicious to keep those treasures safe.

I move my head back and forth in the human gesture as my skin settles back to a dull blue and orange. "Nothing," I chitter back softly.

Olivia moves zha's head up and down, and doesn't speak again.

I spend the rest of the long trek thinking of ways to protect this new hoard. I'm so engrossed in my thoughts that I don't realize we have exited the forest until I stumble on rocks and plunge into the water. After a small moment of panic as I sink into the water—which is never a place a zhasie should ever be—strong tentacles wrap around me.

Eli is once again yellow in zha's pride as zha holds me aloft. I light up purple for a short moment as Olivia asks if I am alright, but then sink back into my thoughts, skin lit blue as I strategize. The soft laughter of the humans after Eli deposits me back on the shore barely registers on my mind.

I don't even balk at being carried in Wroahk's tentacles after everyone points out that I will sink to the bottom of the lake, incapable of swimming. After we move across, I only cast a quick glance at the glittering rocks on the shore and don't complain when the cave they offer smells of some foul beast.

I have never had a more important strategy to think through, and I had the most sought after hoard of all zhasie before ending up here. This is far, far more important than what I had on my home planet.

I will not fail to protect this living hoard. I can't.

32

Olivia

My mind is too tired to be overwhelmed, but Ree sent us to rest anyway before turning back to orchestrate the efficient movement of items into the beautiful little huts that a large, furry alien named Rannek apparently built while the rest of the group were away.

I don't know how he could have built even one of them in that amount of time, but there are three. I try to not think about it, my head already aching.

"We'll meet here at dark to have a campfire-free story time," Ree calls back to us.

I smile when I see how that makes Kroaicho light up bright orange, but just wave back in response.

The wind stirs softly as Kroaicho and I walk back toward our new cave. My legs are heavy, and the silence between us feels louder than even Wroahk's howling complaints that started back up as soon as we hit the lake water.

Kroaicho walks a few steps ahead, zha's two upper limbs tucked in tight, the blue of zha's glow faint but present. I glance sideways at zha every now and then, studying the subtle shifts in zha's skin, the colors flickering.

It's strange how quickly I've grown used to this—used to zha. If you had asked when I first crash-landed here, I never would've imagined being this close to an alien down to so much as physiology. But now, here I am, trudging beside Kroaicho, trusting zha far more than I trust this planet.

Still, I know where this is headed now that there is another cave. I can't stay cooped up forever. I can't sit still while my friends are out risking themselves looking for the others.

"Kroaicho," I say, trying to keep my tone light, though I know where this conversation is headed. "I was thinking... maybe we could—"

"No," Kroaicho cuts me off before I can even finish. The blue glow darkens slightly, a sign of irritation. Zha doesn't stop walking, though, and neither do I.

I sigh, letting the frustration wash over me. "You don't even know what I was going to say."

"I do. You want me to take you out into the forest. To look for others." Zha's voice is as steady as ever, but I can hear the underlying edge in it now. That same edge that comes every time I bring this up. "It's not safe."

"You keep saying that, but we can't just hide forever! I can't—" I stumble over the rocks as I quicken my pace to catch up to zha, brushing dirt off my knees as I continue. "I can't stay there, Kroaicho. I'm not like you."

Zha's spikes twitch, and I can see the faintest shift of purple in zha's blue glow. The color of frustration. At least I think it is—after all this time, I'm starting to understand Kroaicho's colors, but I'm still not entirely sure what every flicker means.

"I will search for the rest of the hoard," zha says finally, slowing zha's pace.

My heart skips a beat, annoyed we are still talking about trinkets. "I'm not talking about bits of metal, Kroaicho, I—"

"I'm not either." Kroaicho stops then, turning toward me, zha's tall frame towering over me, spikes and all. Zha's skin flickers again, the faint purple still there, but something else—something softer—pushes through. Orange, then red.

"We are two now, but I see now that we also have a hoard," zha starts.

"I don't want a—"

Zha interrupts me again. "No, listen. A living hoard. Of beings, not rocks."

My eyebrows lift. "That's… a huge shift for you, Kroaicho," I mutter, mind still catching up.

"Yes." Kroaicho's spikes twitch again, and a new color, yellow, begins to bloom across zha's skin. At first, I can't place it. It's brighter than anything I've seen on Kroaicho before, like zha is glowing from within.

I stare, fascinated. "What's… what's that color mean?"

Kroaicho tilts zha's head slightly, regarding me with those ever-watching eyes. "This is pride. I made a good decision and I am proud of it."

Pride. The realization makes me smile, and before I can stop myself, I reach out, letting my fingers hover just above zha's skin. He looks down at my hand, and I pull mine back, not willing to touch when I don't allow the same.

"That means a lot to me, Kroaicho," I whisper.

The yellow deepens, spreading slowly across zha's limbs. Kroaicho's eyes shift back to me, a flicker of orange flashing across zha's chest for the briefest second.

Without thinking, I blurt out, "Can I... touch you?"

I cringe, annoyed with myself, and waiting for zha to point out that I don't allow the same.

The question hangs in the air between us, and for a moment, Kroaicho doesn't respond. Zha's spikes twitch again, and I see the blue of confusion flash briefly before fading away. Finally, zha speaks.

"Yes."

I take a hesitant step forward, my hand trembling slightly as I reach out to press my palm gently against zha's arm.

Kroaicho has held me tight, but I always turned my palms in, so I never really knew...

Zha's skin is warm—softer than I expected, with a faint hum of energy beneath the surface. I can feel the rhythm of zha's pulse, steady and strong.

Kroaicho watches me, zha's eyes narrowing slightly as if it's studying my reaction. I run my fingers along the edge of one of zha's spikes, marveling at how smooth zha is. There's a gentleness here, hidden beneath all the sharpness.

I pull my hand back, curiosity satisfied, but suddenly self-conscious of how unfair it is that mixed in with the good feelings is my mind wanting to pull away from the contact.

And then, out of nowhere, my own body reacts, lighting green, making me realize I haven't been hounded by the arousal since zha used expellant on me.

I feel a surge of warmth flood through me, and I look down to see my skin glowing bright skin. This must be natural, then, and it catches me by surprise.

"You are green, Olivia," Kroaicho says, zha's voice betraying zha's own surprise.

But when I look up, I see the answering green thrumming along all of zha's limbs and segments.

Without another word, we turn and head toward the cave again, the green light still flickering softly across both of our bodies.

As we enter, zha's pink eyes land on me with a surprising level of intensity and I feel my breath catch in my throat.

I hold up a hand. "First... what do you mean by a living hoard? People aren't things, Kroaicho."

Zha's skin lights up purple. "Of course people are not things. I didn't say that."

I don't really believe it. "I've been treated like a thing before you, Kroaicho."

"I didn't—"

"Let me explain," I say, cutting zha off. "Well," I start, my voice shaky with uncertainty. "I guess... I should start from the beginning. I'm the youngest of four... uh, zhannel. Which is already a pain in the ass, but it gets worse. My siblings are all much older. One sister, two brothers. All from my mom's first marriage to this guy who, well, let's just say I'm glad wasn't alive long."

Kroaicho listens intently, zha's body shifting slightly, blue starting to light up on zha's skin.

"He was rich... I mean, he had a giant hoard, but wasn't my, uh... zhann. That was a māori guy. That's my biological father." I stop for a moment, my throat tightening as the weight of the truth settles in my chest. "I won't ever know who he was."

Kroaicho's confusion deepens, the soft blue glow intensifying. Zha doesn't understand human relationships and I know I need to skip past all of that.

"My mum, my zhann, spent a lot of her... hoard trying to fix whatever is broken inside of me."

For a moment, I'm lost in the memory of those days—sleepless nights, doctor's visits, the meds that turned me into a zombie, the never-ending exhaustion. And the constant guilt. Always the guilt.

"My siblings," I say, forcing the words out through clenched teeth, "they hated me for it. Because it was their inheritance. Most of the hoard came from their zhann, so they think I don't deserve any of it. As if I asked for that money, I mean hoard, to be used like that. After a while, it was clear that I was just a thing to spend money on until she fixed me. When I tried to leave, she would guilt me back into her life. Talk about her illness and how it was my fault and I'd end up caring for her."

Kroaicho's glow shifts again, a deep purple of irritation this time, as if zha is angry on my behalf. It gives me confidence to keep talking.

"They hate me, but they don't get it," I whisper, my voice barely audible now. "They don't understand what it's like to give up your life for someone. My mum... she could've hired help. She could've spared me from all of it, but she didn't. She expected me to be there for her no matter what. And I was. Because of guilt over money I didn't ask to be spent in the first place."

Kroaicho leans in slightly, zha's glowing eyes locked onto mine. Zha doesn't interrupt, just listens, and for some reason, that makes it easier to keep going.

"I missed out on everything," I admit, my voice cracking. "Friends, parties, college... not that I wanted those things, but I wanted the choice, at least. And for what? For a woman who couldn't even treat me the way a mother should. She was so focused on herself, on her sickness, that she never saw what it was doing to me. But I still wanted her to see me and appreciate me. It's just... complicated. It's not healthy. It never was."

There's silence for a moment, just the soft light of our glow filling the cave as I process my own words. I don't know why I'm telling zha all this. Maybe it's because I've been bottling it up for so long. Or maybe I just needed to say it out loud to someone—anyone—who wouldn't judge me.

"I did not understand a lot of that," Kroaicho admits and my heart sinks, "but I gathered enough to know that you were treated poorly. But that is not how I see you. Anything in a hoard is not a 'thing.' It is... a treasure to be protected. A treasure worth time and attention. A treasure that cannot be replaced. What I realized, just now, is that no treasure fits that description better than you. There is never more than one person that is exactly the same, and you are the most valuable among them."

My skin lights with orange to hear zha's words, but then I realize there is another unsettled matter tied to my story. "My two zhann," Kroaicho twitches at that, still getting used to the idea. "Did not raise me together and it was terrible for me. I mean, it happens to a lot of people and they are fine, but I don't want to do that. If we are two, then if you have a zhannel, then we become three... or four. I'm not ready for that," I add hastily, "even if it was possible, but you need to know that there is definitely a 'we' when it comes to that."

Kroaicho nods, the movement awkward for zha and it makes me smile. "I will agree to us being three... or four, instead of one. When the time comes to share our hoard."

33

Kroaicho

I know there is no miscommunication or misunderstanding now. Olivia's skin is purple with zha's rage, but also with the light that zha got from me. And we are both thrumming green, and not just because of this confusing arousal that zha spoke of or something done to zha by the genali.

No, this is our own glow, and this time I plan to enjoy it and not allow the doubts that hit me before—that zha would take my hoard—distract me.

With that thought, I can no longer wait to touch zha and surge forward, eliciting a shocked squawk from Olivia before my limbs tighten enough to pull out that sigh of contentment as I squeeze.

I take in a deep breath, impatient to hear the sounds zha makes when I let out my expellent, but zha interrupts me. "Wait!"

I close the flaps of my expellent with great difficulty, skin thrumming with my annoyance. "What now? I would like to feel you writhing again."

Zha makes a choking sound, then speaks again. "I want that too, but I don't want this to be one sided."

My tusks start grinding together that we are back to this argument. "You don't have expellent, Olivia."

"I know that, but don't think I forgot that you almost told me somewhere I could touch," zha snaps back, zha's skin lighting up purple to match my own.

"You do not like to touch," I retort.

"I wouldn't be offering if I didn't want to do it. It's easier when it's me touching someone else. I want this, Kroaicho. Tell. Me." The last two words are clipped and forceful and I relent.

"Inside my nostrils," I explain.

"Say what?" zha responds, skin lighting up blue.

"The flaps that hold back my expellent. Some zhannel find something soft to hold and stroke in there," I say with a huff.

"Oh, 'some zhannel'? Never you?" zha responds, mocking in zha's voice.

"As I said, it is not necessary that—"

"Stop talking and shift me around so I can do this, uh... thing," zha says with conviction.

I move zha farther up onto my upper segment as I push my head back and lower my snout, ensuring that zha's limbs can reach.

"There are four. All of them or just one?" zha asks.

"One is sufficient, I am sure," I chitter back.

"Four it is, then. Luckily I have four hands now," zha says while reaching up toward me.

My spikes tingle and my middle segment twitches in anticipation.

"You are going to have to squeeze me harder than that or this might be more violent than pleasurable," zha tells me and I quickly comply.

The idea of zha's wrist claws near such a delicate area while zha is angry is horrifying. My body is rigid as each of zha's hands make gentle contact with the fluttering edges of my nostrils. The first touch sends waves of feeling through all of my segments and I relax.

I trust zha, and there is something about the purple of zha's skin mixed with the thrumming green of zha's mating signal that is very exciting. Zha gently moves zha's soft, deliciously clawless hands into my bottom nostrils and I let out a long, chittering moan.

"The top ones are tight, Kroaicho," she whispers in manticorid. "I don't want to hurt you."

"You won't," I click back, falling back to my native language in my excitement.

The pressure against the slits of my upper nostrils increases, and then my whole snout is throbbing with pleasure as the tips of each of zha's fingers find the edges of my expellent flaps.

"Yes," I hiss out, then lose the ability to communicate.

Zha has found each ridged edge and is stroking in long, slow glides. Zha's skin is slightly rough and it's making me let go of my tight control. Not long after, enough expellent leaks to help each stroke of zha's fingers glide in a smooth, continual oval.

I hold my segments rigid and pull zha's soft body closer to me, tucking zha tight to me as the pleasure builds in stronger and stronger streaks of feeling from my snout down the the end of my last segment.

Zha increases the speed of zha's stroking, zha's own breath coming fast as I keep my flaps closed tight, but revel in the warmth of zha's hands and zha's scent as my breath bellows in and out along the upper reaches of each flap.

I never thought a scent would be pleasurable, but with each stroke and each deep drag of breath, my segments get continually tighter. When each flap finally seizes, sending waves of pleasure from my snout, I lose control of my flaps and on the next exhale I flood my expellent into zha's face.

My segments are quaking as Olivia lets out zha's delicious sounds of pleasure and zha's body writhes against me.

As the pleasure settles into a contented thrum along my skin, I shift my body so zha can lay against me. Zha's pleasure has made zha sleepy and it's not long before I can no longer see the pink glow of zha's eyes.

I'm still awake, eyes roaming over zha's beautiful, treasured features when zha wakes up again.

"That was amazing, Kroaicho," Olivia whispers to me.

"It was," I agree.

"Aren't you glad you get to do that more than twice?" zha teases.

"I am," I agree again. "Now let's sleep so there is some time before the sharing of stories."

Zha laughs. "You and your stories. That would have normally freaked me out. The idea of being out there with a group, I mean... but I'm looking forward to it too. For now, just hold me?"

And so I do.

34

Olivia

My skin is lit up like an orange Christmas tree when I sit in the center of the buildings Rannek built. I hadn't noticed the lovely benches before and it's soothing to run my fingers over the carvings of odd, alien animals on the sides of them.

It's almost too much to take in at once, so I focus on the details.

I glance over to the big, shy purple furred male, who is still actively whittling away at a bench across from me, using a combination of sharp rock and claws.

I just meant to take a walk down the shore, but the artistry drew me in. When I glance down, I see a long, thin piece of shale in the dirt and drop to the ground, inspired to draw another *tā moko*.

I get lost in the process for a while, thrilled with how fun this is with two right hands, and as I finish up I realize that Ree is seated on the bench behind me.

"Oh... hi. Uh, have you been there long?" I ask, feeling self-conscious.

"Yes, but don't worry," she says in a light tone. "That's beautiful. Is it tribal? Oh, right. You're from New Zealand, aren't you? Māori?"

"That's right," I say, still keeping my eyes downcast, embarrassed for someone to see my art. "I am... uh, half that. Māori, I mean."

It's the first time I've told a human and it feels good to claim it.

"Olivia..." Ree says, trailing off and then speaking again. "Not to sound rude, but are you autistic?"

My eyebrows furrow, memories of a string of psychologists surfacing. "No. I'm too empathetic to be autistic."

"Are you? Did someone tell you that?" she asks gently.

"Yes, an expert," I reply, confused.

"I rather doubt they were an expert, Olivia," she says. "Most likely they were narrow-minded and only knew what autism looked like in men."

"No, you don't understand," I argue. "I'm just... angry... violent. I was a terrible—"

She cuts me off. "Stop for a moment, please. When did you get angry?"

Kira and Rin walk into the clearing right as she asks and I freeze up when I see others moving toward us, but then make myself let it go.

I'm sick of pretending.

"I get angry when people touch me. Sometimes I hurt people," I say, feeling miserable to admit it. "I kept getting moved from one boarding school to the next, each time getting expelled for fighting."

"I see," Ree says. "And are sounds too loud and lights too bright sometimes?"

"Yes..." I trail off.

"What happens, besides sometimes being violent, when you get overwhelmed?" she asks.

I swallow hard. "Sometimes I shut down... I mean... I just can't stay awake because it all just feels like too much."

Ree nods. "You said you're empathetic. How do you know how people feel?" she asks.

"Well, not always with their faces, that's confusing a lot of the time, but from their voices. From context and knowing how it would make me feel. See? Not autism."

"That is autism, Olivia," Ree says gently as more people take up seats around us. "Sometimes it isn't that someone can't recognize emotion or empathize. In fact, for some people they empathize so much it is painful for them."

What? I blink, what she's telling me suddenly resonating.

"But... I thought we had healing nanites. Why don't they fix my broken brain, then?" I say, reeling.

"Because it's not broken, Liv. Just different. Just like all of their..." Ree pauses to gesture around at all of the hulking aliens around us. "... brains aren't broken."

"I think a case can be made for Drasuk," Kira breaks in dryly.

"Shut up, Kira," Ree says, but not unkindly. "Look at them. Their brains are just like they should be. Just like yours is how it should be."

"Am I an alien now, though?" I ask, still catching up.

"Well, we all pretty much are at this point," Rin says, laughing.

"But you aren't like me," I insist, "and it's just getting worse since I met Kroaicho. Now I also want to hoard things, even though I know it's stupid and I just... I..."

"What?" Kira asks softly. "You what?"

"I know you'll get sick of me. Everyone does," I admit, voice breaking.

Ree lets out a long breath fists clenching, but Kira laughs. "Livie, my green, green girl. Have you met Drasuk? Have you met Wroahk? We love those idiots and you are a cute little ball of fluff in comparison."

Ree chuckles, no longer tense now. "Listen to me, Olivia. I doubt we are going to be able to leave this planet, which means we are making a new world. Right now. With every choice we make. A new culture. We won't have a neurotypical world you have to bend yourself into a pretzel to fit into. It's going to be full of aliens, which includes us, by the way. Just be you."

"It isn't normal," I mutter, still unconvinced. "The rage."

"That's the wrong way to think about it," Eli's voice calls out.

It takes me a moment to realize that she's in a wooden tub that I thought was the start to some new project and hadn't looked inside of. When did she get there?

I don't figure it out before she starts speaking again. "Instead of asking yourself why you get upset when people touch you, the better question is why are people touching you without permission? That's what isn't normal."

Rin winces. "I did that. I'm sorry, Liv."

"No, it's really okay, like I said," I reassure her. "You didn't know and you were terrified. I can control the anger when I need to."

"Of course you can," Kira says, pride in her voice. "You are really fucking strong. Mentally, emotionally, and physically. You are a great fucking ally."

"Community member!" Eli calls out.

"Friend," Rin adds with a smile.

"The greatest treasure of the hoard," Kroaicho chitters from behind me in zha's native tongue.

I whirl, skin moving from blue back to orange. I grin and Kroaicho's skin lights up orange too.

"Fuck," Kira quips. "Who needs night vision with these two around?"

Everyone laughs, me with them. Kroaicho settles down in the cleared space behind one of the benches, which I just now notice each bench has behind it. Plenty of space to fit all of the big beasts. There's even a two-tiered bench that has Kuret on the higher part and Rin on the lower so they can both sit comfortably.

I blink, finally getting what Ree is trying to say. Rannek has been busy, paying close, quiet attention to everyone around him, steadily making everything as perfect for each of them as he possibly can. As fast as he can.

After dusting my hands off, careful to not cut myself with my wrist claws, I move to the bench in front of Kroaicho. Zha puts zha's arms around me and squeezes me just the right amount.

I brace myself for someone to point out that it doesn't make sense that I let Kroaicho touch me, but no one even looks our way, wrapped up in getting settled and making fun of each other.

I look down and notice that my clawed feet are perfectly level with the ground. This bench was made for me, I realize... and I just met Rannek. We barely even spoke.

Tears are swimming in my eyes as the stories start up.

"You should have seen his fucking face," Kira barks out. "He kept saying *pet* like it was some sort of insult and then I fucking stabbed him."

Drasuk lets out a rock grinding sound of rage. "That is not how it happened!"

"I like this story, Kira," Kroaicho breaks in. "It matches Drasuk quite well. Zha is the perfect conceited treasure."

"See, even glow bug sees it, you big blue lump," Kira says as she punches the grumbling drakonid on his shoulder, then hisses.

"And Kira is the best treasure at insults," Kroaicho adds and Kira puffs out her chest and wiggles her bone-crowned head.

"Fuck yes, glow bug," she says pumping a fist in the air.

"What kind of treasure am I?" Eli asks, water splashing out of the tub in her excitement.

"You are a glittering orange glow," Kroaicho responds.

Eli sinks down in the water, making a sound of confusion.

"Zha means you are cheerful, like the orange glow of our skin. A treasure of joy," I translate.

"Oh, I like that," she says, back to grinning. "I do try."

A flash of purple from the corner of my eye catches my attention and I glance over in time to see Rannek place a small wooden sculpture on the bench beside me.

"For you, Kroaicho," the purple male whispers.

Kroaicho looks down at it, then carefully extends a middle limb to gently take hold of it. "You made this treasure? It is beautiful. Olivia spoke of art and you are clearly well versed."

Kroaicho speaks louder. "Rannek is the treasure of thoughtfulness," zha announces.

The soft-spoken purple male's fur puffs up so much he looks nearly double his already formidable size.

"Th-thank you," Rannek stutters, then hastily walks off into the woods.

"Aww," Eli says. "He is so adorable."

"Tell that to Wroahk already," Kira grumbles.

Eli snorts. "Wroahk stopped insulting him, Kira. I don't know what happened since they've been working on the Many Teeth protections, but they must basically be best buddies now if Wroahk isn't complaining about Rannek being a pacifist."

"I see your point," Kira says with a laugh. "Tell us what kind of treasure Wroahk is, Kroaicho."

"I don't know yet," Kroaicho says in a serious tone. "I must spend more time assessing before I can tell how zha fits in the hoard."

Ree snickers. "Don't we all..."

"What about the argila?" Rin asks, pointing to where the three beasts are sprawled out behind her and Kuret.

And so the rounds of treasure identification continue. Then more jokes. So many of them after that are at Drasuk's expense that soon the tears in my eyes are from laughing, not just from the wonder of feeling a part of something special.

All the while, Kroaicho and I provide plenty of beautiful muted orange glow to make up for the lack of campfire.

Olivia

I open my mouth so wide to yawn that it pops and there is an answering pain that shoots through my sinuses, making Kroaicho startle next to me as we make our way back to the cave. Zha has the small carving held gently in zha's claws, treating it with the utmost care.

Rannek seems even more shy and unsure of how to interact than Kroaicho and I are and it makes me smile to think of just how far we have come. We are almost... sociable at this point.

I can't deny that I'm exhausted from being around everyone, but tonight felt like a turning point. My exhaustion is a pleasant sort of tiredness, like I only need to retreat to recharge, not to protect my sanity. I can't remember a time when I felt this wiped out, but was already planning to come right back out again to see people. I'm looking forward to it, even.

I want to help Rannek build more huts and hopefully get him to teach me how to use my claws to carve like he does. I haven't seen paper since I got here and drawing in the dirt just doesn't provide the same sort of satisfaction... but there is still this constant impulse to create.

Learning how to make three--dimensional art is exciting and for some inexplicable reason, so is the idea of helping Rannek come out of his shell a bit. He reminds me of myself, except far less angry. He isn't the least bit violent, but seems just as socially unsure. Everyone has been nice to him, but I still feel this strong protective instinct when I see just how kind and soft he is.

Apparently even Wroahk, who seems like the ultimate predator, sees it too, so Rannek has plenty of protectors, but somehow it feels right for me to take on the job in a more dedicated way. The innocent should be shielded. I wasn't and I used to be horrified by the violence within me... but I see now that it can be used to protect people.

I hope Rannek doesn't mind having a new body guard. My lips twitch. I hope I don't mind spending that much time with someone.

Then I glance back to Kroaicho and realize that I already am spending time with someone and with a raised eyebrow it suddenly occurs to me that it doesn't drain me. Not like being with others. It's refreshing and it gives me hope that maybe that feeling can be extended to other people.

Tomorrow I'll start shadowing Rannek to test that theory. Well, at least part of the time. I still want to get my four hands wrapped around the throat of the enemy as often as possible.

I let out a moan, remembering the feeling and Kroaicho stops in zha's tracks and whirls to face me, skin lighting up green in response. My mind hadn't been on that, but as soon as I see the glow my own skin flashes green as well.

Both of us instantly pick up our pace, hopping over rocks, and it makes me laugh. Kroaicho's skin swirls with orange among the green.

I'm breathless I enter the cave, still smiling. Kroaicho circles me, then looks down at zha's hand and the sculpture still clutched in it, skin lighting blue and orange at the sight. For a moment, zha simply stands there, thinking, then zha heads over to a cave wall.

I'm about to ask what is going on when Kroaicho pulls back a massive arm, then takes a long, horizontal slice at the cave. Rocks scatter, all of them flying away from me and I jump at the sound of their impact.

"What in the…"

I don't bother finishing my sentence because the purpose becomes clear as Kroaicho very gently places Rannek's sculpture on the newly created shelf.

That's new.

"Why not just start a new pile?" I ask.

"This is treasure of a different kind, Olivia," zha explains. "Something given, not found, or taken, or handed down from a zhann. Something special, with a rich story centered around the person who gave it and the moment they did."

My lips quirk up at the awe in zha's voice at this new concept. "It's called a gift, Kroaicho, and I agree. They are special. Mostly because they remind you of who gave them."

My smile falls when I think of the sketch book my boss gave me. I won't ever see him again, will I? Then I remember what he said he wanted: for me to go out into the world and make a difference. I snort. Well, I went beyond it, but I will still make that difference.

I can make him proud, even if he won't ever know about it.

There is a pang between my eyes and I rub at it. Why would I want to cry? That's a happy thought, isn't it? After another throb of pain and no tears come, I shrug it off, once again distracted by Kroaicho.

Zha is turned to face me, skin lit up almost completely green, but with swirls of orange to communicate zha's contentment. Zha moves forward, taking several long strides on multiple limbs before sweeping me up and against zha's chest.

"This would be the second time, Kroaicho," I tease. "Are you sure you want to use up all two of your mating options?"

After a clack of tusks, zha responds. "Do you plan to steal my Rannek gift?"

"No," I retort.

"Then there will be far more than two matings," zha says with another two clacks of tusks hitting tusks.

Kroaicho settles down onto the knees of zha's back limbs, holding me just the perfect amount of tight against zha.

I reach my four arms up toward zha's face, but then feel self-conscious, remembering how bossy I was last time. "Was all four too much? Was I too rough?"

"You were perfect," zha says. "I never knew it could feel like that."

My heart leaps at the praise and my heart starts beating faster thinking of how good it felt for me, too.

I glance up at the spikes on the left side of zha's head, thinking of my own new spiky additions, which Kroaicho has already adjusted to for this hold, it seems. "I guess we'll never be able to fuck on our backs, will we?" I say with a laugh.

"Why would anyone ever do that?" zha asks, blue swirling in now. "Humans have many strange ideas about mating."

"You have liked them so far," I point out.

"That is true," zha concedes. "What others do you have planned?"

It's odd to be the one who knows more about sex, but it also feels good. Like I have power and control. Similar to how it feels to kill an enemy, but even better.

It makes me feel bold and I reach my lower arms up before I can think much of it and grab ahold of two of Kroaicho's lower tusks. The ones that jut upward.

"I will make you feel amazing," I growl out. "Just do as I say, like a good caterdragon. Just remember: I am in control."

Shivers pass over Kroaicho, pink eyes widening and skin blazing green. "You are. I would give you every treasure," zha breathes out.

"No," I say forcefully. "There is no exchange for this. All I want is you to do what I say."

"I will," zha says, voice soft and eyes still wide, body trembling.

It pleases me, my own skin lighting up to a brighter green to hear the capitulation. The submission in zha's tone makes me pant. I pull on both tusks, moving Kroaicho's massive head closer, pushing zha's head back so zha's neck is arched in just the way I want it, spikes shivering and eyes looking down at my hands in anticipation.

"Don't move," I bark out.

With careful, teasing strokes I run the tips of the fingers of my two upper arms gently around the flaring edges of zha's lower nostrils. Once, twice, and again. Each time zha's breath comes faster and faster.

"You are so soft here, Kroaicho," I groan.

With each stroke and breath, some of zha's expellent starts to coat my fingers, exciting me. Suddenly, I can't wait any longer, moving my hands to the upper, tighter nostrils and easing my way in.

"You take me so well," I pant out.

I throb at the juncture of my thighs as I feel the tight hold and resistance against my fingers. I'm only able to fit two fingers in and fold my ring and pinky fingers close to my palm so I can reach the terminus and the slick, delicate membrane.

From my experiments the last time, I know that stroking from the top then down and around, in a C shape, but with the one on my right backward, elicits the most excited chittering.

With each stroke, I increase the pressure and speed, my clit throbbing in time with my rising excitement. Kroaicho is holding back zha's expellent until zha's release. I want to make this as pleasurable for zha as possible, but the idea of pulling a long breath of that heady scent into my body and exploding with pleasure makes me impatient.

Every few strokes of my fingers I have to remind myself to slow down, but after a while I'm too caught up in how low Kroaicho's chitters are to pay attention to taking it slow.

"Let go for me," I order.

Immediately, Kroaicho starts shuddering and suddenly lets out a bellowing breath, the mist of zha's expellent invading my lungs and making neurons fire.

I thrash, my moans echoing in the cave as the waves of orgasms hit.

36

Kroaicho

Olivia is still holding tight to my tusks as my release pulses through me. As it recedes, I focus on the sounds zha is making. Ones I never thought would ever bring me satisfaction, but they do. Zha has lost control, wriggling in my arms and it is a singularly delightful sensation.

I take in a long breath, appreciating the musky way zha smells as soon as my expellent is released.

Suddenly, Olivia stops thrashing, zha's back arching. Zha's eyes open wide, then zha coughs. And coughs again.

My skin lights blue, then red, but before I can ask if zha needs help, I see the expellent wafting from zha's small nose.

I have no time to wonder at it before it reaches me. Olivia's fingers are still stroking me as the tremors of pleasure hit, rippling along my limbs, making my body jerk.

The expellent is in my upper segment, begging to be pulled in farther. The temptation to open up my inner membranes and pull it all the way down into my lower segment is almost overwhelming.

After all of the missed mating seasons, this is my chance.

This is exactly what a zhasie does. Exactly what my zhann would expect of me. There is no guarantee there will ever be another opportunity...

But then I remember my conversation with Olivia and our agreement and I push back my instinct, ensuring that my middle and lower segment membranes remain tightly shut.

I let myself simply enjoy the thrumming, rolling sensations of Olivia's expellent in my upper segment as long as it lasts, finally realizing that zha is trying to speak with me.

"Kroaicho! What did I do? You said it can be a weapon. Oh my *God*. Kroaicho!" zha says frantically.

When I open my eyes, there is wetness trailing zha's face, skin lighting purple and pink.

"I am well, Olivia," I assure zha. "You used the correct mix."

"Oh fuck, Kroaicho. I don't even know how to fucking mix whatever that is. I could kill you!" zha hisses back.

"No, you can't," I counter.

"Oh no… did I just get you pregnant? I'm not ready for that. I mean, I will, but I'm not—"

I stop Olivia before zha causes mental harm. "There will be no zhannel until we are both ready."

Zha's small forehead wrinkles. "You can control that?"

"Yes, easily," I respond. "We will do this many, many times. I will do exactly as you say."

She snorts. "You can tell me to do things too."

My skin surges brighter orange. "I will. I see now that it is another form of treasure. One that can and will be repeated often."

Zha lets out a long breath. "Yes. Something to exchange with each other, I agree."

"A gift, then," I say with a decisive clack of my tusks, muted by the fact that zha is still holding tight to two of them. "One of the many benefits of being two instead of one."

Zha pulls zha's lips wide at that. "Two really is better than one. One hundred percent agreed," zha replies.

37

Olivia

When I wake up, I'm trapped. It takes me a moment to work out that it's Kroaicho. We are both on our sides, zha pulling me close. I try to wake Kroaicho up, but zha is like an immovable object. I manage to free one arm and give a gentle push against zha's chest, which only makes zha's other arm tighten around me.

Great. Just great. I consider using my new strength, but it would be a rude awakening.

"Alright, buddy. Time to let go," I whisper, half-heartedly trying not to laugh. Kroaicho's skin is a soft, warm hue—somewhere between orange and white—but the big lunk is dead asleep, zha's breathing slow and steady, entirely oblivious to my struggle.

After a few more awkward tugs and some serious contortionist-level maneuvering, I manage to extricate myself. Finally free, I stretch my arms high above my head, muscles protesting from the odd sleeping position.

"Not sure how I'm alive after that," I mumble, a little bemused at myself for managing to escape what felt like a living weighted blanket. A very, very big one.

Once my limbs stop aching from the stretch, I glance around. Not sure how or when... but I can see a pile of treasure starting up in a far corner of the cave and I snort.

That didn't take long.

I shift my gaze to Kroaicho, still peacefully asleep. Zha's long, muscular arms are curled slightly, massive forelimbs resting gently against the ground. There's something oddly serene about watching the lumbering oaf rest like this, the soft glow of zha's orange hue radiating warmth.

I creep closer, cautious not to wake zha just yet now that I extracted myself. Leaning over zha's face, I find myself staring at the soft rise and fall of zha's chest, the gentle flutter of zha's spiked head with each breath. It's strangely captivating, to watch this powerful alien creature at rest. For a moment, it's easy to forget just how dangerous everything on this planet is, Kroaicho included.

I start to prop my chin on the back of a hand, then have to reassess when claws are in the way. Then I'm back to watching him for a few minutes.

Soon the boredom starts to creep in. Sure, watching an alien sleep is fascinating for about thirty seconds, but then it's just... sleeping. My mind drifts, and I consider exploring the island again. I glance toward the cave's dark mouth, curiosity stirring inside me.

But then, the memory of getting lost in endless passages slithers into my brain, and a shudder runs down my spine. Yeah, nope. I'm not wandering alone right now.

With a sigh, I turn back to Kroaicho. There's really nothing else to do, and boredom is quickly turning into impatience. I cross my arms, tapping my foot. "Alright, big zha," I mutter under my breath, "time to wake up."

It's not really needed, I know... I could just go find someone to talk to, but once I get something in my head it's hard to change direction. I poke zha's chest. Nothing.

"Hey, Kroaicho," I whisper, jabbing zha again, harder this time.

Zha doesn't move, just continues zha's steady breathing, oblivious to my poking. I huff in frustration, but I'm not giving up that easily. Leaning closer, I give zha another series of pokes, one after the other, right in zha's side.

"Come on," I grumble, now poking zha like I'm trying to win a carnival game. "Wake up!"

Kroaicho groans softly, shifting slightly, but still refuses to open zha's eyes. I grin mischievously. If this glow stick thinks zha can out-sleep me, zha has got another think coming.

"Alright, fine," I say, poking zha once more for good measure. "You asked for it."

I poke zha's nose this time. Zha finally stirs, eyes fluttering open slowly, blinking up at me with a look that could only be described as alien irritation. Kroaicho's skin flushes a deep violet and I can't help but laugh at the sight of it.

"There you are," I say, giving the alien a cheeky grin. "Good morning, sunshine."

Kroaicho glares at me... or, well, zha's version of a glare, but it's hard to take the big zha seriously when zha is still glowing a soft orange from contentment. "Why?" zha's voice is low, groggy, and mildly accusatory. "That is an incredibly rude place to..." zha trails off, then repeats the question. "Why?"

I raise an eyebrow. "Why what?"

"Why wake me?" the alien grumbles, sitting up with a groan, Zha's massive arms stretching out beside zha. Kroaicho gives me a curious look, eyes flicking over my face, then lower to my glowing skin.

I roll my eyes, then hiss out in pain, clutching at my face and blinking hard.

Kroaicho's glow shifts to white—amusement. "Did I not say that it wasn't natural to roll your eyes about?"

I feel my skin heat up, the glow from my own body deepening to a dark purple—annoyance. I glare at the overgrown candle stick, then take a deep breath, letting out a huff. "I woke you up because I'm bored, okay?"

Kroaicho blinks at me, tilting zha's head in confusion. "Bored?"

"We talked about this. Yeah, you know, that feeling where you're sitting around doing nothing for so long that you start to go insane?" I wave my hands for emphasis. "That."

The alien's amused glow brightens, the white practically jumping off zha's skin. Zha leans back on zha's massive arms, giving me a look that's somewhere between smug and curious. "We have talked about this, yes. And you need... me?"

I scowl, crossing my arms tighter over my chest. "Yes, I need someone to talk to. Is that so hard to believe?"

For a moment, Kroaicho just stares at me, and then zha blinks again, this time faster, before zha straightens up. Zha's glow shifts from white back to a soft orange, and zha leans in slightly, eyes wide with sudden interest. "What do you wish to talk about?"

I freeze for a second, taken aback by the sudden shift in zha's mood. Kroaicho looks almost... eager? I wasn't expecting that.

"Well, uh..." I start, but my words trail off as I try to think of where to even begin. The glow of my eyes reflects in zha's now attentive gaze, and I feel my pulse quicken at the intensity in zha's gaze.

Is it just me or did the temperature just skyrocket?

Shit, what did I want to talk about again? I blurt out the first thing that comes to mind.

"Want to go for a swim?"

Zha's skin flares purple and then I remember the incident when we got to the lake and suddenly I can't stop laughing.

38

Kroaicho

I glare at the human. Again with the laughter. Olivia, bent over clutching zha's stomach, lets out this... sound, an irritating mix of amusement and hysteria, and I feel my glow deepening to an even darker purple. I don't appreciate it. I don't see what's so funny about me sinking like a rock.

I shift my weight, pulling all four of my upper limbs tight against my upper segment as I stare at Olivia, waiting for this episode to end. Zha's laughter continues, the irritating echoes bouncing off the cave walls. Zha looks up, wipes a tear from zha's face, and finally manages to stifle another snort of amusement.

Olivia glances at me, and I can feel zha's gaze softening when zha sees the irritation radiating off my skin. My glow flickers into a deeper purple, and I immediately regret it when I see zha's ridiculous human *smile* grow wider.

"Oh, come on," Olivia coos at me, zha's voice dripping down into lower chittering. "Stop pouting, Kroaicho. It wasn't that bad. Eli snapped you right back up."

"And then you all laughed at me," I point out. "This is a human reaction, isn't it?"

I hate it when zha does this. I shift in place, narrowing my eyes and trying to focus on something else, anything else, other than the way zha is talking to me like I'm a zhannel.

"It is," zha admits.

I huff, turning my head away slightly, though I keep my glowing eyes fixed on zha. "It was highly unpleasant and clearly dangerous."

That finally sobers Olivia up. Zha straightens and gives me a look. I know this look. It's the one that makes me anxious because it often precedes zha's temper flaring up. Whenever zha gives me that look, things tend to escalate. Fast.

This time, it just makes me want to get closer to zha and see what zha will do, not retreat. Maybe zha will grab my tusks and use that gruff tone again. I shiver in anticipation. Maybe zha...

I stop myself there, reminding myself that as much as I have changed, I am still holding on to my insistence to only look at things my own way. Olivia is not a zha. Olivia is a *she*. I roll the word in my mind, pulling up the equivalents in all the languages I have learned, letting the idea soak in until the words and the concept become natural.

I brace myself, but instead of shouting or snapping at me like I expect, Olivia just rolls her eyes. The glow from her pale pink irises pulses with some kind of odd... discomfort? She groans in pain, which makes my skin flair in response. My spikes twitch involuntarily.

"What the hell?" Olivia exclaims, eyes wide.

She rubs her temples. She is so stubborn. "Why does that hurt so much?"

I shoot Olivia a smug flash of skin, letting a low chitter rumble through my chest. "I told you to stop doing that."

She snorts out a breath, then looks at me, skin lighting back to orange. Suddenly, her eyes are far more intense and her skin lights up blue.

"What does that color mean?" she asks.

I'm confused for a moment, skin also lighting blue, but then I look down and see the streaks of black mixed in with it and my tusks drop open.

I stare, mesmerized. I haven't seen black on a zhasie since my zhann...

"Kroaicho," Olivia says. "Is something wrong? Are you alright?"

When I look up, her skin is pulsing red in fear.

"No, I mean, yes. I am well. Black means..." I trail off, not knowing the word.

"What?" Olivia prompts.

"The closest, biggest emotion possible," I explain, looking back at the dark patterns.

"*Love*?" she asks, voice soft.

I don't know the word, but when I glance back up, I see black swirls mixed with orange on her skin and I know whatever word it is, must be the right one.

I point a claw at her. "Yes. *Love*," I agree.

She looks down at her hands, using a finger to trace the black swirls as they solidify into full, dark expressions of feeling between us.

"Two, not one," she says in a whisper and it sends the same thrill through my segments as it did last night.

With a wide human smile, she looks back up. "Apparently, I *love* you. Don't let it go to your head."

"Go to my... that makes no sense," I point out.

She rolls her eyes again, then yelps, holding her eyes.

"I will keep reminding you to not do that," I tell her.

"Forever?" she asks, voice light.

"If needed, but I hope you will learn faster than that," I reply, then let out a shocked breath when her tentacle tail whacks me in my middle segment.

She is laughing now. "Like you learned about your hoard?"

"What hoard?" I ask as I carefully ignore the pile that has already started in the corner, skin lighting up yellow despite my attempts to stop it.

Zha moves around me. "How about I just rearrange this little—"

I whip around, arms reaching out imploringly as her laughter reaches a higher pitch. She is hopping around my hoard, six limbs gyrating in an odd rhythm when I realize it is a joke.

"I should have tossed you in that chasm you were sleeping next to when I had the chance," I grumble, skin lighting up white in contradiction to my statement.

"Don't worry," she chants out. "There will be other chasms."

39

Preview of Ruby

Szhe'ka

She curls her body inward so that she looks smaller than she actually is, and her bright threads are splayed behind her like a carpet of red flowers on the green forest ground.

If I stretch my hand out far enough, I can reach out and touch her again, like I know I really want to, though I decide it's not a great idea. Plus, I already touched her once before and from our short time together, I know she would rather have me as far away from her as possible.

I cannot tear my eyes away from her delicate features, each one so much smaller than mine that it makes me wonder how she gets anything done with them. I come to understand that I'm deeply fascinated by everything this small creature does—how she can breathe, fit bits of food into her mouth or even see.

She probably does all these things normally in a way that is natural to her kind. Still, it is all new to me.

I am especially surprised every time at the amount of venom she can shoot out of her for anything she does not like. She is, in a word, enrapturing, and I am a fly caught in her trap.

She notices me staring and I divert my eyes, expecting her to scold me, but she does not. Instead, she gets up restlessly and drops to the ground with a sigh of exhaustion and folds into herself, this time facing me. Her eyes are squeezed shut but her body is vibrating, and I know she cannot be comfortable.

"Come closer. Stay warm," I sing softly to her and her eyes open.

She shoots me a tired look and I stretch both of my left hands out. Her eyes travel up and down the length of my arms, but she just looks away, not giving me an answer.

I beckon again and her eyes look up to my face for a moment that feels too long. "It is cold. Please."

Without saying a word, she gets up and walks over to me.

She is so much smaller than me, even when I am lying down and I reach one of my hands to grab on to her and tuck her under my wing, forgetting for a blessed minute that I no longer possess my feathery down. The pain from trying to extend them reminds me that there is barely anything of them left and a twinge of painful realization washes over me; I am grounded for life and really will never fly again.

I wave away the thoughts of self-pity and arrange her so that her upper body is mostly supported by one of my arms and not a lot of her is in contact with the cold ground.

She takes over from me and continues to adjust herself until she finds comfort in curling into her body and placing both of her hands between my arm and her head. She only spares me a single glance before drifting off into slumber and I am left to study her once more.

While she is asleep, she looks much more relaxed, her body no longer curling tightly around itself. Her mouth is parted by sleep and her tongue sticks out only slightly, making her look a little silly.

I am left to wonder what she would look like if she weren't so angry with me all the time. What would her pleased expressions resemble? Would her happy songs flutter as much in me as when she approves of a decision I have made, however few times it has happened?

These are all foolish questions, anyway.

The hunters added to her and made her something more valuable, like understanding different languages and who knows what else, but they took the very thing that makes me who I am.

I do not know how much longer I will survive without my wings.

The pain in them is always with me, however hard I try to hide it and I can only hope it doesn't affect my plans with Ree to ensure Ruby is rescued alive.

My arrangement was simple; to get Ruby safe, somewhere she could reunite with the rest of her sisters, and they could support each other. After that, I will never see them again and I will have to live the rest of my days on the ground like a graceless beast, with only the honor of my glory days to warm me.

It doesn't feel good knowing that I am so young, yet the apex of my life has clearly already passed, almost making nothing worth living for, besides the words of my promise, of course.

The sounds that Ruby makes in her sleep take me away from my troubling thoughts and I stare at her face and wonder what she is dreaming of. I hope it is only good things and the kindness of the world that she has experienced before the hunters. That is always what I try to think about before I fall asleep as well.

Images crowd my mind at the thought. Taking to the skies with my brothers one last time as we leave our aeries and descend, one last joint song, and one last bout of chasing thermals. As I occupy my mind with thinking of these simple pleasures, I hope that the dawn will be kinder to Ruby and me.

We deserve that much.

www.ingramcontent.com/pod-product-compliance
Lightning Source LLC
Chambersburg PA
CBHW060352310726

48976CB00003B/788